The Race Girl

A Moretti Racing Family Saga

by

James Herbert Harrison

ISBN# 979-8-9896936-0-3 Paperback

ISBN# 979-8-9896936-1-0 Hardcover

www.jamesherbertharrison.net
jamesherbertharrison@gmail.com

Preface

In 1965 I saw my first coverage of the Indianapolis 500, which was actually a condensed tape delay that was featured the following Saturday on ABC. A.J. Foyt and Parnelli Jones were the household names although the great European champion, Jimmy Clark, would rule the day with pit help from the famous Wood Brothers NASCAR team. There was a new name mentioned during the telecast, a young Italian-American, Mario Andretti, who along with the late Hall of Fame pitcher, Bob Gibson, would become my childhood sports heroes.

A year later the great John Frankenheimer film, Grand Prix, was produced and upon review, I was hooked for life on the sport of motor racing in all forms. We did get TV coverage of NASCAR and Indycar back then, but I had to subscribe to the late Chris Economaki's National Speed Sport News to keep up with Formula One and international sports car racing.

After twenty-plus Indianapolis 500s, I am still in awe of the sheer magnitude of the world's greatest sporting event. Every great race driver should race there at least once, and every sports fan should have it on their bucket list.

I have written fiction novels about crime drama, international intrigue, and even romance, predicating a recent consultant to suggest that I combine them into an explosive tale with a backdrop of my main interest, motor racing. It is my desire and belief that The Race Girl, A Moretti Racing Family Saga, will provide some entertaining value to fans of all these genres.

-James Herbert Harrison

JAMES HERBERT HARRISON

Prologue

Las Vegas, Nevada

Adam Herrera was on the hot seat. All the corporate brass and dignitaries from all over the country were present along with many international business executives. He had insisted the team owner himself be there for the engagement, but racing legend Anthony "Andy" Moretti was still in Saudi Arabia as the team prepared for their second Formula One race, thus he had sent his youngest son to spend the weekend in Las Vegas and do the team proud. It was an altogether innocuous move as Herrera was a fan of both racing Moretti brothers, and Alex was a natural at entertaining in front of a crowd. Team General Manager, Bob Ward, and the hospitality team would handle the setup of the Unibank sponsored display cars, and be there along with Alex to socialize at the team-sponsored cocktail party before the banquet dinner, featuring Alex Moretti as the keynote speaker.

The youngest of the Moretti Motorsport drivers was originally expected to show up with Evelyn Stevens, his teammate and erstwhile girlfriend, a combination that was sure to please the attending crowd as Stevens had become the world's motorsport sweetheart, but as the two had fallen out romantically, Alex insisted that he represent the team himself.

Since his appointment to Vice President of Marketing, Herrera had been the driving force behind getting the corporation into motor racing and for the most part, it had gone very well. Initially, Unibank was a secondary sponsor at many NASCAR events, the main sponsor of two Indycar racing events, their corporate signage appeared in four Formula One races, and was well represented at Sebring and Lemans. In the second year, Unibank co-sponsored the Grand Prix of Long Beach with Honda and expanded their footprint by becoming secondary co-sponsors in sports car racing, both with the World Endurance Championship (WEC) and the North American International Motorsports Association (IMSA).

Unibank's third year of motor racing involvement saw a major expansion by becoming the main corporate sponsor for Moretti Motorsport, a firm whose players were rich in motor racing history and competed in most of the world's racing series which now included Formula One, the pinnacle the team had been aspiring to as a last step toward superteam status. Moretti's teams had finished well last season in the series championships of Indycar, Formula E, and IMSA, despite having a lackluster showing at the single biggest prize, the Indianapolis 500, where none of the three entries finished in the top five, two with handling and tire issues, while the third car was involved in a multi-car crash.

Being preoccupied himself, Andy was cautiously optimistic about having Alex handle the Unibank function, as the boy had recently pushed back on most of the offseason appearances, particularly on weekends. He had become somewhat relieved when his youngest son seemed all the more enthusiastic about flying out to Vegas for this one, the single most important non-racing event on the calendar. Andy had blown off concerns from Ward regarding Alex's reliability, assuring the team's GM that his youngest boy had shown such zeal for the Vegas assignment. Now the team principal was about to blow a gasket when Ward began calling and texting him almost by the minute.

"I can't get hold of him, Andy! This is an absolute disaster. I've got both Adam and Wally asking me what our Plan "B" is. I knew we should have had Evelyn here, too. This sucks!" Ward exclaimed.

"Evelyn is pretty to look at, but she's not that great at speaking in front of a crowd. You know that, Bob," Andy responded, knowing the pressure and embarrassment his right-hand man must now be under.

"Right now, pretty to look at looks pretty good, Andy. You need to call Herrera. At least make him think you care!... Alex is not taking my calls or returning texts... Maybe he'll take your calls. Here they come again, Andy.... Call me back."

This latest stunt would be a catastrophe for the team as Unibank was the most lucrative sponsor Moretti Motorsport had ever landed, potentially dwarfing anything that past tobacco companies had even spent. He and his promotional staff had spent an unworldly amount of time, energy, and expense to land the account, including their settling on a complicated performance-based contract.

The sponsorship, along with their strong new engine supplier, had helped push the team over the challenges of getting into Formula One, and Andy had gone to their F1 facility in England immediately following the season opener in Bahrain to settle an internal dust-up between their two team crews after a pit strategy mishap had cost the team a couple of valuable championship points. Their lead driver was Anthony Moretti, Jr., "Tony", the oldest of Andy's two second-generation drivers, and a young man who had done quite well in Indycar, winning two series championships, and nearly winning the big one twice.

Andy had rung and sent texts to Alex's cell phone continuously for nearly an hour, getting nothing but voicemails, as he had wanted to have one last word with his youngest son before the evening's event. Suddenly, a splash screen on Andy's new Apple iPhone popped up that got his undivided attention.

"This is a Fox News break from the world of motorsports. Earlier this evening in Las Vegas, Nevada, motor racing driver, Alex Moretti, was involved in a serious car accident on Tropicana Boulevard near the MGM

Casino Hotel. Moretti has been taken to a local emergency room, reported to be in serious but stable condition. We also have to report that a teenage girl was a passenger in the vehicle with Moretti and was also hospitalized with serious injuries. Thus far we have received no report on the identity of the young woman. Las Vegas Police have had little to report regarding any pending charges against the famous driver.

Alex Moretti drives for Moretti Motorsport, whose principal is his legendary father, Andy Moretti. The team fields racing teams in series all over the world, having as their chief sponsor Unibank Corporation. Stand by as Fox News has more updates on this breaking story."

A No show for Unibank's dinner as keynote speaker and now this! Damnit, Alex! Andy thought furiously, as he saw the name pop up as a call coming in, a call he dreaded to take.

"Andy Moretti," he answered, gritting his teeth in preparation for what was coming.

"You know why I'm calling."

Andy could tell by his tone that Herrera was steaming. The longtime booster for all things team Moretti was blitzed for Alex not showing up at the Bellagio for the Unibank banquet dinner, a big deal that Adam himself would be under tremendous fire over.

"What can I tell you, Adam? Alex has been in an auto accident as he was heading over. I hate it, but accidents happen."

"What in hell was he doing with Amanda in the car!?" Herrera yelled.

"Amanda? Amanda who? I don't know what you're talking about, Adam," Andy replied testily, knowing he should be getting off and calling the hospital to check on his son.

"Amanda who!? Amanda Cook, Andy, that's who! You recall, Byron Cook's youngest daughter!"

Chapter 1

Recalling a Legacy

The room was dark and devoid of sound with exception of the beeping of the monitor and the small semblance of light as the device screen was emitting the displayed waveform. He didn't feel really bad, incognizant of the amount of pain medication being administered through the IV taped to his arm.

Alex knew something catastrophic must have occurred, but his memory of the accident was fuzzy. He pressed the help button at his side, mostly out of curiosity, the door to his room opened, and in walked the shift nurse. The light woke up the elderly woman sleeping on the chair in the corner, who herself arose and immediately approached his bedside.

"Where am I?" Alex asked, looking around and recognizing her. "Grandmother?"

"You're in a Las Vegas hospital, Alex. You've been in an accident," Matilde Moretti responded as she held her grandson's hand, wearing a smiling face with misty eyes while the attending nurse quickly took the patient's temperature.

"I don't remember,...I don't remember anything," he stated.

"Can I get you anything, Alex?" The nurse asked before sharing a look with Mrs. Moretti and nodding, knowing they would need a private moment when she exited the room.

"No,... No, I'm fine. I just pressed this to see what would happen. Thank you."

"Well, I'm Brittany. Just press that again when you need anything," the young shift nurse stated and nodded at the elder Mrs. Moretti prior to departing.

"Honey, you've been in a bad wreck. You're very fortunate," the Moretti family matriarch stated, having difficulty sharing the rest of the news.

"What happened? What about Amanda?... Please tell me, Grandma."

As she gathered her thoughts, the room telephone rang and the elder Matilde scurried around the far side of the bed to pick it up, as Alex listened intently.

"....Yes, he is doing fine....We haven't heard, but she's still alive and in intensive care....I don't know, Andy. I just got here three hours ago, and he just woke up....We don't know anything, yet....Hang on."

"It's your father. Are you up to talking to him?" Matilda asked as she motioned to hand him the phone.

"Sure, Grandma."

"Be prepared, honey. You know him. He's pretty angry."

"Angry? Angry about what?" Alex asked.

"Just talk to him real quick," she replied.

"Hello," the patient stated, his mind still fuzzy about what had transpired.

"Alex, can you tell me what happened?" Andy Moretti asked rather sternly. "The press are at the door in Huntersville like a pack of wolves!"

"Dad, I don't know anything. I don't even know how I got here."

"The staff told me you're in stable condition. Have the police shown up there, yet?"

Matilde gathered her only son was yelling at her bed-ridden grandson and grabbed the phone out of Alex's hand before the conversation got worse. "Andy! He just woke up! He doesn't remember anything! When can you get here?"

Alex now confirmed in his mind that something serious had happened. His father was very angry with him as he began recalling the Unibank banquet and the fallout it would cause. He could tell the conversation between his father and his grandmother was heated, as witnessed by Matilde looking away toward the window as she talked.

"I know he's in trouble, Andy! How about you forget about your damned cars for once. He needs you!... What about Sabetha? Have you heard from her?"

"No, she's probably running around the Swiss Alps somewhere with another new boyfriend," Andy replied.

"Well, are you going to contact her? She *is* Alex's mother, Andy!"

"I won't have to contact her, Mom. It's all over the world news wire now."

Andy was still in a state of shock at this tragic news. *Byron Cook's teenage daughter! My lord, son! How could you possibly be that careless?*

He would be on a plane in a short few hours heading west toward Las Vegas, having plenty of time for self-study on the intercontinental flight, time to reflect back on where he had come, a family history of Moretti Motorsport's climb to achieve its place among the world's great legendary racing teams. Andy had always wished his father would be alive to witness it, much of it courtesy of Unibank and all about to blow up right in front of his eyes.

Stopping in briefly at the team facility in Huntersville, Andy prepared for the unexpected visit to Vegas and arranged an impromptu meeting with his longtime lawyer prior to departing. Ed Rothman had been Moretti Motorsport's chief attorney since day one.

"It appears the charges, if there are any, will be minor. He tested well below the legal limit, thank God. Expect Unibank's attorneys to be preparing a civil suit, though," Rothman stated. "Their CEO will be on the warpath over this," he added, declining personal comment that he himself could hardly blame the man.

"Who will be handling that for us, Ed?" Andy asked, knowing Rothman's area of expertise was contract law, not civil litigation.

"We'll partner with Fuller, Smith, and Davidson out of Raleigh, as the suit will undoubtedly be filed in North Carolina."

No sooner than he and his attorney had concluded their meeting, the desk phone buzzed. Andy knew his executive secretary, Silvia Francisco, would not interrupt her boss at such a stressful time unless it was someone very important. "Andy, Mr. Penske on line two."

He immediately picked up. "Good morning, Roger."

"Good morning, Andy. Any update on how he's doing?"

"He's awake and talking with no apparent serious injuries," Andy replied.

"And the Cook girl?"

"No news on her yet, Roger."

"I know you have a full plate, Andy, but other than what's being reported, can you tell me anything?" Roger Penske, the CEO and family patriarch of the legendary Penske Corporation, knew Moretti well as the two had competed in all levels of motor racing for many years. As Penske Entertainment Corporation now owned the Indycar series and the Indianapolis Motor Speedway, he would have a keen interest in all matters involving the series' racing teams.

The huge Unibank sponsorship had a huge impact on Indycar and worldwide motorsports as a whole, as such endeavors strongly enticed interest from other corporate sponsors, both domestically and internationally. Indycar was just beginning to recover from the economic effects of the COVID-19 pandemic, a major setback after years of stagnation over the series' sanctioning body feud of the previous twenty-plus years.

"You know about as much as I do, Roger," Andy replied, holding back on admitting their Unibank sponsorship would be in severe jeopardy, but then thinking Penske would know that.

"Andy, you know we're all here for you and know the press is hounding us for information, too. I trust you'll keep me informed."

"I will, Roger. Thanks for calling."

Andy disconnected the call and shook his head as Frank Gower, Alex's crew chief who had stuck his head in the headman's office to inquire about him. "That was Roger. He's worried,…worried about what effect this whole blow-up will have on the series."

"They don't call him *The Captain* for nothing, Andy. Who should handle the press here while you're away?"

"I'll think about that. Just have everyone respond with no additional information at this time until further notice."

Andy prepared to head for the regional airport in Concord, where he would take their private jet for the nearly five-hour flight to Las Vegas. As the plane became airborne and the skyline of Charlotte surrendered to the scenic Smoky Mountains, the veteran racer and team owner began to reflect on his long life in motor racing, passing a silent prayer that his son and Byron Cook's daughter would be okay and this tragic incident wouldn't put an end to everything he had worked his whole life for.

Steve McQueen had a famous quote in the movie, *Lemans*, *"Racing is life. Everything that happens before or after is just waiting."*

That was absolutely true for Anthony "Andy" Moretti, a man whose entire life from the time he was born was centered around the sport of motor racing.

Raised on the Italian Riviera near Genoa, his father drove sports cars for legendary car manufacturers Porsche, Jaguar, and Alpha Romeo. Following a stellar career winning the 24 Hours of Lemans three times, numerous other sportscar races worldwide, and four FIA sportscar championships, the senior Moretti was tragically killed while racing in Nurburg, Germany. Along with many others, the death of Moretti symbolized such events, a sport where nearly half of its participants would not retire alive.

Young Andy would carry the torch of his father's legacy despite vehement opposition from his widowed mother. His father had always felt he would never encourage his only son to drive racing cars, as the senior Moretti had seen the worst of the sport play out multiple times before succumbing to the hazard himself. But he had always seen that competitive spirit in the boy,... that drive to win,... to be the best. The family patriarch knew young Andy would never be content with selling cars, or building houses, or sitting in a swanky office. No, racing was in his blood. Racing is what he would do. In young Anthony's mind, the Moretti name would be synonymous with the sport, spoken in the same breath as Enzo Ferrari or Juan Manuel Fangio.

Coming up through the ranks in the ladder series of the 1990s, Andy got his first Formula One drive in Monza driving for March. An entire season followed that produced mediocre results, but young Moretti caught the eye of some top teams as the entire series paddock saw the March as a very uncompetitive chassis and Andy's few mid-pack and even one third-place finish got him noticed.

The following two years had Moretti driving for Frank Williams and nearly resulted in a world championship. As a free agent, the accomplished and budding young racing star could not come to terms with the team, while believing an open seat awaited him at McLaren, another top-tier team that had yet to secure the services of its two drivers. This was not to be, however, but due to the tragic and untimely death of Marco Santori in a testing crash, Moretti managed to get a ride with Ferrari, the team that every ethnic Italian dreamed of driving for.

Those were lean years for the *Prancing Horse*, however, and Andy Moretti was becoming frustrated. He had tasted victory and a legitimate shot at being world champion at Williams, but now languished in an uncompetitive car that struggled to score any podium finishes, much less wins. After two years of mediocre results, Andy's stock had taken a dive along with his ego, as Ferrari hinted at his being relegated to number two on the team for the next season.

During the winter, Moretti participated in the Daytona 24-Hour sports car event, sharing a ride and winning in the GTO class with two other drivers, including American NASCAR star Mark Martin. Although happy to be involved in winning after so many races, the experience of running in a slower class and getting constantly overtaken by the faster GTP class cars seemed to diminish the win, at least from a mental standpoint. It was the prototypes that grabbed the headlines and dominated the podium as these machines rivaled the speeds of the Formula One cars he was accustomed to, not to mention their somewhat similarity to the legendary Porsche 956s and 962s young Andy had watched his father drive while growing up.

The somewhat laid-back atmosphere in the Daytona paddock became quite appealing to Moretti and led to a decision on his part to sign a one-year deal with Maris-Bentley, a relatively small but well-financed team based out of Indianapolis that fielded cars in Indycar and IMSA, the North American version of the FIA's World Sports Car Championship. This period led to the most successful period of Andy's career with first-year wins at the Meadowlands street circuit and on the oval at Phoenix. Moretti added a co-driver victory in the famous sports car race in Sebring, Florida, and impressed everyone by winning and finishing a close second as a guest driver at the two NASCAR road course events at Watkins Glen and Sears Point.

What followed was a long and fruitful career with Chip Ganassi, one of Indycar's top teams, where Andy won thirty-eight races, including his biggest career trophy at the Indianapolis 500, not to mention being series champion three times.

Retirement is often difficult for any star athlete and Moretti found himself as a fish out of water in the broadcast booth, always having been a bit on the shy side in his life. His off-the-cuff political incorrectness kept getting him in trouble with the sanctioning bodies, not to mention his own network, and he quickly learned he needed a change.

Andy did, however, have a keen eye for talent in the sport and eventually arranged financial backing to purchase his own team from Ben Longmire, an automotive parts magnate who had spent his semi-retirement years running a successful Indycar team. As a young driver, Andy had always seen the sport of motor racing as two-dimensional. It was all about finishing and winning in the car. As a team owner, he quickly learned the real competition in his sport, the competition for sponsors. The costs of fielding a team of racing cars were immense, especially if the team endeavored to win. There were always one or two teams, like drivers, who were simply glad to be there, almost as a hobby. But that was not Andy Moretti. Moretti Motorsport was in business to win, win races, and win championships. To accomplish winning, a team had to have money which meant getting good sponsors, and in most cases many.

The business side of the sport had changed immensely since Colin Chapman had broken ground in Formula One with his famous Team Gold Leaf Lotus cars. Drivers like Jimmy Clark and Graham Hill never had to spend a whole Saturday at a corporate store opening or hang out all day at a show booth. He could just imagine a VP of Marketing asking A.J. Foyt to fly to Nassau for an hour-long guest keynote speaker engagement. David Pearson or Donnie Allison showing up in three-piece suits to shake hands at a corporate sales meeting? Who were they kidding?

That was the way business was conducted now. Competition for sponsorship money was fierce. The drivers themselves had to court their own sponsors and often bring them to a team if they were going to get a ride at all in many cases. The owners and drivers of race teams had to stay as focused on pleasing their sponsors as winning on the track and these sponsors had to constantly be sold, sold not only on staying loyal to that team but often sold on staying involved in the sport period. The business of motor racing was particularly susceptible to national and world economic conditions. When a corporate bottom line went through hard times, the advertising budget for expenses like motor racing sponsorships was among the first to be cut.

This was a part of the business that Andy Moretti despised. He himself had always struggled with it as he didn't care for salespeople generally and had to work very hard at conducting himself in that arena. Too often, he had to admit, his drivers' fortunes would rise and fall nearly as much with their corporate relations abilities as would their driving skills. When his two sons chose to become race drivers, career paths that were never much in doubt, Andy went overboard in stressing this importance to them.

Tony was the oldest and most established of the two boys and had won twenty-three Indycar series races in his seven years, including the marquee event at Long Beach and two Indycar Championships. He was indeed considered a man to beat. Six years younger, Alessandro, or "Alex" as he preferred, was competing in his second season and starting his own legacy. Alex was fast in the car, very fast, but drove hell-bent on winning every race and overdriving at times, still resulting in too many DNFs.

Neither driver had won the big one at Indianapolis, although Tony had finished runner-up in a photo finish the year before, losing by an eyelash to the venerable Scott Dixon, Team Ganassi's ace driver, in an emotional finish for all involved as Dixon had been Andy's rookie teammate with Chip during his last year of active driving. No one in the sport knew at the time the New Zealander would become Indycar's twenty-first century ironman, a racing legend in his own right, and still winning against the next generation twenty-plus years later.

Tony gained substantial success with his disciplined car control and won many races and indeed his two championships by often saving the race car's tires and smart fuel management, a style that had ironically become known as *Dixonian*.

Alex seemed to care less about car management and had a simple attitude toward winning, drive the car as fast as it would go and hope it lasts. *Win enough races and the championships would come,* he kept telling himself. Very sensational at times, Alex was often compared to the late Gilles Villeneuve, and would always be among the drivers to beat, if and when he finished.

On a personal level, although similar in appearance the two sons couldn't have been more different. Tony tended to be on the shy side himself, taking after his father. Always excelling in school, Andy's oldest son was a very disciplined kid and became skilled as a driver through sheer will and determination. Alex had a very extroverted personality, the type of person who had never met a stranger. As a young man, he had never been a good student scholastically, and always had an air of mischief about him. The boy did have his very good looks going for him and was always quite popular with members of the opposite sex.

Both Moretti boys were good with corporate sponsors and each approached public relations in a manner to match their prospective personalities. While Tony lacked the same flamboyance in front of a crowd as his younger brother, he was reliable and neither the team nor its sponsors ever had cause to worry about him showing up for an important event. Alex was credited with some of the most memorable quotes as a keynote speaker, but his father was constantly fielding complaints about him showing up late for events, and in one case not showing up at all.

This latest sponsorship opportunity, one that was huge in its scope and volume, had actually been generated by a chance encounter on Lake Norman, the huge body of water near Charlotte that was extremely popular with the regional motorsports community. Many of the sport's personalities had lakefront properties and boats of every size and shape there, as well as many other individuals directly or indirectly connected to the industry.

Walter "Wally" Remington was an Executive Vice President at Unibank Corporation, enjoying life at his lodge-type home on the shores of Lake Norman, and spent a goodly number of summer days on his fifty-foot Azimut Flybridge yacht. Constantly entertaining a well-known roster of guests, a local Mount Mourne regional bank manager had brought along his new neighbor, Myles Delcanton, the NASCAR team manager for Moretti Motorsport.

During the afternoon excursion, Delcanton had become acquainted and hit it off with Adam Herrera, Remington's right-hand man and newly promoted Vice President of Marketing for Unibank, having recently relocated from Los Angeles to Charlotte. Herrera revealed that he was a huge fan of motor racing himself, particularly Formula One and Indycar, having been to the Long Beach Grand Prix several times while living in Southern California. This connection led to an introduction to Andy Moretti and a subsequent invite to the Moretti Motorsport hospitality tent at the upcoming Indycar weekend in Nashville.

Herrera quickly became friendly with Andy Moretti and his boys, leading to Unibank's involvement in motor racing and discussions of a major sponsorship relationship. As Unibank was in the heart of NASCAR country, indeed a few key NASCAR teams were Unibank clients, Andy's recent investment in a NASCAR team had opened some doors in that community, a discipline that had become America's most popular racing series.

While in Nashville, Herrera spent time making the rounds doing what he did best, networking with people. He met briefly with the Penske Entertainment staff regarding the leasing of a Tower Terrace hospitality suite at the Indianapolis Motor Speedway and visited briefly with The *Captain*, Roger Penske himself.

While enjoying the breakfast buffet with Andy at the Moretti hospitality tent on Saturday morning, Adam met attorney Louis Newberry, who was the newly contracted agent for Evelyn Stevens, the good-looking young Brit who was rapidly becoming the sport's poster girl. The three discussed an overall deal with Unibank becoming the team sponsor and including a tie-in to Evelyn as a driver, whom Moretti would sign at season end as part of a multi-year deal.

Stevens had started out young like most drivers, competing and often winning several karting championships in southern England prior to moving up gradually to the GP3 Series. Her lifelong dream had been to compete in Formula One, a feat that no female had been able to broach with any level of success since Lella Lombardi, who had a sixth-place finish in a Grand Prix nearly fifty years prior.

The European ladder system to Formula One is a fast imitation of musical chairs, much more so than other motorsport series around the globe. While Evelyn Stevens was competitive in GP3, she had indeed finished on the podium three times, her photogenic good looks are what garnered much attention, to the point that other drivers who had scored more success on the track held a level of resentment toward her, fearing she would have an unfair advantage with corporate sponsors over themselves, regardless of their own on-track prowess.

While a couple of Formula One teams did show some interest, they feared a repeat of what had happened in the States with Danica Patrick, the very attractive female driver who had brought in a large measure of notoriety and sponsorship dollars to Indycar and NASCAR. The feeling in the paddock had carried a level of discord toward her as other drivers and team personnel grew tired of the media circus, due in large part to some bruised egos of a few drivers who blamed Danica for their own lack of media attention, a somewhat unfair sentiment as she was very good on the racetrack when given a competitive car.

The general consensus among Formula One teams was their sport didn't need the added attention, as their discipline was recording a near unlimited success. Thus the few opportunities in F1 had become closed to Stevens, and like many talented young European drivers, she sought opportunity in the States. Seeking to increase the market share of its Guinness Draught brand in North America, the British corporation Diageo saw this avenue in Evelyn Stevens, and having these newfound sponsorship dollars she became the second driver for the IndyWest team, a relative newcomer to the sport and struggling to get a foothold following three seasons fielding an Indy Lights team, which was Indycar's ladder series.

Evelyn quickly put her face on the front page by finishing tenth in her first event in Saint Petersburg, Florida, and a very close second to reigning series champion Will Power on the high-speed oval in Fort Worth, Texas. Suddenly she was the darling of the sporting world press, culminating with a feature article and bikini photo on the cover of Sports Illustrated. She naturally caught the attention of much of the male persuasion, including competitor Alex Moretti.

Alex and his father engaged in many conversations regarding the budding romance, fueled by the senior Moretti's concern for how it may affect his son's performance on the track, notwithstanding the fact that Moretti was one of the top-tier teams looking to recruit Stevens, whose star power among sponsors could not be ignored. "You do know she *is* your competitor on the track, Alex," young Moretti had heard more than once.

Andy planned to replace the third team driver, Juan Pedro Cortez, and was courting the services of Evelyn Stevens, as were other teams. A three-way dinner meeting with himself, Adam Herrera, and Louis Newberry was planned for a subsequent Friday evening in Charlotte. On the table was a lucrative contract involving Unibank coming on as the team's primary sponsor and putting Stevens in the third Moretti car, as well as the team featuring her in a car at three major sports car races, Daytona, Sebring, and Lemans.

They had become the hottest couple in the sport, Alex Moretti and Evelyn Stevens, and the press couldn't get enough of them. Like many celebrity romances, a new paparazzi emerged giving the couple, their teams, and the series as a whole a new influx of publicity, which had its ups and downs. The extra journalists and their camera crews were starting to become a flagrant annoyance for an already crowded paddock.

The couple enjoyed a relatively private late-night dinner at the popular Nashville restaurant, quiet in a context that even though the area did have a very successful annual Indycar event, it *was* in relative NASCAR country, and as such most of the Indycar drivers came and went about socially with little fanfare. That suited Alex to a tee, as he badly needed a break from the constant barrage of those seeking autographs and selfies. Even though it was inherent to Alex's personality to appreciate and accommodate the fans, it had gotten to be a bit much, particularly since his newly acquired girlfriend was so popular.

"Quite a happening town here, huh?" Alex stated.

"Yes, and these country *honky tonks*; so very American," the Brit said, smiling. "I'll have to get me some of those cowgirl boots."

"We do have much, what is the right word? *Diversity* here in the States...Tough track today," Alex lamented, as he obviously had more on his mind right then than the local Nashville partying scene. Both he and Tony had struggled to get into the top tier during qualifying. The street circuit was just north of downtown and on the grounds of Nissan Stadium, home of the Tennessee Titans NFL team.

"I'm rather surprised at the crowds, Alex. I always heard that Americans in the South were into NASCAR," Evelyn observed.

"Oh, they are. They definitely are. But this is Josef Newgarden's hometown. He'll be hard to beat, and so will O'Ward... We'll catch 'em tomorrow, though."

One of the things that always seemed to attract Stevens to the younger Moretti was his simple belief in success. The two brothers were very competitive together, but all in such a supportive way. The comparative criticism in the press didn't seem to affect Alex, who in a certain way was his brother's biggest cheerleader, next to Tony's new bride, of course. For a guy who had such a big ego, as did most good race drivers, she admired Alex for his lack of any envy toward Tony, a trait she felt would serve their own relationship well.

As she and Alex immersed in shop talk during dinner, Evelyn would constantly attempt to steer the conversation away from the track and garage toward other things, all in a vain effort to affect romance whenever she could. It was a challenge as she always had her ever-increasing celebrity distractions, and as for him?... He was a racer.

Recalling her easily from social media, their waiter approached along with one of the chefs toward the end of the evening. "Evelyn, if you wouldn't mind, could we get your autograph?" The young man asked sheepishly, and mostly on behalf of the chef.

She and Alex shared a look, thinking their plan for a somewhat private dinner had gone array, at least momentarily. Stevens signed a restaurant menu for each one and then asked if they would also like Alex to sign. The four shared a slight moment of embarrassment when it was obvious the two restaurant employees had no recognition of Alex whatsoever.

"This is Alex Moretti, my competitor and Andy Moretti's youngest son," Evelyn explained, unhappy with herself as an afterthought for bringing Alex's dad into the equation, as if to imply her man could only be recognized because of his famous father, an all too often scenario that Evelyn knew would get under Alex's skin.

The waiter and chef shared a confused look and one replied, "Oh, of course. Thank you."

An uneasy silence befell the table as the waiter and cook walked away smiling. "Oh, don't let it get to you, love. Not everyone on this planet keeps up with our sport."

Alex forced a smile, knowing Evelyn was probably right, but also feeling belittled and constantly having to admit to his girlfriend being much more famous than himself, a reminder that was occurring constantly, and one that a Moretti was unaccustomed to. While he was extremely proud of his father's legacy, this kind of repeated incident was a source of embarrassment and served to fuel an ever-growing and burning desire on his part to make his own mark in the sport he loved.

Andy's Indycar team was progressing with mixed results. Tony had been his usual consistent self, winning three races and finishing in the top six three other times. Alex had himself won twice with four total podium finishes, while the third driver, Cortez, had been a dismal failure since coming over from Formula One two years earlier.

The import of F1 drivers by Indycar teams was no guarantee for success and vice-versa. Legends like Emerson Fittipaldi and Nigel Mansell had come *across the pond* to make immediate impacts, as in effect, champions were champions. Many mid-pack former Grand Prix drivers brought little but sponsorship dollars, as was the case with Cortez. Any third driver in the Moretti stable would tend to blame their lack of success on Andy's two sons getting preference in equipment and personnel, and the Columbian was no exception.

The silly season had begun in earnest as the season headed to the famed Indianapolis Motor Speedway for the only weekend where the Indycars and NASCAR "Cup" cars would be featured together at the same track. The Penske Entertainment folks had promoted the event to have the two series come together in joint support with many fans being supportive of both.

The Saturday Indycar event was run on and off in the rain, always a condition that served to level the playing field and provide some exciting and unpredictable results. When the weather appeared to break, many teams chose to pit late for slick tires. When the field cycled through, IndyWest driver Evelyn Stevens found herself leading the race. As her rain tires began to degrade badly with the track drying, the team chose to roll the dice and have her stay out with three laps to go. When hard chargers Scott McLaughlin and Colton Herta were gaining at a rate of over fifteen seconds per lap, the rain resumed. The second and third-place drivers, both on primary slicks, ran into each other at the end of the back straight and Stevens limped home to her first Indycar victory, only the second female to ever win in the series and the first since Danica in well over a decade.

Gleefully in unchartered waters, team owners Geoff Lynch and Roberto Santos arranged an improvised celebration party in their hotel. Agent Newberry, who generally stuck to Stevens like glue, sent a text to Adam Herrera, in town as Andy Moretti's guest who had already left the track, heading to his downtown hotel for a shower and change of clothes, prior to a planned dinner engagement with Andy, Bob Ward, and two other sponsors.

"Adam, how about coming over to the Indy West celebration party?"

The two kept exchanging messages as Newberry wanted his client to sell herself to this potential gold mine representative, separately from having Andy Moretti or any other team owner present.

Herrera responded. *"I'll message you after I return from dinner. If it works out, fine."*

"Louie, is this really necessary? I'm exhausted," the day's celebrated winner inquired.

"Evelyn! Don't spit in a gift horse's face!" Newberry exclaimed, appearing exasperated. "This guy has a big checkbook in his pocket! With a sponsor like that, you could write your own ticket for any team you wish to drive for! I worked hard to set this up! Let's not blow it."

They all met in the Conrad Hotel's lobby lounge at just past 11:00 PM. Both Evelyn and her agent appeared a bit battle-worn from too much partying, a condition not lost on Herrera who was not offended as he knew this was a big day for her and was quite congratulatory. As Evelyn was quite a striking woman and she and Adam Herrera seemed to connect right away, Newbury became very guarded as if worried their connection may somehow downplay his own importance in any future relationship.

The agent made it quite clear that his client's contract with IndyWest would expire at season's end and they were open to offers from other teams. He attempted to steer the conversation toward Unibank going for a straight driver sponsorship, taking their dollars to whatever team his client chose to work for.

This rubbed Herrera the wrong way as he felt a certain friendship loyalty to Andy Moretti and his team, as they had been his guide to the world of motor racing from day one. In addition, Andy had even been the one who introduced him to Newberry, not to mention hosting their earlier dinner in Nashville where the Unibank Marketing VP had felt they had an agreement to proceed. As such, Adam felt a certain disdain for Steven's agent, who following an evening of consuming a bit too many adult beverages, began to come off as arrogant and blatantly over his head.

For her part, Evelyn displayed an attractive personality matching her physical beauty, and the bank executive had the wheels turning in his mind regarding her extreme sex appeal and marketing potential. Newberry seemed to become agitated when Herrera tended to ask most of his questions toward Stevens herself, an act that Adam found amusing, if not petty.

"So, how about NASCAR, Evelyn? Do you have any interest in running there?" Herrera asked sincerely.

"Well,"...She hesitated to collect her thoughts.

"Of course, she is interested in NASCAR," Newberry interrupted, awkwardly speaking on her behalf.

"Since Andy now has a majority interest in a team there, it may be a natural... Should you sign on with him next year, of course," Adam added.

The evening was getting long and Herrera suggested they connect again early the following week and discuss proposals. By this juncture, Adam was of the opinion that Stevens was doing herself a complete disservice by having Newberry represent her, a man who was totally out of his league. Of course, as one being on the other side of such negotiations, he relished dealing with such an amateur and thus dared not suggest to her anything of the sort.

The talks between the three parties became sophisticated as Unibank was willing to commit to a four-year deal that included Andy's three drivers, with certain funding tied to performance. Newberry could not get the guaranteed money he wanted from Andy, so he had Stevens sign for just two years with another two-year option. This created a gray area with some options in the third and fourth years, arrangements Andy was not at all keen about but couldn't decline because the Unibank commitment overall was just too lucrative. Discussions were even made regarding the possibility of Stevens moving to Moretti Motorsport's NASCAR team in the third year, a future arrangement that all three parties looked upon openly.

Andy watched with mixed emotions as he saw the romance between his youngest son, who had garnered the nickname *Paddock Playboy*, and Evelyn Stevens, with her British accent and photo model looks, drawing together like magnets. He would see in many ways a repeat of himself in Alex, recalling his first meeting Sabetha in Barcelona. She was not a driver but a regular fixture in the Formula One paddock, a beautiful *Grid Girl* as they were referred to, promotional models who worked for each team.

Their marriage was a storybook at first. He was winning and moving up the series pecking order and life was exciting as the young couple traveled the world with the jet-set crowd of Formula One, a sport growing rapidly with the expanding technology explosion and its play to a worldwide audience. The birth of their first child, Antony Jr., had brought additional tranquility to the Morettis. The constant travel slowed, at least for a while, with Sabetha not wanting to attend as many races, even though her mother-in-law, Matilde Moretti, was all too happy to tend to young Tony while they were both away.

His move to Ferrari brought the family closer to their Genoa home, thought of at the time as a personal bonus with Andy now within driving distance of the team facility in northern Italy, while his former employer, Williams, was headquartered in England. He couldn't wait to get home following the Sunday races, and would often not be seen by his team until the following week prior to the next race, generally two weeks later. This was not looked upon favorably by the team, or Formula One in general, to the point where Andy came to believe this may have affected his failure to secure a seat at McLaren, a team also based in England.

The lean years for Ferrari at the time wore heavily on Moretti, as his popularity with the *Tifosi,* the Greek word given to the massive Italian Ferrari Scuderia fanbase, declined. As one of their own, the legendary manufacturer saw Andy Moretti as the man who would put the famous brand back in the winner's circle and compete for the constructor's championship, a status that had escaped the fabled Maranello car manufacturer for over a decade nor had Ferrari hosted a world driving champion since the late seventies.

Formula One in those years became a two-team battle between Williams and McLaren while the other teams competed in mid-pack, a condition that ate at a man like Andy Moretti, who saw the prime years of his life in racing being spent in a car where he had little or no chance of winning. Team Manager, Sean Benolt, became insistent that Andy spend more time at the Ferrari test circuit at Fiorano, a three-hour drive from Genoa. He would sometimes leave before dawn and return near dark while often spending a night or two in local hotels, either way resulting in less quality time being spent with his family.

Recovering from childbirth, Sabetha soon regained her form as a beautiful, vivacious woman and one who couldn't deal with neglect from her husband, particularly one whose career woes were depressing his romantic appeal. For his part, Andy kept feeling more and more pressure from the team, implying that his marital issues at home were reflecting negatively on his performance in their cars. Rumors surfaced of Sabetha having an affair with a wealthy business tycoon from Monte Carlo and the two separated.

As Sabetha's new beau didn't favor her playing full-time mother, particularly since young Anthony reminded him so much of Sabetha's ex, she spent most of her time away with the boys' grandmother, Matilde, becoming his de facto nanny, a role she was all too glad to fill.

Andy and Sabetha had worked at reconciliation and were on and off as an intimate pair for ten years, finally divorcing when their second son was two years of age. Andy never remarried as the scars of the breakup with Sabetha never quite healed. He had engaged in a few on-and-off romances through the years but knew his first love would always be to the sport, a man incapable of giving a woman the full commitment she most assuredly wanted and deserved. This was an inherent weakness, a disease he often felt, and one he didn't wish upon his two sons.

Tony had seemed to do extremely well for himself in that regard, as the entire family just adored his wife, Crissy. He approached his career so businesslike, a man who could shut it off at race end and go home to private life, regardless of the current success or lack thereof driving. His father knew that trait hadn't come from him as he himself had been the total opposite, wearing motorsports on his sleeve 24/7. He certainly didn't believe it came from Sabetha, who had a socialite personality and never fully relished the nuclear family thing, even when her husband was winning and happy. It didn't come from Andy's father, either, a man fully obsessed with racing as young Andy and his mother seldom saw the senior Moretti at all unless they accompanied him to the racetrack. Years later, Andy would reflect on and admire his mother, a woman who remained loyal to his father through thick and thin, enduring the tragedy of his death at an early age, and remaining the true family matriarch to this day. It was her personal qualities that had rubbed off on Tony, Andy was certain.

He saw Alex and Evelyn with different concerns. She was any man's dream, for sure, with that rare quality of beauty, class, and personality. And Alex, with his own handsome appeal and bubbly persona had never lacked for attracting females either, starting at a young age. There was always a side of Alex that admired and envied his older brother, Andy knew however, and had always felt that Alex adored his sister-in-law and saw in her the kind of relationship he wanted for himself someday.

With Evelyn's celebrity increasing daily, which admittedly had the sponsors jubilant, Andy saw this romance between the two as challenging, to say the least. He also saw his own role as father and boss getting more complicated, knowing conflicts would sometimes flair up on the racetrack, and his having to mediate those would get ever more difficult when not only dealing with two of his drivers, but two of his drivers who were also lovers.

The Gulf Coast sunset highlighted a pleasant breeze as Alex sat alone on the twelfth-floor balcony and enjoyed a cocktail. He and Evelyn were able to grab a rare few days off together between venues and their ever-increasing corporate sponsorship commitments. While it was not workable for either to turn off or simply ignore their phone traffic, Alex began to feel the strain of having a romantic relationship with a sports media supermodel, while she droned on and on with her agent, an annoying man who seemed to call every hour as though he was her panicked parent.

"I'm sorry, love," Evelyn decried as she finally appeared through the sliding door, joining her obviously disgruntled boyfriend.

"Why don't you just turn that thing off for the night?" Alex asked as more than a strong suggestion.

"Oh, poor baby. Is he being neglected?" she replied mockingly as her bathing suit top dropped to the floor.

His expression lightened up as she moved toward him, burying his face between her tan-lined breasts. As the two engaged in an intimate moment on the gulf-view balcony, the dark-colored object went unobserved, a small but expensive drone sporting its high-resolution camera.

The high-profile couple had been truly discreet regarding their whereabouts for a few days, and it would come as an unpleasant surprise when the two prepared to head out in the morning of the third day as Alex turned on his phone and received the disturbing message from his sister-in-law, one accompanied by a short video.

"You guys had best conduct business behind closed doors. The entire world is watching."

No more than half a minute went by when Evelyn's own phone began to buzz, indicating what seemed to be an on-the-hour call from her agent. After she had let it go to voicemail twice, she finally acquiesced and answered.

"Evelyn! Have you seen that video?" Louie asked excitedly. "This is not good."

"What video?" she replied anxiously.

"What video!? Oh my god, let me send you this link," Newberry responded hastily.

Evelyn hit the text message button and the link he had sent her, noticing her text box was flooded with previous messages containing comments and the same link. "Oh, my lord! How in the bloody world?"

"I'll have to prepare some immediate crisis management responses on your social media and release a press statement," Newberry stated as a man sounding as though shocked but working overtime to get everything under control.

"Let's just talk later, Louie. I have to pack up," she responded with a mixed feeling of embarrassment and shock. "I'll touch base when we get to the airport." She hung up the phone, knowing by seeing Alex's mood that he must have just been confronted the video himself.

Alex sat on the edge of the bed, just staring toward the balcony. In spite of his reputation as a cavalier playboy, Evelyn knew that deep down Alex had an intense private side when it came to his intimate life, a side of him she actually adored. He would be quite disturbed by this new video that had gone viral.

It could have been worse. The steel bars of the balcony railing served to disguise much of their open exposure although she had displayed most of herself totally, her recent tan highlighting two shapely bright breasts and a tan-lined rear end for all the world to consume.

"Who all knew we were here, Evelyn?" Alex questioned. "I know Dad didn't tell anyone," he added, knowing his father had suggested the private getaway for a few days, recalling his own experience in the limelight, and had advised them to be very discreet about it.

"The only people who knew were my mother and sister. And I didn't even tell them exactly where we were staying," Evelyn declared defensively. "Nobody else I can think of."

"What about Newberry?" Alex asked sternly.

"Of course, Louie knew. But he wouldn't disclose anything. You know how protective he is," she replied innocently.

"Protective, huh?" Alex grunted as he continued to pack his things. "If that twit Newberry is in charge of security, I'll know to sleep with one eye open from now on."

He had grown to have a level of contempt toward his girlfriend's agent, a man who was a constant menace with his countless phone calls and invasion of their privacy. Alex didn't add that he knew Louie had a crush on her, not that he saw the pompous Englishman as a threat romantically, but his constant attention was extremely annoying and would have been an embarrassment to any normal human being, which in Alex's view excluded Louie.

Over a thousand miles away Newberry enjoyed a cigar where he busied himself being the agent of Evelyn Stevens, the woman who may soon replace Oprah as the most recognized female on the planet, a status that he would take all the credit for, so far as he knew.

"Three thousand, Remi. Not a dime less, unless you want this to become a party line. You have competitors." Newberry had informed the paparazzi reporter of their three-day location, one who prepared to transfer another deposit into his bank account.

He would pretend to scold his client about this, imitating that folks like Honda or Unibank would not look kindly upon this type of publicity. In truth, he was tickled pink with the stunt, as hundreds of thousands of would-be fans, those who barely knew what an Indycar even was, much less the sports' biggest star, would be added to the rolls of likes for their videos and links to sponsors. He now relaxed, assuming more of the world's more risqué press publications would be ringing his number.

What neither Louie or Remi knew was the Moretti-Stevens romance would soon become such an explosion, the demand for everything increased to the point of a paparazzi becoming extraordinarily professional, their trackers no longer needing to be tipped off by anyone regarding the pair's whereabouts.

The woman hired to sleep with him exited the bathroom and prepared to leave, standing expectantly as it was customary for her customers to reward her with a generous tip, one that was not forthcoming.

You should have just included that in the price, Newberry thought, always of the opinion such services had much more perceived value at the outset than upon the conclusion.

The hired *entertainer* didn't smile as she departed.

The announcement had come the previous autumn prior to the Belgian Grand Prix at the famous Spa-Francorchamps circuit, where Andy Moretti appeared as part of an effort to show interest in Formula One, which was rapidly gaining popularity in America with the new U.S. ownership group. Evelyn Stevens had signed a contract to drive for Moretti Motorsport the following season, teaming with the two second-generation Moretti boys, Tony and Alex. She had brought in some extra sponsorship from Seagram promoting their evermore popular wine cooler product line.

The extra sponsorship dollars came with a personal cost. The motor racing media fraternity had long adopted Stevens as their poster girl, but now the rest of that world celebrity paparazzi had joined in, putting yet more of a strain on her and Alex's romantic relationship, as well as the Moretti Motorsport team as a whole. What began as a novelty was now causing dissension in the ranks, as the increased media attention had brought some unforeseen problems. The Indycar series had long touted their access to the drivers and teams, taking a cue from the NHRA, but series president, Jay Frye, had little choice but to add a few restrictions at most venues, as crowd control and security became major concerns.

Tony's recent bride, now expecting their first child, had developed a sort of kindred spirit friendship with Evelyn, a relationship strained when a rather sleazy article appeared on social media and a tabloid magazine comparing the five-month-pregnant Crissy Moretti with Stevens, implying that young Alex had made up ground over his older brother with his romantic accomplishments, something he had yet to do on the racetrack. The post went viral, causing a new level of anxiety within the team, and much to the consternation of everyone in the Moretti family. By coincidence, the originator of the offending blog appeared to come from the same source as the blogger who perpetuated the compromising social media video months earlier.

The team endured nevertheless, pulling off an impressive victory in the prototype class at the Daytona 24-hour endurance classic to start the year, followed up by a win at the Saint Petersburg Grand Prix by Tony, with Evelyn joining him on the podium with an impressive third. Alex had led early and ran among the leaders for half the race prior to retiring with gearbox problems.

The grand opening, planned for late January was delayed a few weeks over construction issues. The delay, however, worked in everyone's favor as the team presented a fast start on all fronts with the win at the Rolex 24, their lead NASCAR driver Alan Allison finishing a promising fourth in the Daytona 500, and the stellar showing in St. Pete. The huge event was promoted as a celebration for all the employees of Moretti Motorsport and their sponsors, which really meant it was a huge coming-out party for Unibank Corporation.

Their sponsorship announcement had rocked the world of motorsports, and along with the Ford announcement to partner with Moretti and re-enter Indycar as part of the new hybrid engine formula, the team seemed poised to solidify their competitive status at the top of the sport, build on their new partnership in NASCAR, and push to move into Formula One as an expansion team.

It was a monumental deal, four years with a two-year option, and one that revolutionized the entire Moretti operation. The contract was extremely sophisticated in its size and scope, requiring an overall team performance standard, tied certain drivers to the sponsorship as well as the team, and included ample obligations for commercial advertisements, corporate appearances, etc.

The major dollars from Unibank enabled Andy to enhance the recently acquired NASCAR team, but more importantly, gave the team the financial backing needed to enter Formula One with some of the sport's finest talent. The relationship also predicated a move to the Charlotte area from their long-time base in suburban Chicago, a more centralized location to service all the racing series, tripling the size of their existing NASCAR facility and becoming the team's worldwide headquarters.

The newly transplanted employees loved the area, close in proximity to the mountains and the ocean, as well as Lake Norman. The area had long been the epicenter of the NASCAR world with most of the major teams based there as well as home to many of their drivers, not to mention the nearby homes of iconic legends like Richard Petty and Dale Earnhardt, Jr. Nearly all suppliers of motor racing hardware had facilities nearby and, of course, the proximity to the Unibank World Corporate Office building, located in downtown Charlotte, was icing on the cake.

The new facility, just north of Huntersville, North Carolina, was completely dressed up for the occasion. The 700,000-square-foot facility would have every nook and cranny decked out for the invited guests and their entourage. Much of the corporate brass from Unibank were there, including their CEO Byron Cook, the man who had been a tough sell on rubber stamping the four-year sponsorship deal.

The deferred schedule of the event and more pleasant March weather allowed many of the bank executives, along with their family members, to be treated to a thrilling ride at the nearby Charlotte Motor Speedway with Alex and Tony Moretti chauffeuring their guests around the mile and a half banked racetrack in the special two-seater Indycar at one hundred sixty miles per hour.

One of the riders was Allison Cook, the oldest of Byron Cook's two daughters, while the younger of the two girls, Amanda, stood with her parents and other bank staff, her father suggesting she was still a bit too young for such extremities.

The highlight of the festivities was the unveiling of the new Unibank livery featured on each of the various series cars, NASCAR, Indycar, IMSA, and last but not least, the Formula One model, one which Unibank would co-sponsor with British Petroleum starting the following season.

The car was actually a rebranded year-old McLaren, generously on loan by Zak Brown, the team principal of the legendary team, and one who had given tacit approval for his friend Andy in his quest to enter F1, a support that was yet to be unanimous among his F1 compatriots.

Everyone present would get an ample number of photographs with the cars and team drivers, highlighted by the very photogenic and popular Evelyn Stevens. By evening's end, the bank guests seemed to be all smiles, impressed with the hospitality while totally excited about the Unibank liveries on all the race cars.

In concert with Unibank's recent acquisition of a sizable West Coast bank chain, arrangements were made by Herrera for Cook and his family to join the rest of the bank contingent as special guests of Moretti Motorsport at the very popular and festive Grand Prix of Long Beach the following month in southern California.

As the pilot announced the descent into Las Vegas over the intercom, a directive that all passengers be seated and to secure their seatbelts, Andy gathered his final thoughts on such a memorable past year as he prepared mentally to deal with the present and what awaited him at the hospital, not only his own youngest being injured but facing the Cooks as their youngest child was in critical condition and fighting for her life.

"I knew when I saw those two girls there would be fireworks," Andy had told Ward as he boarded their plane before takeoff. "But I had always just assumed it would be the oldest Cook girl."

Chapter 2

Hospital Reminiscence

W hen Andy walked in there was a moment of silence, reflecting the obvious tension. While Alex had looked better, his father was quite battle-worn emotionally, appearing to have aged ten years in the last twenty-four hours. Matilde stood and shared an emotional embrace with her son, tired as she had been there on watch with her injured grandson since arriving early Sunday morning.

"How are you feeling?" Andy asked as he and Alex shared a brief handshake.

"I've been better, Dad," Alex replied, struggling to find a few words. The enormity of what had just occurred was not lost on any of them. "I'll live."

"They still have him hopped up," his grandmother chided.

"Not so much," Alex stated, the last shot of Demerol having been several hours earlier. "How is Amanda?"

His father and grandmother shared a look, both pausing as if thinking how to tell him. "I was there about five minutes ago. She's still unconscious, Alex, Her mother and father were there outside the ICU," Andy advised. "I didn't receive the warmest of welcomes."

Alex had to glance away toward the window. *Unconscious! Oh my god,* he thought as a tremendous bout of guilt fell over him.

"I suppose you want to tell me what happened?" Andy asked seriously, approaching the side of his son's hospital bed while his mother stood on the opposite side.

"We were just heading back into town from Hoover Dam. I came up Tropicana Boulevard towards the MGM Grand when a delivery truck pulled out in front of us. I heard a crash and the next thing I knew, I was waking up here....I want to see her. Can you take me down there?"

"Alex, are you out of your mind? Her family is getting ready to sue us for every dime we're worth. We're trying to figure out if they will be given grounds to sue and cancel their contract with us." Andy declared, struggling to keep his cool. "Forget about not showing up at their corporate banquet, Alex.... But sixteen years old!? What in hell were you thinking?"

"Andy, don't be too hard on him," Matilde prompted. "I recall when you were young. Sabetha was what, six years younger than you?"

"Yes, Mom! But Sabetha wasn't Byron Cook's teenage daughter, the man who writes the check that keeps the whole team running!... Damn, Son! How could you be that careless!? This little stunt of yours has jeopardized the solvency of the entire company! I don't know how we ever recover from it." Andy decried seriously. "You had better hope and pray that girl survives."

Alex was jolted emotionally, unable to speak.

Matilde was angry. "Anthony Moretti! Would you just listen to yourself? You're just like your father. Everything is just about your racing cars, the rest of our lives be damned! Your son is in the hospital and could have been killed! Get hold of yourself!"

We drive cars at two hundred miles per hour for a living. Getting killed in auto accidents is not that much of a shock to us, Andy thought, a vain attempt to mentally excuse himself. "Yes, racing is our lives, God help us. But it's not just us. We have a lot of families who depend on paychecks from us.... Whatever you do, Alex. Stay away from that young Cook girl... Don't post on social media... Don't talk to the press about her... In fact, just see if you can keep a low profile,...if that's possible. We're all going to be in damage control mode for a while."

"What about St. Pete, Dad?"

"St. Pete?" Andy asked as he paused to share a glance with Matilde. "What about it? I've already penciled Crosby in to take your place. That all assumes we don't get shut down beforehand," Andy replied. The Indycar season's first event, the St. Petersburg Grand Prix, was less than two weeks out. Moretti Motorsport would again field three cars, with Alex previously assigned as their driver in one.

"Crosby!? You should have talked to me first, Dad! I'll be out of here in a day or two!"

"You don't know if you'll be cleared. I had to act. Besides, the Honda people despise these types of media circuses," Andy declared. "Even assuming you'll be fit, we can't have you in a Unibank-sponsored race car while this Amanda Cook lies in a hospital, possibly fighting for her life! You're out on this one."

Suddenly the family conversation was interrupted by a newsbreak on the room's TV monitor.

"This is Bryan Massey of NBC Sports. We are coming to you live from the Elite Medical Center in Las Vegas, Nevada, where Saturday evening, a serious accident occurred involving a sports car driven by well-known race driver Alex Moretti and passenger Amanda Cook, the sixteen-year-old daughter of Byron Cook, President and CEO of Unibank Corporation, one of the world's largest financial institutions. Moretti is reported to be in fair condition while young Amanda is now lying unconscious in an intensive care unit and listed as being critical. We'll now take you live to the hospital where Cook is preparing to give a public statement."

As the cameras zoomed in on the improvised podium, the broadcast engineers filled the waiting moments by showing highlight videos of Cook and Andy Moretti shaking hands in a photo op of the unveiling of the Moretti Unibank-sponsored Formula One car, More quick spots were shown featuring the Unibank co-sponsored F1 car with Tony Moretti driving, a second Unibank sponsored Indy car with Evelyn Stevens driving, and a third with Alan Allison driving the Unibank badged NASCAR model.

"This tragic accident has cast doubt on the monumental sponsorship deal that last year had rocked the entire world of motor racing. We go now to the gathered crowd as it now appears the shaken banker is approaching the microphone."

Appearing solemn and obviously stricken, Byron Cook stepped up to the improvised podium where he worked to adjust the microphone. "We have just left the hospital intensive care unit where my daughter Amanda remains unconscious, a state that has not changed since the accident. We believe her injuries are serious but we remain hopeful and pray for her full recovery. I wish to thank you all for the outgoing support that we have received worldwide. I will now make time for a few questions." Cook nodded to ESPN motorsport analyst Josephine Myer.

"Mister Cook, have you spoken to Andy Moretti and how do you see this affecting the sponsorship relationship between Unibank Corporation and Moretti Motorsport moving forward?"

"I have spoken to Andy just briefly a few moments ago, although we did not have a cordial conversation. I know our marketing people have been in close communication with them. Right now, my wife Sarah and I are focused 100% on Amanda's recovery, and any further comments regarding our ongoing relationship with a motorsport team would be inappropriate at this time."

"Mister Cook! Do you know how long Alex Moretti and Amanda have been seeing each other?"

"I do not know. Amanda cannot speak as of yet," Cook replied testily.

Andy held up the remote and hit the mute button.

"Relationship with *a* motorsport team! That pretty well sums it up," Andy reacted while shaking his head. "Let's not make this any worse than it is, Alex. You just concentrate on getting well and do not talk to the press! I need to get back to the hotel and take care of some business."

Matilde stood up and gestured to push Andy toward the door. "Yes, you go take care of your *business*."

The two walked out and stood momentarily in the hallway. "You need to lighten up on him, Andy. The boy has been through a lot."

"I'm trying to handle this as calmly as I can, Mom. But this is serious. God forbid, if this poor Cook girl dies, he could be charged with vehicular homicide... And speaking of Sabetha, have you heard anything from her?"

"I was going to ask you the same thing. No, nothing... Maybe she doesn't know about it, yet." Matilde replied with a sigh.

"She would have to be on top of Mount Everest or at the South Pole not to know about it, Mom. It's headline news worldwide now."

"I know not hearing from his mother eats at him. That's why he needs his dad's support right now."

"I have a full plate with this. You know that," he answered.

"Yes... Now go!"

Emotionally exhausted, Matilde shut the door and walked slowly back toward Alex's bedside. "You two are just alike," the Moretti family matriarch said to him, shaking her head. "As mad as I get toward your father, he's right about one thing. You've had nearly every girl on this planet chasing after you your whole life, Alex,...and you had to somehow get entangled with this sixteen-year-old?"

Alex stared back with a blank look. His grandmother was quite correct. Both Moretti boys always had girlfriends as their ethnic Irish and Italian good looks had served them well. While Tony had always one girlfriend at a time and had recently married, Alex had a reputation for being quite a lady's man, one who seemed to have a different girl in every port.

"How did you end up in the car with this bank CEO's daughter, anyway? Do you want to tell your grandmother about it?"

Alex couldn't help but force a smile. He loved his grandmother and had always been able to tell her anything. "It started back not long after the deal with Unibank was announced"...

"Wait, Alex! You mean this has been going on for a while?"

"It began last year at Long Beach.... We kind of crossed paths at a cocktail party in the Renaissance Hotel. It was Amanda and her sister Allison.

We shared some small talk, I hung out with Allison some later, and then Amanda and I took a long stroll together on the beach past midnight,"

"Those two girls are both lovely and practically look alike," Matilde injected curiously. "But Allison must be close to your age. Why the sixteen-year-old?"

"It's kind of a long story, Grandma," Alex answered timidly, not mentioning the fact that Amanda was actually still fifteen at the time.

Matilde motioned as if to check the time on a watch, one which she did not have on, and dragged the corner guest chair over next to his bed. "All I have is time, my grandson."

Long Beach, California, a year earlier...

The atmosphere in Long Beach was electric and the hotel was buzzing with activity. The Grand Prix of Long Beach was the area's busiest tourist event as the famous auto race took hold. The Renaissance Hotel's main banquet hall was all decked out in racing décor as the most significant corporate sponsorship in recent series history was to be highlighted.

The annual Grand Prix through the streets and along the shoreline was the most prestigious event on the series calendar outside of the Indy 500 itself. Established as a race featuring the old Formula 5000 series in 1975, the event subsequently turned into what was affectionately titled the U.S. Grand Prix West, a second American race for Formula One and grabbed the imagination of North American racing fans when legend Mario Andretti won in the famous John Player Special Lotus two years later. Monetary issues predicated the venue switch to the more domestic Indycar series several years later and the event remained extremely popular, not only with fans but for corporate sponsors as well.

Unibank had used the occasion and connection as a major sponsor to offer a promotional contest for their regional bank managers and much of the corporate brass from Charlotte were on hand as well, all guests of

Moretti Motorsport. The contingent was larger by double than any group they had hosted prior, predicating an extra investment in non-racing staff, both full and part-time, to accommodate them.

One popular cocktail reception was held annually and hosted by Racer Magazine. A virtual who's who of motorsport team owners, drivers, and dignitaries were gathered at the party, including Evelyn Stevens, recently returning from Tahiti following a lucrative photo shoot for Elle Magazine.

While the crowded ballroom was buzzing with chatter, two young women, appearing to the distant eye as being identical twins, looked about merrily, catching their share of attention as the old adage, *her momma's good looks and her daddy's money,* fit the two girls to a tee. Allison was four years older than her younger sibling Amanda, and the family had used the occasion as special guests to visit their oldest daughter, who was nearing completion of her sophomore year at UCLA.

"Look, Amanda. There's the two Moretti brothers, one for each of us," Allison stated giggling.

"I think one of them is married, Allison," Amanda replied.

"Oh? You've been checking them out, huh Amanda?... Well then, that still leaves one."

Like a gold band ever held you back, Allison, the younger sister thought to herself. "It's such a shame Aaron couldn't be here for this."

"Yes, such a pity," Allison commented, tongue-in-cheek.

Aaron Williams, Allison's longtime boyfriend, was in his second year as a cadet at the Citadel, the famous military academy in Charleston, South Carolina. He had strenuously pressured Allison to attend nearby Charleston Southern University, a personal endeavor on the part of him and his family that failed. Spending her exciting years at a Baptist College was not an option for Allison Cook, a beautiful young woman from a rich family who possessed a certain zest for life, one that begged to flourish beyond the horizon of her native conservative South Carolina.

While many journalists and their staff wanted photographs of Evelyn Stevens and Alex Moretti together, it was apparent to all observers that he was quietly annoyed by it, as he circled the ballroom in a constant effort to escape while causing a strain in the relationship that could hardly be disguised. Catching him in an isolated moment, the two sisters., one in particular, was quite forward while the other younger and shy one followed in tow.

"You look like you need a break from all the publicity, do you not, Alex?" Allison asked as more of a suggestion.

Young Moretti smiled at the two, recalling them vaguely from the team's facility opening a few weeks earlier, but feeling at a disadvantage and degree of embarrassment at not recalling their names. "Yes, it does get a bit much, sometimes," he replied, still mentally attempting to recall the two, catching a break when the crowd all quieted briefly as the girls' father was about to be interviewed by an NBC Sports reporter, along with Adam Herrera and Andy Moretti.

"This is Leigh Diffey, coming to you from Long Beach, California on Friday night, kicking off the world-famous Long Beach Grand Prix, the longest-running street circuit race in the Western Hemisphere and a crown jewel of Indycar. I have here three very special guests, Byron Cook, the President and CEO of Unibank Corporation, Adam Herrera, their Vice President of Marketing, and racing legend Andy Moretti, team owner of Moretti Motorsport. It is a very exciting time in Indycar as Unibank enters the series as the major sponsor for Moretti Motorsport. Adam, I'll start with you. Could you share with our worldwide motorsport audience why Unibank has chosen to get involved with racing and what the corporation hopes to achieve?"

"Thank you for having us, Leigh, and let me state how excited we are at Unibank to partner with Andy Moretti, and expand our footprint in this exciting sport. We started our involvement in motor racing two years ago, and as you know, we felt it went well and chose to expand. We are so happy to be here and involve Unibank with Moretti Motorsport, a name that has meant so much to motorsports internationally for so many years. Being from Charlotte, Unibank has always been close to the sport of motor racing and we really feel the Moretti team to be such a great association for us with their presence and record of success in so many different forms of racing."

"And Andy, you must be very excited about getting an iconic sponsor like Unibank onboard, yes?"

"I'm very excited about it. As you know, Leigh, our sport is so competitive in all venues. Having Unibank as our major sponsor will allow us to expand and bring in top talent worldwide. It's a great move forward for our team and I believe very good for motor racing overall."

"So Byron, the Unibank focus will be mostly in the Indycar series, at least initially it seems. Can we assume that is a measure of great things to come from a series that has gradually recovered from the woes of the Covid pandemic?"

"Well, Leigh, you know Unibank has been involved with NASCAR for years, although certainly not to this level. We're all about gaining customers and we see new opportunities here. Of course, since Andy has now purchased majority ownership in a NASCAR team, we will be increasing our footprint there as well."

"Adam, I understand this isn't your first Long Beach Grand Prix," Diffey continued.

"Oh no. I'm originally from this area and this event was always a *must-do* event on my personal calendar. Many of us at Unibank have long been fans of Indycar, and racing in general. As you know, California has a very rich history in motor racing. In my garage sits my pride and joy, a 1965 Shelby Cobra coupe, a very rare car with a 427 racing engine. While it's true that Indycar has faced some strong headwinds over the past twenty-plus years, since Roger Penske and his company took over the series we see some great things happening. Of course, the Covid pandemic set back the series, as it affected many sports enterprises, but we see Indycar as being on solid ground now. Understand, the great staff at Unibank supports all forms of motor racing. As you know, we're also doing some marketing at the new Formula One race in Las Vegas."

"Andy, one last question for you before we go to break. It's no secret you have a strong desire to field a team in Formula One. Can you shed any light on how that initiative is progressing?"

"We're working on it. You know Formula One is the world pinnacle of motor racing and it is a rather exclusive club. We're hoping our franchise will be finalized by mid-year and we'll be on the grid a year from now."

"There is the expectation that one or both of your sons will be the drivers on that team. Can you tell us anything about that?" Diffey asked.

"There will be many opportunities for drivers, Leigh. I'll leave it at that for now," Andy replied smiling.

The buzz in the crowd resumed, while Alex and the two Cook sisters smiled at each other, waiting to break the ice.

"I am Allison Cook. You gave me a spin in that two-seater race car in Charlotte," the older of the two introduced herself, holding her left hand up in a motion to imply he should conclude the introduction with a gentlemanly kiss.

"I apologize, but I think the last time we met you had a driver's suit and full-face helmet on," Alex responded smiling while glancing toward the obviously less forward younger sister, who blushed and held out her hand to simply shake his.

"Oh, and this is Amanda, my little sister," Allison added rather awkwardly, while Amanda gave her a disapproving stare.

Alex studied for a brief moment. "Allison and Amanda Cook, Byron Cook's daughters, of course. Pretty cool, you two coming all the way out here for this."

"I actually attend school in LA and even arranged for some of my sorority sisters to be here, too," Allison added quickly.

"Oh, that's impressive," he answered. "What college?"

"I'm in my second semester at UCLA," Allison replied proudly.

"And what about you, Amanda?" Alex asked, genuinely interested.

"She's a freshman at Fort Mill in Rock Hill," Allison replied on her sister's behalf, and much to her dismay. "It's a high school in our hometown."

"My dad flew me out for this with the family," Amanda added, attempting to disguise a hidden disdain for her older sister constantly belittling her.

"Well, how do you two like it? The racing, I mean," Alex asked, a question directed more toward Amanda, perhaps in an effort to get her to open up.

"Love it," Allison answered falsely. Her father had taken the girls to many NASCAR events in Charlotte over the years, supporting a former team owner who was a huge bank customer and giving Allison a level of disdain for the sport. "Such a party! Speaking of parties, I'm hosting one later with some friends at the Tower Penthouse. Would you like to join us? I mean,...of course, you and Evelyn."

"We may just do that," he said. "I'll see what's on the hit parade for later, anyway. Could just be me, if that's okay?"

Allison quickly gave him her best flirtatious smile. *Oh, trouble in paradise, it seems,* she thought. "All the better. We could head over in an hour or so!"

"I'll have to hang on here for a while until this reception ends. Give me the location, if you care to," Alex stated, smiling neutrally toward the two.

"I'll text it to you, if that's okay, Alex?" Allison replied, accustomed to getting her way with the male persuasion and already confident the two had established a personal connection. She then pulled her phone from her purse in a prompt that he should give her his number.

"Well, if you will both excuse me, I had best get back to team socializing," Alex stated, giving the two an approving nod. *What a beautiful smile,* he thought to himself. *Both of them! And both look so much alike,... yet so different somehow.*

At just past 9:00 PM, the Racer cocktail reception wound down. Evelyn's agent had arranged for her and Alex to visit a hospitality suite at a top-floor Renaissance suite sponsored by Merkim Vallez, a well-known Hollywood publicist. Alex resisted, suspecting more and more that these appearances were as much to forward the career of Louis Newberry as an agent than to benefit his client, Stevens, and the youngest Moretti was getting evermore tired of being a part of Evelyn's social life,... in effect, standing in her shadow.

"Alex, come on. You have to come!" she stated forcefully. "I need you there."

"Why Evelyn? For more photo ops? You're a stand-alone celebrity now, baby. You don't need me there."

"Alex! Don't get weird on me! Do you have any idea what this could mean to our future?"

"You mean *your* future. And I have a *very* good idea....And more and more, I begin to see I want no part of it," he added. "We have a busy day tomorrow. Let's blow this off and head in," he added suggestively, although doubting she would follow. *That was probably a word or two too far*, he mused. *But some things just have to be said.*

He walked away as the sport's most popular driver stared at his backside,... before Newberry grabbed her by the arm, escorting her away.

At just past eleven, Alex lay awake staring at the ceiling alone as Evelyn had gone off with Newberry without him. This was nothing new. She had gone to Paris in December without him and he had more recently declined to accompany her to Tahiti.

He wanted his picture on the front of Racer and Autosport magazines, not Vogue or Cosmopolitan. And he wanted the pictures and articles to be about him as a racer, not as Evelyn Stevens' boyfriend.

Just one time, he would like to move through the checkout line at a grocery store without seeing his and her photographs pasted on nearly every tabloid magazine. He would hear the whispers behind him; "Look, that's Evelyn Stevens' boyfriend."

He pondered over and over about the party invite as he lay there agitated, and finally said to himself. "Oh, what the hell."

He then got up to get dressed again.

Twenty minutes later, he knocked on the door of the fifteenth-floor penthouse apartment and was greeted by two rather wild-looking young fellows, one sporting lime green colored hair, while the other appeared to have every gold colored ornament sold at a flea market kiosk attached to his head. "Hey Mon, come on in! I assume you know somebody here, right Mon?"

Moretti was a young man accustomed to being recognized, particularly at the various series' venues, finding it strange that not a soul in the large suite did, nor seemed to act as though they had a clue about the weekend event he was part of.

Allison spied him from afar and the wheels were already turning. *He's here alone! Evelyn Stevens' boyfriend.* Accustomed to having her way with members of the opposite sex, she saw this as an opportunity she could hardly resist and zestfully came running. "Alex!"

He smiled and greeted her casually, still looking around and wondering if this was such a good idea.

"So Allison, did you say this is your first time at a race?" he asked, attempting to get comfortable.

"We used to go to the Charlotte Motor Speedway, several times I believe. Sat up in a corporate suite."

"Oh, that's right. I think you may have mentioned that. We just got into NASCAR," Alex stated, moving the conversation.

"It's much different than this. I can tell that," Allison added. "Will you race there?"

"Not this year. I volunteered to run a few next season. They run nearly twice as many races as we do. So I would like to run Daytona and maybe a few more NASCAR races if the schedule works out."

"So, what happened to Evelyn?" she asked gleefully, sort of indicating she had interests at the moment other than motor racing.

"Oh, she had prior commitments," he replied neutrally.

"I guess that means you're my date, then," she responded and grabbed him by the arm, leading him around the room and introducing him to some of the crowd, as she was obviously fairly well-known.

"Who are these people?" Alex asked. Generally, when one showed up at any of the circuits' weekend parties, some of the personnel from the paddock would be familiar. The younger team members, like himself, were among the late-nighters. He didn't recognize a soul.

"They're mostly from the university. One of my sorority sisters is from here and invited a few of her friends to join us. Look, that's Isaac Menori. You know, Marc Menori's son, the well-known movie producer?"

"No, not really. I don't frequent movies much," Alex replied.

Out of nowhere, a wild-looking blonde rushed up and gave Alex a strong lip lock. Surprised, he grabbed her gently around the waist, forcing some space between them. He had come to expect some bazaar behavior from fans, but this chick had given it some new meaning.

"Oh, sorry, baby. I thought you were someone else," the young woman spouted and then reached around Allison's neck, practically spitting in her ear. "I want one."

The two spent the next few minutes drinking champagne while she continued to introduce him to her many acquaintances from college. While he found Allison quite good-looking, she came off as quite bold, if even a bit raw for his tastes. He wrote it off as her having too much to drink.

"So, how long have you been screwing Evelyn?" she asked, a confirmation she was getting lit up.

"Oh! Now come the more subtle questions, right?" Alex replied, having given some quick thought to just saying it was none of her business, but thought better of. "Uh, how do you know I have been?" Alex answered with a neutral smile.

"Oh, I'm sorry," Allison replied with a roll of her eyes. "How long have you two been together? Is that the way I should ask it?"

"Several months, I think," he replied. "Why do you ask?"

She studied him a moment, unsure she could control him yet, something she was unaccustomed to with members of the opposite sex. "When an attractive young woman like me meets a handsome and famous guy like you, one does wonder about such things."

He nodded while avoiding her stare, knowing a come-on when he saw it, but strangely relieved when another of Cook's spaced-out friends approached and immediately imposed himself into their conversation.

"So, you're one of those drivers, huh?" The young man asked, somewhat condescendingly.

"He drives for my dad now, Terry," Allison stated. "Right, Alex?"

"Yes! I got it now," her classmate, Terry, declared before Alex had an opportunity to respond. "You're that Evelyn Stevens' boyfriend. Lucky you. Man, is she hot... Is she here?"

Alex stole a glance toward Allison, one of tacit disapproval. "Could we get some air?" he inquired, put off by this Terry character and feeling the room was getting a bit noisy, not to mention the various aromas circulating.

"We're heading outside to the balcony, Terry," Allison told him sternly. "Alone!"

"Tell him I do threesomes, Allison!... If he's into it," he screamed at their backsides as they exited his company, with Allison escorting Alex away with her left arm while reaching behind her back and giving her outspoken classmate the middle finger salute with her right.

The two stepped out onto the balcony overlooking the harbor and beach. They were not alone but it was not as crowded outside, nevertheless.

"So, do you want to tell me about it, Alex?... Evelyn, I mean."

"Evelyn and I have kind of evolved, I guess. We're close. We live together. But we're teammates and competitors, too. It's not easy to blend all that."

"I suppose it isn't. Does she know you're here with me?" Allison asked, a bit presumptively as she looked away toward the beach.

"She probably doesn't know where I am. And at this point, we sort of quit asking," he replied, as much to himself as to Allison.

"I have my own room, on a different floor at the Westin," she quickly added.

My, you are straight to the point, aren't you? He caught her drift but wasn't to that stage, yet. *And that Terry's retort, implying that he had a history with Allison? Not sure I'm all too keen on what this gal's into.* he thought feigning a smile. "This used to be a much better vantage point up here in the old days before they changed the circuit. I remember back when my dad raced here. Have you been here before?"

"No," she replied, annoyed that he wasn't taking her bait and changed the subject, a ploy she had used many times herself but was totally unaccustomed to the same treatment. "You seem kind of stiff, Alex. Come on, let's loosen you up." She guided him toward another small cadre of friends at the other end of the balcony.

The smell seemed like a substance different than regular Marijuana, he thought. "What is this stuff?"

"Best crack you'll ever smoke, Mon," a rather fried-looking young student answered.

He looked at Allison seriously. "This is not my deal."

"Oh, come on, Alex. It'll help you forget about Evelyn," she stated plainly. *And more about jumping me!*

"I have a race car to set up tomorrow."

"Alex!" Allison screamed. "What's wrong with you?"

"Nothing that will get resolved with this," he replied, eyeing those around him who were obviously getting blitzed and thinking a few were a bit too cavalier in hanging over the railing from fifteen floors up. "Thanks for the invite, Allison. I'm out of here."

She followed him all the way to the door. "You've only been here for a few minutes!"

He just nodded and stated again that he had a car to drive in the morning, headed toward the hallway, and shut the door in front of her.

Allison was completely stunned. *You don't shun Allison Cook in front of her friends, you bastard!* She thought vindictively. "My daddy writes your paycheck! I own you, Alex Moretti!" she yelled at the door, loud enough to think he surely would hear her.

Alex departed from the elevator in the building lobby and walked out the door toward Shoreline Drive, quickly of a mindset that Allison Cook, as attractive as she was physically, had completely lost her allure, at least regarding his interest. He strolled out toward the street, preparing to make his way back to his hotel, when he noticed a lone figure out on the beach, a barefoot female casually stepping in and out of the ocean waves as they casually lashed against the sand. She stood out in the moonlight on the late-night shoreline as the evening was mildly cool in the spring here, and the beaches were yet to be crowded, even during the day. He studied the lone female for a moment, thinking there was something familiar about her.

He casually walked across Shoreline Drive to satisfy his curiosity and as he made his way across the beach parking lot the young woman saw him, freezing momentarily as the unknown figure seemed to approach.

Is that the young Cook girl? He pondered. "Amanda?"

She looked up, still uncertain, and began to move briskly toward the yacht harbor.

"Amanda, it's Alex! Alex Moretti!"

She then stopped and waited for his approach. "Hi," she said plainly.

He looked at his watch, seeing it was just past midnight. "Amanda, I'm not sure it's a good idea, you walking out here this late at night all alone. Do your parents know where you are?"

"No," she replied. "They went to bed about an hour ago. I went down to the hotel lobby for a soda and just decided to get some air. It's so nice out here, and quiet.... And pardon my saying so, but you don't seem like the fearful type, driving cars for a living at three hundred miles per hour," Amanda commented smiling.

"It's actually just over two hundred, Amanda, and this place won't be quiet for long," he grunted. He thought again about Allison, mostly how much the two sisters resembled each other. *But they were so different.*

"And speaking of quiet," she asked curiously. "Enough nightlife already?"

"You could say that," Alex replied, finding himself enjoying the conversation with the younger Cook girl, one who seemed to have shed her shyness. "You're at the Westin, aren't you?"

"That's right," Amanda replied.

"Me, too. I had better escort you back there."

She looked at him, not wanting to appear as the lost kid, but happy he was with her. "So, you didn't go to Allison's party?"

"Yes, I actually did, briefly. I have to run setup on the car tomorrow, so I didn't stay long."

"You know she wanted to sleep with you."

He hesitated, suddenly not so comfortable in having this conversation with a girl this young, speaking so boldly about her sister and only having met them a few hours earlier. "Did she tell you that?"

"No. She didn't have to. I know my sister."

"Sounds like you don't approve," Alex said, half-jokingly but genuinely curious.

"Her life. She's just,... well, different than me."

"Oh, I thought you liked me," Alex joked.

"That's not what I meant."

"I know... You two sure look alike. I mean that as a compliment."

"That's what everyone says," Amanda replied. "Like you and your brother. You guys look alike."

"True enough, I suppose." *But you and Allison could almost pass for twins,* he thought. "But we're sure different, too."

"His wife is very pretty," Amanda stated sincerely. "How old is the little one?"

"Chrissy? Yes, she's a real sweetie. My new nephew, Adrian, is seven weeks old."

"So, what about your girlfriend, Evelyn?"

"What about her?" Alex asked, curious himself now about her curiosity.

"Are you two serious?" she asked, somewhat presumptuous considering they had just met, what,...four hours earlier? Amanda assumed there must be something going on if he was partying with her sister,... *or perhaps he indeed was the Paddock Playboy,* she pondered.

"I thought so, for a while at least. Not sure we're right for each other," Alex answered, pausing his thoughts for a brief moment and looking away to the sea, as though answering the question for himself and not just the curious teen at his side.

The two strolled along the yacht harbor, pleasantly chatting and not realizing the circuit fence would not allow them past the Shoreline Village and around the northwest corner of the track, unless they wanted to go for a long swim.

"Oh oh, we can't go this way. We'll have to turn around," Alex stated, somewhat embarrassingly.

For her part, Amanda was thrilled. Alex was the best-looking guy she believed she had ever laid eyes on, not to mention she actually did feel much safer since he arrived. "If you showed up at Allison's party and didn't stay long, she'll be pissed."

"Yes, I gathered that," Alex replied, curious about where this conversation was headed. "What's she going to do, tell your dad on me?"

"She can be a real bitch, Alex,...capable of anything. I hate to say that about my own sister, but she is."

"Been there, done that. Can't make 'em all happy....Let me guess, you're a real sweetheart yourself, huh?"

"I'm sure I am no match for Evelyn Stevens. That woman is gorgeous," Amanda replied.

Alex felt a strange emotional rush, as this Amanda was so forthright in speaking her mind, belying her earlier façade as the shy little sister. "I think you just need to be yourself. Amanda, You don't need to emulate anyone else. Be true to yourself and you'll be just fine," he stated, believing Amanda was quite attractive herself even though she and her sister so strongly resembled each other. *There was just something about Amanda,* he kept thinking.

"How old are you, Alex?" she plowed on.

He continued to get amused, in a good way, that he and this teen girl were having such a visit. "Just turned nineteen, Amanda. And you?"

She thought about lying but then thought better of it. "I'll be sixteen in February."

Which means you just turned fifteen, Alex thought, amused but chose not to belittle the girl over it, and thinking she could have passed easily for seventeen or so. "Sweet sixteen and never been kissed," Alex replied smiling as the two approached the Westin Hotel entrance.

"I don't know about that," she said, returning his smile while looking around.

He looked around himself, looked at Amanda grinning, and picked her up off her feet. "Let's just remove all doubt then." The two engaged in a long and passionate kiss as they seemed drawn together like magnets.

Back on her feet, she looked around again while resetting her emotions, assuring herself the both of them weren't being watched. She then hugged Alex again heartily and kissed him again. "Please, don't tell Allison."

"Jealousy, huh?"

"Worse than that. She would tell Mom and Dad," Amanda replied seriously. "I'd be grounded for the rest of my life."

Yes, being out here this late, caught with this particular fifteen-year-old would probably not go over well, he thought. "Don't worry about it... Our secret."

The two prepared to depart when Amanda asked for Alex's mobile number. "Can I text you?"

"Sure, Amanda. Just give me your number and I'll look for it."

"How many Amandas do you have saved?" she asked smiling.

"Oh, hundreds," he joked. "But you'll be the only one tagged simply as *Amanda*... No last name... You had best walk in through the lobby ahead of me, you know?"

"I do....Well, Alex Moretti, I hope you win Sunday," Amanda said parting as she headed for the lobby doors, looking back one last time at him and smiling.

She then headed toward the elevators, suddenly upbeat about the weekend and hoping she and Alex would connect again somehow. She entered her room, which had been reserved for her and her sister, together. She knew Allison would be quite late getting in, if at all, and if the party turned out the way she gathered from Alex's reaction, she knew her sister would be in a bad mood.

I need to text Trisha, Amanda thought of her best friend as she searched online for a picture of Alex to attach. *"Trisha! Check out who I met tonight!"*

Alex returned to his hotel room minutes later, not surprised nor even strangely annoyed that Evelyn was still out on the town. He got to sleep quickly after some mixed and emotional feelings regarding the two Cook sisters. *Pity they can't just swap personalities, though,* Alex pondered, knowing the older of the two must be about his own age.

His thoughts kept returning about his late encounter with Amanda, the younger one, an experience that reminded him of a first love years earlier. There was an obvious rift between the two siblings, one that he was genuinely curious about. He found himself wishing Amanda was older, if only by a couple of years. *What if a passerby did see us out in front of the hotel tonight?* Alex thought. *Oh my god, there would be hell to pay over that. Fifteen years old,... and the daughter of the Unibank CEO! I'd best get her out of my mind and get some sleep,* he told himself. *But there was just something about Amanda,* Alex kept pondering... *Something quite enchanting.*

Chapter 3

Strained Romance

The next morning, Alex awoke early with Evelyn lying next to him. He had slept so soundly that he hadn't even noticed her arrival, and was oblivious to the time. The mood was awkward while he prepared a coffee pot, as she expected some sort of token inquiry about how her night had gone, an interrogation not forthcoming. Much to the contrary, she noticed Alex seemed aloof, as though nothing out of the ordinary had happened between them. It had been a habit, if not customary, for the two to arrive at the track garage area together, and she was surprised when he headed out early without her.

Evelyn did show up a half hour later and joined Alex among the other team members and guests for the buffet breakfast, served at the Moretti hospitality tent in the paddock garage area. The two chatted casually with Tony and Crissy, the new baby still with Matilde back at the hotel. Both Alex and Evelyn avoided any inquisitive remarks about the night before.

Nearby, Andy and team manager Bob Ward sat with the company of Adam Herrera and the Cook family, Byron, Sarah, and the two girls. A third young woman sat at that table as Allison had invited one of her sorority sisters, Kim Davidson, who happened to live in nearby Malibu Beach.

The girl kept giving Alex a flirty glance, one not lost on Evelyn. The young woman then got up and strolled over to their table. "Alex Moretti, Do you remember me from Allison's party last night? We didn't get a selfie together. Would you mind?"

Stevens had to force a smile, angered and somewhat embarrassed by this clandestine party divulgence. It was the same for Alex, but for other reasons. He did recall vividly this wildly forward female from the party the night before. How could he forget? *What kind of game are they playing?* He pondered while seeing Evelyn was not at all happy with this unfamiliar and admittedly wild-looking babe.

"All of us wanted a photo with him," Kim stated, mostly for Evelyn's consumption. "But Allison just wouldn't let go of him, not even for a second. She's such a lush," Davidson spoke while laughing.

"I hate to leave good company, but duty calls," Alex stated abruptly, wanting to exit the conversation.

As if on cue, Allison approached just prior to Stevens herself preparing to exit. Acting as though nothing unforetold had occurred, she sat down next to the series' lone female driver. Allison had a mentality that she held some sort of implied power over Stevens, as well as all of the Unibank-sponsored drivers, as the daughter of the corporate sponsor's CEO, and was still angry that Alex Moretti didn't quite understand that, yet. She had been planning a sweet revenge ever since Alex had so flagrantly embarrassed her the night before, starting with using her so-called college friend Kim's intrusive performance just a few moments earlier.

"So, Evelyn, do you miss England?" Allison asked, feigning interest. "I always wanted to spend time in London. It must be a blast!"

Evelyn was seething with discomfort, knowing she couldn't lash out at Allison or her flirty friend, at least not at the present. She bit down hard while thinking of a proper response. "It's like many bloody large cities, I suppose. It has its high points,... and low points."

All during breakfast, Amanda had kept to her parents, wishing she could somehow connect with Alex, but having to settle for the slight but significant rush she felt when their eyes met. She couldn't keep from breaking a pleasant grin as she thought about their late encounter the previous night as she listened intently to the distant chit-chat between her sister and his girlfriend.

"Well, if you all will excuse me," Evelyn stated, as she herself had the need to get with her crew.

Allison put a subtle hand on Steven's arm prior to her preparing to back away from the table and began speaking in lowered tones. "Evelyn, I am sorry you couldn't make the party last night. I insisted that Alex bring you and he said he would tell you about it. All my friends there were so disappointed," she added disingenuously. "I hope that our being together wouldn't give you any false impressions."

"Oh, Evelyn's fine," a boisterous Louie Newberry blurted out as he had come onto the scene a few minutes earlier. Speaking on his client's behalf, her agent was the type who always believed his word would add credence to any conversation. He knew Evelyn would not be happy with this previously undisclosed party business involving her boyfriend and Allison Cook, so he had to keep reinforcing her on the value of a budding friendship with Byron Cook's outspoken and quite hot-looking daughter.

Allison held back a condescending laugh, seeing this Louie was quite buffoonish as an agent for the popular Stevens. *He could be useful, though,* she thought in a devilish way. *We'll toss his card in the bottom of the deck,... to be pulled and played when needed.*

The buffet crowd emptied the garage/hospitality area as all of the crews and drivers headed toward their perspective pit boxes in preparation for the morning warmup session, where teams had a final pre-race opportunity to tweak the setups on each car in race trim.

Ever conscious of the moods and attitudes of his team members, Andy overheard a bit too much of the hospitality chit-chat and chose to table an issue that went against his better judgment of generally dealing with such issues after a race. Waiting until the right moment, he pulled his youngest son aside. "Alex, what are you doing, chasing Allison Cook now?"

"No, I'm not chasing Allison, Dad," Alex replied, looking away as if in denial and not wanting to continue the conversation right then.

"What about this party? And now the Cook girl apologizing to Evelyn that you didn't tell her about it! Look, Alex. I'm not blind. I know you're tired of all of Evelyn's constant media attention. The good lord only knows that I'm tired of it myself. And I know Allison Cook is a babe in her own right.... Yes, I'm still a guy, too. But she *is* Byron Cook's daughter, the man who basically funds this entire operation now. You cannot get involved with Allison Cook! If you're going to fall out with Evelyn, there are a million other gorgeous young women out there, son. Do you hear what I'm saying?"

"I will not mess with Allison Cook! You have my word on it, Dad. Now, can I check in with my crew?"

"Of course," Andy replied in a lower tone as he watched his youngest boy walk away, conscious of the wandering eyes and ears of the crowd. *Your word on it, huh?* Andy pondered, certainly not expecting such a response.

The overall ambiance of the seaside circuit with its festive atmosphere had a positive effect on the Cooks in general, as Byron could see many casual fans who were not even into the racing itself on hand. "Potential customers all," Herrera kept reminding him. Their improvised canopy-covered suite overlooked the Moretti pit stalls and they felt as though they were right on top of the action.

Sarah and the girls seemed to really enjoy it themselves, especially since they had someone to root for now, with Allison suddenly appearing to be an enthusiastic Evelyn Stevens fan, while Amanda centered her more tempered attention on Alex Moretti. Sarah simply chose to pull for Tony Moretti to lend support to a little inner-family competition, convenient on her part as her driver seemed to be favored by all the pundits to win.

The Long Beach circuit, often referred to as the Western Hemisphere's Monaco, was similar in respect that passing on most of the track was difficult at best, thus qualifying took on an added importance. Alex had always been fast on the circuit, but today it seemed he and his crew could not get the right balance in the car and were running a full second off the pace of the leaders during qualifying, surprisingly failing to make the fast six, the drivers who would compete in a final session to win the pole position.

Conversely, Tony Moretti and Evelyn were both fast all weekend and Alex's older brother set the fastest time in winning the pole, lowering the track record by four-tenths of a second. Evelyn would start on the inside of row three, a favorable position in her own right, while Alex languished near the back of the field, over a second and a half slower than his brother in a tight, competitive field.

During the Sunday morning warmup, Alex and his crew made improvements to the car in race trim, convincing him that he had a winning chance, in spite of starting so far back. Evelyn was quite fast, too, and Tony was seen simply as the man to beat, starting on the pole and being the event's defending champion.

As midday approached starting time for the race, the excitement heightened as the various teams' VIP guests, including the Cook family, were all invited to walk out on the track during the pre-race period, mixing in and observing the various TV journalists and their camera crews meander through the starting grid, looking to interview the various drivers and other celebrity personalities.

Amanda appeared anxious as she wished to approach Alex's car, disappointed it was so far from the first few rows where her parents and their team guides seemed to want to gather. Struggling to remain nonchalant, she did wait until a short instant when her parents and sister were preoccupied to shoot Alex a short smile and wave, a brief but emotional rush hitting her when he raised his gloved hand from a distance to wave back at her.

Things didn't start off well in the race for Moretti Motorsport when hotshot rookie, Cam Raeburn, attempted a first turn inside move on Tony, braking too late and sliding right into the side of the pole sitter, taking both cars out of the race. Andy would complain bitterly to race officials, but the shunt would be written off as a racing incident and the first four laps would be run under caution.

The race was marred by multiple accidents and through sheer attrition and some timely pit strategy, things were looking up for Andy's team as Evelyn and Alex were running second and third going into the final segment and one pit stop remaining. Will Power, a driver possessed when tasting the checkered flag, led with two lapped cars between him and Evelyn, and would be a man who would be very difficult to beat. On lap 61, all of the lead cars came in for their final stop for fuel and a fresh set of tires. Power pitted a few spots ahead of the Moretti cars and with a very proficient stop appeared to have retained the lead when a lapped car unexpectedly swerved in pit lane, running into the back of Power's car and damaging the rear wing. Power would proceed onto the circuit, but the crash brought out the race's seventh caution flag and Will would have to re-enter the pits on the very next lap for repairs, ending any chance of the impassioned Aussie winning.

When the race went green again on lap 64, Evelyn led going into the first turn, followed by fan favorite Helio Castroneves, gaining a position during the last stop, with Alex Moretti trailing close behind in third. One advantage for Moretti was his reserve of the Push-to-Pass, a feature on Indycars giving each driver an extra reserve of boost to be used throughout the race at their discretion. Drivers who do well in conserving much of this reserve will have a straightaway advantage at the end of a race, and Alex had most of his allotment remaining, while his teammate Evelyn and Helio had little. Moretti dogged the cagey Castroneves, a man who had won the event a generation prior and a sports legend as one of a select few four-time Indy 500 champions.

With ten laps remaining, Helio began to lose air pressure in his left rear tire, allowing Alex to easily pass him on the Seaside Way backstretch and ending any chance of winning for the man affectionately known as Spiderman. With only a lapped car between the race leader Stevens' car and Alex, it appeared team Moretti was in for a rewarding one-two finish, a thought ecstatic for owner Andy Moretti, who endured a few laps of nausea following the opening lap incident taking out his oldest son.

Alex quickly passed the slower-lapped car and closed on Evelyn when she encountered some lapped traffic of her own. Taking the com from his two crew chiefs, Andy got on the radio, instructing his drivers to drive clean, no mistakes, and bring it home. With three laps remaining, Evelyn had completely exhausted her Push-to-Pass while also running to conserve fuel as an issue on her last pit stop resulted in a miscalculation and short fill condition.

Alex began to complain that Evelyn was slowing him down while Andy kept repeating to both his drivers to race clean and bring it home. On the white flag lap, the two cars drove past the flag stand side by side. Alex had the lead by a half car length and had the line going into the first turn, but broke late and nearly hit the first turn barrier while Evelyn passed him again on the inside of the first turn while he struggled to regain momentum. Comfortably leading after getting through the roundabout at the Aquarium Fountain, Evelyn appeared headed for victory when her car began to sputter on the Pine Avenue short straight. Trailing by a full four car lengths as he came out of the turn onto Seaside Way, Alex closed rapidly on his intimately close teammate and moved to pass her on the inside when she broke hard to cut him off. The two cars collided in the apex of the turn and both slid into the tire barrier, a shocking and devastating development for Moretti Motorsport.

As the yellow caution lights immediately lit up assuring the race would end under yellow, Pato O'Ward, a half a lap behind earlier and destined for a comfortable podium third place finish, slowly passed the two disabled Moretti cars, making his way around the final turns to victory.

An enraged Evelyn Stevens unstrapped her safety belts, jumped up out of her cockpit, and stormed toward Alex, screaming expletives and slamming her helmet to the ground. "Alex. you arse! That was my bloody corner! You took us both out!"

For his part, Alex was equally ticked off. "What kind of dumbass move was that, girl!? I had the line! Do you know what mirrors are for?"

The press couldn't get enough of it, and the image of the two at each other's throats soon became a front-page photo on a majority of sports press outlets worldwide, carrying over on social media for several days afterward.

The aftermath in the Moretti Motorsport garage area was not pretty. Andy went off on both of them, but mostly his son, who in his mind had robbed the team of an easy one-two finish.

Alex had his share of vitriol to throw back at his father. "What was it you always said, Dad!?... Morettis always race to win. How many times have I heard that?"

Alex kept reviewing the race film over and over, unconsciously blaming himself for the racing incident. Evelyn had her second major win in an Indycar within her sights. The team had the one-two in the bag. *If I would just not have pushed it. Was it because I just wanted to win that bad,...or did I just want to take it from her?....Aw, I'm a racer. Screw it!*

As Alex prepared to head out for the airport, he began to sift through the many text messages on his phone, a strong mixture of anger, sorrow, and tough breaks from many of his and her fans and acquaintances. He got a rather snide text from Evelyn's agent, one whom Alex had always known had the hots for her anyway, and sent Newberry a quick reply. *"Stick it where the sun don't shine, Louie!"*

He did receive one text that caught his attention and a brief smile. *"So sorry you didn't win. Maybe I'll see you around Charlotte sometime? Amanda."*

In more ways than one, Long Beach had seemed to seriously damage the nearly year-long romance between Alex Moretti and Evelyn Stevens. In the brief layoff before Alabama, she had only spent a few nights at home with him in North Carolina, and the two had shared no intimacy. As if to add credence to their personal rift, she announced she would make other living arrangements for the month of May. For the coming weeks at least, the two appeared to be strictly teammates,... and nothing more.

On Thursday evening the following week, the Cooks sat down for their formal evening dinner, a rare vestige remaining from an old conservative custom that much of society had abandoned, limited to the three of them since Allison was back in school at UCLA.

The topic of college football somehow came up, and as the family were big Clemson fans, much of the dialog always seemed to surround the Tigers and whether they would face Alabama in the upcoming season.

One who didn't say too much at the dinner table, Amanda surprised her parents a bit. "Speaking of Alabama, are we going to the race in Birmingham next weekend?"

Sarah shared a confused look with her husband. "Race in Alabama? What race, Amanda?"

"The Indycars. They race at Barber Motorsports Park, just outside of Birmingham."

"Barber Motorsports Park?" Sarah asked.

"Yes, Herrera is heading down there with Andy Moretti," Byron stated. "We'll be more represented at the NASCAR weekend in Delaware, though. We don't have facilities around central Alabama, although we are looking at an acquisition... So maybe next year. I knew Allison was getting friendly with Evelyn Stevens, but I didn't know you were into that racing stuff, Amanda. What's gotten into you?"

Amanda hesitated, not wanting to express too much. "Oh, that race out in California was so much fun," she replied. "I just kind of got interested in it."

"Speaking of sports," Byron interjected, changing the subject. "My golf pals and their wives are coming over for a barbeque Saturday evening. The Williams are bringing their son as well."

He then smiled, expecting a bit of enthusiasm from Amanda. Bud Williams had dropped some hints on the golf course that his son Kyle wanted to rekindle the relationship with Amanda, one that seemed to have stalled since the Cook's annual friends and family Christmas party. Kyle Williams was the local star quarterback at Fort Mill High and a favorite to win the Gatorade Player of the Year, a nationally sanctioned award for each state's outstanding high school athlete in each major sport. Williams stood to be the first student in forty-two years to win the prestigious award for both football and baseball.

Amanda didn't immediately reply, much to his father's surprise, if not disappointment.

"Bud told me Kyle has been badgered by over twenty universities offering him scholarships, including Alabama, Oklahoma, Florida State, UCLA, and of course, South Carolina and Clemson. I told him we haven't decided where you would attend college, Amanda," her father stated expectantly, his statement coming across as more of a question.

Amanda looked toward Sarah as the table endured a brief moment of uncomfortable silence. "I'm going to Brittany's slumber party on Saturday. I told you about it, Mom!"

"But there will be some kids, here! Kyle Williams included," Byron replied immediately. "You won't want to miss that, Amanda."

The whole table got momentarily and uncomfortably silent.

"May I be excused?" Amanda said finally. "I have a ton of homework to get done."

"Certainly, honey," Sarah replied as she and Byron watched their lone resident girl get up from the table and head quickly upstairs.

"What's going on around here, Sarah?" Byron asked, rather sternly. "Every teenage girl in the state would walk through fire to go out with Kyle Williams. I remember when Allison was that age. We couldn't keep her away from the boys. I can't recall Amanda even mentioning Kyle Williams' name for what seems like months."

"How long have you known about this? You can't just drop something like this on us with two days' notice, Byron," Sarah inquired.

"I invited them on Tuesday. I thought I had said something," he answered, flustered. Being the man of the house, he wasn't accustomed to being questioned like this.

"Amanda has been looking forward to this slumber party, Byron."

"Well, Bud won't come right out and say it, but he is worried about his son, thinking his issues with Amanda may affect his athletic performance. I don't know what to tell him."

"You don't have to tell him anything, Byron," Sarah added, wanting to say that issues with their daughter were none of Williams' nor his boy's business, but held her tongue.

"You do know Bud is one of my best clients, Sarah."

Sarah froze momentarily and shot looks of daggers at her husband. "Byron Cook! This isn't the old Antebellum South! Engagements and marriages are not arranged!"

Byron froze and was momentarily speechless. "I just want what's best for her, that's all."

"Best for her? Or best for you,...and Unibank? Do you know how you sound?"

"I don't believe I like your tone, Sarah," Byron responded sternly.

Sarah stood up, preparing to exit early from the family dinner table, a motion deemed inappropriate in the Cook household. "I don't like my tone, either,... or yours."

Amanda laid faced down on her bed as Sarah gave a soft knock on her door prior to entering. She knew her mother wanted to discuss the dust-up at the dinner table and didn't really want to talk about it.

"Amanda, you know your father means well, even if he does display that old southern male chauvinism occasionally."

"I know, Mom."

"We've never talked much about you and Kyle Williams, baby. Did you two actually break up?"

"We were never really dating, Mom. Dad always insisted we never date until we were sixteen, anyway," Amanda answered.

"Your father is just worried, that's all," Sarah came back. "You seem to just want to spend all your time with Trisha. He just remembers when Allison was your age."

"I'm not Allison, Mom," Amanda replied, trying to keep her voice calm, but struggling to do so.

"You used to get excited when you were around Kyle, Amanda. What did happen between you two? Are you just not interested in him?"

"Nothing happened between me and Kyle, Mom." Amanda fibbed. "And so far as me still having any interest, maybe you should ask Allison."

"Allison? What does she have to do with anything?" Sarah asked, an answer she wasn't 100% sure she wanted answered.

Amanda looked away and lowered her tone. "Nothing, Mom. It's nothing. I shouldn't have said that. Don't worry about me, Mom, Okay?"

"Sure baby," Sarah said as she and her youngest embraced just prior to her leaving to retire.

Chapter 4

Team Hospitality

The month of May was the most important on the series calendar. Historically, the month had been the entire focus of the motor racing world. On the whole, May in Indianapolis had become somewhat diminished from years earlier when Pole Day was two weeks before the 500 and drew over a quarter of a million fans itself. That phenomenon had abruptly stopped in the mid-nineties over the sanctioning split, and the series had since spiced things up by adding a mid-month race on the speedway's road course.

While some of the teams had based their operations in the Indianapolis area, the Morettis adapted by renting a large waterfront home on Geist Lake, with all splitting the cost. Evelyn had planned to stay earlier, but the rift between her and Alex predicated that she chose to get her own small condo in Zionsville, a northwestern suburb of Indianapolis and a much closer commute to the speedway.

Inner-team relations had remained strenuous for the past few weeks. Since their withdrawal, neither Alex nor Evelyn had appeared to be with anyone else romantically, at least so far as the paparazzi could tell, fueling speculation the spat that occurred in Long Beach was temporary, and Stevens herself refused to believe their split was permanent while thinking a few weeks cooling off period may not be such a bad thing, particularly when her schedule between the on-track sessions and her other promotional sponsorship commitments during May would keep her fully occupied.

For his part, Alex was all too happy to have a break from much of it, even taking the time to pull his boat all the way up from Lake Norman up to Indy for the month. He enjoyed his boating after hours and would often take his team members out, knowing their long hours spent in Gasoline Alley at the speedway could wear them down. Now that his older brother was a family man, and with Newberry always keeping Evelyn so occupied, Alex had become quite popular with the crew, and the time spent with many of them off-hours seemed to keep him occupied, taking away at least some of the loneliness in not being intimately attached to his teammate.

The Grand Prix on the speedway road course turned out to be the best single race result ever for Andy Moretti, as his two boys, Tony and Alex, finished one-two, and defending circuit champion Evelyn also came home with a solid third. The three all shared the podium for the first time ever, and there were shouts, hugs, and the spraying of champagne abound.

Alex and Evelyn seemed to put any dissension aside, at least for the moment, and one image went viral on social media of the two in an embrace with ample captions ranging from *"Back in the love nest?"* to *"The first couple of motor racing returns"*. As happens often in motorsports, as with many other things in life, one's highlight is always what happened lately, and the sour mood from Long Beach just a few short weeks earlier seemed like old news.

The post-race celebration winding down, one of the mechanics on Alex's team, Mathew Ralston, had recently married and had brought his new bride up for a long weekend from Charlotte, along with another couple who were close friends. Alex invited the four for a Monday evening cruise on his boat, and as both the girls were big Evelyn Stevens fans, he took the opportunity to invite her, also. Whether Alex was motivated to further thaw any rift team-wise that was left over from Long Beach, or to test the waters on rekindling romance, he wasn't totally sure himself. But Evelyn readily accepted and all agreed to meet at the Moretti's waterfront leased home at 7:00 PM.

The four Morettis, Andy, Alex, Tony, and his bride Chrissy, pulled into the driveway at half past six. Alex had invited his father but the patriarch declined, never overly comfortable in the role of boss and being around his son and popular female driver engaging in anything other than business. Following a quick change of clothing, Alex scurried down to the dock in order to prep the boat a bit for company, when he heard his phone beep with new messages.

The first message from Evelyn read, *"Louie has a last-minute network interview for me, Alex. I'll have to ask for a raincheck"*. He read the message and shook his head, not one accustomed to this kind of rejection from women. Not too upset, though, he shook it off, thinking this to be a sign, one that reminded him of all the reasons their intimate relationship had soured in the first place.

He casually opened and browsed through the rest of his messages, spying one that caught his eye he had missed the night before, *"Great race, Alex! Looks like you and Evelyn are back together, huh?"* The message was from Amanda and had an attached cropped photo of him and Evelyn appearing all the more cozy together on the victory podium. He smiled and pondered a moment about how to respond.

"Thank you, Amanda. Yes, great race for us, but I would rather have swapped places with Tony. Evelyn and I are just teammates now, nothing else really. So, did you watch it on TV?" SEND.

Immediately she replied. *"Yes! We're all coming up for the big race in two weeks! I'm so excited. Are you going to win the Pole?"*

Wow! He thought. *Race girl question!* *"I'm impressed! You're really getting into it, aren't you?"* Alex pecked back, enjoying the little exchange. SEND

"I'm learning. Pulling for you, though!"

"Glad to hear it. What's your schedule?...At Indy, I mean?" Alex replied, as he looked up and could see his guests approaching the dock. SEND

"Not 100% certain. I think we fly in on Friday," Amanda texted back.

"Well, I'm sure I'll see you up here. Gotta run." SEND

Amanda put her phone down, mildly disappointed this digital dialog was coming to an end, at least for the evening. She had received two missed calls and a text from Kyle Williams lately, ones that she had not returned. The young man was frustrated with Amanda, as she had become evermore standoffish toward him since Christmas, especially since she had gone to Southern California a month earlier.

She had become infatuated with Alex Moretti from the moment they had met. He was the first attractive guy who had totally rejected her sister, Allison, one she knew to be quite sexually *suggestive*, and had paid attention to her, the little sister. Allison was angered by the put-off, a fact that somewhat amused Amanda. *Is that why I am so attracted to Alex, because of Allison? No, it's more than that. He's so good-looking, so adventurous, so famous, yet so down-to-earth.... I can't wait to see him!... Maybe he'll text me first sometime. That would be nice.*

Geist was a relatively small lake, at least for someone accustomed to Lake Norman. The traffic after hours during mid-week in May was light with mostly a few small boats and pontoons belonging to lakefront residents. The newlyweds and their friends were a bit disappointed for not getting to party with Evelyn Stevens, but the five water skied, swam, and carried on well past sundown when Alex finally decided to put in. The Carolinian tourists had taken multiple photographs and videos and all would have sufficient fodder for their social media for days to come.

Alex walked in through the back entrance and found his father lounging in the family room, a notebook computer on his lap and cranking away on the keyboard, always the consummate businessman.

"I didn't see Evelyn's car out front," Andy commented. "I thought you had invited her up as your date on the boat?"

"I did invite her, Dad, but to say it was for a date may be a stretch. She overheard me talking about it with Ralston, so I asked her out of politeness," Alex replied. "She blew it off at the last minute. Business with Newberry, she said."

"Uh-huh. So tell me what's going on with you two."

"Not sure. We haven't been together, as a couple I mean, since Long Beach," Andy's son answered.

"Well, take this the right way, but I need to know these things. It affects the team you know." Andy asked, attempting to walk a fine line between being Alex's father and his boss. "You don't appear to be all that upset about it... This evening, I mean."

"No, Dad. I guess I'm really not. I'm going to crash... Good night."

"Make sure you don't wake up the baby."

Andy took a last sip of his cocktail, knowing he had best get up to bed, himself. The highs of the previous day's victory would be short-lived. The days this week would be super busy for his team, as well as all of Gasoline Alley, as they prepared for Pole Day. He was cautiously optimistic, though. Both of his boys were fast in today's practice but Evelyn was two miles per hour off the pace, and he worried that her spat with Alex, if it could be labeled as such, was affecting her concentration.

No, she was good yesterday. I just need to dwell on what I can control, he thought. Andy's stress level was extremely high as he not only had to deal with the big race, but he had to worry about Unibank's entourage coming in for the whole weekend. Long Beach had been a precursor of the kind of crowd Unibank could bring to bear, and Herrera had indicated the guest crowd for Indy would double that.

It had been assumed that most of the Unibank brass, at least all who were into racing, would attend the Charlotte World 600, a major NASCAR race held on the same day as the Indy 500, since it was a hometown event for them. Delcanton and his team had long prepared for this, a much less complicated project to manage since little travel and related hotel accommodations had to be handled as most of their guests were local. As this year's special guests of the 500 were announced as former presidents Bill Clinton and George Bush, the entire Board of Directors at Unibank, as well as much of their senior management staff, would make the trip along with their families and a host of their own selected customers from all over the world. It would be far and away the largest contingent of sponsorship guests the team had ever hosted at one time.

When added to the fact that Herrera had only given them a few weeks notice, the team's business manager, who was also Andy's sister, Marie, had to jump through hoops just to arrange hotels, as rooms of any kind for the 500 weekend were at a premium, to say the least. Andy about hit the ceiling when she handed him the corporate bank Visa account statement reflecting all the charges. Herrera had joked that Unibank was collecting poetic justice as Moretti's business accounts, including most of his credit line and all the company Visa accounts, were held by none other.

Most of their corporate executives would be on hand, including the headman himself, CEO Byron Cook with his family. While Cook was friendly enough in their few meetings and had seemed to truly enjoy the hospitality at Long Beach, he was a pure bean counter and not as outgoing as Herrera, who attended nearly all of their events, including NASCAR. He and Andy would generally keep to the same schedule, which included alternating back and forth between the Indycar and NASCAR venues. Competing in the two series, there were virtually no weekends off for much of the year.

I just hope that Allison Cook doesn't screw with Alex's head, Andy considered. To a certain extent, he felt as though things may be more stable if his son and Evelyn Stevens were still sleeping together. *No rest for the wicked,* Andy joked to himself. *I did choose this life.*

Alex made his way to his bedroom, mindful to be quiet as he thought about Tony, Crissy, and his new nephew, Adrian. He was very happy for his brother as his life seemed so settled, so stable. He took a quick shower and laid down, hoping for a good night's sleep while staring up at the ceiling. He glanced over at his phone, half expecting Evelyn to call him, or at least maybe send him a text message.

He thought about his father's questions and would subconsciously ask the same things to himself. *Do I really miss her?... I suppose I should. We did live together for nearly a year.... But Long Beach! Maybe I should take the high road and call her.... No, ridiculous. We see each other every day at the track, side by side... Dad is right, though. The rift between us has the whole team sort of on edge. Maybe I'll send her a text.*

Alex grabbed his iPhone and started to send Evelyn a message, just some funny pics and a video from the lake, kidding her about what she missed. He pecked out a message that read, *Newberry couldn't be this much fun!* He started to hit SEND, but then something stopped him. He looked at the time – 11:40 PM. He changed the word *Newberry* to *Rock Hill,* then proceeded to change the send to contact,... SEND.

Amanda heard the alarm on her phone and reached over to her nightstand to turn it off, suddenly awakened by the message notification that popped up on the screen, *Message from Alex.* Sitting up in bed abruptly, her fingers moved rapidly as she retrieved the text which read, *"Rock Hill couldn't be this much fun!"* She was so excited when she also noted the time, 11:42 PM.

She scrolled through the various attached photos and chuckled when she reviewed the short video. There was Alex multiple times with four others, two guys and two girls, all appearing to be around Alex's age, or early to mid-twenties. Her first thought was that one of the females was with Alex, but upon repeated review of all the images, it appeared maybe not. She thought she saw a wedding band on one of the girls. *And where was Evelyn Stevens?* She thought. *And would he have sent me these at that hour if she was with him?...Well, maybe,* she thought as the devil's advocate briefly. *But probably not!*

She quickly cranked out a reply: *"Looks like a blast, Alex. Where was this? Are those two other drivers?"*

Sarah peeked in on her, reminding her daughter about the time, as she would drive Amanda to school in thirty minutes.

Alex was already on I-465 heading around the north side outer by-pass and on his way to the track. His iPhone, attached to the car stereo on his new Acura NSX, buzzed as he saw a message come in from *Amanda.* He pressed the button on his steering wheel to reply, and smiling, sent her a response. *"Good morning young lady. No, one guy works for the team. The other guy is his buddy from North Carolina, up visiting for the week. The girls are their spouses."*

Amanda was beaming when she received such a quick response as she sat in class craving the break so she could check it. She wanted so much to ask him about his own possible date but hesitated. *Calm down, Amanda,* she thought. *He's not your boyfriend. You hardly know him. But we are texting each other! And he texted me first this time! Can't wait to show Trisha!*

Pole Day at Indy promised to be exciting, as competition in the series was more competitive than at any time in the history of major open-wheel racing. The better-established teams, Penske and Ganassi, were always to be dealt with. Ed Carpenter, team owner and oval racing specialist, was a threat to win the pole. Now McLaren, with their storied history at the speedway, had returned as a team featuring former champion Alex Rossi and series hotshoe Pato O'Ward and were also quite a force as were the Andretti Autosport drivers Colton Herta and Kyle Kirkwood. Andy approached qualifying with a strong mix of anxiety and optimism. No single driver was strongly favored nor had any driver/team combination been truly dominant year after year since the days of Rick Mears driving for *The Captain* back in the eighties.

Approaching the last hour, Tony Moretti had the provisional pole, Evelyn Stevens had posted the fourth fastest time, and Alex had struggled in tenth, knowing he had a bit more in reserve. He and the team made a late and risky decision to get in line again and blow off the first run.

As the last car on the track with just two minutes to go, Alex found speed and blistered the track record on the first two laps at over 235 miles per hour. If he could maintain for two more laps in the speedway's four-lap qualifying structure, he would have the pole, not on par with winning the

500 itself but still the most lucrative and prestigious qualification in racing, not to mention the extra points awarded toward the championship.

Coming through the first turn, the precision split timing reflected his speed was holding. Everything was smooth entering turn two when something on the rear suspension let go, sending the car into the wall at well over 230 miles per hour. The entire right side of the chassis was completely wiped out as the car finally came to a stop on the center of the track entering the backstretch.

The crowd, numbering some fifty thousand, stood on their feet as the speedway safety trucks and ambulance raced toward the wreckage. The TV broadcast cameras zeroed in, seeing no movement in the cockpit. The announcers spoke in a stressful tone, waiting for the paramedics to extract Alex Moretti from the car.

A few moments of the broadcast were filled with dialog regarding the tremendous safety improvements the speedway and the sport in general had made over the years, noting that many such crashes had resulted in catastrophe at much less speed. Several moments still passed with no movement and one commentator made the unpleasant reference to the hard crash that took the life of Ayrton Senna in Italy nearly three decades earlier, a crash with an estimated impact of 160 miles per hour. Some dialog was added regarding the terrifying accident nearly twenty years earlier when the legend Mario Andretti had hit some debris at nearly the same speed, endured a 360-degree airborne flip, and happily walked away, shaken but mostly uninjured.

Six hundred miles to the south, Amanda sat in the family room and stared at the large TV with horror as her eyes filled with tears. Her mother, Sarah, had heard her cry out from upstairs and came running down to check on her.

"Amanda, what is it?"

"Mom! It's Alex. He crashed!"

Sarah looked quickly at the monitor, never recalling her youngest daughter having such anxiety over a sports injury. "Alex who, Amanda?"

"Alex Moretti, Mom! You know, Moretti Motorsport!?"

The two sat impatiently on their leather sectional and watched the coverage while the medical crew worked, with Sarah holding Amanda's hand as the mother could see her visibly upset. After nearly fifteen minutes, the paramedics manhandled the driver up out of the car and lifted him onto a gurney. Just before four of them worked to move Moretti up and into the back of the ambulance, the driver raised his head slightly and gave a courtly wave to the crowd, which erupted with cheers. Amanda buried her head in her mother's chest as she now shed tears of joy.

Good god, where has this emotion been? Sarah thought as she comforted her youngest.

Andy sped on his scooter through the garage area and to the speedway medical facility, one world-class by any standard, finding Alex conscious and responsive to all the preliminary examination procedures. He was able to freely move all of his limbs without difficulty, a good sign that he had sustained no serious injury.

"How lucky can we be, Dad? I had it. I had that pole! What happened?"

Andy smiled, so glad to see his youngest boy alive and well, as the matter of race qualifying had sunk to mere insignificance. Having his two boys both starting on the first row would have been historic, but they would both likely be starting at opposite ends of the grid now. "I'll have Crosby qualify a car for you. It's a long race... You'll be fine. How's he doing, Doc?"

The on-staff physician stated that he was a bit shaky but quite fortunate, considering.

"I'll be good to go, Dad. Crosby isn't fast enough!"

"Doc?" Andy asked as a follow-up while all awaited.

"He'll have to pass the computer-based ImPACT test and then be signed off by the Medical Director. I don't know. They usually want at least ten days after a hit like that."

Minutes later, Tony and Chrissy walked in, his brother giving Alex a hefty handshake, while his sister-in-law followed, handing Tony the baby before giving Alex an emotional hug as Andy stepped away to take a call.

"Scary ride, huh?" Tony asked, jokingly.

"I had to kick you off the highlight reels, brother."

"You always were one for theatrics," Tony retorted, as they all shared a laugh.

Andy informed Alex that Roger Penske just called to check on him, expressing his well-wishes. No one mentioned anything about Evelyn, who had left the speedway an hour before, her starting position in the second row being well secured. She did send Alex a text forty minutes later and called Andy, stating she had been in the hot tub and had just learned about what happened.

Alex's phone kept buzzing for an hour with non-stop text and email messages. Every driver in the paddock was sending him well wishes, along with a myriad of other fans, current and former sponsors, girlfriends, and close friends. He was even receiving well wishes from a few of the same people who had just weeks earlier blasted him for what happened at Long Beach.

Finally catching up with them all, he spied yet another text message from Amanda. *"That was scary, Alex. I was afraid and cried. So glad you're okay!"*

Cried? He thought. Alex hesitated, unsure of the best reply, and wondered why he was concerned about it. *"Thanks for your support, Amanda! It means a lot to me."* SEND

Byron returned from an afternoon of golf, greeting his wife Sarah with a customary embrace before noticing her being somewhat distracted, if not disturbed, about something. "Sarah, what is it?"

"Oh, one of those Moretti boys crashed a while ago. Could have been serious," she replied.

"Well, race drivers live by the sword and sometimes die by the sword. When did you get so worked up about that?" Byron asked, genuinely confused.

"Oh, Amanda and I were just watching a little of it. Looks like he's okay, though. Got a good bit of Unibank on the screen, anyway. Is Lasagna okay for dinner?"

"Sure. I'm heading up for a shower."

"Byron, we are going to Indianapolis for the big race, correct?" she asked as he headed out of the kitchen.

"Yes. We'll fly up on Friday. Why?"

"Just checking. Are most of the bank's senior staff are going up there this year?" Sarah stated.

"We're guests of honor at Indianapolis this year for Moretti Motorsport. We're meeting two former Presidents themselves. Should be quite exciting."

The night had been very stressful in the Moretti garage. The team had a backup car prepared by Sunday morning and ready for Miles Crosby, the team's Indy Lights and test driver, to shake it down. There were a mere half dozen cars still waiting and hoping to qualify in the last row, all running less than three miles per hour off the Pole speed and Crosby wasn't measurably faster in the early warmup than any of the rest, despite being in a car that had exactly the same setup as Alex's car that had broken the single lap qualifying record just a day earlier.

A stressed-out Alex had not been cleared to drive the next day and it was looking possible, if not yet likely, that Alex may miss the race altogether. By late morning on Sunday, the team made a bizarre decision that team principal Andy Moretti, who had not run a hot lap in a car in well over a decade, would attempt to get the car up to speed and qualify it himself.

Adam Herrera sat ecstatically on the Moretti pit stand as the entirety of the pitlane looked on. All the press pit reporters scrambled to get a microphone in front of Andy, Alex, or Crew Chief Mike Alberry to get comments. Herrera couldn't resist sending a text to all the Unibank board members and executive vice presidents. *"Are you guys catching this? It's practically Unibank Day at the speedway!"*

A meeting with track officials occurred, deciding whether Andy would have to pass the Rookie Orientation Program, generally required for any driver who had not competed on an oval race since the previous year's 500. Track officials considered waving the requirement since the veteran Moretti had been a former 500 pole and race winner, series champion three times, and indeed had won forty series races. Bob Ward pitched in and also made the case that his boss had another three runner-up finishes, fully three other 500s where he had led the most laps, and had never been in an accident on the speedway seriously involving another driver.

Following official clearance, Andy took a few warm-up laps and had the car within two-tenths of a second a lap off Tony's pole time in short order. The legend felt very good in the car after the team tweaked the front wing and rear stagger a bit and by mid-afternoon he was ready to go, a last-minute attempt to get the third car in the field.

Alex couldn't sit still and strolled back and forth behind the pit wall. He felt a buzz and checked his phone, spying yet another text from Amanda. *"So proud of your dad! We're all watching. Good luck, Alex."*

It was getting late and three cars remained in line to qualify, including Andy, his number "5" Unibank-sponsored Honda-powered Dallara, primed and ready. The first two ran in the 229 to 230 range, bumping one car off the last spot. The whole Moretti team was tense as this was it. The speedway could give and the speedway could take away with no guarantees.

In the mid-nineties, *The Captain,* Roger Penske, had dominated the 500 one year with Al Unser Junior and Emerson Fittipaldi, running a powerful Mercedes pushrod engine. When the engine was banned a year later, the weakness of the Penske chassis showed it could not run effectively with a more conventional Ilmor Indy engine against the Lolas or the new

Reynards, and did not qualify for the race altogether. If that could happen to *The Captain*, it could happen to anyone.

Andy took his two warm-up laps and sped past the flag stand, hitting over 240 miles per hour entering the first turn. The car was very smooth and driving down the backstretch, he couldn't help but think about old times, just briefly. Finishing his first lap at just over 233 miles per hour, he finished with a four-lap speed of 232.9, the fifth fastest speed recorded. Of course, with the change of drivers, the car would have to start last. But lo and behold, Alex Moretti and his number "5" Unibank car was in the 500!

Sarah answered Allison's call, as the girl mainly wanted to request money again. The two had their goodly bit of small talk when the subject of the racing came up, as Sarah asked Allison if she had been following it any, and her first daughter declined, claiming she just didn't care for it.

"Well, would you believe Amanda is now into it, and big time?" Sarah indicated.

"Why Mom? What brought that on?"

"I don't know, Allison. She was watching yesterday late in the afternoon when she started hollering, no screaming actually, when one of the Moretti drivers crashed. You'd have thought he was her brother or cousin or something."

Hmm, Allison thought. *Or something.* "I'll have to ask her about it....Well Mom, if you could transfer a couple thousand for me. The sorority is getting a house for the weekend in San Francisco."

"Allison, you are still so welcome to go to Indianapolis with us. Your father says we're to get the red carpet treatment, and even meet two former US Presidents."

"I'll have to pass, Mom. I can't miss Harley's wedding. Is Amanda going?"

"Oh yes. She is super excited about it, for whatever reason." Sarah replied. "The transfer should be done in ten minutes. You be good. Love you."

Not even a minute passed when Amanda's phone buzzed...Allison calling.

"Hello, little sister. I hear you're really into this racing now."

"Yes, I'm into it, I guess," Amanda answered cautiously, not wanting to say that much to Allison, who could do nothing but somehow cause trouble.

"I remember when Dad last took us both to the Charlotte NASCAR race. You appeared bored stiff. What's got into you?"

"Well, we sponsor a team now and I have a driver to pull for," Amanda stated proudly.

"Evelyn's not likely to win, Amanda. Tony Moretti might, but he just got married." Allison smirked back.

"You forgot Alex Moretti," Amanda replied, a bit too boldly.

"Alex! I heard he's starting last, Amanda. Not a chance."

"Maybe so, Allison, but I'll be there rooting for him regardless. Have fun in Frisco. Bye now."

Allison was annoyed in staring at her phone now belching out a dial tone. After all, she was the one who always did the hanging up on people.

The Cooks landed at Indianapolis International Airport on Friday afternoon, transferring to the Hyatt Regency downtown at just passed 7:00 PM. Maria had arranged the reservation for two rooms, a king suite for Byron and Sarah, and a queen double for the two daughters, as it was assumed at the time both Allison and Amanda would be attending. Dinner reservations were made right down the street at St Elmo's, the city's oldest and most famous steak house.

When they entered the establishment. there was Adam Herrera there to greet them. "Byron, you and your family are welcome to follow me as we have your table all set."

They all proceeded to a corner table in the back, where Andy Moretti waited, along with his sons, Tony and Alex, and Evelyn Stevens. All stood to welcome them, while many of the establishment's other patrons looked on.

The four hosts sat on the opposite side facing their guests, with Amanda on the far end next to her mother and opposite Alex, while Evelyn sat between the two brothers. Alex and Amanda shared a brief smile, one that she took as a bit too neutral, while she found herself consciously focused on Alex and Evelyn's interaction.

Are they here together as a couple? Amanda kept thinking while the group all engaged in small talk. As one of Unibank's sponsored drivers, Evelyn, as well as the Moretti boys, would probably be expected for dinner anyway. Still, Amanda felt unpleasant about her and Alex, although they didn't appear as intimates. *Don't be presumptively foolish, Amanda,* she kept thinking to herself. *We traded a few texts, not rings.*

While Herrera and her husband chattered away over dinner with Andy and Tony, Sarah engaged mostly with Alex and Evelyn. "Amanda and I sat nervously while that ambulance hauled you away to that medical building, Alex. Must have been a harrowing experience."

"Yes, before that I had a pole-winning run going when something in the rear of the car let go. I hit the wall hard and just held on for dear life."

"Oh yes," Sarah quickly replied. "I thought Amanda was going to scream. We were so happy when you waved at the crowd."

Amanda blushed as she and Alex made eye contact, a sparkle between the two not expressed until that moment, and looks that were not lost on Evelyn.

"Sarah, Allison and I have become friends through social media," Evelyn stated, feeling comfortable addressing her on a first-name basis. "She won't be joining us?"

"No, she's in San Francisco with friends. Not into car racing, at least not to the same degree as Amanda," Sarah added, giving her youngest a smile, and a prompt to comment.

When the shy Amanda hesitated, Evelyn asked, "So, Amanda, you're a fan now, are you?"

Amanda shifted her eyes back and forth between Alex and Evelyn as she collected her thoughts, not wanting to disclose her singular interest in Alex

Moretti, as opposed to the sport in particular. "I just caught the accident last Saturday,...and me and Mom watched for a while....It was scary."

"I'm her favorite driver now, Evelyn," Alex injected jokingly, feeling he needed to take some pressure off of Amanda at that moment. "She's always for the underdog, right Amanda?"

The table had a brief chuckle over the lite comment while Evelyn felt a tinge of disappointment, wanting to hear and gauge the young woman's answer outright.

As dinner concluded, the group gathered outside the restaurant entrance and Amanda was keen to observe the commuting arrangements. While she and her parents prepared to take the short walk back to their hotel, she noticed Evelyn and Tony getting into a car with Andy, while Alex stood separately out on the curb by himself, waving goodbye to them as they drove down the street toward the expressway. *Interesting,* she thought.

Ten minutes later, Alex sat at the bar in a small place called Cleo's, actually owned by a small oriental woman named Hae, who used to date one of Tony's crew members, and she and Alex had remained very close friends. Nearing 11:00 PM, he checked his messages and sent one out.

Sarah insisted she escort Amanda to her room, which was on a different floor than her own, while Byron chose to hit the lounge for a nightcap with a few of the other executives who were there as part of the Unibank contingent. As Allison always tended to be the wild one, Sarah didn't worry much about her youngest daughter and left her room within five minutes to retire for the evening.

Amanda prepared to hit the sack herself when her phone buzzed with a message from her best friend, Trisha. She hit the app button and dialed.

"Hey girl! How's the trip going?"

"I'm tired, Trisha. The flight and a huge dinner at this old restaurant, you know. We were with the Morettis and I sat across from Alex!" Amanda replied back to Trisha's face on her screen.

"What happened, Amanda? You don't look too excited," Trisha asked anxiously.

"I didn't really get to talk to him. I mean, I was sitting right next to Mom, and he was right next to his girlfriend, that Evelyn. My gosh, Trisha, she's so beautiful."

"Hey Amanda, so are you!"

"I'm not even old enough to drive, Trisha. And she's....Oh my god! He just sent me a text! I'll call you back," Amanda exclaimed excitedly.

She then opened the message that read, *"Are you asleep yet?"* To which she quickly replied, *"No."*

After a minute, she received a return message. *"If comfortable, call me then."*

Amanda's heart skipped a beat. *He wants to know if Mom or Dad are with me.* She then dialed and Alex answered on the first ring.

"So, what are you doing now?" he asked with a chuckle.

"Well, I just got up to my room and I was talking to my best friend. Where are you?"

"I'm just hanging out down the street. Do you want to get together for a while?" Alex asked.

Amanda could hear music and a crowd in the background. She didn't want to head down the street alone this late and doubted she could even get into any nightclubs. *He surely knows that,* she thought. "I have my own room. You could come up here, if you want."

"I don't think that's a good idea, Amanda. If your parents see us,... probably wouldn't be good. Can you get away for a bit? I'll meet you out on the street in front of the hotel in ten minutes."

Knowing her father was due to head up for the night, Amanda avoided the elevators and used the stairway down to the first floor, careful to make her way through the hotel lobby while out of eyesight to the lounge. She was nervous and excited as she strolled out toward the street, startled when a man came up from behind her, putting his arm around her shoulder to motion her forward.

"Let's head down this way, Amanda."

"Alex? You scared me. What's with the hat and sunglasses?" she asked dubiously.

"People recognize me, Amanda. I don't think we're ready for that, are we?"

"I suppose not. Where are we going?" Amanda asked, just curious.

"There's a small bar a few blocks over. I was there when you called. I know the owner and it's busy, but not as busy as every other club around here tonight.

The two entered Cleo's and Hae had reserved the far corner booth for him. As they walked through the crowded and narrow bar, a young woman with two friends, all of whom were quite liquored up, put her arm out and grabbed him. "Hey! Alex Moretti! We've been worried about you since the crash."

"Oh? Well, I'm fine," he answered, checking a moment to see if he knew them. "Thanks for asking. Now, if you will excuse me?"

Undeterred, the woman spat. "Wait! Could I get a picture?" she said, as she stepped up beside him and handed one of her friends her phone.

Alex put his hand up, blocking the flash. "Please, no pictures!" He then moved in closer to the woman's table and spoke into her ear.

Following the exchange, he and Amanda moved forward and took up station in their corner booth, which afforded the two a slight measure of privacy.

"What did you say to her?" Amanda asked.

"I told them you were married and we were incognito," Alex stated.

"No! You can't be serious. Like I really look like a married woman."

"Hey, it's dark in here," Alex replied smiling from ear to ear. "It worked, didn't it?"

Hae came up to check on them and introduced herself. Amanda replied in kind, pleased the Asian woman didn't seem to pass any judgement on her, and watched as Hae brought out two mixed drinks.

"What is this, Alex? I better not get drunk," Amanda asked, not too seriously. "Why didn't she ask me for an ID?"

"It's mostly fruit punch, Amanda. Hae's cool. She knows you're younger than me," Alex replied.

Amanda raised her eyebrows a bit, thinking he must have set this all up in advance. *I guess I should feel good about that,* she pondered.

"So, how have you been, Amanda?" he asked genuinely, as he considered this the first real meeting for them.

"Fine. But how about you? That crash!"

"Not missing a beat! How come you have a room all by yourself?"

"Because Allison didn't come. Mom and Dad offered to stay in my room with me, but I refused. Mom was cool about it. They'd freak if they knew I was here, though....You could have come to my room, Alex. It's not even on the same floor as Mom and Dad's room."

"Are you disappointed?" he asked.

"No, but are you?... Sneaking around downtown with a girl my age? I suspect you have other,... options."

"Well, I do drive race cars at 235 miles per hour. I guess you could say I do live on the edge, Amanda. Honestly, you don't look that young. I still say you and your sister could almost pass for twins."

"That's what everybody says," Amanda replied for the millionth time, as she gathered more thoughts. *Time to be a bit bold, Amanda.* "So, what's the deal with Evelyn?"

"There is no deal. We're teammates."

"She's such a beautiful woman," Amanda stated, looking for his reaction.

"Indeed she is.... So are you."

"Flattery will get you everywhere, thank you. But you didn't answer my question. Are you disappointed you didn't come up to my room?"

"We could head back there now, if it would make you feel better," Alex said.

"Not really. It's good to see you, though. Strange that we have to meet like this, six hundred miles away when we don't live that far from each other," Amanda replied, getting more comfortable in their conversation with every word.

"How do you know that?" he asked.

"My dad is the CEO of a huge bank. Many of my relatives around Charlotte work there. I just assumed you had accounts there. I know you live in a condo overlooking the lake up past Huntersville... Are you mad at me?"

"I don't know. What else do you know about me?"

"Not too much. I know you're from a famous racing family. I know you were living with one of the world's most beautiful and famous women."

"Go on, Amanda."

"I know you shunned my sister in Long Beach. No guy has ever done that."

"Never?"

"None that I know about."

"Well, that's more than I know about you," Alex declared.

"There's not too much to tell. I was born and raised in Rock Hill, South Carolina. My parents are rich. We live on a lake. I went to a girl's catholic school until last year. Now I'm a freshman in high school."

The two spent another hour chatting and laughing. Amanda had two more mixed drinks, which were purposely weak, as Alex had requested of Hae. Approaching 1:00 PM, she brought out the tab and informed Alex she was about to close.

The two strolled back out onto the street, still fairly crowded at the late hour, as the 500 weekend would be the busiest downtown of the year. As they got closer to the hotel, they stopped in front of a restaurant and sat down on a bus stop bench.

Amanda looked at him with her pretty blue eyes. "You are welcome to come up to my room for a little while. But we won't have sex, Alex."

He looked back at her, searching for the right words. "Okay....It's getting very late and I have a busy morning."

"I want you to know, I'm not like my sister."

"I know that, Amanda."

"You sure you're not disappointed?"

What a conversation, Alex thought. "I thought we had a good time tonight....No?"

"I have!... I mean we have," she replied immediately. "I just know that you... I just meant",... Amanda couldn't complete her response and just turned and pressed her head on his chest.

Does this girl think I would go to all this trouble, indeed risk the wrath from my own father, not to mention hers, if all I wanted was to get in her pants this weekend? Is that the image my persona projects? "No Amanda,

I'm not disappointed. There will be plenty of time for that, I think," Alex stated softly, and pulled an encore of Long Beach by lifting Amanda up off the sidewalk and pressed his lips against hers. Time seemed to pause in an animated state as passersby glanced at the two with amused envy.

"Well, I guess you had better go. Geist Lake is what, almost an hour's drive?" Amanda asked after composing herself.

"Not quite that far, but I'm staying down here, tonight. I have a place reserved above Cleo's. I'll see you early in the morning. We're all meeting your family before the parade. You can ride with me."

"You're going to drive *me* to the parade?" Amanda asked, confused.

"Not driving you *to* the parade, Amanda. You're riding with me *in* the parade."

The three Team Moretti drivers all met in the Hyatt's main restaurant at 9:30 on Saturday morning, awaiting the Cook family. Andy Moretti and Adam Herrera had discussed and agreed that each of them would accompany the featured drivers in the 500 Festival Parade, an annual event downtown the day before the race, and all part of their VIP treatment. All of the thirty-three drivers would be featured in new Camaro convertibles, with most having their own spouses or other special acquaintances on board with them.

The arrangement as to who would ride with who would be decided over the morning breakfast. As Tony would be riding with Crissy and the baby, Byron, Sarah, and Amanda would all three ride with Alex and Evelyn.

In order to head off any debate, Alex started the conversation. "Since I'm now Amanda's favorite driver, she can ride with me. Mr. and Mrs. Cook can ride with Evelyn, who will have a much more prominent position in the parade, starting closer to the front. What do you think?" he asked the group generally.

Everyone seemed agreeable to the assignments, as Byron seeing himself featured beside the famous Evelyn Stevens expressed a blatant approval.

Sarah smiled neutrally, simply throwing Amanda a glance to check her reaction. In spite of her best effort to disguise her excitement, Amanda was beaming, an expression not lost on Sarah, nor also on Evelyn.

The parade kicked off with a few floats and local high school bands, followed by Alex's car, as he would be the thirty-third starter. Amanda felt like she was in heaven, perched up on the back of the convertible and waving at the huge crowd that lined the streets as though she herself was some sort of celebrity. She knew these fans were all really waving at the well-known and popular Alex, but here she was right next to him. She wasn't a hundred percent sure yet that she was his girl and he was her guy, but right at that moment in time, she surely felt like it.

Allison was awakened by the beeping signal on her phone and she sat up in bed with a severe headache. The young man next to her was snoring and the smell of his breath was atrocious. She took a moment to rekindle her bearings as the room didn't appear to be one in the rented condo she and five other sorority sisters had set up through VRBO. She could vaguely recall the club where she had met the guy, and had less recollection of what occurred after the place had closed down.

You must not have been that good, buster, she thought with an air of cynicism.

She grabbed her phone, preparing to call one of her fellow travelers, seeing a message from her mom. It was a phone video of her and Allison's dad appearing with Evelyn Stevens in the back of a convertible in a parade, one that she now recalled hearing about. A sudden thought came to her as she repeatedly reviewed the panned footage. *Where's Amanda?*

Seeing the time was 9:35 local and realizing it was past noon back home, she dialed her mother's number.

"Allison, you should have come with us. We are in the 500 Festival Parade riding with Evelyn Stevens, got to meet Peyton Manning, and that girl who won the American Idol last year. It is so much fun," Sarah expressed, obviously bubbly and out-of-character for her. "How's San Francisco?"

"Oh, we're having a blast, Mother," Allison replied, now rolling her eyes as she looked over at her overnight sex partner, wishing he would wake up and take her back to their condo. "Where's Amanda? You surely didn't leave her at the hotel all alone."

"Oh no. She got to ride with Alex Moretti. They are way ahead of us."

"Well, have a good time. Give everyone my regards," Allison responded, her hungover mood now worsened.

The two disconnected and a shrill of anger overcame the oldest Cook sister as she began to poke the still-sleeping guy in the ribs. "Hey, get up! You need to take me home!"

"What do you mean, take you home? I only have a small scooter," he grunted. "You can call Uber."

Allison got up and headed for the bathroom, realizing now what a dump this jerk lived in. *I must have really been drunk last night,* she lamented. Disgusted with the shower that hadn't been cleaned or sanitized in ages, Allison passed on it and simply got dressed before heading outside to the street, indeed contacting Uber.

Amanda parading around with Alex Moretti? Allison thought angrily. *That little bitch! That creep! You're out of your element, little sister!*

Amanda thought she was on top of the world as the convertible moved slowly through the downtown streets of Indianapolis. Here she was, a young high school girl riding side-by-side with the most handsome guy she had ever laid eyes on, waving to the crowd on both sides of the street as though she was a superstar. Alex continued to sign autographs and give selfies while he and Amanda waited at the end of the parade route for the back of the procession to catch up.

One voice from back in the crowd, yelled, "Hey Moretti! What happened between you and Evelyn!?"

Another rowdy hollered, "Hey Alex! What's with the new babe!?"

Not wanting Amanda to feel belittled or uncomfortable, he declined comment and motioned for her to come over next to him, as he put his arm around her waist and included her in the rest of the remaining selfies and photos the crowd shot.

A good half hour later, the rest of the Cooks and Morettis assembled along with Evelyn. A lunch buffet was arranged and awaited them at the Moretti hospitality tent at the speedway. Transportation to the track was discussed and a chauffeured shuttle bus was on stand-by at the hotel.

"I could take someone," Alex offered. "Of course, my NSX only has two seats."

Byron and Sarah shared a hesitant look before deferring to their daughter, who was smiling while nodding up and down at the prospect of riding in the exotic Acura sports car. "Come on Mom, Dad. Say yes!"

Knowing Byron would have his natural fatherly reservation, Sarah put a hand on his shoulder while whispering in his ear. "Come on, Byron. She's not a small child anymore. Let's not embarrass her in front of these people."

He gave his wife a defeated look before turning his glance toward Alex. "All right young man. But you save that heavy foot of yours for tomorrow's race. Got it?"

"Of course, sir," he replied. "I'm parked in a garage just a few blocks over. We'll see everyone at the track."

Alex and Amanda headed west on North Street a block and turned south on Illinois Avenue past the Masonic building. Once comfortably out of sight, they strolled hand-in-hand, a small gesture but one that gave her a warm feeling nonetheless. Passing a few on-lookers, a couple of autograph and selfie seekers couldn't be ignored and she noticed that Alex had a knack for pleasing his fans, and he overlooked the many side comments from passersby such as, "Where's Evelyn Stevens", and "Looks like Moretti's got him a newer model".

Finally making their way to the parking garage and a pittance of privacy, Amanda asked, "Is this how it is all the time?"

"Pretty much," he answered. "It's much more pronounced here at Indy. In places like Detroit, or even Monterey, I don't get noticed as much. Blame a lot of it on that crash."

Amanda buckled herself in, amazed at his sports car, which must have cost a fortune. Her dad had a Porsche 911 in the garage at home that she had ridden in, *but it was nothing like this,* she thought pleasantly. She had wondered but chose not to ask about Evelyn's transportation, noting that Alex's former flame had sort of quickly disappeared when the parade concluded.

They pulled out on the street and noticed the crowd staring. "Relax, Amanda. It's the car, not us. The windows are tinted."

As the two exited the downtown area and made their way northwest toward the speedway, Amanda began to envision a life with him, trying to decide if she would like all of it. No stranger to catcalls, she revisited the comments made earlier in her mind. *"Looks like Moretti has a newer model"? Should that bother me?...Or should I bask in the adulation? Is this real?...Or is this just some novelty?...Calm down, Amanda,* she kept telling herself. *Let's just see what happens next.*

Amanda took in the surroundings of the Moretti team hospitality, the huge buses, the makeshift tents, the fine buffet, and then a walk-through of Gasoline Alley and a quick tour of the fairly recently constructed Winner's Circle platform and the impressive Pagoda tower. She had been to the Charlotte track a few times, a place always considered big time, but this place did have a certain *magnitude* about it. She became somewhat let down most of the afternoon, as she couldn't really be close to Alex and had to hang out with her mom and dad, although all of the Morettis sort of took turns playing host to all the Unibank people there.

As they stood in the fan area behind the Pagoda, TV cameras and press crews were conducting ongoing interviews with various people, including drivers both past and present, celebrities, and others from the motor racing community. She and her family got some close-up photos with Helio Castroneves, the one they called Spiderman who had won many times, and Mario Andretti, probably the most famous personality in racing. They also got to meet A.J. Foyt, another legend and a big fellow who gave quite an entertaining interview.

She did have the opportunity to spend a little time with Crissy Moretti and the new baby, Alex's nephew, Adrian. The beautiful and bubbly little man was all decked out in his Unibank Racing infant outfit, a visual that became a main photo attraction and even pleased her father, Amanda noticed. For her part, Crissy was a very attractive woman in her own right, having quickly gotten back in shape following the pregnancy. Not only did she look good, but Crissy was such an outgoing person, and Amanda could quickly see why Alex was so fond of her and so happy for his brother.

"Where did you meet Tony?" Amanda had asked when the subject of drivers and their families had somehow come up.

"We met in Seal Beach, my hometown," Crissy responded. "I was waitressing at a little bar on Main Street. They had a big car show and he was there as a celebrity for one of his sponsors and Alex was with him. I'll never forget it. Credit Alex for us getting together."

"Really? Tell me about it, if I may be so bold, I mean," Amanda asked, obviously sincerely interested.

"Well, I was waiting their table, the two of them and two others. Alex was young back then, like in his teens," Crissy explained. "I thought they were both so cute, and I had my eye on Tony, who struck me as being shy compared to Alex who was so talkative. I found myself trying to flirt with him but he sort of wasn't responding. When they got ready to leave and I brought out their check, Alex just kind of blurted out that if I put my phone number on the back of the receipt, his brother might call to ask me out."

"Oh my god! That is so cool. Then what happened?" Amanda asked with an intrigued excitement.

"Tony turned beet red and I thought he was about to punch his brother in the nose, but the next day I got this call from him, and he kind of asked me out," Crissy explained cheerfully.

"Kind of ask you out?" Amanda inquired, now seriously wanting to hear about it.

"He said they were racing the following weekend up in Long Beach, and would like me to come as his special guest. Of course, I was excited about it. I got to hang out with all the other VIPs when he was on the track, and Alex was with me, too. He was still racing Lights back then and the two of them were never on the track together at the same time. I remember getting all dressed up for the Racer cocktail party. It was the first race like that I had been to and it was great. He finished third and had me come up on the podium for pictures with him. The rest is history and you see the result," Crissy went on as she smiled at Adrian, the grinning baby boy who had become the hospitality tent's center of attention.

The Saturday schedule included a driver's autograph session, where fans could line up and get signed photos from all the drivers. Grouped together by teams, Evelyn and Alex sat together, engaging in limited small talk while they each signed what seemed like thousands of cards and pictures placed in front of them.

"Those Cook sisters are quite pretty, aren't they, Alex?" Evelyn asked, throwing up the question out of the blue and stumping her former lover.

"Indeed, they are very attractive girls," Alex replied in as neutral tone as he could muster.

A few busy fans passed some time, giving Alex the false mindset that Evelyn's inquiry was limited. "Pity Allison didn't make it. Then she could have ridden with you this morning," Evelyn added.

Alex ignored the suggestion, much to her chagrin.

"Give that young Amanda a few years, and she'll be a hot item, won't she?" Evelyn kept on.

"Coming from you, she may be glad to hear that," he answered, not giving in to anything.

"So Alex, you don't agree?" Evelyn questioned more, to the point of tedium.

"As I said, they're both nice-looking girls," he responded again, and Evelyn could tell he was starting to get annoyed.

The afternoon festivities were drawing to a close and the Unibank guests were all gathering to depart back downtown to the hotel. An evening dinner reservation was arranged by Herrera at the hotel exclusively for all of the Unibank entourage, and much to Amanda's consternation. Sitting through a formal dinner and listening to a full evening of banking lingo was not on the teen's hit parade, especially now.

Unable to have a private conversation with Alex, even though they were all together for drinks and chatter at the Moretti hospitality tent for the last forty minutes prior to leaving, she overheard him mention to others that he was taking his crew out for an early dinner and that all hoped to get a good night's sleep before the big day tomorrow.

She and her family arrived back at the hotel just past seven, with all due in the restaurant an hour later. She quickly bathed and prepped with a fine formal dress that Sarah had picked out for the occasion, and with plenty of time to spare, she sent Alex a text. *"Could you come here later?"*

Alex and his crew, who were all pizza and wings types, gathered at the Union Jack, a popular Speedway pub off Crawfordsville Road that was packed during the race weekend, as were all local food and beverage establishments. The place was noisy and he didn't catch Amanda's message for over half an hour. He replied. *"Can't do it tonight, Amanda. Have to turn in early–big day tomorrow."*

She sat at the restaurant table next to her mom, seeing that Alex had finally replied to her. She read it, disappointed but understanding. Feeling she had to respond, she pecked in a reply that read, *"I understand. Miss you already"*, and couldn't keep from smiling when she got an immediate reply.

"Me too."

The Unibank suite was just north of the Pagoda with a clear view of the flag stand hanging out over the row of bricks, representing the start/finish line. Attendees enjoyed a full-service buffet and could sit in air conditioning and see the race on the main straight from behind large glass windows or sit outside in the open-air reserved seats.

Amanda looked on anxiously, as Alex's Unibank-sponsored car sat on the end of the line in the pit lane while the speedway worked through a whole agenda of structured pre-race rituals, such as the *Back Home Again in Indiana* song and the Air Force flyover in concert with the singing of the national anthem.

The field finally got the command, *Drivers, start your engines,* and the field slowly made its way forward, The cars all ran slowly the first lap, held up by the Chevy Camaro pace car. The third time around the green flag fell and engines roared, the entire crowd on their feet as Tony Moretti's lead Unibank-sponsored number "2" Dallara raced toward the first corner.

Almost as fast as the loud start, the yellow flag was waved as a massive wreck occurred at the entrance of Turn One. The yellow flag quickly turned into red as the race was stopped before it even completed a lap. Amanda looked on in shocked horror as she witnessed the replay on one of the large monitors inside. It appeared one car had collided with another in mid-pack, sending both into the wall and one flipping upside down as four other cars, drivers having no place to go at over two hundred miles per hour, crashed hard into them, including the third Unibank sponsored car driven by Alex Moretti.

Her heart skipped a beat as continuous coverage focused on the six drivers, two of which climbed up out of their machines right away, Alex's car had the whole right side taken off and sat up against the wall right in the center of Turn One. The surviving roster of cars all came around and into pitlane where they were stopped in running order, awaiting the track to be cleared and a restart. The safety crew worked to extract the other drivers involved, and Amanda was overwhelmingly relieved when Alex got up and out of his cockpit, mostly under his own power, and was escorted to the back of the speedway ambulance, taken for yet another visit to the medical facility.

It took the track safety crew nearly thirty minutes to remove all the wreckage and prepare the track surface for another start. One at a time, the speedway announcer called out the names of drivers who had been cleared and released from the medical building. Andy Moretti's name had not been announced by the time the depleted field was fired back up to resume racing. Not knowing what to do and throwing caution into the wind, Amanda exited the suite and scurried down the elevator to the ground behind the stands. Getting directions from the VIP suites security guard, she began to run headlong, passing the host of souvenir trailers, a fleet of parked buses, and team semis toward the medical building, located near the speedway museum and a good hike on foot.

She approached the entrance and was abruptly halted by speedway officials. Examining her VIP credentials, the security agent listened as she claimed to be Alex Moretti's fiancée, and was somehow allowed in. She was led to a room where she found Alex sitting upright on an examination table. Without even thinking, she rapidly approached him teary-eyed and gave him a huge hug and kiss before the resident physician re-entered the room and began to ask questions, namely who was this unfamiliar young woman, how did she escape protocol, and manage to even get into the place.

"That's okay, Doc. She's with me," Alex stated, mentally brushing off the huge disappointment of being taken out of the race and glad to see her, nonetheless.

"I'm sorry, Alex. Is she a member of your immediate family?" The doc asked, already having learned of the story she told the security agent, and most skeptical as to whether this young woman was indeed Alex Moretti's fiancée. Like most of the motor racing establishment and fanbase, the doc thought Moretti was still romantically involved with Evelyn Stevens.

"I'm so sorry," Amanda responded. "I'm just a close friend and big fan. I was just worried about him."

Thirty minutes later and following an escorted exit out of the med center, a winded Amanda re-entered the Unibank suite, confronted by a concerned set of parents, predicating an explanation that she had stomach cramps from too much of the buffet and had to hit the restroom. Her story seemed to satisfy her father, as Byron had been outside in the open-air seating and had only missed her being absent from the suite a few short minutes earlier. For her part, Sarah wasn't quite so gullible but chose not to press her daughter on it, as it had been months since she had seen Amanda this bubbly about anything.

The 500 was history with the very popular Pato O'ward winning his first Borg-Warner Trophy for Zak Brown and McLaren, but a disappointing result for Moretti Motorsport as Andy's team had so much hope going into it. The Grand Prix had been a highlight for them and so was qualifying, despite Alex's Pole Day crash, although made somewhat noteworthy with Andy actually qualifying his car. Race day itself was a letdown as Tony had led on and off for over four hundred miles but an ill-handling car on the last set of tires had relegated him to a seventh-place finish. Evelyn had run consistently in the top ten, also, but a late pit stop incident hurt her, and she had to settle for seventeenth. Add Alex's first lap disaster and the Indycar division of Moretti Motorsport had pulled out of Indianapolis all the worse for wear and lamenting on what could have been.

All was not lost, however, as even though their team had not made a great showing, overall the Unibank people had left Indy quite pleased with the Moretti hospitality and Herrera was already talking about next year's plans. He had also seen their star girl, Evelyn Stevens, in a new and unfamiliar light...*A somewhat sad one.*

Chapter 5

Summer Heat

In the long period between Long Beach and Indy, things were not good for Evelyn Stevens emotionally. Regarding her and Alex, most casual observers believed that spending the month at Indy after a moderately successful if uneventful race in Alabama, and with both being separated for a month, the track notwithstanding, their relationship would heal up and they would be back in the love nest. After all, the shunt at Long Beach, though devastating, was just a racing incident and drivers did get over those, unless the same two drivers would still be at it week after week, which had not been the case.

For her part, Evelyn held a deep sadness over the rift. Still upset over this Long Beach late-party business, she constantly kept blaming herself, knowing Alex despised her volume of celebrity engagements. Following Indy, she informed Louie that she wanted to be left alone for a few days, something that would not come as a natural act for him. Evelyn wanted her relationship with Alex to get back to normal, if there was such a thing for a pair like them. She did hold out a smidgen of hope as she technically still lived with him at his condo on Lake Norman, although she had not actually been to the place since departing for Birmingham. *But he hadn't asked me to move out,* she often pondered and noted that he hadn't been seen with anyone else lately, or at least that she was aware of.

In the week following Indy, the Morettis had a few days rest before they would run in Detroit the very next weekend and follow that up with running the 24 Hours of Lemans, the world's greatest sports car event. As the IMSA cars could run with some modification, and the Indycars did not run at all that weekend, Andy would run two cars and a total of six drivers, including all three of his Indycar pilots. The previous summer, Tony and his wife Crissy had vacationed a few days in Paris along with Alex and Evelyn, a trip interrupted all too often by Newberry calling all the time and scheduling appearances with her in front of the French press.

The drivers thus headed back home to North Carolina before the upcoming packed schedule, Tony and Crissy's lakefront home in Sherrill Ford, and Alex's condo in Davidson, which he had shared with Evelyn. This would come as a moment of truth for the two, as she decided to show up for the first time in over seven weeks, not knowing what would happen.

Alex walked through the door late on Monday evening, somewhat surprised to see Evelyn's Corvette parked in the building's parking garage. He immediately caught the aroma of one of his favorite Italian dishes cooking readily on the stove and there was Evelyn, just having showered and sporting her soft Union Jack bathrobe he had given her for Christmas. He also heard the washing machine going and figured correctly that she had gathered up his dirty shirts and jeans, all indeed due for a cleaning.

"You got down here early," Alex observed. "What's going on?"

"Oh, I don't know. I do still reside here, last time I checked, Alex."

"I'm going to take off a bit, maybe do a little fishing."

"Bloody fishing?" she asked cynically. "You?"

"You should try it sometime. It's relaxing."

She stirred around a bit, suddenly uncomfortable in his presence and not expecting this reunion to play out this way. "Are we splitting up, Alex?"

"It appears we already have, Evelyn."

"It was your bloody decision,...not mine," she replied, her voice getting emotional. "Do you expect me to say I'm bloody sorry about Long Beach?"

"It's not about Long Beach. We're both to blame for that. That's water under the bridge now," Alex said, realizing that having this conversation was more difficult than he thought it would be. "You're a big star now, Evelyn. You don't need a guy like me."

"Please don't tell me what I bloody need, Alex!"

"We don't always travel in the same circles, Evelyn. Only when we're at the track, that is."

She began to lower her head, having difficulty looking Alex in the eye for an instant, her own eyes beginning to well up. As hard as it was to face the truth, she knew he was right. So long as she had Louie as an agent, who always had a full-time schedule for her, she and Alex would have issues. She could drop Louie, she supposed. *But what would a new agent do? Nothing?*

"Are you sure this is all about Louie, Alex? You're not involved with that young Cook girl are you?" she asked, returning a stare.

"Now you're getting paranoid, Evelyn," Alex replied while rolling his eyes in gesture. He felt guilty for being deceitful but knew the ramifications of his being honest about it.

"Don't belittle me, Alex! I saw the way she looked at you at St. Elmo's, and then the next morning when she found out – no, you decided – that she would ride with you in the parade. That wasn't the look of another star-struck fan... No, it was something more," Evelyn stated accusingly, no longer wearing an expression of sadness but more one of rancor.

"Are you finished?" Alex asked.

"I guess I am," she answered, becoming misty-eyed again. "I'll need a few days to move my stuff out."

"No hurry, Evelyn. I'll make arrangements."

Her expression changed to one of blank resignation as she watched him while he worked to pack a few personal belongings before heading out the door. She picked up her phone, momentarily ignoring the messages from Louie. *My god, if Alex would just pay as much attention to me as he does,* she thought, and then fired off a text to another contact.

"Allison, call me when you get a minute, please."

She then broke down and wept.

It was late night in Barcelona when she returned Evelyn's call. "What's up, race girl?"

"How's the trip, Allison?" Evelyn asked, still emotional but a bit more composed by now.

"Having a blast, girl! What's happening?" Allison asked, curious she was hearing from Stevens like this. They had kept in relatively close touch since Long Beach, but mostly through social media and text messaging.

"How long are you going to be over there?" Evelyn asked, curiously.

"I fly back a week from tomorrow. Why?"

"We're all heading to Lemans early next week. I thought if you were still in Europe, we could hang out together, Maybe do London a few days after the race,... or maybe Paris."

Allison was giddy. *This was one of the most recognizable women on earth. What an opportunity!* "So, Evelyn. What about Alex?"

"We sort of parted ways, Allison. He'll be there as my teammate for the race, but nothing more," Evelyn stated.

"Well, girl. Count me in!" Allison added. "You've got a date! I'll inform Aaron and the folks I'm going to extend the trip for another week. Is that enough?"

"You know I'll be racing the following weekend for four to five days. I know you're not a big fan of it," Evelyn said.

"Nonsense! If you're racing, I'm a fan, Evelyn. I'll find a way to keep busy while you're out there chasing the speed of light."

"Okay then, I'll text you the info on where I'll be."

Evelyn disconnected the call, now happy that Allison had not called her back right away. She had been so emotional that she was prepared to spill the beans to Allison about what she suspected about Alex and her younger sister. Upon reflection, she knew that disclosure, if true and made public, would likely destroy the whole Moretti Motorsport-Unibank relationship, which would not be in her best interest, in spite of all her personal vitriol.

She had known by their varying social media exchanges that Allison was due to return from her sorority group vacation the same day she would arrive in France and felt it harmless to invite her, figuring their schedules wouldn't match anyway. Now that the girl surprised her and had taken her up on the offer, she bit her tongue and just hoped to make the best of it.

Trying to look upon the upcoming trip positively, Stevens would be Alex's teammate in the same car, along with Vito Caruso, the team's full-time IMSA sports car driver. She still needed a distraction now from Louie, and maybe Allison Cook would provide that. After all, her agent had pushed her to befriend the bold young woman, all in the interest of business, of course.

It may be interesting to see how Allison and Louie would mesh together, Evelyn thought, smiling if ever slightly for the first time all day. She had seen firsthand the way Louie's tongue would almost snap off of its rollers at the site of Allison Cook, somewhat blind to the fact that her agent would constantly do the same thing at her personally when physically behind her back.

Amanda was so excited. Trisha had turned sixteen and got her driver's license. Her parents were cautious for a couple of weeks but finally relented on allowing their spirited teenage daughter to take her mother's car, a new Ford Explorer, out for shopping during the day. It was hot on that first Wednesday in June and the two girls could hardly contain themselves as they drove up I-485 toward the Charlotte Douglas International Airport's second exit, where Trish proceeded west on US Highway 74, using their GPS to guide them toward a development called the Vineyards on Lake Wylie.

Amanda dialed out a stored number on her phone, receiving a quick answer. "We just pulled in here. Are you close?"

"I'm almost there, probably five minutes. The boat is blue and white with a checkered flag on top. Just wave at me from the dock," Alex responded, excited to see her again after their brief but fun encounter in Indy, as both of them kept their emerging relationship alive mostly through text messaging. He rounded the bend and into the cove, spying the two teen girls as the one with whom he was quite familiar was waving wildly as he slowed to a troll in the No Wake zone.

Trisha had volunteered to just drop Amanda off and let her be with her new budding boyfriend alone for a couple of hours, but Alex declined, believing it was too much to ask Amanda's best friend to drive her all the way up to the north side of the lake and just hang out while the two of them cruised around. He edged up to the dock as the two girls boarded before backing away and heading back out to the main body. Amanda was proud to show Alex off to her longtime friend and while Alex looked forward in navigating out of the narrow cove, Trisha nudged Amanda with her elbow, just to steal a glance and give her a big thumbs-up smile.

For his part, Alex was long used to having good-looking young women around him, and Amanda and her friend, Trisha, both in their colorful skimpy bikinis, didn't disappoint. Alex's boat, a thirty-seven foot Four Winns cabin cruiser, was quite nice but not overly impressive to the two girls, both from well-to-do families and living on the lake themselves, were quite accustomed to such crafts.

Alex and Amanda were somewhat tentative around each other, having spent limited time together physically and indeed it had been weeks. Neither were quite sure if they were actually a couple, per se, but seemed to share a mutual feeling they wanted to be.

Anchoring at a small island out in the middle of the main channel, the three were quickly relieved from the sultry hot weather by jumping into the water. The lake was shallow as Alex approached Amanda from behind and embraced her as she felt like heaven was upon her and looked forward to the day she would have her own license and see Alex often, and more to the point of not having to be so discreet about it. Alex held her snug and turned her around for an emotional kiss. Amanda's quick surprise and natural shyness quickly evaporated as she seemed to melt in his arms.

Trisha showed slight embarrassment and swam away to the other side of the boat, wanting to give them a few moments at least. She had known the two Cook sisters since her family bought their lakeside home twelve years earlier. Amanda had shared the tale about Long Beach and Indy, along with the fact that Alex had shunned Allison, one whom Trisha well knew as a female openly capable of wooing the lust of boys and men of all ages. With Alex and Allison being nearly the same age, and his being a former intimate of the famous Evelyn Stevens, Trisha could appreciate all the things Amanda was so proud of. For all of that, she did hope that Alex wouldn't hurt Amanda, as his being a famous international racing driver, and an extremely handsome one at that, she could just imagine the temptations he would be exposed to, and the sacrifices he would have to make on Amanda's behalf to even have a relationship with her.

Anchors up, Alex gave the two girls a brief orientation on piloting his boat, suggesting that Trisha play captain for a few miles while he and Amanda lounged on the bench seat in the stern.

"So Amanda, tell me. Your family has no clue about our late-night rendezvous at Indy?" Alex inquired casually.

"No, not really. Are you worried about it?"

"A little bit. I trust you have no one there checking your text messages," he replied.

"No, I keep those rather guarded," Amanda added.

She wanted to ask him some really straight questions, questions about his relationship with Evelyn, and anyone else. She was feeling rather possessive already, constantly reminding herself that she shouldn't be. *I'm a teenage kid. He's a famous star. How could he travel to all those places, be confronted with all those young women, and remain faithful to someone like me?*

"This is a pretty nice lake, not as choppy as Norman," he observed, believing their conversation needed to steer away from their having to constantly hide from prying eyes.

"How often do you use this boat? I mean, during warm weather, do you get many days off like this?" Amanda asked.

"Not enough. My dad thinks I should be at the shop every day with the techs. Says it makes for better relations... Tony does that," Alex stated casually.

"Maybe you should take your brother's advice. Seems to work for him," Amanda added.

"It does work for him. He's smarter than me, Amanda. He's able to channel all that mental energy that way. Doesn't work for me. I need to be at the track to focus on all that stuff. We're two different people. We may look alike and we may do many of the same things, but we're different. Have you ever heard such a thing?" Alex asked rhetorically, as he looked at her chuckling.

"What about Evelyn? Is she at the shop every day?" Amanda asked, wanting to get her in the conversation somehow.

"Ha! Are you kidding? She almost has to GPS the address every time she does go in. Her schedule is so busy with that Newberry and all."

"You mean that agent guy?" she asked.

"That's right."

"You don't like him very much, do you?" Amanda asked, searching.

"I think he's a sleazeball. If I could buy Louie for how good he is, and sell him for how good he thinks he is, I could retire tomorrow."

"I think he doesn't like you because he's jealous. He has the hots for Evelyn," she added.

Alex kept getting more and more impressed with her mental perception, seeing she had pegged Newberry to a tee and trying to recall in his mind how many times she had been around him and Evelyn. "Well, he shouldn't worry about Evelyn, at least as far as I'm concerned... And neither should you, Amanda."

"She does still live with you, though," Amanda stated, expectantly.

"Not really, Amanda."

"We don't have to talk about her, Alex. I don't want our time clouded with that," she responded,

"No, it's okay. You've got Evelyn Stevens on the brain, so let's clear the air on it," Alex declared. "She is so busy, she rarely comes to Charlotte between races. We actually had a formal parting of the ways and while she takes time to move her things out, I live there," he added as he stared forward.

"What do you mean, there?"

"Come on, I'll show you," he said and stood up, taking Amanda by the hand and leading her forward and down into the front cabin.

The space had ample room with a queen-sized bed, shower and toilet, a TV monitor, small refrigerator, microwave, hot water, heater, and air conditioner, complete with side tinted windows. She hid a strange sensation while looking at the tinted small windows and small curtains that would cover them.

"Alex Moretti, do you really expect me to believe you live on this boat?" Amanda stated skeptically as she stood just inside the cabin doorway. "Trisha, check this out."

The three all gathered inside the boat's cabin, as drops of rain began to fall. The three gathered around the small table and snacked on Alex's meager rations of cheese crackers while the pattering of rain drops pelted the fiberglass ceiling above them. A talkative Trisha rambled on, asking Alex endless questions about life and racing while mixing in a few tales about Amanda, who relaxed up close to him.

"I wish I could see you more," Amanda said when Trista had a break in her action.

"I know. With you living on this lake, there ought to be a way," Alex replied thinking.

The girls chatted briskly as Trisha accelerated down the southbound entry ramp toward the expressway. She wanted to plant a seed about her own boyfriend coming next time, but Amanda strenuously objected as she was quite paranoid about having anyone else in the know. Trisha provided little argument as Jeremy, bless his heart, couldn't be trusted to keep his mouth shut if his life depended on it, and was also a relatively close friend of Kyle Williams, a young man who still had aspirations toward Amanda.

"So, when are you going to do it?" Trisha asked, knowing the question weighed on her friend.

"I'm not going to do anything while you're with us, Trisha."

"I know that. And I know you're scared. But I know you want to," her friend buzzed. "I wasn't going to say anything before today, but I can see it written all over you, girl. And he's a nineteen-year-old guy. You can't expect him to hold out forever."

Amanda stared out the window. She was thinking about it but she was anxious. She was still a virgin, sort of, but never felt this way about a guy, and found herself conflicted in a societal evolution where half of her classmates were openly having sex and the whole concept of celibacy was only a myth, slowly facing extinction along with the whole idea of marriage itself. She had a severe stain in her recent past, a recurring reality that she wished was only a dream, fearful that she may somehow hold that against Alex.

She had long looked upon her own sister with disdain, particularly in her attitude toward Aaron, a straight-as-an-arrow guy, morally and ethically, who worshipped the ground she walked on, only to have her cheat behind his back at random whenever it served her wills, which often had nothing to do with emotion, but her unending quest for power over others. In Amanda's mind, if her boyfriend was an eight hundred pound gorilla, Allison would find a way to sleep with him just for spite.

Amanda still held to an old fashioned belief of connecting with that special guy who would love her as her own and receive the same in return. She still had hidden suspicions about Alex, telling herself repeatedly that he had done nothing to deserve them. How could they carry on a relationship together? If they were caught, she knew there would be hell to pay for them both, but mostly for him. *Would he accept just seeing her a few hours every other week or so when my best friend has to arrange it?* Amanda thought seriously. *If he wants to see me right after he gets back from France, I'll have to figure out a better way.*

"Just make sure you don't spill the beans to Jeremy, Trisha. Promise me!"

"My lips are sealed, baby."

After Alex had dropped the girls off he checked the lake map on his phone, thinking he might look into getting a slip on Wylie, or maybe even check out some rentals. Down the lake a piece was the closest marina up on an opposite cove which he cruised down to, pulling up to the gas pumps and choosing to just top off while he was there.

He jumped up onto the dock and while the attendant pumped his fuel, ran quickly up to the office. A smiling young woman stood facing him, ready to sell him anything from a replacement prop to an ice cream bar. He noticed the name on her name tag, Tammy. "I was just curious if you had any slips open to rent?" he asked.

"All of our monthly slips are taken. We do have our daily slips without lifts. Would that be for tonight?" she replied, smiling at the handsome guy, not familiar as they didn't get many strangers during midweek.

"No, I'm just asking generally. How much notice do you need for one of those?"

"During the week, none. On weekends, the more the better. No guarantees.," she responded.

"And what about your rentals? What do they run?" he asked, thinking of an alternative as the act of pulling his boat out of Norman, trailering the dual-engined cruiser clear down here, launching it in and out, and then pulling the thing all the way back. *Good to know the options.*

"Here is one of our brochures. We have everything from jet skis to houseboats. And all this is online with availability, too."

"Okay, I'll check it out and get back to you," he said while studying the colorful handout.

"Where's that accent from?" she asked grinning.

"I actually live up past Huntersville now. But I recently relocated down from suburban Chicago," he said casually.

"I knew you didn't sound like you're from down here. What brought you to the Carolinas?"

"I'm in the automotive industry. Performance parts," Alex replied, avoiding her stare and not wanting notoriety.

"Well, they have a lot of that up in Huntersville, I know that," she stated, still smiling.

"How about parking my truck and trailer overnight?" he asked, observing this may be a bit more convenient than where he had launched clear up at the north end of the lake in Belmont.

"We don't get many of those," Tammy responded. "When you put in, just let us know. If you park on the far side of the lot, no problem."

"Yes, surely. Well, thank you," he said as he walked away. *That southern belle accent. It does grow on you,* he thought, thinking of another thing he liked about Amanda. "I don't suppose that place next door allows boats to dock there overnight, do they?"

"Papa Doc's?... I kinda doubt it."

"Is that a good place?" Alex asked, observing the lakeside establishment just next door.

"Best wings on the lake," she replied. "It gets packed on weekends. I love their oysters, too."

Oysters, huh? He pondered as he smiled at the clerk and departed.

Lemans, France

The entire team arrived on Tuesday and checked into the Hotel Concordia Lemans Centre, a historic four-star hotel in the center of town and a short drive north of the legendary track. All the drivers and their boss, Andy, had separate rooms, a last-minute change necessitated by Marie's travel staff as Alex and Evelyn would not be rooming together.

As Andy stepped up to the counter he was greeted by Montagne Toussaint, the hotel manager. "Bonjour, Monsieur Moretti. Welcome back to Lemans. I did arrange Mademoiselle Cook's special request for a room adjacent to Monsieur Alessandro Moretti. You will please bring anything else you need to my special attention. I trust your stay in Lemans will be most enjoyable and good luck with the racing."

106

Andy looked up from signing the various registration documents, smiling but with a confused look. "Mademoiselle Cook?"

"Oui, Monsieur. The Mademoiselle called earlier this morning and I was happy to handle the arrangement personally," Toussaint replied proudly.

Allison had taken the train through the French countryside and arrived at the hotel late on Wednesday afternoon, settling into her room as she heard the roar of motor racing cars off in the distance, as practice for the weekend race had begun earlier. She looked forward to the next several days, seeing Evelyn Stevens as a key to bigger and better things for her, while at the same time dealing with another very personal matter, a box that needed to be checked off.

While Allison was still bitter toward Alex Moretti after what had happened in Southern California two months earlier, she was determined not to let it show and keep a close eye on him. From all that she had gathered, Allison knew that her sister, Amanda, no doubt had a crush on him and why wouldn't she? He was handsome, famous, and now apparently available, a quality her sister would see as *necessary*.

But how could they even carry on a real relationship? Allison pondered amusingly. *Yes, they didn't live that far apart now, but she cannot drive up there, and he most definitely wouldn't be welcomed by our parents, particularly our father, an old-school conservative who was hell-bent on Amanda taking up with Kyle Williams, a young man Allison knew was a snake.*

I'll catch that playboy Alex in something this week, I'm sure, even if I have to stir the pot myself.... Don't worry, little sister, I'm always there,... to save you from yourself.

Allison strolled into her room's bathroom and stood in front of the vanity mirror, her cunning mind in motion and unable to keep from smiling to herself.

During the team practice session, Andy looked for the best chance to have a frank and uncomfortable conversation with his youngest son. While his teammate Evelyn Stevens passed in front of them with her second shakedown lap, He spied Alex with two technicians, motioning his head left to request a private conversation. The two then stepped outside to the back of the pit garage.

"Alex, you promised me. You gave me your word. This has nothing but trouble written all over it," Andy stated sternly.

"Dad, what are you talking about?"

"You know what I'm talking about. Allison Cook, that's what. Did Marie know she was going to be here?" Andy asked, disappointed that his sister would not have made him aware of such arrangements.

"Dad, I found out Evelyn invited her! I had no idea she was going to be here. You need to ask Evelyn what the deal is!" Alex answered, not happy that Amanda's sister was in Lemans nor the fact that his father thought that he was behind it.

"Why did she request a room adjacent to yours, then?" Andy asked, still skeptical. He wanted to believe his young son, truly concerned that he would go back on such an important promise, although he himself knew the temptations posed by beautiful young women.

"Dad, what do you mean, she requested? I'm telling you, I had no idea she was coming to Lemans, none!"

Andy saw his son in a full state of being perplexed. Something strange was going on with this Cook girl, something he would like to get his arms around. With all the stress of trying to run a team here with two cars and six drivers, not to mention the army of support personnel involved, this strange issue involving a family member of his major sponsor was the last thing he needed right now. He would attempt to query Evelyn about it,... when the time was right.

The Moretti team contingent returned to the hotel at just past 9:00 and all visited their various rooms to shower and change prior to heading out for a late dinner, with all dining at a small bistro called The La Vieille Porte. Now learning that Allison Cook was in Lemans as Evelyn's special guest, Andy insisted that she join them as part of the added stress of having to entertain unexpected sponsors. As a sidebar, he hoped to get a measure of Allison Cook's motivation behind this mysterious room request.

Alex tried to appear relaxed but was extremely uncomfortable with Amanda's sister being in such proximity, especially since she was invited by Evelyn and his having no knowledge of just what or how much his former girlfriend may have shared with the older Cook sister regarding their own breakup. What his father had brought up regarding her room preference was another strange article that served to add to this intrigue. *Is she here to spy on me? If so, was she doing so on Amanda's behalf?... No, that possibility was inconceivable. So what is her game here?* He wondered seriously.

The dinner conversation was naturally dominated by the first day of practice for the 24-hour marathon race coming up. Crissy attempted to inject some small talk to entertain Allison, a young woman she really knew little or nothing about. As dinner progressed, Tony's wife couldn't help but notice that she kept looking at her brother-in-law, Alex, while he seemed to avoid even glancing at her. Knowing that he and Evelyn had just broken off their relationship, Alex's paying little or no attention to a woman whose vanity rivaled Stevens' own just wasn't a natural act for him, notwithstanding his father's unspoken rule that none of his drivers fraternize romantically with their sponsors or their families.

Evelyn tried to act gleeful but she herself could hardly ward off a sour mood as she just kept reminding herself of her and Alex's broken romance and now having to deal with Allison's expectation toward being entertained. Following dinner, Evelyn declined Allison's suggestion of going out on the town, stating her strong desire to get a good night's sleep for a change.

Allison was escorted back to the hotel with the rest of the team's name players, all having rooms on the third floor. Departing the elevator, she headed for her room which was 824, the last door on the right, noting with a smile that Alex had entered room 822, just next door. *How charming.* Up the hallway were Evelyn and Tony's rooms, and Andy Moretti was just across the hall in 825. Allison had wished for the two to be somewhat secluded from the rest, but even she couldn't have everything.

She chose to take a walk around the town, a charming French village that was already buzzing with the gathering of a massive crowd arriving for the famous race. Knowing it was still mid-afternoon back home, she filled the rest of her evening messaging her college friends and then thought she would send one to her sister.

Amanda checked her phone which beeped, catching a new text alert from Allison. *"I'm in northern France now, Amanda. Went out on the town with Alex and Evelyn. This place is packed with people from all over the world here. Having a blast."*

She suddenly felt a bout of concern, angry that Allison was in Europe, freely hanging out with her guy while she sat in South Carolina, unable to even speak out about it. She had sent Alex a series of messages pretty much all day, with only one reply hours earlier informing her that he was in the team pit garage preparing to hit the track. She was about to send Allison a reply when her phone rang,...a number UNKNOWN?

"Hello," she answered curiously.

"How are you doing, baby?"

"Oh my god! Alex? What is this phone?" Amanda replied with a 180-degree change of mood.

"It's my phone, going through an exchange over here. I know it's not possible, but I wish you were here, Amanda."

"Oh, me too. Did you get my messages?" Amanda asked.

"Yes, that's why I chose to just call you," he stated. "We had a shakedown of the cars at the track from 4-8:00 PM. All of us just had a late dinner in town and knowing the time would be hours behind, I thought I would just wait and call. So, how are you?"

"Who all had dinner with you?" she asked expectantly.

"All of the team drivers. You know the three of us, plus Crissy, Dad, and the other three, Caruso, Crosby, and Blair. I wasn't aware your sister would be here," Alex stated genuinely.

"I just found that out myself. She and some college mates were vacationing in Spain, but I thought she would be back yesterday. She sent me a text that she had gone out on the town tonight with you and Evelyn," Amanda expressed, curious how he would react.

"Gone out on the town?" Alex replied quickly. "I don't know how she ever got that idea. We all went down the street for dinner at a restaurant. She and Evelyn may have gone out afterward but I doubt it. We all spend so much time in the car here, I suspect Evelyn is bushed, as am I."

"Please don't get into trouble with my sister, Alex," Amanda said emotionally.

"Amanda, stop worrying. I'm here to race. Scout's honor."

Amanda listened intently, feeling a sudden bout of guilt. *Settle down, girl,* Amanda scolded herself. *You need to get a grip. Trust him.* "I miss you," Amanda stated emotionally.

"I miss you, too. Make sure nobody gets hold of your phone, Amanda," Alex told her as the two prepared to disconnect. "Are you positive that Allison doesn't know anything?"

"Alex! Nobody knows, except my best friend, Trisha."

Lemans was the world's most famous sports car event. Similar in format to the Rolex 24 at Daytona, each car would run for twenty-four consecutive hours while employing multiple drivers. Perhaps due to the travel and time change, the summer hot weather, or the pressure of winning such a prestigious race, Lemans just seemed exhausting in comparison.

Alex had thought about requesting his father split him and Evelyn, having each run in different cars, but held back as he'd been telling his dad for a year that his personal connection with Evelyn would have no bearing on their role as teammates. He was now seeing the wisdom of his father's advice, cautioning him about that very thing, and worked hard to suppress his anxiety, at least openly.

Friday was another busy day, with the various practice sessions mixed in with the supporting events, and the team entourage had a light dinner, choosing to turn in fairly early which was much to Allison's repeat consternation. She had fully expected Evelyn to show her a good time and thus far it had been far less, especially for a wild college girl accustomed to burning the midnight oil.

Alex woke up early on Saturday morning, showered, and stood in front of the bathroom mirror preparing to shave. He suddenly felt repeated drops of water on his head and looked up, noticing a steady water leak coming from his bathroom ceiling. *Some sort of plumbing leak in the room above,* he acknowledged and called down to the front desk, advised that the hotel staff would check on the problem immediately. Prior to his departing for the track, he checked with the front desk and was told the repairs would be time-consuming and that the staff may have to transfer him to another room, to which he patiently replied in kind by informing the desk clerk he wouldn't be returning until after midnight.

Caruso would run the opening stint on Saturday when the green flag dropped at 4:00 PM, with Alex following and Evelyn pulling the third and final shift with the Toyota motorsport staff salivating at the prospect of their car taking the checkered flag with the lovely and world-famous female driver at the wheel. It was decided that each would run twice for four hours, assuring they would each be well spent toward the end.

As Alex was set to be on at 8:00 PM, he planned to be there in the team pit garage, studying the progress of the race and gathering information from Caruso and the team to be better prepared for his stint behind the wheel. The team's Toyota prototype was fast and promised to be durable, as was the reputation for Toyota-branded products. The competition was stiff, however, and doing well at Lemans meant a combination of speed, efficiency, and luck, all ingredients similar to the 500 at Indianapolis, but in a race that lasted eight to nine times longer.

Allison hung out around the pit garage, annoyed at first that track officials would not allow her in, but Andy had chosen to intercede and provide her with proper credentials as though she was actually a member of the crew, all in much to his chagrin. Sporting an outfit best described as little more than a bikini, she became quite a distraction for the team at large, while all the while catching the ire of track officials.

Andy could tell Alex was quite nervous around her, adding to his confusion, noting that the Cook girl headed out and upstairs to the VIP suite where Tony, who would run the final stint on the other car, enjoyed dinner with his wife.

The two chatted at length with Allison as Crissy again enjoyed sharing her story about how she and Tony had first met, noting that Allison seemed quite interested in Alex's part in it. The two initially had a warm attitude toward their guest, confused a bit when she disclosed that she was engaged to a young man she had gone to school with, an admission that appeared in conflict with her carefree attitude and seductive attire.

Her curiosity satisfied and getting bored after a bit, Allison waited until late when Tony left the suite to prepare for his shift in the car, asking Crissy to join her for a late night out. Tony's bride declined, beginning to see Allison Cook as potential trouble, the large diamond on her finger seeming to have little meaning to her. While she escorted the team guest back to their hotel, Allison chose to head out on the town on her own.

The various restaurants and clubs were less crowded now as most of the fans were at the circuit and she couldn't believe that people would actually hang out there for the duration. She browsed a few boutiques for a couple of hours before entering a bar for a few mixed drinks. At first glance, the patrons assumed by her attire that she must be a prostitute, but she didn't quite look the part as being *too* attractive and having too little makeup on for a common street hooker. She shared a mixed feeling of ego, disgust, and amusement when a couple of half-drunk locals tried in vain to hit on her while she consumed the most expensive cocktails in the place, all on their tab.

Since coming to Lemans, she had seen little of Alex, other than being in such close quarters at the track. His behavior became somewhat of a mystery for her, in her mind no man could be that consumed with racing cars and ignoring all of life's other *opportunities*. Evelyn had told her that she would relieve Alex at midnight and that he would be off until 8:00 AM Sunday.

Returning to the hotel at just past 11:30 PM, an intoxicated Allison Cook sat alone on her king-sized bed, dejected that she had traveled all the way to northern France on the guise of connecting with Evelyn Stevens and getting her own picture on worldwide social media as a result. While she was not a rabid fan of motorcar racing, she would be there cheering as the winner crossed the finish line and was willfully available when the champagne was being sprayed all over everyone. But sitting in the stands, or even in a VIP suite, and watching loud and fast cars pass by repeatedly for hours on end just wasn't her idea of entertainment.

She opened her purse and extracted some white capsules from a small plastic bottle, labeled a prescription antibiotic which was a convenient mask when traveling internationally. She swallowed a pair and then moved to open the French doors leading onto the small outdoor balcony, as she leaned against the wrought iron railing while she waited impatiently for the narcotics to take effect. She observed the crowd below which had been drawn back into town from the race track after sundown, wondering to herself why she wasn't down there partying with them. As the high began to counteract her oncoming headache, she checked the time on her phone and displayed a sly smile. Allison was waiting on something... She was waiting for two other French doors to illuminate,... the exterior French doors just one balcony over.

Alex returned to the hotel at 12:44 AM, informed by the front desk clerk, a young man named Pierre, of some alternate arrangements for him. "I am sorry for the inconvenience in your room, Monsieur Moretti. The repairs to the bathroom cannot be completed until Monday morning. We have taken the liberty to move you to a suite on the top floor. It does not have a balcony that looks out over the downtown area, but it is much larger and has a large jacuzzi hot tub for your enjoyment. We will also award you a voucher for dinner for two at our diamond star restaurant. I hope that will be satisfactory, Monsieur."

"That will be fine, Pierre."

"There will be two bottles of champagne on ice in the suite, compliments of Monsieur Toussaint for your enjoyment," the clerk added, assuming the handsome and recognizable Alex Moretti would be entertaining another guest. "The lovely Mademoiselle Allison Cook,, who is staying in 824, had asked me to notify her when you came in. Should I contact her room and advise her of your room change?" the expectant hotel agent inquired.

Alex was frozen a for moment. *Allison wants to know when I get in? What's her game, anyway? What was it Amanda had said? She's capable of anything....Please don't get into any trouble with my sister.* "You may let her know I'm in, but make no mention about my change of rooms, Pierre. And I won't be needing the champagne, either. Nice touch, though," Alex replied, tired and just wanting to get to his room, shower, and sleep. As he grabbed the new key off the counter and prepared to walk away, a thought entered his mind. "Say, Pierre. When, may I ask, does this dinner voucher expire?"

"I believe they are good through the end of the year, Monsieur."

"Oh," Alex replied with an obvious look of disappointment.

"When do you feel it would be of use to you, Monsieur?" Pierre asked, not wanting this patron to be disappointed, and knowing he was part of a team that would be back next year.

"I don't know," Alex replied casually. "Maybe next year, maybe the following year. Could be three years from now."

"I will discuss it with the manager in the morning. I think we may accommodate you," young Pierre related, smiling while envious of Alex, a young man known for his romance with the well-known British driver Evelyn Stevens, and now this other hot brunette was after him as well. *Where did you go wrong, Pierre?* He thought smiling and shaking his head.

"Whatever you can do, Pierre," Alex had replied, casually strolling toward the elevator, and by the time he put his key in the door of his newly assigned fourth-floor suite he had forgotten about the dinner voucher altogether.

Exhausted from the driving, he enjoyed a quick hot shower and prepared to crash, fabricating a quick text message to Amanda. *"Long day, Amanda.*

I just got in after four hours in the car. We're running third right now and on the same lap as the leaders. Had a bum room but they gave me a larger one on the top floor because of it. Too bad you're not here. This appears to be the honeymoon suite. I'm very tired and will crash. Wish us luck! Alex." SEND.

He immediately received a return text from Amanda. *"Alex, I know you're tired but please call me."*

Alex leaned back on his bed, extremely tired from four hours of driving the long 8.5-mile road course at speeds exceeding 200 miles per hour. Although he kept himself fit, just the driver's fire-resistant suits alone in Lemans would serve to drain a man or woman. He knew tomorrow would be tough with the daytime heat. Of course, Evelyn would have the worst of it from noon to finish.

"Alex! Thanks for calling me. I know it's really late over there," Amanda answered her phone, quickly lowering her voice as she had lost awareness of the fact that her mother was upstairs and perhaps within listening distance.

"Yes, it is. I'm beat. This is the toughest race I've ever driven. You tend to get numb after a couple of hours and start to get tired. But you also have to stay really alert after dark because of the different classes. I'm constantly having to approach and pass slower cars, and some are much slower. It's not like racing around a track where all the cars are running at about the same speed."

Amanda had spent the whole day on and off downstairs in the game room catching the 24-Hour Lemans coverage on Motor Trend TV, a subscription channel she had added to the family's TV package, assuming her parents would surely not notice the extra five bucks per month.

"I've been watching," she stated proudly. "It looks like you're doing good. You went from fifth to third, I believe."

"Very good, Amanda. That all happened between 8 to 11 PM." *She's a race girl, all right.*

"How's everyone else doing," she asked, meaning, *What's my sister up to?*

"Everyone's fine. Tony had a brake problem after six hours and lost four laps. Evelyn is doing okay. She's not as fast as me, but she's very smooth and easy on the car. Allison was in the pit garage earlier, but I didn't see her much later on."

"When will you be back in Carolina?" she asked.

"Won't be for several days. I'm going to Silverstone, just northwest of London, with Tony this week for a Formula One test. We'll be there for a couple of days and then we're heading to Elkhart Lake in Wisconsin to race next weekend. and from there we're heading to Mid Ohio. Should be home two weeks from Monday, I think. Just keep the faith, Amanda. I'll see you soon."

"Okay my love, I know you're tired. Get some sleep... Bye now," Amanda closed. *Oh my god,* she immediately thought. *Did I just say that?*

Alex hung up and prepared to crash. *Did she just say that word?*

Allison pranced back and forth between her bed and the balcony, always glancing to her right and looking for a light or anything indicating activity next door. She knew the team's schedule and Alex's driving stint was to end at midnight. She looked at her watch for the hundredth time. *1:50 AM. Where is he?*

At just after 2:30, Allison strolled out onto the balcony again and finally saw light shining through the room 822 French door curtains. *Alex is back! She thought for a few moments about what to do and then grabbed an extender device to use for selfies. She attached her iPhone to the end of it, hoping to hold it out over the adjacent balcony and somehow see or hear what was happening inside. If he has a woman in there, maybe even a prostitute, I'll get proof of it.*

Allison leaned over the side of her balcony, holding the end of the shaft as she endeavored to position it in front of his balcony's door windows. Her phone just did catch the nearest edge of the glass, but in front of folded sheers on the inside which filtered out any discernable images. Pulling it back, she reviewed the brief recorded video, which reflected movement inside the room but was so blurry nothing could be made out. She stepped back inside her own room, examining the French doors and noticing the

117

curtains were bound on each end, allowing an open center. *I have to get my phone cam just a bit more extended,* she thought.

Back outside and leaning over the railing even further, Allison was close to getting a better shot when she heard shouts from down below on the crowded street.

"Mademoiselle! You should have a drone! You are going to fall and kill yourself!" A voice from the street yelled up at her, supported heartily with much laughter.

Allison jerked the black metal stick back quickly as the edge of her phone caught the top of the room 822 balcony railing and broke loose from its bracket, falling through the open balcony grate toward the ground three floors down.

"Oh crap, Allison!" She spoke to herself as she leaned out over her own railing in an attempt to see where the iPhone may have fallen.

"Oh no, Mademoiselle! If I find your phone, will you marry me!?" The drunken partier yelled, following even more laughter.

Three minutes later, Allison showed up in front of the hotel. The historic building was ornately landscaped with a square-shaped hedgerow up against the structure, and as her phone did not appear on the lawn bordering the sidewalk and the street, she began to immerse herself through the stiff shrubbery in a frantic search for it. After a lengthy few minutes of endless folly, she entertained the crowd on the street with her battle with the wide and prickly trimmed hedges, her colorful language becoming all the more amusing to an ever-swelling number of rollicking onlookers.

After several minutes of embarrassed frustration, she immerged onto the lawn itself, having been quite a spectacle with her frantic effort to rid herself of the many twigs, insects, and other various vegetation while leaving a sizeable section of the hotel's landscaping in a sad state of disrepair.

"Oh, Mademoiselle, you should have used a drone," the same heckler rambled on.

"Stick it up your ass, you drunken frog!" Allison stated angrily, as she approached the young man and his cadre of friends who couldn't stop laughing.

"Oh, my Mademoiselle is an American....She sounds like a southern belle from Georgia. Oui?"

"You pompous ass.... Would one of you please call my number?" Allison asked, quickly changing her tone when she needed the drunken party animals to help her and reaching into her purse for a pen and notepaper to write it down.

"My American Mademoiselle,... my southern belle, would this make you happy?" The young man declared smiling from ear to ear as he held up her iPhone."

She reached forward to grab it and he backed off. "Maybe you will kiss me first, my American Mademoiselle."

"Give me my phone, asshole, before I call the police!" Allison screamed, as her patience and embarrassment were at a fever pitch.

"I tell you what, my beautiful Mademoiselle. Could my friends and I at least get a selfie with you? Something we can always use to remember each other by?"

Allison was tired of the theatrics, but not wanting to further engage with this bunch she relented and stood with the ring leader and his band of party animals, taking pictures with several of their phones, many with the partying guys and gals hanging all over her.

"Okay, enough. Now will you please give me my phone, Monsieur?"

"It is Antoine. And you will want a photo with us both on your phone, Mademoiselle, something to hold in your heart forever," the bold Frenchman exclaimed in slurred and accented English.

Allison had to force a smile as the cackling crowd cheered. Antoine handed her phone to a pal who stood back a few paces and shot a photo of just the two of them.

"Oh, my love!" Antoine exclaimed now down on a knee. "I will not sleep a single night until you marry me!" He then fell over sideways, the crowd gathering to help him up as he struggled to stand and looked around... But to his bemusement, his American southern belle was gone.

As she moved quickly back toward the lobby entrance, Allison stared up toward the third-floor balconies, now seeing the lights in Alex's room appeared to have gone dim. She didn't think he would have left and surely couldn't have crashed that soon, could he? She made her way back into the hotel and up to her room, fully planning to salvage something out of what had thus far been a disastrous evening.

She quickly showered and applied just the right amount of makeup and mascara. Her dark long hair shined and accented a perfectly white smile and bright blue eyes. Having shaved completely, Allison adorned her favorite lingerie, a blue-colored corset, complete with matching blue stockings, and a see-thru brassier. By all measures, Allison was an extremely sexy-looking woman and one that no self-respecting male could turn down, she thought confidently.

Popping another narcotic and washing it down with champagne, Allison psyched herself up for the next act, one that she had performed numerous times before.

She stood a moment in front of 822, quite confident that no one would stray down the hallway at this hour. She then knocked on the door gingerly. and after a brief moment, someone looked through the peephole, indeed in complete surprise.

The door was opened and before Allison stood a young woman, one overdone with makeup but quite shapely as she stood naked in front of her new guest. The wild-looking French female waved Allison on in and after a brief hesitation, she followed, disappointed on one hand that she would not have Alex Moretti to herself, but cynically excited to see the shocked look on his face when she suddenly appeared.

The prostitute took Allison by the hand, leading her down the room's short hallway before the two stood in front of the occupied king bed, a sight that had Allison wide-eyed and stunned even in her animated drug-infested state.

"Monsieur Toussaint! I did not know you ordered extra service," the street hooker, who introduced herself as *Danielle*, exclaimed excitedly. "Come, Mademoiselle, let's get you out of that outfit and down to business."

Allison jerked away as she witnessed the shocked hotel manager, a man who sat up on the bed, naked, overweight, and somewhat embarrassed, but salivating at the sight of his erotically dressed and quite sexy-looking American guest.

"Where is Alex Moretti!?" Allison demanded.

Toussaint and *Danielle* looked at each other in mild confusion, before he finally stated, "He was moved to a suite on the top floor."

Allison stomped out the door and retreated back to her room, angry, totally humiliated, and more determined than ever to get even with the one male on earth that she just couldn't seem to control, Alex Moretti.

Chapter 6

Stunning Disclosures

While Alex continued to share his Romeo and Juliet tale with his grandmother, Amanda gradually improved and on day five regained consciousness. Her prognosis was positive, and although her left arm had been broken in the crash and was in a cast, her head injuries appeared to be all superficial and were steadily healing. The results of all the various tests for traumatic brain injury produced the desired results. Her mother had remained in attendance throughout her stay while her father had flown back to Charlotte and was relieved the previous day by Amanda's older sister, who had driven up from Los Angeles.

Doctor Mammoud Assani, a resident neurologist, entered the room accompanied by a senior nurse carrying a tablet. Assani and another resident physician, Doctor Mark Halbert, had attended to Amanda from the minute she had been transferred from the emergency room to the IC unit. The Cook's longtime family physician, Doctor Ronald Barrows, had also been in very close communication from his office back in Rock Hill.

"Your results from the MRI and CT scans are negative," Assani declared, speaking to Amanda and her relatives generally. "There appears to be no apparent brain damage. You are a very fortunate young lady," the doctor added smiling.

"When can she be released and ready to travel back home, Doctor?" Sarah asked.

"Doctor Halbert will discuss that with you soon, I believe. Amanda, do you have any questions for me?"

"How is Alex?" she replied immediately as if shouting a question she had held in reserve too long.

Assani hesitated, sharing a look with Sarah as a signal that she could better handle that question.

"You shouldn't worry about Alex Moretti, Amanda. Put him out of your mind." Sarah chose not to mention that Andy Moretti had approached them three days prior, expressing his genuine concern and asking rather sincerely if they would object to his bringing his son down in a wheelchair to check on Amanda, offering a concerned regret for what had happened. Byron had been outright rude to the man, claiming he would demand a restraining order on Alex, and in spite of the circumstances, Sarah had felt somewhat embarrassed and sorry for him.

Amanda became misty-eyed and couldn't help but wonder in disappointment why Alex had not even sent her a message inquiring about her well-being.

"I heard some gossip from some of the nurses. That arrogant ass has been busy flirting with them the whole time you were in Intensive Care, Amanda, not even knowing if you would live," Allison claimed, feigning extreme anger.

Sarah reached over and firmly grasped her oldest daughter's arm, a signal that she should back off now, as Amanda continued to tear up.

Later that afternoon, Doctor Halbert received a return call from Doctor Barrows. "I am sorry for the delay, Doc. Busy day."

"That's quite all right, Doctor. Very busy ourselves." Halbert responded, preparing for an intimate conversation.

"Of course. So tell me, how's my girl?"

"Amanda is doing quite well. All of her tests have come back favorably. She's now wide awake and completely alert and talking to everyone. She'll have those skin wounds to heal for a few more days, and of course that broken arm. She should be good to travel home in a couple more days."

"That's very good news. I'll update her father later today that we've spoken and I appreciate your work out there. I guess I had best get".....

"Hold on, Doctor! There is something else I need to discuss with you and I am counting on your confidence," Halbert stated seriously.

After a long pause, Barrows replied. "Of course, Doctor Halbert. What's on your mind?"

"You know, Doctor Barrows, here in Nevada, the legal age for patient consent is sixteen, other than in cases of emergency. Of course, when Amanda entered the emergency room such restrictions were waived and her parents signed all the consent forms necessary and were advised of everything at that time," Halbert stated, pausing for an acknowledgment.

"Yes, go on," Barrows answered, curious where this was headed.

"Now that Amanda is out of trauma and I have a release by our neurologist, I must get her to sign another consent form personally, in order to discuss any further prognosis and treatment."

"I'm not following you, Doctor. Get her to sign whatever you need. She'll have no problem with that."

"What I have to discuss is of a nature that may be rather uncomfortable," Halbert added and proceeded to share with Barrows some other pertinent medical issues regarding their patient. "I'm going to have to ask the mother and sister to leave the room before we present the forms, Doctor."

Barrows was temporarily speechless as if news regarding the accident thus far hadn't been enough. "I see. Perhaps you could have Sarah leave the room at that time and take a person-to-person call from me."

"That may be a good idea, Doctor Barrows.... The sister, too. But listen, getting back to our earlier agreement, what I just shared with you could get me in really hot water as I don't have Amanda's signed consent form in my hand just yet. Do you understand?"

"I suppose I do. I will just advise Sarah about the privacy procedures and you and Amanda will have to handle the aftermath."

"Deal. I appreciate it, Doctor. And I'll have the staff send over all the updated records soon."

Doctor Barrows hung up the phone, staring blankly at the floor....*Oh my god!*

The staff nurse entered, showing Amanda some documents she needed to authorize.

Sarah and Allison were confused and somewhat angry when they were asked to leave the room momentarily before Doctor Halbert entered and proceeded to ask Amanda how she was feeling, taking a few minutes to closely examine the injuries, all of which were healing up nicely.

"What am I signing?" Amanda asked.

"In accordance with state and federal law, at sixteen years of age you have a sole right to privacy regarding health issues. You may authorize us to share your information with others, such as your parents, other medical professionals, clinics, and so forth. Or you may choose not to."

Amanda began to sift through some of the forms, looking somewhat confused. "I don't get this, Doctor. I've been in here for several days and everyone knows what happened to me."

"Well, Amanda, certain privacy stipulations in the law are waived in the case of life and death. We were covered in sharing everything with your parents and getting their approval for tests and treatment, as long as you were confined to the Intensive Care Unit. Once you were transferred up to this floor, some new rules kick in. I must share something with you now that may affect your decision and how to fill out a couple of those forms."

She just looked up at him from her bed, still confused.

"Amanda, did you know about your pregnancy?" Doctor Halbert asked solemnly.

She was stunned at the news. "Oh my god!... No!" She answered, unable to hold back her tears.

"I'm afraid so. It was about six or seven weeks. Did you not have any indications? Any symptoms?"

"No...At least I never thought." *That's what it was...*

"The fetus was terminated as a result of the accident and you becoming temporarily comatose," Halbert explained.

Amanda welled up and began to sob, unable to speak.

"Well, if you wish your medical information to be disclosed to your family, or anyone else, including medical staff and facilities, you can see on the forms where to indicate so. You may decline, Amanda. Then you'll choose what to tell your parents,... and others," Halbert informed her. "I'll give you a few moments, if you need it, Amanda."

"I'll sign your forms," she declared in resignation. "But I would like to tell Mom myself."

"Of course, Amanda."

She looked over the forms, signing below the verbiage authorizing the sharing of medical data with all other medical facilities, physicians, and medical staff. She went through the remaining content, checking and initialing boxes, not thinking clearly at the moment. In the section listing any other non-medical individuals authorized to have access to her records, she listed her mother and father, then paused a moment and thought, *Should I add Allison?... No.*

"Does the father know about this, Doctor?" she asked.

"Amanda, I have to ask this. Do you know for certain who the father was?"

"Of course I do!" She replied rather loudly. *You must have me mixed up with my sister,* she thought angrily. "He is Alex Moretti."

"No Amanda. He has not been informed. Your parents prohibited any information regarding your health to be discussed with anyone outside your family," the good doctor advised. "Of course, you may list the father as eligible to receive your records if you choose."

"So, do Mom and Dad know about this?" Amanda asked, an afterthought entering her mind.

"No. This prognosis was documented in the lab *after* you were released from the IC Unit. So again, due to legalities, you are the only person thus far, aside from doctors and medical staff here, that knows anything about it," he explained clearly.

"I really do not want anyone else to know about it, Doctor. At least not now," she exclaimed. "Is that possible?"

"It's possible," Halbert responded. "The hospital had to submit some required forms to the Coroner's office. If they choose to issue a legal death certificate, it will then become a public record."

Amanda fought back emotions as she struggled to complete the documents, which she finally handed back to the doctor. He left the room, examining the documents as he walked, noticing Amanda did add a name that wasn't Cook....*Alessandro Moretti.*

By Thursday afternoon, Alex was somewhat better and the attending physician indicated he would probably be released the next day. He had become well acquainted with the floor station nursing staff by now, and nearly everyone had given him a heady amount of sympathy and attention. The Moretti family had long been very well known to worldwide motor racing fans, but now with the unfortunate accident a few days earlier, he had become universally well-known to the masses, most of whom had never followed the sport, including the entire hospital which was awash in the headlines regarding their two patients, both who had become world famous overnight.

The shift nurse, Brittany, had become quite friendly, if not outright flirtatious, and Alex took advantage of that to get some random updates on Amanda.

"I have some news, Alex," Brittany stated. "Amanda Cook has awakened and is speaking now. SHe was released from the IC unit yesterday and transferred to a private room. She's now able to stand and walk with some help."

Alex felt a huge emotional lift at this news. His worst fears, that Amanda could permanently exist in a comatose state, or worse, was a possibility that he just couldn't comprehend living with. He asked this nurse, one who had seemed to have his best interests at heart, "Brittany, is it possible for me to see her, or maybe at least speak to her on the phone?"

"I would not advise it. Her mother is at her side and would no doubt pick up the phone. I hear you're not exactly on their Christmas list right now. There is something else," the nurse added, hesitating as she looked toward the door, as if needing confirmation they were not being overheard.

Matilde raised an eye, sensing something important was about to be disclosed. "What is it, Miss? Something the whole world doesn't already know?"

"Maybe not yet," Brittany responded. "Alex, as a result of the accident, Amanda lost her baby."

He and his grandmother sat speechless, neither able to even move.

"Did you know she was pregnant, Alex?" Brittany asked seriously.

Alex just looked up at her, struggling to even find words. "Oh my god!"

"Do they know how far she was along," Matilde asked following a moment of silence.

"Six to seven weeks I heard," the nurse replied.

As Alex temporarily turned to glance out the window as if not wanting to look anyone in the eye, if just momentarily, Brittany gave Matilde a quick eye motion to follow her outside to the hallway.

The aged woman could barely hold back her own tears as she followed the nurse, one who was sharing very confident information, down to the end of the corridor where they could sit down by the huge exterior window.

"Mrs. Moretti"...

"Please, Brittany, call me Matilde."

"Okay, Matilde. I'm afraid this could be serious trouble. Your grandson may be charged with involuntary manslaughter."

The Moretti family matriarch stared down at the floor, unable to respond.

"I am so sorry to bring you this news. But I thought Alex should know before the police show up," Brittany said softly to avoid passersby as she briefly held the stricken grandmother's hand.

"Oh my god.... Oh my god," Matilde replied finally as she now broke down.

"It is not definite, Matilde. It has to be determined by the coroner that the fetus would likely have been carried to full term by the mother. When an accident induced miscarriage occurs at such an early stage there is the question of reasonable doubt. But there is also a judgment made about the health of the mother"...

"And I'm sure Amanda Cook has no previous health issues," Matilde replied, knowing the point Brittany was about to make. "When do you believe the police will arrive?"

"The coroner's office usually takes a few days to issue a death certificate. Alex may even be released before then."

"I'll tell him, if you don't mind."

"Of course, Madam. I am so sorry, and please do not openly disclose that I told you," Brittany responded, now forcing back her own tears.

Returning to his room, Brittany completed her tasks of getting an update on Alex's vitals and departed.

Never the type to just lay around and wait for something to happen, Alex picked up his smartphone and began punching in a message. *"How are you feeling? I miss you."*

Amanda's mother escorted her to the bathroom when the small beep sounded on her smartphone perched on her nightstand, picked up immediately by Allison. She proceeded to forward the message to her own iPhone prior to deleting it and checked for any other messages in kind while her sister and mother were preoccupied. She also took time to go into Amanda's phonebook list and swap the sixth and seventh digits on Alex's phone number, just after setting the Block Caller on his real number. She also set a block on the swapped number, having no clue if it was even active but assuming an actual user of that number would reply to Amanda's messages eventually. *Not perfect,* she thought deviously, *but someone has to save Amanda from herself.*

Matilde finally got control of her emotions, at least superficially, and took it upon herself, despite all advice to the contrary, to head over to the South Wing. She approached the nurse's station hoping to acquire the information regarding Amanda Cook's room number. As the recovering young woman was released from Intensive Care and moved to a standard room, she assumed visitors would be allowed in.

She entered the room and was recognized instantly by the Cooks, Sarah, Amanda, and Allison when the latter immediately stood up to confront the emotional woman.

"Mrs. Moretti, I don't think it's in good taste for you to"....

"Wait Allison," Sarah interrupted. She could see Amanda's expression brighten at the sight of the unexpected visitor.

Allison gave her mother a stern look and then quickly chose to exit the room.

The patient, mother, and their new guest shared a few seconds of emotional silence as Matilde looked at Amanda, laying in the hospital bed, her one arm in a cast and a few bandages still covering much of her face, but slightly smiling in spite of it all. Matilde started to well up yet again as did Sarah, prior to both women moving to embrace one another.

"I am so sorry," Alex's grandmother expressed with a squeaky voice.

Without words, the two women parted slightly as both faced Amanda. Matilde wished she could just pick up and hug the child, and as if Sarah could seem to read her mind, she stood aside from Amanda's bed while simply nodding.

Amanda formed tears herself as the aged woman, one whose expression so reminded her of Alex, grasped the teen's hand.

"I have been praying for you, Amanda... Praying for us all," Matilde continued as she smiled and glanced at Sarah. "I hope we can all see each other again someday, amid better circumstances, perhaps."

"How is Alex?" Amanda asked anxiously, oblivious to what her own mother would think at the moment.

Matilde and Sarah shared a brief look, each knowing the answer to that question carried some varied context. "He is fine, Amanda. He has been"....

Sarah put her hand on Matilde's shoulder as if to communicate that Amanda's question couldn't fully be answered, at least not currently, and that her visit, while personally appreciated, should conclude.

The two senior women briefly embraced again as Matilde turned to walk away. As she headed back to Alex's wing, she felt better that she had made the effort. Passing Allison in the corridor, she attempted a brief smile, just a nod of acknowledgment, but was met with a deceitful stare.

Recalling the two sisters from Indianapolis the year before, she hadn't formed much of an opinion of them back then, only that she remembered their looking so much alike. But now following this brief reacquaintance, she could readily see why her grandson recognized such a difference in the two. Even in her current state of recovery, a girl who hadn't fixed her hair or donned an ounce of makeup in many days, Amanda presented such a feeling of warmth and love, traits so strongly and sadly missing from the older sibling. Much of her previous consternation related to the thought that her grandson would risk everything for such a romantic connection had become somewhat diminished.

There was just something about Amanda, the Moretti family matriarch considered.

Following Matilde's exit from Amanda's room, the three Cook women were tense. Amanda could barely stop sobbing and the whole family seemed to be at war with each other over this latest revelation. Byron couldn't contain himself when Sarah had phoned to inform him of the elder Mrs. Moretti's visit. Exhausted by now from lack of sleep, she wouldn't allow him to speak directly to Amanda, knowing both of their emotional states.

Allison held back thoughts of her own bitterness, playing the part of the loving, caring sister. "Mom, why don't you go to the hotel and get some sleep? I'll stand watch here with Amanda."

Sarah looked questionably at her youngest daughter, never having recalled seeing her so stricken. "Yes, perhaps I will," Sarah responded, thinking the next long conversation with Byron may be better served in private.

Allison walked her mother out of the room and down the hall toward the elevator. "Get some rest, Mother. I'll be here with her."

"She has been asking about that boy on and off ever since she regained consciousness. Your father is ready to shoot the young man, God help him."

"He hasn't even called to check on her, Mom!" Allison practically yelled back.

Sarah stated sadly. "Well, his grandmother came. I think that may have done Amanda some good, don't you think?"

"Please, Mom. Go rest," Allison replied without further comment.

Seeing her mother off as she stepped into the elevator, Allison walked down the hall and into a restroom, locking the door behind her. She then took out her phone to check the forwarded text message.

Oh, how sweet, Allison scornfully thought as she read the incoming message intended for Amanda. *I'm just protecting you, little sister,* Allison thought, crediting herself with a devious smile. *You'll have one hell of a time playing footsies with him while he's behind bars.*

"Where is Mom?" Amanda asked as soon as her older sister walked back into the room.

"I sent her to the hotel to get a regular night's sleep. You have just about worn Dad and Mom out here."

"I want to ask the nurse about Alex."

"Amanda! Are you blind? You were in a coma for days! You even didn't know if you were going to live! And that asshole didn't even bother to call, or send anyone from the staff by to ask about you...Nothing!"

Amanda just looked out the window, staring blankly and speechless.

"Did he even know you were pregnant, Amanda?"

Amanda just stared back at her. *How would he know? I didn't even know.*

Matilde returned to Alex's room emotionally exhausted. She had not felt such devastation within her family since her husband had been killed nearly forty years earlier.

"So Alex, I assume you were getting to the part about how Amanda became pregnant.... And I know how those things are done; I'm just curious as to when and where," Matilde stated, suddenly much less thrilled with her grandson's fascinating tale, but yet wanting to hear it.

Late June, 2021

The team returned from Europe in mixed spirits as Alex and Evelyn's car finished third at Lemans while Ferrari took the checkered flag in the legendary event they had once owned over a half-century earlier. Both Moretti brothers had a very successful and rewarding Formula One test, a step to just get the team acclimated to the discipline in a year-old car leased temporarily from McLaren, with Alex surprisingly outperforming his more experienced and celebrated brother by all of three one-hundredths of a second on the famous Silverstone circuit.

Following a top-five showing at Road America, Alex chose to fly home for a precious few days, while the rest of the team traveled directly to Ohio, with many stopping off for brief family and friends visits in the Chicago area on the way.

Alex and Amanda spent another afternoon together on Lake Wylie, again with Trisha's company. As the two were now extremely close and possessed a mutual desire to be together more often, this became all the more challenging as both were now looked upon with surprise and suspicion from friends and family regarding their perceived lack of outside romantic interests.

Alex had fended off such questions in the guise of a new interest in fishing, claiming he needed relaxation from the weekend rush of the racing schedule. Spending more time around Lake Norman, he had become closer with Tony and his family while even surprising his father by suddenly spending more time at the team facility.

One individual who wasn't buying this ruse was Evelyn Stevens, who had obviously gotten to know him quite well on a personal level, particularly his insatiable appetite for private intimacy. Her suspicions were easy for him to sidestep, however, due to her ever-busier schedule propagated by Newberry, a man who saw new opportunities in his client, both financially and romantically.

For her part, Amanda had more difficulty managing the secret and would-be forbidden romance, drawing skepticism from all quarters. Her father, a man who believed she should be planning a future with his pal, Bud Williams' boy, was now worried about her sexual orientation. Her mother was more sympathetic but constantly attempted to question her and dropped subtle hints here and there about potential boyfriends, not to mention her surprise at Amanda's newfound interest in auto racing, never seeming to miss selected broadcasts, even at the expense of a sunny Saturday or Sunday afternoon on the lake with family and friends, an activity Amanda had seemed to die for in the past.

Adding to the challenge of concealing her romantic connection was her best friend, Trisha. It was not so much that Trisha would intentionally disclose Amanda's secret, nor had she even accidentally done so, but since the two girls had been best friends since kindergarten and they were inseparable, acting more like sisters than even toward their own siblings.

The two were always seen by friends and family chatting and pursuing mutual interests together that seemed to mirror everything. The mere fact that Trisha had a steady boyfriend meant she was constantly interrogated with questions about Amanda's romantic status.

Amanda's biggest concern by far was her sister, as Allison would constantly bombard her with uncomfortable questions and often go out of her way to arrange for Kyle Williams, her own boyfriend's younger brother, to constantly be in her physical proximity, to the point where it seemed he was being tipped off about her personal schedule and bordered on stalking her.

She began to think of how she and Alex would spin things once the cat got out of the bag. Her answer would always come back the same. *Not an option. That cat must never get out.*

The team rolled into their North Carolina home base on Monday following a stellar weekend in Ohio where Alex caught a break when race leader Romain Grosjean lost a gearbox while taking the white flag, allowing an opportunistic Moretti to win for his first season victory, and brother Tony joined him on the podium with a steady drive finishing third.

Amanda had been in Myrtle Beach with the family out deep sea fishing during the day, and thus Alex was somewhat chagrinned that he hadn't received an *attaboy* text from her while he and the team celebrated his dominating win. Two hours later, her iPhone back in range, Amanda couldn't hide her glee and sent Alex a late but emotional message. *"I was so excited to watch your win, Alex. I am out on a fishing boat right now and just got back in range for my phone. Hope to see you Tuesday when we get home. Love you!"*

Following such a busy two-month run, the team had a rare weekend off, and considered the midseason break as time for a battery charge. Alex spent the bulk of Tuesday at the team facility, and as Tony took the opportunity to take his family to the beach, he and his father chose to have a rare lunch together. The two entered a popular bar and grill and were seated when the waitress approached, a young lady who looked somewhat familiar to Alex.

"Hello, my name is Tammy. I'll be taking care of you fellas today," she began. "Say, do you remember me From the marina on Lake Wylie a few weeks ago?"

"Oh yes, how have you been?" Alex replied, pointedly staring down at the menu in hopes of shortening their conversation.

"Doing fine. Changed jobs, as you see. Did you ever reserve a slip down there?" she asked, thinking she would impress him by remembering their conversation.

Andy looked at both, confused. *What is she talking about?*

"No, still thinking about it. I'll have the Philly Steak sandwich. How about you, Dad?" Alex declared, hoping this gal, Tammy, who seemed to like talking, would move on.

"Okay, and you, sir?"

"I'll have the special, no onions, and the water is fine for me," Andy stated, still curious about this marina.

"Water for me, too," Alex added, again hoping to shoo her away.

"That sure is a nice boat you have. We don't get many that cool on Wylie. I'll be back with your waters right away," she added as she walked off.

"I think that's one of Rick Hendrick's crew chiefs over there," Alex claimed, motioning to the left in a vain attempt to avoid any more questions about the waitress.

"What's she talking about? Slips at some marina? Lake Wylie?" Andy asked.

"I was thinking about going down there and doing some fishing," Alex replied.

"Fishing?... You?" Andy thought the whole slip rental was pretty bizarre. After all, Alex had a fully covered slip with a lift as part of his membership fees at his condominium complex.

"I just took the boat down there one afternoon, the week before we went to Lemans. Somebody at the club bar told me the fishing was better down there, not as choppy."

Alex's father thought the whole fishing thing sounded corny, coming from a fiery young charger like Alex. *I just hope those fish down there aren't married,* he thought.

Andy was pumped as the new Formula One car was coming together nicely and he wished to share his plans for much of the upcoming season with his youngest son, whom it seemed he seldom spent time with anymore, in spite of their racing together. "I'm not going to sign Crosby for next year. As Tony will be the number one driver in F1, I plan to bring over Marcus Newsome to team with you and Evelyn; Bring in two new drivers for Indy Lights."

Newsome was the current points leader in Formula E, thought by some as the driver to team with Tony Moretti as their F1 duo, but Andy had signed Geoff Leland for one year with an option, a former F1 pilot recently squeezed out by Haas, thinking he needed an experienced driver for their first year in Formula One, perhaps taking some pressure off Tony while he gets a year under his belt.

"Sounds like a plan to me, Dad. I remember you telling me before that you were talking with Leland's agent about coming to Indycar before you signed Evelyn," Alex replied.

"It will likely be for next season only. About this time next year, you and I can have a conversation on whether you're ready for Formula One."

"I'm pretty content right now where I'm at, Dad. Tony has been in Indycars for seven years, not counting this season. I think I would be good for at least that. Maybe even go for the NASCAR Cup championship first."

"Seven years?" Andy replied. "NASCAR? I thought you would even be disappointed that you weren't going to F1 next year," Andy asked, always believing a Moretti would dream of that.

"Well, since we are Italian I guess that is the end game. But I'm in no hurry. Right now, I don't need the pressure," Alex answered.

The pressure? Andy thought. *You always thrived on that.* "You could run a limited NASCAR schedule next year on the Indycar open weekends. You wouldn't be competing for the Cup Championship, but then you could make a decision for the following season," Andy offered.

"Something to think about, I guess," Alex answered nonchalantly as though his mind was elsewhere.

"What's going on, Alex? You seem as though your mind is on another planet. Are you missing Evelyn?"

"Not so much, since I do see her all the time anyway. Though I must say, I don't miss that horse's ass, Newberry. I feel sorry for you in having to deal with clowns like him," Alex stated.

"Yes, well it goes with the territory, I guess. Listen, Alex, I want to apologize for our little dust-up regarding Allison Cook," Andy began, knowing the best time to discuss problems within a team or family was immediately after a big weekend victory. "You may not care about her, but she seems to have a thing for you, although I'm not at all certain what that thing is."

"What can I say, Dad?... Twisted steel and sex appeal," Alex replied jokingly.

"You know, starting with the aftermath of Long Beach, I didn't know how you could stay away from her, especially since you and Evelyn were at each other's throats," Andy reflected. "In fact, I honestly thought she was the reason you and Evelyn were having problems, that race-ending squabble aside. Those Cook girls are both gorgeous, aren't they? Take after the mother, I think. Anyway, after the trip to Lemans, I can kind of see why you came to resist her temptation. There's just something about that girl. I can't put my finger on it. Seems like she's got a rather arrogant and almost sinister confidence, the kind of woman I never much liked. I think her dad may be like that."

You don't know the half of it, Dad, Alex mused. "You're probably right."

"But speaking of Evelyn, have you two fully parted ways? I mean, she took her time moving out, didn't she?"

"Yes, sure looks like it," Alex came back.

Tony and I are not all that different, Dad, Alex thought seriously. *Not at all.*

The two wrapped up their lunch as Andy pulled out his credit card. "Here, you take care of the tab. I need to hit the can.'

Alex waited impatiently as the waitress approached. He handed her the card and watched while she ran it through her little slider.

"I thought so," she commented seeing the name on the card. "You're Alex Moretti, and that's your dad, right?"

"Yes, that's right."

"I'm a big fan. Are you still dating that British gal, Evelyn?" Tammy asked innocently.

"I was. We're just teammates now. Do you go to the races?" Alex asked, trying to get her off-subject.

"Not yet. I haven't been able to"...

"Oh, there's Dad," Alex stated, rising from the seat. "We're kind of on the run. Nice seeing you again."

On Tuesday mornings, Sarah drove into town for a weekly charity meeting which would generally last until just past 1:00 PM. As Allison was in Charleston, Amanda had to be home with her visiting grandmother until Sarah returned, when she then rode her bike down to the clubhouse pool where she parked it inside the secured gate. She then called Uber.

Alex opened the front door expectantly, excited and picked Amanda up off the floor when their lips came together as if they hadn't seen each other in months. This was her first time being at his place, or any male's place for that matter, and as such she was a bit anxious. *Just another step in life,* she told herself.

"Relax Amanda," Alex instructed. "What do you think? It's not your mansion on the lake but"...

"It's nice," she spoke, a bit spooked looking around while thinking about Alex and Evelyn and all the times they would have had here.

It was a different décor than she was used to with racing stuff all over the place. "Oh, how cute!" Amanda exclaimed as she picked up a small stuffed bear on the couch outfitted with a Long Beach Grand Prix tee shirt.

In one corner of the front room, Alex had a tall glass cabinet full of all kinds of model race cars. On the main wall, a large framed painting hung with three autographs scribbled at the bottom.

"Is this your signature, Alex? Looks like a doctor, as you can't even read it."

"No, that's my dad winning his first Formula One race in Austria. It's signed by him, Frank Williams, and the artist," Alex replied, standing close to her as she seemed to want to know about everything.

"Frank Williams? Who's he?"

"He owned the Williams Formula One team. Very famous guy who passed away a couple of years ago. He had periods of time where he dominated Formula One," he explained.

"Why don't you race in Formula One?"

"I may someday. It's a very exclusive place. Dad just got a team and Tony will race there next year," Alex replied, so pleased that Amanda had such interest in such things.

"I thought the Indycar was exclusive. Is this Formula One bigger than Indycar or NASCAR?" she asked as she continued to explore the many memorabilia items arranged around the place.

"Formula One is the pinnacle of motor racing. Huge worldwide, Amanda."

"I thought the Indianapolis 500 was the best?" she asked.

"The 500 is the world's biggest race. Formula One is the biggest series. I know, it can be a bit confusing. I'll probably be there eventually," he replied, now getting distracted by Amanda's denim shorts and well-tanned shapely legs, as he continued to follow her around the room.

"So, all these cars?" she asked, returning her focus to the curio cabinet. "Are they Indycars or Formula One?"

"Both," Alex answered, taking the time to explain which were which.

"They look about the same to me. I guess you'll be good in Formula One, too. Do they ever race in Charlotte?" she asked. "And how come the Indycars don't race here?"

"They did once, back before I was born, two or three years, I think. There was a huge accident that killed three or four spectators. Bruton Smith had Wheeler shut it down after that."

The late Bruton Smith was a longtime owner of the Charlotte Motor Speedway and his General Manager was Humpy Wheeler, a man best known for his role as "Tex" in the Disney movie "Cars".

She halted the walk-through motor racing history tutorial and turned to look at him. "Alex, I don't have much time. I have to be home before the clubhouse closes and locks my bike inside. And it took almost an hour to get up here," Amanda stated. "Can I come here this weekend? I want to spend the night with you."

Alex placed his hands on her two shoulders. "You sound serious. How are you going to manage that?"

"I am serious! Why, do you already have plans?" she asked.

"No, of course not. I was actually thinking of taking the boat back down to Wylie again, and"....

"I would rather come here, Alex," Amanda declared, cutting him off. "We can go out on the lake early, or play tennis, or whatever you want," she said, looking up at him with those pretty blue eyes he couldn't resist. "I just want to be here with you.... I want to wake up next to you."

Alex took it all in, attempting to process her mood. He figured they would get together eventually but held a very cautious view about the when and where, as he thought she did. Suddenly, she seemed to have some sort of now or never vision about it.

"Amanda, I'll ask how you're going to pull this off. But first, are you sure you're ready for this?" Alex asked, finding himself wanting more from Amanda than her just checking off a box on the road toward womanhood.

"What do you want me to do, run outside and say that I love Alex Moretti at the top of my lungs, or maybe jump up on your coffee table and dance naked for you? Just tell me. Yes, I'm nervous, I'm maybe a little scared. But I'm ready, Alex, if you are."

Alex sat on his couch, momentarily speechless. *Like wow! This girl never ceases to amaze. Did that whole shy little sister façade just seem to disappear right before my very eyes?*

Amanda stood before him with her hands on her hips. "Well Alex Moretti, say something!"

"Hey, sign me up!" He complied. "Now my festy one, tell me how you are going to pull this off. I assume I'm not just going to pull up in your driveway and say, Hello Mr. and Mrs. Cook. I'm Alex Moretti, you know, one of the race drivers you sponsor. I'm taking your youngest daughter out to shack up in my condo for the night."

Amanda slapped him hard across his leg. "Don't say shacking up. It sounds sleazy," she said as the two shared a light moment.

"Okay, Mr. and Mrs. Cook, I'm Alex and I'm taking Amanda for a sleep-over, just a friendly chat you know, about the birds and the bees or something like that. May I have your permission?"

Amanda couldn't help but really laugh now. He was glad to see it as she needed to lighten up and stop worrying about everything.

"Okay, smarty pants. I'm planning a sleepover with Trisha. Her folks and mine or going to Hilton Head for the weekend and our house servant is off on vacation. We have the house all to ourselves. I even thought about having you come down, but Allison is due back sometime this weekend. Besides, I really want to stay with you here. I do. You can come and get me at the clubhouse pool. We'll have fun, I'll have some drinks like that Hae made me in Indianapolis, and we'll go to bed and make love. Since I've covered my butt, Alex, what have you done? Are we completely safe here?"

My lord. Wind this girl up and she just goes and goes, he pondered, getting more excited by the moment.

"Yes, but I was kind of hoping we'd spend the night on the boat," he suggested.

"No boat! I want to stay here. Please, Alex. Give me what I want just this one time. Then next time we can do what you want to do. Deal?"

He then saw Amanda stroll into his bedroom, an unmade bed with dirty clothes about. "Don't worry, it will be clean, Amanda."

"I'll straighten it up when I get here, Alex," she openly retorted, studying some of the interesting framed posters and photographs he had displayed on the bedroom walls. One in particular caught her eye, a color photograph of Alex, his brother, and Evelyn all three on a winners podium together. She fantasized quickly about having her own picture on these walls someday, suppressing a downer feeling and disappointment about Alex's ex-lover being so flagrantly on display right in his bedroom.

"You do have a washer and dryer? I know guys can be pigs," she commented humorously.

"Hey, we have our moments. You saw how nice the boat looked?"

"I need to go. Just one last thing. This will be the real deal for me, Alex. You know I'm not my sister. I'm doing this because you're my guy and I love you. Now, can you reciprocate, Alex Moretti?"

"I snuck you out of a hotel for chit-chat over weak drinks at Cleo's. A man can't love a woman more than that," he replied smiling.

"Alex, be serious. Please, you know this is a big deal for me." Amanda said.

"Do you really think I would jeopardize my career to fool with a girl I didn't care about?... Okay, I love you, Amanda Cook. Is that what you want to hear?" Alex blurted out convincingly.

She ran forward and wrapped her arms around his neck, planting her lips squarely on his. "Yes, I like to hear it."

As the two passionately engaged, Alex reached up to grab her left breast when she pulled away. "Not yet. I know you think I'm old-fashioned, but I want this to be very special.... Please, Alex."

Amanda called another Uber driver and Alex stood outside his door, staring down at the front complex parking lot, sharing a wave with her prior to her departure. He walked back inside, his mind contented and full of anticipation for Amanda's next visit.

Dance naked on my coffee table, huh?

He pulled up to the pool clubhouse and waited for a few members and their kids to disperse from the parking lot. He then sent Amanda a text. *"I'm here. Look for the dark grey Chevy Tahoe."*

Amanda quickly opened the passenger door and jumped in, welcoming Alex with a kiss. "Illinois plates?"

"It belongs to one of our crew chiefs," Alex answered as he backed out of the parking space and headed toward the exit. "He hasn't registered this in North Carolina, yet."

"I thought you said nobody else knows about us," she stated, giving him a serious look. "What, have you dropped your guard?"

"Not to worry your pretty little head, Amanda. Dominic and I just traded vehicles for the weekend. He has a supposedly hot date with a girl he met from Gastonia, so I let him use my car. He thinks I'm doing him a huge favor."

"Oh, the sneaky one, you are."

"Hey, it's a win-win, right?"

"I do know you're all about winning, Alex Moretti," Amanda replied.

Alex got juiced when she would sometimes address him using his full name. It seemed to add a sexy personal touch from her, as though only she could.

The two cruised north toward Lake Norman, chatting away casually. He noticed her decline a couple of incoming calls, something he liked as always wishing Evelyn would have done that more.

As they proceeded past the airport, she interrupted. "Sorry, I have to take this." Trisha had agreed not to call unless it was something important. "Hello."

"Amanda, I'm still here at the pool. Your sister just walked in with Aaron. She asked me where you were," Trisha stated.

"What did you tell her?"

"I told her I didn't know and also told her you were staying at our place tonight."

"Oh my god! Trisha, did she see my bike there?" Amanda asked, wishing now she had just walked the half-mile distance to the community clubhouse and not ridden and left her bicycle there.

"I don't know, Amanda. She didn't mention it. If she does see it and ask, I'll just keep telling her I don't know."

Allison will see through that. She knows Trisha knows everything going on with me. "Okay, Trisha. Keep me posted if anything else comes up. Thanks," Amanda told her, closing.

Amanda then stared straight ahead silent for a moment. "Shit!"

"Oh oh, what's going on, Amanda?" Alex asked, knowing it to be totally out of character for her to use such colorful language, as he himself had cleaned up his own tongue because of her.

"I'm sorry. My sister is already back in town. I wasn't expecting her until tomorrow," Amanda stated in a tone that Alex could tell had changed.

"Well, Aaron is with her. So long as he's home, that will keep her busy," *Hopefully,* she thought but didn't say.

"If it's going to be too big a problem we could change plans and I could get you back today. Just have to be careful that Allison would not see us returning," he responded.

"No way. I'm done with her ruining my life! I'll worry about the consequences tomorrow. Let's just not think about it, okay?" Amanda requested, a stress blackout she herself knew was impossible.

They arrived at the condo late afternoon. Amanda was pleasantly surprised that Alex had the place spotless although she was actually somewhat disappointed as she was looking forward to sprucing up his pad on her own for some reason. She did notice something else different, though. That framed picture, the one on the podium with Alex and Evelyn together. It had been replaced with one of just Alex and his brother. *Two brownie points for you, my love!*

Alex was amused and curious about the luggage bag she had brought along, wondering what she needed for just a single night. He then noticed she unpacked several clothing items and began to place them in his chest drawers, rearranging a few of his things in the process as if to signal that she had established a second home. A side of him wished that were true, *but we're years out from that, Amanda.*

"Come on, we're taking an evening cruise," he instructed. He loved running on Lake Norman later in the evening as the surface would smooth out with less smattering of boats running all over the lake. "Here Amanda, put this on,... with your big sunglasses."

He noticed her shutting the guest bedroom door to change into her swimming suit. *She's still shy,* he thought to himself. *I hope she didn't forget about what will happen later,* he mused, trying to remain unconcerned.

"I don't burn, Alex," she stated, standing now before him in a bright orange bikini.

"The hat is for disguise, baby. No need to push it," he claimed while trying not to show that she was literally taking his breath away.

"We could just stay here the whole time, Alex."

"No, we can't act as prisoners, Amanda. We may just run into a few of my neighbors down at the doc. They're used to seeing me with..." Alex didn't finish the sentiment, knowing that Amanda was still uncomfortable regarding Evelyn. *It'll pass with time,* he told himself confidently.

They boarded the boat without incident and left the dock. Alex opened the throttle past 5,000 RPM, as the racing driver would come out in him, even away from the track. He enjoyed standing straight up behind the wheel, face above the windshield to catch the strong wind.

"This is my relaxation, Amanda," he declared loudly as if speaking over the sound of the motors and breeze. "When I'm out on the water, I forget about all of life's challenges."

"Is that what I am, a challenge?" she replied, loudly herself as sure to be heard.

"Of course you are!" he responded. "It's not easy having a girl I can't see very often."

"I know." She clutched his arm tightly and hugged his shoulder. "Absence makes the heart grow fonder, right?"

"Not to worry. We just have to get more done when we are together," he replied in an off-the-cuff effort at humor.

Amanda turned to look away toward another passing boat shaking her head,... and smiled to herself.

They passed by the many shoreline mansions that adorned the lake. It reminded her somewhat of Lake Wylie and their place but to a much higher level. She had been here before on Wally Remington's yacht, but it had been three or four years. They passed by a few crafts that blew horns and waved wildly. A couple even slowed as to signal a desire that Alex stop for socializing. But he just waved and passed on with the throttle pushed down harder.

"How do all these people know you? You haven't been down here that long, and we're going so fast."

"They recognize the boat, my lovely." He didn't add the fact that many assumed he still had Evelyn Stevens with him.

"How far are we going?' Amanda asked, seeing the sun getting lower in the west. "I don't really want to be out here too much after dark."

"I'm just going to pull into my favorite cove just up ahead. I have super running lights for cruising at night and there won't be that many boats out. We'll be fine."

Amanda just squeezed his arm tighter and tightened her lips, watching as the boat slowed to a troll before Alex dropped anchor.

"Come on, let's cool off," Alex said, and before she could even reply he dove over the side.

"How do you know I won't just leave you stranded and steal this thing?" she yelled down at him, laughing.

"Come on. Turn the music up and jump in!"

She dove in after him, agreeing the water was so refreshing. The two engaged in a friendly water fight while treading toward the shore and shallows. They came together, embracing each other while their lips met repeatedly. Amanda had a thought in wishing she could just stay like this forever.

Back on the boat, Alex entered the cabin and fired up the small stove. "Come tell me how you like your burger," he yelled out to her, still up on the aft deck.

"Everything but onions!" She yelled back. "Just bring them out here when you're finished."

A few minutes later, Alex poked his head out from the cabin door. "Come on down, Amanda. I have a surprise for you."

"It's so nice out, Alex. Let's just eat out here, okay?"

Alex looked up at her, confused and disappointed. "Amanda, I have a romantic candlelit table set up for us. Come on, you may never see this side of Alex Moretti again," he joked with a welcoming handout.

Amanda relented and the two occupied the boat's cabin where surely as advertised, Alex had the small table outfitted with a white tablecloth, candles, and crystal wine glasses, all to compliment his serving of cheeseburgers and French fries. "I would have done better than burgers, but I race cars, Amanda. I'm not a gourmet cook."

Despite his attempt at humor, her mood had seemed to darken and he noticed it right away. "Amanda, what's the matter?"

"Nothing, Alex. Why?"

"I don't know you that well, baby. But that girl who was in the water with me a few minutes ago is not the same as the one across from me now. Come on, talk to me."

"I just don't like being out on the water after dark. Could we head back?" Amanda asked, now forcing a smile.

"Amanda, I have tons of lifejackets onboard and have strong running lights. I can assure you"...

"It's not about that. Could we just please?"...

Alex sat in stunned silence as Amanda began to tear up, obviously upset about something. "We can head back now, Amanda. You're afraid. It's about Allison being home, right?"

Amanda started to cry, unable to speak but slowly shaking her head. He moved forward and sat down near her, pulling her head toward his chest as she responded in kind by putting her arms around him and squeezing him as tight as she could, wanting to tell him in unspoken words that her breakdown had nothing to do with him personally.

"I'll be okay. Just give me a minute," she spoke finally as she sat up, grabbing a napkin to wipe the tears from her eyes.

Alex stood and began to clean up in preparation for getting the boat underway. He had his back to her as Amanda began to speak.

"It was real late at night," she began, radiating a tone that something serious was about to be disclosed. "It was at my parents' home Christmas party, one that we have for friends and family every year. I remember it was quite pleasant outside for that time of year. Allison's boyfriend, Aaron, and his family were the guests of honor, so to speak. Of course, everyone knew the Williams quite well as Mr. Williams and my dad play golf together. Aaron's brother, Kyle and I, had gone to his homecoming dance and were kind of dating after that. Aaron and Allison were both home from school for the holidays.

The adults were upstairs and kind of lost track of us. It was only us kids down in the game room bar and we were sneaking into Dad's liquor cabinet. Allison took Aaron by the hand and they went to the downstairs spare bedroom and closed the door. We were starting to get drunk and Trisha took Jeremy, her boyfriend, into the storage closet of all places. It was just me and Kyle and he started to kiss me. I told him we couldn't do anything there. It was an open room with an open stairway, right there. And I knew Trisha and Jeremy would come out of the closet any minute. I was still a virgin,... but I was blitzed and liked Kyle.

He suggested we go out to the boat, which was out back at our dock and up on a lift but not covered up yet. It's a small yacht with a closed cabin like this. Kyle was all over me and I began to feel suddenly light-headed. Trisha told me later he had slipped a date rape pill into my drink. Before I knew it, we were naked and he was trying to push inside me. I wasn't ready and it hurt,... hurt bad. I kept calling for him to stop and he just kept pushing. It wasn't working. I wasn't ready... I started screaming. He put his hand over my mouth so no one would hear me. I managed to bite his hand, and bite it hard..."

Alex sat in a frozen state taking this all in, fairly certain he was the first individual, at least the first male, who had heard any of this previously.

"... I remember looking to my right at the cabin windows, wanting someone, anyone, to see us and come save me, but at the same time felt so ashamed lying there naked and crying and not wanting,... It was so dark outside and the windows had the small curtains, just like those," Amanda stated, nodding toward the small rectangular tinted windows in Alex's boat cabin.

This all explains why she is like she is, the boating after dark, the not wanting to even come into the cabin. My god! Alex was now thinking.

"I'll never forget," Amanda continued. "Just as Kyle stood there before me and was putting his pants and shirt back on, he looked down at me and said, Why doesn't your sister ever have this problem?"

"My lord, Amanda. I don't know what to say.... I had no idea. Don't worry, we don't have to"....

"No, Alex. I want to."

"Amanda, if you're worried about me walking out on you"....

"Alex, I'm not worried. Okay, I admit that when I found out Allison was going to Lemans....It isn't that I didn't trust you, but I know what my sister is capable of. How many times have I heard, even from you, how much me and my sister look so much alike? And I've seen the way you look at me, so"....

"Hold on! Time out, Amanda. Let me tell you, I've always seen you two in a different light. It started that night in Long Beach, the night with that young girl on the beach. You and Allison may both be pretty on the outside, but I see you as beautiful on the inside," he told her as they both were quite emotional.

Amanda's mood had changed course again. She couldn't believe this, a guy who she could share such things with. "You know, Alex, when Allison returned from Europe a few days later, I could tell,...whatever she had up her sleeve had failed. You could have slept with her if you wanted to. We all know it, but you didn't. And I'm sure you knew then that would have ruined us. She would have rubbed it in my face. I love you so much, Alex Moretti," she confessed as tears began to form in her eyes again, but in a good way. "We can make love right here, right now if you want."

She's done it again! Melting me down, he thought to himself. "No, I spent half a day getting my condo all shined up for you. We're pulling up anchor and heading back," he declared with all the resistance he could muster, still thinking how good Amanda looked in her skimpy bright bikini. "Just promise you won't fall to sleep on me."

She woke up the next morning to the smell of fresh coffee. Amanda crawled out of bed, rummaging through the chest drawers for her new XL-sized tee shirt, entering the kitchen and sporting it over little else. "Why didn't you wake me up?"

"I wanted to let you sleep," Alex replied as the two embraced. "I like your shirt," he added, noting she had on a Moretti Motorsport licensed tee shirt, assuming she bought it at the speedway in May. "We had quite a night. How do you feel?"

"I feel wonderful," she responded sincerely, not openly relaying the sentiment to suggest they do it again while she was still there. "How was I?"

You're not supposed to put it like that, Amanda, Alex thought grinning. "Which part, the one about you asking all the questions or the part about you getting out your little notepad and writing everything down?"

She abruptly grabbed the Long Beach bear and threw it at him, both laughing as he jumped back, spilling half his cup of coffee all over himself.

..."So you and Amanda managed to keep seeing each other in secret from summer last year all the way until now?" Matilde asked, wanting to smile but unable under the current circumstances. *I wish he could meet with this girl,* she thought sadly.

"We did have some close calls. And as hard as it was, we would go weeks sometimes without seeing each other, relying on mostly phone calls and text messages. Her father got really crossways with her mother over it. She's a really popular girl at her school but didn't want to date anybody. I suggested she go to their high school homecoming dance, which she did, but her date was upset with her because she kept texting me the whole night, not to mention that this Kyle Williams wanted to take her himself but she wouldn't even look at him," Alex stated, breaking a smile.

The tale paused as Brittany, back on shift, was making her rounds and entered the room.

Chapter 7

Carolina Vengence

S arah and Amanda sat in the second first-class row as the plane passed over northern New Mexico. a direct flight from Las Vegas to Charlotte. Amanda was healing up nicely and should have been feeling better physically, but the deep pain she felt mentally dominated her thoughts, extreme sadness in learning about her pregnancy and an ever-increasing disappointment that she had heard nothing from Alex, not a text message asking how she was, not a call stating he missed her, nothing.

Was what we had for almost a year nothing? It certainly was real for me. How could he just turn away like this, as if flicking off a light switch? She thought over and over while staring out the window at the mountainous terrain below. She had sent him a text message while at the airport but still no response. She had even tried to call while Sarah was in the airport restroom but Alex had changed his voicemail to that generic greeting with no name, and had not replied to any of her messages.

Sarah knew her daughter was not much for conversation and kept it temporarily at a minimum, simply placing her left hand on Amanda's knee as a sign of soft love and support. She knew Byron was on the warpath and had already been in touch with half the lawyers in Rock Hill, Charlotte, and Las Vegas it seemed, hellbent on putting Moretti Motorsport out of business, not to mention demanding that young Alex Moretti be locked up. She also knew by pure intuition that Amanda still had feelings for the young man and was crushed by what had happened.

She had received a call from Byron right after Alex's grandmother had left the room, chewing her out for even allowing the elder Moretti woman a minute's audience. She had known that Allison must have immediately notified him and out of character, Sarah sternly chastised her oldest daughter over it.

"We already have too many secrets in this family, Mother," Allison had recoiled, one not feeling the least bit guilty knowing that she harbored many if not most of them herself.

Byron had instructed Sarah that under no circumstances should Amanda have any communication with anyone named Moretti again, ever! Always a person who attempted to see the good side of everyone, Sarah knew it was an accident. She didn't know if Alex was driving too fast, or just didn't see the bus ahead, or what could have happened. *But he didn't test with any alcohol, and it's not like he purposely attempted to harm Amanda,* she thought.

Following the visit from Mrs. Moretti and some reflection afterward, Sarah had a mind to contact the young man herself. After all, Byron didn't say anything about anyone else communicating, she pondered slyly. And she wanted to know for her own gratification why he had not reached out to Amanda.

Another hour passed and Sarah wanted to handle some things between her and Amanda before they landed and were met by Byron at the airport. "Honey, talk to me, please.... You were in love with him, weren't you?"

Amanda kept looking away and out the window for a few moments before turning to face her mother. "I still am, Mom," she replied emotionally and began to weep.

"How long have you been seeing him, Amanda?" Sarah asked, all in a tone to signify understanding.

Amanda didn't reply, fearing the wrath of her father with what was already known.

"Please, Amanda. I promise I won't tell your father. It makes little difference now anyway," Sarah continued, genuinely curious.

"It's been almost a year. We just kind of connected while we were at Long Beach last year," Amanda stated, recalling the pleasant memories of their late-night stroll together on the beach.

"I wish you would have come to me, Amanda. I would have gotten you some protection," Sarah stated solemnly.

"I couldn't do that, Mom. Dad was trying to push Kyle on me, and with Alex being four years older? Come on." Amanda replied, not disclosing the fact that Trisha had helped her get on the pill and that something must have just gone amiss.

Sarah felt a shade of anger, always thinking both her girls would share everything with her. *Be real, Sarah Cook. You were a sixteen-year-old once,* she scolded herself. *And you surely didn't tell your mother everything.*

"Do you have Alex Moretti's phone number?" Sarah asked, pulling out her own iPhone and ready to input it.

Again, Amanda hesitated.

"Honey, I'm just going to try and get hold of him," she stated. "I want to know why he hasn't contacted you, myself."

The 757 landed at Douglas International in Charlotte just after 8:00 PM. Sarah couldn't hold back, and as soon as the aircraft pulled in toward the concourse and the fasten seatbelts lights went out, she retrieved her phone and dialed. Not wanting to leave a voicemail, she hung up and declared, "I just got a general voicemail, Amanda. I assume he'll see the missed call and call me back,"... *Maybe.*

Byron greeted his wife and daughter at the gangway exit, arranging to have a chauffeur with a wheelchair to escort the recovering girl down to baggage claim. Amanda started to put up some resistance, pushing back against it and claiming she was okay to move freely on her own now, but her father was adamant. He did not admit to the fact that Edmunds had been insistent about having her in that wheelchair and had reached out to the local media outlets, all of which sent their camera crews and reporters to the airport in order to film and get comments from the injured teenage girl, one whose saga was now well known worldwide.

Sarah was not happy with all of them flocking in front of her daughter while she was still in such a state of mental stress. "Byron, can't you just make them leave? Amanda's not ready for this right now."

"Sorry, honey. She's a public figure now."

"This is just all too much," Sarah responded.

The ride home seemed long as Amanda stared blankly out the window. It was just ten days ago that she had accompanied her parents to Las Vegas for the bank convention and banquet. As Byron and Sarah were quite busy all day on Saturday, her mother had given her the okay to just hang out in the indoor pool and game room all afternoon while she arranged for Alex to pick her up and the two spent the afternoon together. All things were great until the accident had now changed their lives, seemingly forever.

It was nearly 10:00 PM when they arrived home, and Sarah helped her up to her bedroom as Amanda indicated a desire to turn in. In reality, she just really wanted no part of too many more questions from her father, a man who seemed all too anxious to now seek retribution upon the entire Moretti family.

Byron and Sarah both retired to the master bedroom shortly thereafter as Sarah had the same sentiment.

"So did she say anything else important after I left Las Vegas?" Byron asked anxiously.

"Like what, Byron? We already know she was seeing Alex Moretti and the two got together and had sex. We know now she was pregnant and we now know they were in a serious car accident and Amanda spent over a week in a hospital. What else do you expect her to say?" Sarah replied, obviously disapproving of her husband's overbearing and vengeful attitude.

"Ohhh lots, Sarah. You do realize that Unibank's sponsorship of Moretti Motorsport led to this immoral affair with our own young daughter," he responded. "This cannot stand."

"Need I remind you how young I was and how old you were when Allison was conceived?" Sarah challenged.

"We were in love, Sarah. And if you recall, without hesitation I did the right thing," Byron replied, recalling a generation earlier the two having a very strenuous and emotional conversation with Sarah's parents.

"And you know what's in this Alex and Amanda's hearts?" Sarah responded quickly.

"Moretti barely knew the girl! Taking advantage of my beautiful young daughter, and that damned Andy. I know he knew about it! It's sinful!"

"You're not going to shoot them, Byron, so what are you going to do? Don't you think they feel terrible about what happened themselves?"

"Well, they most certainly should! James Edmonds will be here tomorrow morning to talk with us. We're going to sue that outfit for all their worth, and I want criminal charges filed against this Alex Moretti. He has scarred Amanda for life!" The man was fired up.

"Oh my god, Byron. Go to sleep."

The family attorney pulled into their drive at 9:30 AM. Byron and Sarah were already engaged in an ugly dispute over it.

"She's not ready for any of this, Byron!" Sarah kept saying over and over until nearly screaming.

"Edmunds says we have to get on top of this now, while it's still hot in the headlines," Byron yelled back. "We're all going to have to face the music on this sooner or later."

The family attorney walked in and was greeted as Sarah offered him some coffee, although her facial tone toward him was not all that welcoming.

He sat around the kitchen table with Byron and Sarah, her insisting they have a brief discussion before Amanda joined them. For her part, Amanda would have preferred to just go back to school, although also anxious about how her classmates and the teaching staff would behave towards her.

Byron had pushed the longtime lawyer to pressure the local Solicitor General's District Attorney to press charges of statutory rape, but Edmunds required more information, which was the purpose of this visit.

The family's attorney had requested they conduct the interview here at the residence, keeping Amanda as comfortable as possible.

Sarah left to collect Amanda, already extremely uncomfortable if not angry regarding the nature of what was coming. Amanda entered the room a few moments later along with her mother and sat with her in the front room on the leather sofa opposite the men.

"Amanda, Mr. Edmunds has some questions to ask about what happened to you," Byron led. His attempt to warm a frigid atmosphere having little effect.

The girl just stared, having no reply.

Following a questioning glance to all present, the counselor began. "Amanda, allow me to confirm the information I have, if that's okay?"

She shrugged her shoulders.

"On Saturday, March 13th of this year were you a passenger in a car accident in Las Vegas, Nevada?"

"Yes."

"And the vehicle was driven by a Mr. Alessandro Moretti, correct?" Edmunds continued.

"Yes."

"To your recollection, your next conscious thought was waking up in a hospital room five days afterward?"

"Yes." Amanda's short answers indicated her attitude toward this exchange.

"Amanda, I know this next series of questions is going to be uncomfortable. I'll try to keep it brief," Edmunds explained. "When you were admitted to the emergency room and subsequent IC Unit, you aborted a new pregnancy. Was Alessandro the father?"

"Of course," Amanda answered, not happy with the question.

"Do you recall the exact date when that conception took place?" Edmunds asked. while Sarah began to give both him and her husband a very stern look.

"I think it was January 20th," Amanda answered affirmatively.

"The day after your birthday!?" Byron interrupted as Edmunds gave him a cautioning glance.

"Yes, the day after my birthday."

Edmunds shuffled a bit, as though pondering. "Amanda, are you quite certain about that?"

"If that was the day after my birthday?" she replied as if confused.

"No, I'm sorry. Are you positive that was the exact date your pregnancy was conceived?"

Amanda paused, looking uncomfortable as her parents looked on anxiously. "The doctor said it was six to seven weeks, so that would have to be it."

Edmunds added some notes. "Amanda, was that the first time you and Mr. Moretti had intimate relations?"

She and Sarah shared a look as though Amanda was searching for guidance on what to say. Sarah was tight-lipped, looking her daughter in the eyes and simply nodding.

"No. It was not."

Byron's face became flushed red, barely capable of controlling his anger.

"Did this always happen in one location?" Edmunds plowed forward.

"Why?" Amanda asked, her first immediate response.

"Is this really necessary, James?" Sarah blurted out, now getting upset herself.

"Sarah! Let the girl"... Byron yelled before Edmunds cut him off, holding up his left hand toward Byron as a signal.

"I'm sorry, but this may be important."

Amanda changed her tone, giving both her parents stern stares. "I don't recall."

"Amanda! You have to answer the man's questions. He has to do his job," Byron stated, unable to remain silent.

Amanda began to tear up. "I'm not feeling well. May I be excused?"

Sarah escorted Amanda back up to her room, where she closed the door and the two sat together briefly on her bed. She could tell Amanda didn't wish to talk about any more of it, thus Sarah chose not to press it.

Downstairs, Edmunds attempted to calm Byron down, as the attorney could see the man was on edge.

"So where do we stand, James?" Byron asked, still agitated.

"Well, here is the way it is. If it's proven in a court of law that your daughter and Moretti had sex in the State of South Carolina prior to her sixteenth birthday, the Solicitor General can bring charges of statutory rape against him. That probably means Amanda will have to testify to that."

Byron sat shaking his head. Of his two daughters, he had always thought Allison would cause this type of grief and not Amanda, the girl who was the more polite and quiet of the two.

"If we place Amanda under oath, would she testify?"

"We'll work on that," Byron stated.

"Have the two communicated in any way since the accident?"

"No, not that I'm aware of, James."

"Well, let's hope that doesn't happen. She's obviously very emotional right now and her testimony would be too unpredictable. Her stating she doesn't recall something like that may cast some doubt in front of a jury, and perhaps reasonable doubt. If she can detach herself emotionally from this young man, she would more likely be a better witness. Are you sure you wish to put her through this, Byron?"

"No one's above the law, right James? After I signed to bankroll that whole Moretti operation up there for four years, those sons of bitches think they can get away with this? Huh, not a chance!"

Edmunds nodded while smiling at his long-time client and friend. He would have to push this to the Solicitor General, knowing they truly didn't care for cases like this, one in which the rape victim appeared all too willing. "Let me know how you would like me to proceed, Byron. I suspect you'll know when the time is right. I'll adjourn from your hospitality for now."

Byron showed their lawyer to the door and turned to face Sarah, obviously one who was not happy with the whole affair.

"We have to get Amanda to testify that Moretti had sex with her here prior to turning sixteen," he told her.

"How do you know if they did?" Sarah asked as if playing devil's advocate.

"Oh hell, Sarah! You heard her. I don't recall? Give me a break," he stated, rejecting the notion out of hand.

"Watch your mouth, Byron Cook," Sarah told him sternly. "You're not out on the golf course with your cronies. This is a Christian home here!"

The Unibank building in downtown Charlotte had two entire floors occupied by Hampton, Mason, and Morgan, the resident law firm for Unibank Corporation. They were preparing to file a two hundred eighty million dollar lawsuit with the U.S. District Court Clerk in Charlotte against Moretti Motorsport for damages, claiming breach of contract pertaining to language in the original contract stating that neither party shall engage in any activity, unethical or illegal, that may be deemed as detrimental to the reputation of the other party.

The fact that Alex Moretti had been terminated from his father's race team shortly following the incident in question had complicated the lawsuit, placing the outcome somewhat in doubt. James Edmunds, the Cook family's personal attorney, entered at just past 10:00 AM where the meeting was arranged in the law firm's main conference room. In attendance were Byron Cook, Reggie Morgan, who was the grandson of one of the firm's original founders, one of the firm's paralegals, and Edmunds, who had traveled into the city from Rock Hill.

"I want Moretti behind bars!" Cook stated emphatically. "She's barely sixteen years old and he nearly got her killed, not to mention that miscarriage or abortion,... whatever they would call that."

"It's complicated, Byron. The age of consent in every state in question *is* sixteen," Edmunds responded.

"We know the two had sex before that. You guys just have to find the proof," Byron demanded.

"He's clear in North Carolina. Even if someone would testify they had sex prior to her birthday, they have what's referred to as the Romeo and Juliet Law, which renders a defendant immune from prosecution if they are no more than four years older than the victim. Moretti is four years older than Amanda, less two weeks.

In Nevada, their cutoff is eighteen for the defendant. But with no sworn testimony, the evidence to indict is based on the expert opinion of the hospital medical staff making a determination that Amanda's pregnancy occurred prior to January 19th. That case is now in the hands of the Clark County District Attorney out there. There is some positive news out there, however. The coroner has issued a death certificate on behalf of the aborted fetus. That could very well warrant an indictment for manslaughter. But as they have hardened criminal cases on the docket and Moretti is not considered a flight risk or a danger to the public, his case may not see action in the next six months, and that's being optimistic."

"You gentlemen are giving me nothing but bad news. What about our own esteemed Solicitor General?" Byron asked, desperately wanting to hear something positive happening. "I guess you're going to tell me we have Romeo and Juliet down there, too."

"Actually, no. As we discussed before, South Carolina law is pretty straightforward. I've spoken to John about this," Edmunds began, referring to John McCall, the Assistant to the Circuit Solicitor General who just happened to be his son-in-law. "The entire case hinges on whether they can prove that Moretti had sex with Amanda in South Carolina and that it happened before her sixteenth birthday. The forensic evidence from the hospital proves Moretti was the father, but the date of conception is only an approximation that it occurred around that date, give or take a day either way. That's a tall order unless Amanda is willing to testify to the fact herself or get some strong corroborating testimony from a third party. Without Amanda's testimony or other irrefutable evidence, Ferrell wouldn't prosecute. These cases have become extremely rare in recent years."

"I don't give a damn how rare they are," Cook responded quickly. "We're talking about my teenage daughter here! I know that Ferrell has his sights on State Solicitor General and then the governor's mansion. You let the right people know that we're a strong lobby." By *we* Byron referred to Bud Williams, the state's largest car dealer and a known force in state politics.

Edmunds knew it was a consensus in the legal community that third-degree statutory rape in the case of a fifteen-year-old willing victim, given the state of modern-day society at large, was a law that was viewed as long past its time. Should this law be enforced to the letter, half the teenage males in South Carolina would be behind bars. He also knew that he couldn't tell Byron Cook that, not in the current climate anyway.

Morgan informed Cook in no uncertain terms that if the District Attorney in Las Vegas or the local Circuit Solicitor General in Rock Hill, South Carolina, failed to prosecute and convict Moretti on something substantial, the entire Unibank corporate lawsuit against Moretti Motorsport would likely fail. As such, they may be wise to just get some sort of settlement out of court, and if that included a termination of Unibank's sponsorship, a payment to settle would likely be awarded to Moretti, and not Unibank.

"Out of the question!" Byron stated emphatically. "I will not have my daughter's reputation sullied by this cocky little son-of-a-bitch? I don't care what it takes, I don't care how many judges we need to get this in front of, I want this Moretti outfit to pay for this, and I want our Unibank name and logo gone off those damned cars!"

"We're still waiting on all the documentation from your health insurance provider to move forward on the personal liability suit," Edmunds added. "You may wish to make a call or two personally to push them on that."

The attorney knew a large insurance company would tend to have their own legal counsel to represent them, basically taking over the entire personal injury case, and seeing dollar signs evaporating right before his eyes, this was the last thing James Edmunds wanted. He was counting on Cook to go to bat on his behalf, using the entire basis of the Unibank health insurance account as leverage. The local attorney did, however, feel certain that he needed to have Byron see more action from him on the local front as motivation to make such a call.

"Whatever it takes, gentleman," Cook answered seriously. "Right now I have a sixteen-year-old daughter at home in an animated state of depression while that Moretti outfit is still racing cars all over the world on my dime. You're all my lawyers. You work it out on who represents who and who does what. I want results!" The bank executive slammed his fist down hard on the table, an act unforeseen and out of character for a man seldom witnessed as showing emotion.

"Now, I have a board meeting to prepare for."

A Mecklenburg County Deputy Sheriff hand-delivered the envelope, which Andy opened in the privacy of his executive office. The room was well adorned with polished marble tile, a plush checkered flag throw rug, his large oak desk, comfortable furniture, and walls adorned with many of his awards and photographs. One wall had a large cabinet that included the many trophies from his long career, both as a driver and team owner. Being a man of great pride, his throat became dry as he reviewed the first page of the document, realizing it had the potential to ruin him financially, costing him everything he had ever worked for.

Named as defendants in the suit were he himself, Alex, and Moretti Motorsport, Incorporated. He was receiving tacit support from most of the other team owners, for whatever that was worth, but he wasn't naïve and knew when his sponsors started to bail and talk to his competitors, they would be all ears. He also knew some of his very finest technicians and engineers worried about their futures and would be soon talking to other teams, if only initially in private.

It was a conversation Andy just dreaded to have. As angry as he was with Alex he was family, his own flesh and blood. He had given him everything afforded to a kid growing up, a good home, education, job training (if driving race cars were labeled as such), and finally a job, something he now had to take away. The misty-eyed father had suggested he create a quiet background position on the team, somewhere doing something, but the attorneys all advised against it and his still proud son wouldn't accept something of that nature anyway. He was still a racer.

Andy wandered around the facility aimlessly to the different departments. He had a measured confidence in all of his various team managers, but always had a habit of interfacing directly with the many engineers and technicians. After all, he had come up through the ranks in the cockpit of a race car.

On this day Andy Moretti was a very bothered man and all of his employees felt it, each nervous that their own jobs were now in jeopardy, and indeed uncertain whether the entire team would survive. Andy himself even wondered what his future occupation would look like. He had certainly blown opportunities for being a broadcast commentator. Many retired drivers had set up their own podcast shows with varied success. He doubted the guest speaker market would warm up to him, either.

No, he thought. *I just have to ride this out and survive,... Survive and win,... Win to survive.* Both words were always related in the sport of motor racing, but now on a very direct level.

The attorneys were due to arrive in one hour, a meeting Andy almost dreaded. In all of his years of racing, both as a driver and now owner, he had never been confronted with anything like this. It had been weeks and he had seldom spoken with anyone from Unibank other than Adam Herrera, a man who now seemed fearful of his own future. It was perhaps the most uncomfortable state of relations between a team and its key sponsor in the history of the sport. The team hospitality functions at the various races were almost dead, except for a few small associate sponsors and Herrera himself, who was the program administrator for Unibank and would show his presence so long as any semblance of a contract still existed.

Even worse than the sparse number of guests were the actual conversations that dominated the atmosphere within his teams. They were not talking about practice speeds, qualifying, or driver standings. No, they were all talking about Unibank. And even though most of his team members and guests were sympathetic, Andy was just plain sick of hearing about it.

He had spoken to a few local Unibank mid-management executives at some venues who had quietly stated their own desire to attend their own local races but were discouraged from doing so. The attorneys, however, had insisted that Andy and Bob Ward not change anything regarding their side of the contract. The nature of Unibank's agreement called for their liveries on the cars to be nearly exclusive, with the exception of the BP co-sponsorship of the Formula One program. For now, the colorful brand logos were still intact and the press loved it, always having an ear for a good ongoing scandal. They were to keep their communication with Unibank open, even if it was now limited to Herrera only, and make certain all of the normal invites to all events were sent, and to honor any and all requests for appearances, though none had been forthcoming on that front since Vegas.

As Alex was technically injured in an automobile accident, the team did have a common option to replace him with a driver approved by Unibank, which previous to the Vegas incident would have happily been Adam Herrera, but not now. He would send all documents related to their contract with Moretti straight up to the head man himself, who would immediately send copies to their lawyers.

He decided to call a full company meeting on Wednesday morning, where most of the teams would be in-house. The rest of Moretti Motorsport personnel, most of whom were in England, would join the meeting online. He and Alex discussed the upcoming meeting and whether the son should be there but Alex declined, knowing he was the main culprit of the crisis and not wanting to be any more of a distraction. The meeting would begin promptly at 9:00 AM Eastern Time, which was 2:00 PM in the UK. The full domestic contingent all gathered in a large temporarily cleared garage section, hastily arranged with a lectern as Andy stepped up to the microphone.

"Thank you all for gathering here this morning and this afternoon at our facility in the UK. You are all aware of the tragic accident in Las Vegas involving my son, Alex, and the teenage daughter of Byron Cook. We thank God both have seemed to fully recover from their injuries," Andy stated, choosing not to mention anything about the Cook girl's lost pregnancy.

"It is unfortunate the incident occurred, as Alex was on his way to the Bellagio Hotel for the Unibank annual awards banquet guest speaking engagement, which has added fuel to the fire.

On Monday, I received notice of a lawsuit from Unibank Corporation. I will not disclose the amount of the suit, only to say they are suing the team, as well as myself and Alex personally, to get out of their sponsorship agreement as well as substantial liability damages. I have a very reputable law firm representing us and nothing will be decided by tomorrow or next week. In fact, it is our attorneys' view that nothing substantial will change this season, and we may even win in court. Of course, I will not assume for a minute that we will come through this totally unscathed.

It is with sadness and a heavy heart that my son, Alex, will be leaving Moretti Motorsport indefinitely, partly at the insistence of our attorneys, and he may also face criminal charges related to the incident and involvement with Amanda Cook. Hopefully, this litigation will run its course favorably and Alex will someday be back.

As such, these next couple of years may be some tough sledding for Moretti Motorsport. We are already talking to a few new and some previous sponsors. But as you all may imagine, we're not exactly the flavor of the month right now. This Unibank suit is a major black eye that has and will give pause to potential sponsors.... People, there is one cure and one cure only for this disease and that may be summed up in one word – winning.

This team has to win at all levels. You've all given me 100% week in and week out and now I'll need 110%. Win people, and win often. Let's win races, and when we don't win, score points and win championships.

A couple of driver changes are in store. Former IMSA sports car driver, Jon David Hill, will take over on road and street courses in the Indycars and I am talking with Tony Kanaan to pilot the number "5" car on ovals for us. Marcus Newsome's "6" car will inherit Alex's former crew as his crew will move to the "5" car, as half of you have worked well with Kanaan in the past. So as of now, our number one from last year's points standings is the "7", Evelyn Stevens."

Andy chose not to mention that he had reached out to a couple of other veteran big-name drivers but The Unibank blowup had them all spooked.

"Thank you again for all of your support."

Alex knew this was coming. He never intended for this to happen, and never wanted to hurt the team, but it was what it was. He had already made some opening gestures about other opportunities to drive in the series but had received little response. It seemed he was now toxic in the sport he loved. He couldn't even get a low-budget sponsor to back him at the moment, something the small teams required at a minimum.

He reached out to Tony Stewart about participating in his upstart and ever more popular SRX Series, but even the racing legend, who fancied himself as sort of racing maverick, pushed back. "I'd welcome you in, Alex," Stewart had told him, a man sympathetic to his plight. "But you need to get past your legal problems first, as the rest of my series' drivers are concerned."

He even explored starting up his own team, but financiers wouldn't talk to him. He was popular in St. Louis with the Bommarito Group and thought perhaps they may entertain a partnership in an Indycar team, but Frank didn't want his negative publicity, either. The banking world was all too aware of the fallout with Unibank, not to mention the rumor mill in the press that he may still face criminal prosecution.

Having been one of the most popular personalities in the Indycar paddock, going back to when he was a small boy, even the various teams' personnel wanted no part of him, at least publicly, not so much out of disdain but leery of all the press reporters badgering everyone and asking questions about him.

The exception seemed to be Evelyn Stevens, who still carried a soft spot for Alex, despite everything that had happened over the past year. But once a few photos of the two taken together made their way into the media, courtesy of her foolhardy but trusted agent, Newberry, the Moretti team lawyers pitched a fit and demanded that Stevens stay clear of her former teammate and boyfriend, at least until the lawsuit with Unibank was settled.

While he had enjoyed his first year in the Carolinas, he now was in dread of going anywhere, catching public stares and angry comments that ranged from disparagement to outright hate. His father had agreed to keep his NSX with the popular license plate MORETTI-5 in the shop temporarily while Alex applied for and waited for a replacement plate, driving a nondescript seven-year-old Chevy Impala to run around in. Without his robust salary and bonus money coming in, his Acura sports car and beloved cabin cruiser boat would have to go up on the auction block before long anyway, it seemed.

He lay in bed for hours on end staring at the ceiling, his thoughts oscillating between his shattered career and the girl behind it all. *I wonder what she is thinking right now,* Alex often pondered. He couldn't stop torturing himself mentally for what had gone down. Like many of life's temptations, he had always feared the cost of his relationship with her becoming exposed. It would surely damage the team, probably hurt his own career, and likely get Amanda in hot water at home, at least in the short term. But Alex hadn't fathomed anything like this. In spite of it all, his agony was divided between not being behind the wheel of a race car and his now being prohibited from even sending Amanda a simple text message.

After spending a few more weeks sulking in his Lake Norman condo, constantly half-crocked with too much weed and liquor, a close friend and retired driver, Tim Malloy, called and invited Alex to come down to Sarasota for a few days. The weather in early April was beautiful on the Gulf Coast and he advised Alex that a change of scenery might do him some good. Alex had known Malloy for years as he had driven for various teams, never one of championship caliber, but very good with sponsors, and was well-liked and respected up and down the paddock. Although the two were friends, Tim was closer to his dad's age and actually knew Andy much better, thus Alex suspected his host had something in mind other than just lying around on the beach and reminiscing about old times.

Alex arrived in the early evening the following day, choosing to drive and having left for the six-hundred-plus mile trip earlier that morning. Tim invited him in and he was introduced to the recent new girlfriend, Sherri, a gal slightly older than Tim, but nice looking, *inside and out* Tim claimed, and had money from a recently deceased husband who died of lung cancer, as well as having her pension as a retired paralegal.

The three chose to head out to a popular beachside bar and grill for some dinner. For his part, Alex was now well-recognized and the looks from other patrons were still not all that complimentary. Keeping to themselves in a corner booth, the three ordered some oysters and drinks with some small talk. Sherri was curious like everyone else about the accident and his personal relationship with the young Amanda Cook, if he didn't mind sharing.

"There was just something about Amanda," Alex claimed. "She looked just like her sister, both beautiful girls. In fact, Allison is less than a few months younger than I am. Now everyone, including my own grandmother, wondered why I didn't just take up with her."

"Well?" Sherri boldly asked. "Why didn't you,... just take up with the older of the two sisters?"

"Well," Alex grinned, "There was just,"...

"Something about Amanda," Sherri and Tim sang in tune. "Are you two still talking?"

"No, we're not. I sent her a couple of texts while she was still in the hospital. How are you feeling, that kind of stuff. She never replied."

"Maybe she was sedated and couldn't use her phone?... Or perhaps her phone was taken," Sherri added.

"Looks like her parents aren't exactly adding you to their Christmas list, buddy," Tim joked.

"Well, you know I'm facing a possible criminal indictment over this, not to mention Dad and the team getting sued for all he's worth. All of the attorneys insist that I have no communication with her... None."

"You miss this girl, don't you?" Sherri asked sincerely.

"I feel terrible remorse for what happened. But why do you think that?"

"It's something a woman can tell," she responded while nudging Tim.

Alex pondered a bit, searching for the right words. "Yes, I miss her."

"Not to change the subject, but what are your plans? Employment wise, I mean," Tim asked, as he *did* genuinely want to change the subject.

"Try to get a ride somewhere, I guess. This season's looking bleak, though," Alex stated, an expression of resignation reflecting his concern. "I want to drive. I'm a racer, Tim."

"I know you are, purebred. I also know you've never had an agent, either."

"I've driven for my dad my whole life, Tim. I never needed one."

"You're not driving for him now, though," Tim replied. "You still have one of the most famous names in motor racing. There are bound to be opportunities out there, so long as you're open-minded."

"Open-minded?" Alex asked.

Tim looked at Sherri as if her cue.

"I worked for a lawyer here in Sarasota, Donald Petree. His main business was that of being a booking agent for well-known sports figures, past and present," she explained prior to Tim cutting back in.

"I want to be *your* booking agent, Alex. I know the sport of motor racing and many of the players at all levels. Sherri has all the legal expertise. What do you say?"

Alex leaned back in his seat, surprised. In the back of his mind, he had pondered on the drive down that perhaps Malloy wanted to discuss starting up their own team, a venture that he had mentioned in passing before. But that had been years earlier and gathering from looking around, he knew Tim wouldn't commit to all the pressure, travel, and sheer effort involved.

"I'm not opposed," he replied, knowing he had received no other offers since his termination from the team. "Honestly though, Tim, I've already contacted your old pal, Dennis Reinbold, Juncos Hollinger, and Dale Coyne, as well as every race team in NASCAR, and IMSA. I've had nothing but smiles, thanks, but no thanks. Do you really think your smiling face could do any better?"

"I'll have to think out of the box, and you'll have to agree to be rather flexible," Tim stated, not adding that he had also reached out to Dennis and Dale, both of whom he had excellent relationships with.

Alex collected his thoughts and stared back and forth at the two of them sitting across from him. "Out of the box?"

"Like you said, you're a racer, Alex. Would you consider other disciplines? Say, Trans Am or World of Outlaws, for example?"

Alex leaned back. "Outlaws? Those sprint cars that run on dirt tracks?"

"That's just one consideration. We could also explore off-road, or that newly formed Can-Am series I read about," Tim added, gauging his reaction.

"Those sprint cars; I know a lot of drivers over here who cut their teeth on those," Alex reflected. "Tony Stewart, Kyle Larson, and Jeff Gordon come to mind. I always thought they looked like a lot of fun. Some of those races like Knoxville or Tulsa pay really well to win, don't they? You could get me booked in one of those?"

"They certainly do, Alex. But you would need to get a bit of experience on some smaller, less-known tracks first," Tim answered. "I know you're a Moretti, but you can't expect to race with guys like Brad Sweet right off. Them boys aren't going to give you anything. You'll be that famous *outlaw* yourself that every gunslinger will be out to beat. They race to win, too. We'll work on building your new brand. You'll be the guy everyone; drivers, teams, and fans alike, will love to hate. It'll probably start a bit slow and you'll have to be willing to travel zig-zag from one series and venue to another, at least for a while."

Alex took a drink of the fruity cocktail, mentally attempting to sell himself on what the two sitting across the booth from him were pitching, not having given much thought to his reputation which had always been stellar in the past. "I never thought I would have to *build my brand*, so to speak."

"You're a Moretti, a brand that has always been great over the years. You will have to repair that," Sherri stated. "Part of that is where I come in. Your social media needs some work. It had been self-perpetuating in the past, in a good way. It's busy now with a lot of vitriol. In the short term, we'll use that to our advantage, and over time you'll build it back," she added, not mentioning the challenge of overcoming the whole criminal investigation thing.

"What happens when a sheriff shows up at one of these dirt tracks to strap the handcuffs on my ass?" Alex asked dubiously, as much to himself as to Tim and Sherri.

"Definitely wouldn't help our cause, Alex. Would you prefer to lay around and pout, waiting for that knock on the door?" Tim asked, with a rare serious expression on his face.

Chapter 8

Freelance Racer

Alex flew into St. Louis, where he rented a car and headed west on I-70 toward the Highway 54 exit, the route heading southwest through the Missouri capital and onward to the Lake of the Ozarks, a place that reminded him somewhat of Lake Norman, with many lakeside mansions, waterfront resorts, and busy with boats of all sizes and shapes.

The deal Tim had cut included lodging at Margaritaville, a very popular resort formerly known as Tan-Tar-A, Thursday through Sunday, and a fair travel and meal allowance., plus five grand in appearance money split between the track and car owner.

An hour south, the speedway seemed to be out in the middle of nowhere, but the owner had promoted the event heavily with Alex Moretti as the headliner, an outsider and newly branded motor racing's outlaw against the local circuit regulars. Alex's car owner, Troy Cornwell, was a used car dealer from Tulsa, Oklahoma, a man himself accustomed to stepping out of the box when it came to marketing. He had taken Malloy's offer of half the take from the race purse, to add to the till for Moretti showing up.

All of the parties agreed to allow Cornwell to have access to the facility on Thursday and give Alex ample track time to get a feel for things. The owner charged a flat ten bucks a head admission to witness the session, pleasantly surprised when over four hundred showed up and paid it. The team's full-time driver, Randy Tarwater, was along to add advice to Moretti as needed, an arrangement none to the tall raw-boney Sooner's liking. For his part, Alex was not made aware he was taking the ride away from an active series participant and struggled to convince himself that he would not have taken the one-off gig had he known such.

"Hell, Troy, he's a full half second off my best times," Tarwater snarled, not at all happy with playing pit help while this big-name interloper had his ride. "This is all bullshit."

"I don't want to hear it, Randy," Cornwell retorted. "You do want to run next season, right?"

"Of course, I want to run next year. But I'll lose the points for this race. I don't see how that helps us."

"This is only temporary. If Moretti gets us some headlines, that means sponsors. I can't afford another season on my own. Now you need to suck it up and show support."

The front-engine sprint cars were quite intriguing to Alex. The chassis themselves were much shorter than what he was accustomed to and each had a huge wing placed right over the cockpit with settings that could be adjusted by the driver. The engines themselves were all of the small-block Chevy variety, at first glance no different than what powered the old Formula 5000 cars his grandfather raced periodically in the seventies, and had nearly as much horsepower as an Indycar or Formula One car. These drove more like *drift* cars and Alex quickly learned the whole art of these sprint cars was getting into the corners late and how fast one accelerated out of them. He also surmised that the best drivers were good at manipulating the top wing as the tires wore, something he was having to learn on the fly.

He completed thirty more laps around the short track circuit, gradually getting faster by the minute and wearing a broad smile when he pulled back in. "This is such a hoot! How did I do?" He asked Cornwell while Tarwater looked on with a cynical scowl.

"You're near Younger's track record," Cornwell replied happily while showing his guest driver the stopwatch reading on his smartphone.

"Who is Younger?" Alex asked, curious as to who this local hot shoe was.

"Chasity Younger, a girl we just can't ever seem to beat," Cornwell replied.

"A girl, huh?" Alex quizzed mostly to himself, suddenly thinking about someone else.

"Don't get to having too much fun," Tarwater snarled. "It'll be more intense out there tomorrow night, with twenty other cars fighting for that same piece of dirt."

The session wrapped up as Alex prepared to leave the track and head back northwest to his lakeside hotel. He had just headed toward his car when Tarwater approached, the effects of a few beers evident in his manner.

"Moretti, I want you to know that I don't like your kind coming in here, all high and mighty with your big-time family name, thinking you'll just shit all over us rednecks. I hope you flip over and break your damned neck. What you did to that girl was criminal, you bastard!"

Not wanting a brawl with this guy nearly twice his size, Alex replied, "See you tomorrow, Randy. Have a nice evening."

He then walked away as the intoxicated Tarwater came up from behind, grabbed him by the arm, and whirled him around. The angry sprint driver took a hard swing at Alex's head, which he alertly ducked and avoided, following with a very hard kick to Tarwater's groin, putting him on the ground, balled up in a sideways crouch and agonizing in pain. Alex reached down to help him up but Tarwater twisted out of his grasp as if refusing any help. Satisfied the little brawl was over, Alex decided to head out before more fireworks got started.

During the drive up the state highway back to his hotel, Alex struggled with his emotions, as if all of the awful things that had happened to him over the previous few months were suddenly hitting home. Now here he was, taking a one-race dirt track drive away from this Randy Tarwater, a young man who probably saw this local weekend sprint car race as his pathway to the Daytona 500.

He was using his name to scratch and claw his way from one race to another, working for a pittance of what he was used to getting, all to get behind any steering wheel on any kind of race car he could find... After all, he was a racer.

Following a shower and change of clothing, donning a hat and dark sunglasses, he made his way outside and over to the Margaritaville tiki bar for a beer, noticing all of the suntanned, bikini-clad females when it hit him. It wasn't the change of race cars or race tracks that bothered him. There was something else missing.

He looked at his phone parked on the bar, thinking about calling her,... or maybe texting her. All the lawyers had stressed vehemently that he should under no circumstances contact Amanda Cook, or anyone in the Cook family for that matter. *What was it about her?* Alex pondered.

He had ample opportunities from the opposite sex. Despite their celebrity issues, Alex felt confident he could resurrect the relationship with Evelyn Stevens, undeniably one of the most attractive women on earth, and most assuredly the hottest female in motorsports. Of course, she somehow triggered thoughts about the Cook sisters, who were quite beautiful in their own right. But that wasn't all of it, he thought. *There was just something about Amanda.*

He picked up his phone, just in his own mind wanting to go back and review all of their back-and-forth messages. He had sent her three messages while still in that Vegas hospital bed and not one reply. The last one was after he had gotten the great news of her awakening. He knew he had to move on and seek female companionship somewhere else. His brain told him that was what he should do, but that organ beating in his chest held him back.

Alex quickly sucked down three draught beers, clenching his fist. He so wanted to call her or to send her a text. But his limited but remaining logical sense stopped him. All the phone records from all parties could be subpoenaed, the attorneys had stressed. The term *witness tampering* had been thrown out at him. There had to be a way, somehow, for him to communicate with Amanda without harming himself legally. *What must be going through that girl's mind?* he asked himself. *She must have been under tremendous pressure not to contact him, too, if for different reasons. Who knows who would see her texts? Or a reply from him?*

Alex arrived at the track early on Saturday, planning to meet with Cornwell and the track officials regarding the pre-race warmup. The session would start with a half hour of "hot laps" prior to the start of race heats. A record crowd assembled in the stands to add to the normal attendees as many had made their first visit to the rural speedway or even a first sprint car race of any kind, to catch a glimpse of the now infamous celebrity driver, Alex Moretti, a young man now best-known for the Las Vegas auto accident.

This young female driver, Chasity Younger, had done yeoman's work promoting herself as it seemed half the fans had on her tee shirts and hats, not to mention the many *Chasinator* banners displayed all around the track. Many of the regulars begrudgingly paid the extra ten bucks per ticket to cheer her and their other local heroes on and to show this big-name showboat how it was done on the dirt.

Cornwell was already there along with Tarwater, a young man who had revenge on his mind but planned to wait until the racing was over for them, which he assumed would be early, believing Moretti wouldn't last ten laps on a crowded track.

Alex approached both straight up. Gentlemen, I want to talk to you. I find myself in unchartered waters here, running one race and taking a ride away from another driver in the middle of a points championship."

"We've already talked about this, Alex. The team, if you can call it that, needs sponsors. We need notoriety. That's where you come in, even if it is for just one race. Randy knows he'll be looking elsewhere next year without more backing," Cornwell stated as Tarwater held his tongue.

"Hear me out, fellas," Alex broke back in. "I want Randy to run the first fifteen minutes of the warmup. He knows how to set up these cars better than I do. If his best four-lap average is faster than mine, the ride is his. If you want, I'll visit the announcer booth upfront and broadcast the arrangement to the whole crowd."

"That's not our deal, Moretti! The crowd wants to see you race. Honestly, they want to see their favorite drivers, particularly Chasity Younger, run and beat you," Cornwell stated strongly.

"I know that. But this will add a bit of extra drama to the festivities, don't you think?" Alex added quickly.

"Come on, boss!" Tarwater loudly stated. "Ain't that what these celebrity drivers are supposed to do, beat us country boys at our own game? Have him prove it."

Cornwell could tell Tarwater was chomping at the bit, not only to exact revenge for their altercation last evening but to redeem his tattered image, that of a driver who couldn't carry the team on his own merit. The car dealer also had an ongoing curiosity about how good his cars were, and in a related respect, how good Tarwater was as a driver. "All right. But if you lose this hot lap timing contest, I get my part of the appearance money back, and there will be no purse share, Moretti."

"Agreed," Alex replied, surprising both Cornwell and Tarwater with his quick response.

Bud Reinhart, the track owner, agreed with the last-minute arrangement under the same terms as Cornwell. If Moretti lost out against Tarwater in this impromptu time trial competition, he would get all of his part of the appearance money back, also. Unlike Cornwell, Reinhart was tickled with the new deal. He had already collected his record ticket sales, the biggest crowd in the local speedway's history, an extra thirty-five grand made on the added ticket prices alone. He knew he would get a bit of pushback if Moretti didn't run in the feature race, but he advertised the now-infamous driver would appear, and nothing more.

Alex ignored the mostly snide remarks as the infield became crowded with the other owners, drivers, and mechanics. Insults like showboat, wop, and even felon were bandied around, although mostly uttered in low tones as word had gotten around on what he had done when provoked by Tarwater. Adding to his consternation was the reaction he would get from Tim and Sherri should he lose, as he had basically bet the take from his entire contract on this stunt. *Oh well,* he thought off-handedly. *I've always lived my life on the edge. That's how I got myself into this predicament and that's how I'll get out of it.*

True to form, Alex entertained the crowd and indeed created quite a buzz by getting on the track PA system and announcing this special competition within the team.

"Good evening everyone and welcome to this special event. My name, for all of you who may not have heard, is Alex Moretti. Most who have heard my name associate it with either speed or criminality and perhaps both. I hope to prove the speed part tonight and so far as the rest, I look forward to clearing my name in court if necessary. Having said that, I was paid to show up here as a stand-in for one of the track's regulars, Randy Tarwater. As Randy is competing for the series championship, I have offered a challenge that he out qualify me, and if so, the ride this evening is his and I will be his biggest fan. During the thirty-minute hot lap session, Randy will run the first fifteen minutes and I will run the last, both in the same car, the Cornwell Motors Special. Thank you all for supporting this great facility and the great sport of sprint car racing."

Alex re-entered the infield with the buzzing crowd in the background and approached Cornwell as Tarwater was already strapping himself in. Before pulling out onto the track, the driver, still feeling the effects in his crotch, looked up at Moretti, giving him a slow but distinct nod.

Alex began to realize the high risk of it all. This hot lap session on the three-eighth mile oval track would have upwards of twenty cars out there at the same time. He and Tarwater would have to complete their individual four lap times in a crowd, which told him a good bit of luck was involved and Randy was hell-bent for leather to prove that Alex Moretti was all sizzle and no steak. For his part, Alex simply saw himself as a racer, not interested in showing up anybody, but in effect showing up everybody by winning.

Tarwater's best four-lap average was 48.216 seconds, or just over twelve seconds per lap, indeed better than he had ever run at the track, and so far, a full two-tenths per lap faster than Chasity Younger had run before in hot laps, the local favorite who led the points championship.

Alex began slow, spending the first few laps getting comfortable and feeling out the setup changes made since his previous stint in the car. With five minutes to go, he prepared to give it his best shot but was slowed by the car in front of him, who by chance just happened to be Younger. After six laps, Alex saw that she was running full speed on the straights but slowed down immensely in the corners, hugging the inside and getting around just fast enough to stop Alex from getting by. It appeared to him as an obvious ploy to prevent him from putting together a series of four fast laps. Alex attempted to slow down and put some distance between her and himself but the series master responded in kind by slowing in front of Alex herself. If he was to have any chance at all, he had to get by Younger. With less than two minutes to go, Alex trailed the speedy female driver, who was coming up on a slower car. Timing his move perfectly, Alex waited until both cars ahead of him entered the first turn just tight on the bottom and then scrambled past them on the outside, a bold move by any measure. Breaking free and having a small bit of clear track ahead of him, Alex picked up the pace rapidly, mastering the drifting of his car through the turns. He finished the final few laps with Younger right on his tail as the crowd roared.

Cornwell held his stopwatch while Tarwater looked on with waning confidence. At the end of the session, Moretti had beaten Tarwater by two one hundredth of a second, coming in at 48.011. Cornwell was shocked and pleased that both of his drivers had broken the track record.

"I wish I had a second car for you now, Randy. Helluva job out there!" Cornwell declared.

"I can't believe he beat me!" Tarwater stated dejectedly. "I have to admit, I'm impressed. That was one helluva move he made on Chasity," Tarwater stated, mentally tucking it away for future reference.

Alex climbed up out of the car, smiling, and took off around the infield area in search of Chasity Younger, stunned when he came upon her pit crew, which amounted to her father, Ray, and mother, Michelle.

Seeing him approach, Ray moved out in front of Chasity and put up his hand. "Not here, young man. Your reputation precedes you."

"Ray, come on," Michelle interrupted. "What's he going to do, molest her out here in front of all of us?"

Chasity walked around the side of her car and approached, staring at the well-known stranger neutrally. "You're one hell of a race driver."

"So are you. If it hadn't been for that second car, I'd have never passed you," Alex stated.

"You weren't giving me nothin' either," Chasity replied.

Alex was quite amazed at what he saw. While none of the teams and drivers had all of the transportation rigs, equipment, or staff that he was accustomed to, nearly all had much more than the Youngers, and yet this girl, who happened to be the same age as Amanda, was definitely the one that every other driver strived to beat.

"I'll be gunning for ya," She told him smiling as he walked away.

The feature race would be forty laps with eighteen cars competing and thus the three-eighth mile track would be crowded. Alex followed Chasity into the first corner and the two soon became the class of the field, trading first and second places every other lap. The fans were on their feet and mostly cheering for the Younger girl as the pair started to pass the slower cars. On the white flag lap, second-place Chasity attempted an outside pass on Alex when a lapped car spun and T-boned her hard, throwing her into the back of Alex's car and causing both to flip over twice as Alex was also slammed by oncoming traffic.

A track red flag appeared while Alex was immediately able to extract himself from his car, who then began running headlong up the banking toward Chasity, whose car had stopped upside down with fuel spilling out right from under her. With some quick communication confirming that she was still conscious, he and an on-sight track official grunted and shoved Chasity's car over and upright as moments later she herself appeared from out of the cockpit, standing and waving to the arousing cheers of the crowd.

Both Ray and Michelle Younger came running out onto the track, each giving their daughter a haughty embrace. Ray then turned and looked toward Alex, giving him a single approving nod.

"She would have gotten you on that last lap, Moretti," he stated half-jokingly as he placed his hand on the young man's shoulder.

"Very distinct possibility," Alex replied smiling.

"How about a beer?" Ray offered, temporarily putting out of his mind the damage to the *Chasinator*, the family nickname for their now battle-worn and damaged sprint car.

Following the heat, a multitude of fans came pouring onto the track toward the infield. Reinhart himself held back his track staff in an unprecedented move seeing a Brazilian-like soccer crowd, a headline photo opportunity that was just too priceless to pass up. Alex and Chasity were accommodating and allowed the crowd to take photos and selfies of the two dirt track gladiators up until way past midnight.

Cornwell approached Alex with Tarwater in tow, waiting for a break in the action to shake his hand and hand him a roll of cash. "Let's plan the next race, Alex!" Corwell shouted over the noise, as the car dealer saw dividends of bringing in Moretti paying off beyond his wildest dreams. We could organize a full tour, you against Randy here and the Chasinator. What do you say?"

"What, will I drive for somebody else?"

"No, I'll enter two cars, both identical," Cornwell claimed assuredly.

"You'll have to go through my agent, sir," Alex replied, so glad to be receiving some positive accolades from race fans again.

"I called him and it just went to voicemail."

"Well, you know it is past 1:00 AM in Florida right now. I'm sure Tim is fast asleep," Alex responded, smiling for a few more photographs.

The crowd eventually dispersed and the six of them, the Youngers, Cornwell, Tarwater, and Alex gathered in folding lawn chairs and shared stories together over a few beers and grilled burgers. Alex got a new appreciation of the opportunities he had been given since childhood by virtue of his famous family name. Here before him was another racing family, be it on another level altogether, and realized that racing meant just as much to this fine family as it did to the Morettis. He also appreciated what a racer Chasity was and how far she could go given the right opportunity.

As he got more and more comfortable around the Youngers, the subject of Alex's legal problems became open for discussion, and they became quite fascinated with the whole saga, believing by this time that Alex Moretti may not be the felonious pedophile that certain media had made him out to be, especially since Chasity had a boyfriend five years older, herself.

"When are you coming to race us here again?" Chasity asked while her folks had started to pack up.

"Not sure. I have an agent now," Alex replied.

"We'll get him back," Cornwell broke in. "Count on it. Come on, Randy. We have a long drive ahead of us."

Tarwater had been quiet, taking in the whole conversation, happily assured by the boss regarding the two cars. He approached Alex again before leaving with Troy. "I apologize about the other night, and I thank you for you did for us," Randy stated humbling himself, and then held out a hand.

"Tell us," Michelle asked. "How do you like this? It's a long shot from the Indy 500."

Alex declared smiling. "I haven't had this much fun since I raced go-karts as a kid."

"Well, next time I'll have a new car... I'll really be ready to smoke your butt then," Chasity stated.

"Hey, girl. I won't be a rookie next time."

The bunch shared a final laugh before departing. Alex was anxious to get out of the hot driver's suit. *There's no trackside motor home waiting for me with a hot shower this time,* he thought with a final wave, feeling grungy but good to be racing again.

Chasity was intrigued by Moretti's story, thinking about the part of his being ordered not to have any communication with Amanda. She could also tell her one-night competitor still had deep feelings for the girl. As she and her parents traveled the nearly three hours back toward home, Chasity's curiosity got the best of her and she pulled up the Facebook app on her phone, finally finding Amanda Cook after some cumbersome searching. *You should have a name like mine, Amanda. I had no idea there were so many Amanda Cooks in this world.*

She hit the *Friend Request* button and then her mind shifted to other things,... like her new race car.

The dirt track rivalry between Alex Moretti and Chasity Younger went viral as Tim and Sherri were now turning down races as they couldn't accommodate all the requests. As a benefit for their success, the two signed on as Chasity's agent, also, the price kept going up, and in short order Younger's car, the Chasinator II, was a brand new chassis with a 5.7L high-powered engine. Her popularity nationwide exploded and by season's end, Ray and Michele were making enough money on just selling tee shirts, hats, and banners to pay nearly all their expenses.

For his part, Alex wanted no part in owning a car and all the related equipment involved as he had no shortage of car owners standing in line to hire him to show up and race Younger, along with all the other local fans paying double and triple the normal admission to pull for their favorites up against this new duo of *Moretti and Younger,* or as Chasity liked to say, *Younger and Moretti.*

Both now had a GoFundMe page, Moretti's to help pay his legal bills, and for Chasity simply more sponsorship dollars.

In a four-race series in Minnesota, Chasity won three out of four feature events with Alex taking the fourth and second in all of the other three. Using the old Formula One scoring system where points were allotted on a 10-6-4-3-2-1 basis, Younger took the series 30 points to 28 for Alex.

Several other contests were run through October at local dirt tracks that normally drew a Friday or Saturday night crowd of four to five hundred were now packing the house while doubling the price per ticket. The two ran nip and tuck with Moretti winning one event and Younger the next.

By year's end, the top Outlaw Sprint Car events were demanding the sprint car stars participate in two highest paying outlaw sprint car events, in Knoxville and in Tulsa.

While Alex flipped his car in Knoxville, Chasity finished a very respectable fourth, while in Tulsa Alex finished second while Chasity came home in the top ten. The stage was set for the Youngers to run the following season on a much larger stage. On his end, however, Alex's pending legal problems predicated that he could only commit short-term for a few weeks in advance.

Sherri had taken over management of Alex's Facebook page which was quite busy with both fan and hate mail. Her frequent ad posts stating he was available for driving on a free-lance basis received ample attention. While most of the posts were not worth responding to, one message stuck out.

Team Dymoquest, a privateer outfit that had finished in the top six in the World Rally Championship the previous year, needed a driver. Owner Franz Scholl lost his man, Max Francour, who had signed a lucrative deal with the factory Subaru team, a driver seen in many circles as the sole reason for Scholl's team success, a tag on his reputation that Franz was determined to shed. Having worked years earlier for the Williams Formula One team,

Franz knew Andy Moretti quite well and having now learned that his son may be available, put in a call for his recommendation. Andy agreed that his youngest boy's driving style, wild and wooly as it was, may be well suited for that type of racing.

The team had performed poorly in the first two championship rounds, including a last place finish in the snow-covered roads of Sweden, making Dymo the only team to finish in the bottom six in every round thus far. Scholl fired his replacement driver, Pierre Marquez, a journeyman racer who paid his way onboard on a one-off deal. The Mexico round of the World Rally Championship was the only visit to North America and Franz was confident going in that Alex Moretti would give his struggling team a lift.

Alex had never driven a rally car, much less competed in this type of discipline, one that differed quite radically from any other kind of racing he had been involved with. He also knew that coming into a totally different racing arena and expecting to run roughshod over its own established stars was a tall order, regardless of how famous your name was, as he had found out repeatedly on the small dirt tracks. There had been drivers who had stepped into alternative arenas successfully in years past, legends like Andretti, Foyt, and more recently Tony Stewart, but it was extremely challenging and just not done in today's world, largely due to restrictive contracts.

The race venues scheduled a couple of days of practice where all the rally teams could show up and test their cars on the circuit. Alex's first day out in the rally car was contentious as he had sideswiped a couple of trees and ran through a roadside wooden fence, not to mention plowing through a few of the covered hay bails placed at strategic points around the circuit. But unlike his days in Indycars, where a brush with the wall could be tens of thousands in damage and potentially dangerous, these types of occurrences seemed routine here and even laughed off.

The reasons were obvious. The World Rally Championship was not run on purposely constructed racing circuits or even professionally prepared street circuits. These were common and mostly single-lane roads through towns and rural areas with no runoff areas and few safety barriers at all.

In some cases, the car would almost squeeze between two trees having a narrow path between them. The cars would speed through small villages and right past small homes and businesses. Spectators would stand and watch right by the track, reminiscent of the old Grand Prix circuits from the 50s and 60s which resulted in the deaths of so many great drivers and more than a few of the spectators themselves.

In spite of these revelations, Alex found this style of racing quite exhilarating and was having fun driving while enjoying yet another challenge. An additional observation was the relatively relaxed rivalries between drivers and teams. Like all forms of motor racing, WRC events had an overall winner, a driver finishing second, third, and so forth. But drivers never ran with or near each other on the various rally circuits at the same time, as scoring was based on a cumulative timing of segments with the overall winner determined by the lowest combined times in the various stages, like so many rounds of golf. Alex began to see the competition as more comparable to qualifying in other forms of racing, with the benefit that a driver could make up for a poor performance or even shunt in one or two stages by excelling in others. Since the drivers were never actually competing side by side, the rivalries tended to be friendlier as the cars never hit each other or drivers never cut each other off on the track.

As each car had a driver and co-driver, the whole series reminded Alex of the Mexican Baja 1000 race, the famous off-road event held annually, and one of the few North American racing events the Morettis had never been involved with. Franz's co-driver was his son-in-law, a young Dane named Luka Jensen, and he and Alex quickly developed a strong level of comradery.

The team was upbeat having finished a surprising third in Guanajuato, ahead of some of the better-funded factory teams and an astounding accomplishment for a *rookie* driver to the series. Franz was particularly all smiles when his new pilot finished two places ahead of Francour, raising quite an eyebrow among the series' elite teams.

As Franz didn't have the budget of the factory teams, such as Ford and Hyundai, the team tended to travel light and stayed in inexpensive hotels. The Bolfan Vinski Vrh was a quaint bed and breakfast and winery just a few kilometers outside Zagreb, Croatia's capital and host city for the rally series next round. The driver and co-driver gathered on Wednesday evening for a couple of beers in the lobby bar late after hitting a couple of loud clubs in the city.

"Did you ever find out what kind of money Francour got, Luka?" Alex asked.

"No, they haven't disclosed that. But Max told me last year he would shoot for 1.2 million Euros plus incentives. That's about what the top drivers are getting now."

"Not bad. Is it true that half the drivers here basically pay their way in?"

"Oh, at least," Luka replied. "The big money here has gone since the tobacco and beer companies were forced out. Of course, most of the big sponsors in racing are with Formula One. McRae made it big here, but most of his money was coming from his racing sim game."

"It's the same in America. My dad made more thirty years ago than my brother and I made last year combined, even discounting inflation."

"Antonio seems to be doing okay for himself now, yeah?" Luka added. *I'm sure you are tired of seeing his face on all of the European racing media by now,* he thought.

"He's doing all right," Alex replied, noting that he had become more of a celebrity than Tony,... and for all the wrong reasons. "He's still getting used to Formula One."

"Oh, he's a Moretti, Alex. Piece of cake, right?"

"He's been used to starting with the exact same equipment as everyone else," Alex replied. "I know he keeps bugging Dad about when our car will be on par with the Red Bulls, Mercedes, and Ferraris there."

"Well, your brother will be in good company. At least a dozen other F1 drivers are whining about that," Luka reflected.

As the season progressed, Alex was maintaining himself financially as his earnings in WRC, mixed in with some sprint car stints in the States on off-weekends, were paying the bills, the final tally for his attorney notwithstanding. However, his personal life remained somewhat of a wreck as he dealt with an ongoing feeling of guilt regarding Amanda that would not go away. He had mixed feelings of fear and hope that she had somehow got past the accident and perhaps had gotten serious with another guy. He hated the fact they hadn't had so much as a goodbye or even a good-luck conversation since that horrid incident.

The two sat at the small metal table under the old-style rollout awning shading the front of the quaint cafe below their rental studio. Jolanda had seen a change in Alex over the past race weekend and she wanted to press him on it. The mood was very somber and the two had difficulty carrying on a normal conversation, as a divide had developed between them that was gradually getting worse.

They had met in Croatia and she had quickly been attracted to him. They seemed to be right together, at least at first. She was a party girl from a wealthy family, brought up in a broken home since she was a toddler. Living with her mother, Jolanda was basically raised by her nanny and seldom ever saw her father, but the man was quite well-to-do and had supported the family financially since the divorce. She had no interest in getting serious and having a family, something she and Alex had seemed to share common ground on from day one.

For his part, Alex had taken up with the Swede in a vain attempt to move on with his life, replacing the memory of Amanda Cook. It wasn't working but he didn't have the heart to tell Jolanda he wanted to end things, just yet. After all, they had mutually agreed, at least in spirit, that they would just be friends who happened to share a bedroom during the World Rally Series season, a series of races that occurred all over the world.

The events were generally three to five weeks apart and the two would tend to go their own respective ways in between. She never spoke of it, but Alex pretty much assumed that she would sleep around during their absence, and found himself perfectly content with that while never seeing the need to question her on it. This seemed in her view to be a perfect way to conduct personal business, at least initially, but his lack of curiosity toward the subject started to bother her as she had gotten more and more emotionally attached to him.

This had been the third time in the past week, a recurring dream that haunted him like a demon. The scenes would vary in places and times but all had the same theme. One nightmare would repeat over and over, him at the wheel of his boat cruising at full speed, always at a place on a lake he didn't recognize, and always a severe storm overhead. He kept hearing her voice, pleading from inside the cabin for him to come while he couldn't slow down. Somehow he just couldn't stop and open the cabin door while he kept hearing Amanda's pleading voice.

Another bad dream had Amanda standing at his front door, soaking wet from the falling rain and standing before him in a hospital gown with blood running down her left leg. He kept telling her they couldn't see or even talk to each other while they stood facing on opposite sides of the threshold as if it were a forbidden barrier. Sometimes his grandmother would be there, standing with Amanda and crying herself. It had always ended the same way. Amanda would start to cry even more and he himself would break down and weep, with Jolanda finally shaking him to awake.

Each time she would attempt to have him talk about it, Alex would turn away, not willing to open up to her. She had been hinting the past couple of races about her desire to accompany him back to America, a place she had little experience in other than a couple of junkets taken, one to New York City and one to Miami, subtle suggestions he wasn't biting on.

Jolanda decided the time was right to test their relationship by suggesting she may take a break from the rallies, maybe travel to Bali or something.

Alex stared out across the boulevard toward the morning beach, thinking it was time. "I think that's a good idea, Jo. I need some time myself to sort out some things anyway."

The two both shared grim smiles, realizing this was the end for them. He had never seen her as a permanent fixture in his life, just someone to help fill in a gap, and on her side, she had always presented herself to him as a carefree spirit, wanting to travel the world and not getting too serious with anyone. She now looked away and out toward the beach herself, wanting to disguise the fact that her eyes were welling up, coming to grip with knowing that her racer was now leaving her forever.

Tony's wife, Crissy, reserved a nice vacation rental earlier in the week and prior to the Monaco Grand Prix for them to spend a few days in Genoa together, inviting Alex, also. She had never visited the Moretti's original family hometown and thought the two brothers needed the time together, which had rarely happened since the accident. She knew her husband felt close to and bad for his younger brother, but also carried a hidden anger toward him because of the potential damage his actions had done to the family name and future financial well-being.

The four, which included Tony, Crissy, Alex, and the baby, enjoyed a late lunch together at a sidewalk cafe right across the main thoroughfare from the harbor. While the Moretti brothers failed to notice themselves, Crissy was struck by the city as being extremely local and not as touristy as nearby Nice and Monte Carlo, observing the prices for hotels, restaurants, and taxis being much more affordable, items that Alex seemed to appreciate more lately.

Crissy had hoped the brothers' time together would boost their overall morale, herself included. She missed the friendly atmosphere of the Indycar paddock, where the drivers' *others* were welcome almost as part of the team, while everything seemed so much more assigned and formal in Formula One. She also missed the sister-like friendship she had with Evelyn

Stevens, which had naturally diminished since she and Alex had split up and Crissy's own man had been *promoted* to the Formula One Grand Prix circuit.

Typical of a Moretti discussion, talk of the team and Tony's probable last-row start in the upcoming week's Indy 500 dominated their conversation, as well as both brothers' other state of affairs, all related directly or indirectly to their racing pursuits.

"Do you think I would like it, Tony?" Alex asked regarding Formula One.

"Depends on the car,... and the team, Alex," Tony replied. "When we entered a race in an Indycar, We both raced to win and always had a certain confidence that we could win as we were all driving the same equipment. Winning consistently *across the pond,* as they refer to the States, truly gets down to how good the team operates, how well they set up your car, how good the driver is in sync with his crew chief, and how well the driver can go fast consistency while managing the tires and fuel between stops. You do have all those things here, except for the equipment part.

In Formula One, the teams are given a basic set of parameters they must stay within, but every team can produce their own individual chassis and engines. So while these cars appear very much identical, there are small differences, most one cannot see. And because the technology is so precise, that change that is a half second per lap may be the difference between pole and eighth or ninth starting position. When a driver starts in row five, he knows he's not going to win unless something catastrophic occurs, a rain downpour, something like that. It's more a competition between engineers than drivers and your main competition as a driver is between you and your own teammate as much as the rest of the field. I'm racing in the mid-pack right now, Alex, and if I start ninth and finish fifth, it's akin to almost winning, especially if my teammate finishes eighth or ninth. This all goes in reverse, of course, and if your teammate is consistently better than you race after race, your career in Formula One will be quite short-lived. It's really about improving and eventually getting hired by Red Bull or Mercedes or Ferrari, or eventually hoping next year is the year when your own engineers come up with something that bridges that gap," Tony explained.

"I don't know how I would take that, not believing I could win from the start, brother."

"I think you would tend to drive the car faster than it's capable which will usually put you in a wall or sand trap, at which point your day is done," Tony added. "So, how will I avoid that first turn mess next week?"

"You'll be better adapted to starting back there," Alex stated, thinking about his own experience the previous year. "You have to be a bit patient, avoid trouble, and not try to win the thing on the first lap."

Tony listened while knowing this was the exact words their father had told Alex last year. Whether Alex's aggressiveness on the opening lap had made a difference regarding the disastrous first turn accident, no one would ever know. What Tony did know was how much his brother's not being there was eating at him.

"It's been over a year since Las Vegas, Alex. Is there any girl out there lurking in the shadows that we don't know about?" Crissy asked, sort of joking but genuinely curious. She had known Alex for more than three years now and had rarely seen him without a female around somewhere, other than most of last season, when she never took seriously his newly found love of fishing.

"I had a brief encounter with a Swedish girl. But now, not so much," he replied.

"And still no conversations with Amanda?"

"Crissy! He knows he's forbidden to have any contact with Amanda Cook again, at least until all these lawsuits are over with," Tony scolded.

The next WRS event was in Portugal, by coincidence the same weekend as the Formula One Grand Prix of Monaco, as rarely was the marquee Grand Prix run on a weekend subsequent to the race at Indy. It was a busy and volatile time for the Morettis as this was also the weekend of qualifying for the 500. Andy was a nervous wreck as his race team was in turmoil over the pending lawsuits, all while attempting to get the three team cars in the race, while also qualifying a fourth car for Tony to drive as a *guest* F1 pilot.

Despite the Unibank fiasco and the stress of the owner's youngest son facing a possible prison term, Moretti Motorsport salvaged some success during a trying year. Evelyn was having her best season ever, giving a strong showing at the big one in Indy by finishing third in the 500 and winning three other series' races, two seconds, and two other top-five finishes, ending up an impressive second in the Indycar championship to Andretti Autosport star, Colton Herta.

The two drivers replacing Andy's sons on the Indycar team were not as competitive, however, and he and Ward discussed replacing at least one. The press and social media were adding fuel to the fire by now claiming that Jon David Hill may keep his ride over Marcus Newsome due to his personal relationship with Evelyn Stevens and his related position of Louis Newberry being both Stevens' and Hill's agent. This was despite Newsome having displayed consistently more prowess on the track than Hill, although neither's performance would seem to warrant consideration for new contracts next season.

Their first full season in Formula One was not an unbridled success, at least by Tony's standards nor as few new teams ever were, but the rookie Moretti had gradually moved up one or two places per race and was gathering notice of future stardom by consistently running in the top seven by season's end.

The NASCAR team had a mixed season with driver Alan Allison winning twice but failing to make the final points chase. Their second driver, Michael Lariat, was more consistent in his finishes but could never crack the top five in any event. Talks had occurred in Huntersville with Newsome about a potential switch to NASCAR, but the former Formula E champion, now in his mid-thirties, balked at the idea of spending a year or two in the NASCAR Infiniti series, which was basically the sanctioning body's ladder series.

Andy had held out hope that perhaps Alex's legal issues would be over by season end and the door possibly open for his return, but Herrera was adamant that Byron Cook wouldn't hear of it and so long as he was Unibank's CEO, Alex Moretti could have no connection to their sponsorship, an idea echoed by Andy's own corporate attorneys, who were slow-walking the lawsuits with Unibank.

Chapter 9

All in the Numbers

Sarah held her arm around Amanda's shoulder as the two exited the building and made their way to the year-old Cadillac Escalade, Sarah's personal vehicle. Lorraine Angelino was one of the most reputable therapists in the Carolinas and had been counseling Amanda weekly for two months.

While the recovering teen tended to support the hour-long visits, she herself thought they were a colossal waste of money, but worked to cooperate as the process seemed to calm her mother, despite her father's recent mumbling about the amount they were spending and the perceived slow progress she was making.

Amanda had been semi-grounded from spending time with Trisha, as it was a given the neighboring friend had known all along about the illicit romance between her and this reckless young race driver. The two would speak frequently by phone, however, and with the summer months and school being out, the girls would spend ample time at the club pool, even though Amanda was still forbidden from leaving with Trisha by car.

Sarah pulled up to the clubhouse entrance and she and Amanda embraced prior to her mother departing. Byron and Sarah had endured some severe disputes over Amanda ever since the day James Edmonds was there with his lawyerly questions. The mother was nearing forty and her warm and attractive smile had begun to show the telling lines of stress.

Sarah answered the call she had so looked forward to, their weekly conversation following Amanda's visits. She and the doctor had jointly chosen to speak by phone hours afterward as not to give the appearance of discussing Amanda in her presence.

"She is slowly beginning to open up, Sarah. Understand, she has been through a lot," Angelino began.

"Do you see any light at the end of the tunnel for her, Doctor?"

"I do, Sarah. But I sense Amanda has this deep fear of something, and that has me worried."

"Well, that crash,...it had to be terrifying," Sarah replied.

"It's something else, Sarah. For whatever reason, Amanda insists she has no recollection of the accident. Only waking up in the hospital. I know this may sound awkward, but I think it may do Amanda some good to get away for a bit. Away from her domestic surroundings."

"We are all going to Hilton Head for the July Fourth weekend," Sarah offered.

"I'm sorry to say, Sarah, but I think perhaps a vacation from immediate family is in order," Doctor Angelino stated, knowing her patient's mother would be hesitant.

"Oh Doctor, my husband wouldn't hear of it right now. I mean, with everything that's going on and what has happened. Byron hardly wants to lose sight of her."

"Sarah, I must tell you that her father is the main reason she needs this break."

Amanda came home from an afternoon at the pool, entering through the garage door and giving Sarah a brief hug prior to heading up to shower. Donning her silk bathrobe and as she strolled down the hall to her bedroom, Amanda could hear her mother and father arguing below.

"Out of the question!" Byron could be heard yelling. "Our daughter is sick, Sarah! And you want to send her away for a while? How could you even consider such a thing!?"

"Stop yelling. The therapist believes a change of scenery may do Amanda some good."

"Sarah doesn't need to be away from her family right now, Sarah. I think we've had about enough of that quack woman, if that's all she can come up with," Byron declared, by now worked up into a near rage.

"Our daughter needs a break, Byron.... She needs a break from you!"

Amanda was saddened yet again. For what seemed like the millionth time, she would open her phone's texting app, just to see if just possibly he had replied. She would send out a text every few days, just a simple, *"Hi"*,... and nothing. *I can't believe he could just move on like that,* she would think, while always tearing up.

Twice she had actually called and left voicemails. He had changed his message to that generic, "You have reached 847-567-8956. Please leave a message."

She found herself constantly checking his webpage and social media pages, just her own way of keeping a connection. But she noticed the traffic had gone depressingly dark with hate messages. She supposed he got tired of seeing it all and just turned away from it.

Trisha had come home from her job at the mall and called. "Hey, Amanda. How did your visit with the shrink go?"

"As usual, Trish. She thinks I'm crazy and have shut out the whole world," Amanda replied as the two shared some slight laughter. "She actually told me she thinks I should go away for a while, like two or three weeks."

"Probably so, but where would you go, Amanda?"

"Good question. Doctor Angelino even suggested that I go to Charleston and visit my sister, of all things."

"Yikes, Amanda! What did you say to that?" Trisha asked, curious as always.

"Not much. I haven't discussed Allison with her at all. She would just tell Mom and get her upset over it."

"I don't guess you've heard from him?" Trisha asked, knowing what was really bothering her longtime friend.

"No," Amanda replied sadly. "Nothing."

"I think it's a good idea," Sarah exclaimed. "I always wished we would have done something like that ourselves."

"I don't like it," Byron responded. "That Shyree girl is the one who helped Amanda get in trouble in the first place."

Trisha's family took a trip to Gatlinburg every summer, where they rented a log cabin near the Smoky Mountains National Park. Her mother had reached out to Sarah and offered the invite for Amanda, all after being prompted by Trisha, who had long tired of the family vacations without her friends anyway, but went along so as not to hurt her parents' feelings.

"Byron, do you think we can just lock Amanda up here for the rest of her life? She needs a break, Byron! She needs to stop hearing you pressure her about giving that deposition!" Sarah stated in a raised voice.

He was stunned that his wife of twenty-two years was lecturing him in such a way. "You know this will never end for her, Sarah. It'll never end until he goes to trial and is then locked up!"

Sarah looked at him, shaking her head. "It will never end for her, Byron?... Or you?"

Amanda and Trisha arrived at the party early in the evening, crowded to the point it seemed their entire senior class was on hand. The music was loud, the weed abundant, and two sixteen-gallon kegs of beer set up in the pool bar with the tap running almost continuously in a first come first serve mode.

Stephanie Fulton, the party hostess, had the home to herself as her parents had taken a weekend cruise to the Caribbean and as teenage kids will do, turned their rural York County home into a place to party. Fulton and Amanda were part of the high school cheerleader squad, though just casual friends.

Amanda became extremely uncomfortable when Trisha's boyfriend arrived with Kyle Williams, who seemed to keep his distance from her, that is until the various party effects began to hit him.

"I'm glad you seem to have recovered, Amanda, from that accident, I mean," Kyle stated. The handsome young athlete, now a red-shirt freshman at Clemson, was the envy of every female in the place, except Amanda it seemed.

"Why did you have to bring him, Jeremy?" Trisha asked, her tone reflecting her displeasure with her longtime boyfriend. "You know Kyle just uses you to try and get to Amanda. You should choose your friends better."

"Hey! Don't you think it's time for her to bury the hatchet? Think how much better off Amanda would be if she had been with Kyle that whole time, instead of being a playmate to that asshole race driver."

Trisha slapped him,... hard. "Stick it, Jeremy," she added, and then walked away with him standing there holding his right cheek, looking stunned and foolish before the entire crowd.

Half of the teens ended up in the pool later as Trisha and her boyfriend avoided one another the rest of the night. Williams snuck up behind Amanda while in the corner of the pool, tapping her on the shoulder. She turned an about-face when he attempted to force a kiss.

"Get away from me, you creep!" Amanda screamed, suddenly quieting the entire party, and encouraging Stephanie to mute the sound system.

"What's wrong with you, Amanda!?" Williams yelled back. "Moretti just used you for his whore, nearly killed you, and now that you're damaged goods, he's nowhere to be found... Do you hear that, everybody? Amanda's panting for her little wop race driver, and he's nowhere to be found!"

Williams' snide remarks generated a myriad of laughs and jeers, while he started laughing at her himself as Amanda climbed out of the pool, quickly heading toward her best friend. "Please, take me home, Trisha."

Later that night, Amanda lay on her bed, so happy to be in the safety and solitude of her home again. She knew she should put Alex out of her mind. It had been so long and not a peep out of him. She had sent him a few quick texts over time, but nothing. *Maybe he does look at me as damaged goods now,* she pondered. *But I'm not damaged!... Except in my heart.*

The bank CEO appeared to all those around him as having aged ten years in just over a few months. A man of great pride, it was eating at him that his youngest girl, one who should be a near seventeen-year-old high school beauty queen, had turned into somewhat of a recluse. The accident, the injuries, and indeed an illicit pregnancy and miscarriage had seemed to ruin her life. At the same time, his efforts with the board to get Unibank completely out of motor racing had fallen on deaf ears.

All because of those damned Morettis! He kept telling himself 24/7. *Yes, Andy Moretti had fired Alex right after the accident. But that wasn't good enough. His youngest boy was screwing a minor right under his nose, and he didn't do a damn thing about it! And now he is still in business, still winning races, and that kid of his is still racing! Maybe not under our banner, but still racing when he should be behind bars!* Cook was working himself into a frenzy and hit the intercom.

"Bernice, get James Edmunds on the phone for me!" he barked at his longtime secretary.

She, along with the whole staff, worried about him. He was once such a moral and ethical executive who was just wonderful to work for. This incident with his daughter had gradually turned him into a hard and bitter man. She also knew the Unibank Board of Directors had its share of sharks who smelled blood in the water. She dialed the attorney's Rock Hill office, assuming at 1:00 PM that Edmunds himself may not be accessible on the spot. To her pleasant surprise, the lawyer returned the call within ten minutes.

"James Edmunds on line two, sir."

Cook was fidgety, trying to prepare the right tone for his attorney, one who had disappointed him thus far in his ability to get action on all fronts regarding litigation against his new arch-enemies, the Morettis, and was not telling him what he wanted or needed to hear.

"What the hell do you mean, Edmunds!? We'll all be six feet under in a pine box by then!" Cook practically yelled at the speakerphone.

"Byron, you're going to have to calm down. Do you have any idea what the backlog is out there? We're talking about Sin City," the family attorney replied, trying to recall if Cook had ever addressed him by his last name before, a sure sign of disrespect.

"Find out when that Martinez is up for re-election," Cook demanded, obviously distraught at how slow the Clark County District Attorney in Las Vegas was moving on indicting Alex Moretti.

"She's actually running for State Attorney General. She's in a tough race out there and won't likely pursue anything this controversial until after the election."

"Well make some inquiries! Imply that we may support her campaign, or let it out that we may back her opponent. Be discreet, James, but get on it! I want a call by Friday on what's being done!"

Edmunds heard a distinct loud click as Cook hung up on him. He had been dealing with the Cook family for almost twenty years and had never experienced Byron Cook, or any client that he could recall, get so obsessed with a case.

Byron Cook was not a happy man. So far as he was concerned, the bank continued to get hosed for work on their lawsuit against Moretti Motorsport, with no favorable result in sight. The case against Alex Moretti in Clark County, Nevada ended in major disappointment to say the least, as a guilty plea for misdemeanor traffic violations resulted in a mere fine and the civil case had since diminished to a pending settlement between the injured parties and the vehicle owner's insurance company.

"Don't blame the messenger," Edmunds kept telling him as though the angry banker thought the local attorney could simply change the law at will. It now appeared that any possibility of affecting criminal liability toward young Moretti was up to the Sixteenth Judicial Circuit Solicitor General in Rock Hill, an office also moving at a snail's pace.

It seemed as though Byron couldn't even look at his smartphone without some message or news bulletin related to the accident and affair between Alex Moretti and his daughter, Amanda, and was making him all the more bitter by the day. He couldn't shake an undeniable feeling that Moretti had destroyed Amanda's reputation and ruined her life while also causing serious damage to what he considered a once very tranquil Cook family household.

An ever-impatient Cook instructed his executive secretary to have the *gentleman* enter his office. The spit-polished, clean-cut CEO, sporting his expensive dark blue suit and silk tie, stared dubiously at the stranger who just walked in, one who wore faded jeans and a battle-worn black leather jacket, covering a black tee shirt silk screen printed with a smiling Hank Williams Junior image.

"Please sit down, Mister James, or may I call you *Eugene*?"

"I go by *Cotton*, Mister Cook," the Private Investigator replied, catching the bank executive off guard.

"Oh yes. I see that here on your card, Eugene "Cotton" James. How long have you known Edmunds?"

"Since he was a young public defender in Columbia. Before he started making the big bucks," James replied. "May I refer to you as *Byron*?"

"I prefer Mr. Cook," the CEO stated stoically. "What did he tell you about my situation?" Cook asked, not wanting to waste too much time discussing anything James already knew."

"Only that you're not happy with the level of energy Ferrell's office is throwing at this Moretti case," James answered.

"I assume you're familiar with what Moretti did to my daughter, Amanda. Correct?"

"Only to the extent of what's been in the press. In other words, what Ferrell wants everyone to know about it," James replied.

"So tell me, Cotton James. What can you do for me?" Cook asked seriously, cutting to the chase.

"You want evidence that Moretti screwed your daughter, prior to her sixteenth birthday, and somewhere in South Carolina. Am I right?"

"Mister James!" Cook exclaimed. "We're talking about my daughter. A little decorum, if you please."

James appeared unfazed, a reaction Cook took offense to as he was accustomed to dressing down subordinates and seeing remorse. He chose to let it go for the present.

"Okay, so let me just say the two had sex south of the border. Are you confident that happened, Mr. Cook?"

"As confident as I need to be. Now again, what can you do for me? I'm a busy man, Cotton."

"Well, if you want me to find evidence that will nail the bastard;... Is this conversation being recorded?"

"No, of course not. Why do you ask?" Cook quizzed the rough private investigator, a man who seemed to lack any semblance of ethical character.

"I don't know where you're coming from, Mr. Cook. I'll find evidence, if there is any, that Ferrell's office wouldn't touch. It may not be pretty and I don't have rules. I charge two hundred an hour plus expenses. You'll pay me weekly."

"I can do that," Cook responded as he reached for his wallet and extracted his personal Unibank Visa credit card. "Just charge it to this."

"I only deal in cash, Mr. Cook."

Cook hesitated, not liking the sound of this. Edmunds had warned him that James was a piece of work, but just the kind of man he needed for a case like this. "All right, Cotton. But this won't be open-ended. It will be week-to-week."

"I expected no less. I'll need a thousand upfront," James stated arrogantly. "For expenses."

The bank executive squirmed in his seat, not accustomed to dealing with anyone on a basis that seemed to be quite underhanded. "If you won't take my card, I'll have to write you a check."

"Sure. Make it out to *Cash* and endorse it on the back. I assume I can get it cashed here," James responded sarcastically.

Cook gave the flippant Cotton James a less than agreeable look prior to opening a desk drawer and pulling out a blank check. "All right, Cotton James. Let's get on with it."

"I have some questions," James stated, pulling out a small notebook and ballpoint pen. "I have all the contact names and address information, I think. What is Amanda's cell phone number?"

Cook hesitated. "Listen Cotton, I would really prefer my daughter or anyone else for that matter know nothing about your investigation."

"Byron, it's not like I'm going to call Amanda on the phone. If you want to know anything and everything about a teenager, you have to access their cell phone."

"So what will you do with her phone, Cotton?" Cook asked nervously.

"We'll need to know who she's communicating with back and forth, when, and where."

"I'm not comfortable with that, Cotton. That's a very private thing."

"Mister Cook, you have to make a decision here. Do you want to know what happened between Moretti and your daughter or not? You'd never eat sausage if you knew how it was made. Now, do you want your check back?"

Cook sighed in resignation. "All right Cotton, do what you have to do. Her number is 803-675-1098."

James noted the number and now asked, "Who is the carrier she has service with?"

"Southern Wire, as is our entire family," Byron replied, regretting that disclosure once it came out of his mouth. I thought those iPhones were secure and a guy like you couldn't access that information."

"The iPhones, no. But these third-party mobile carriers, maybe," James stated with a devious smile. "So your whole family's account, with all the phones, is in your name?"

"Yes, that's right. They're based right here in Charlotte and a big client of ours," Byron explained.

"I'll need your login... For the Southern Wire account," James directed as he pulled up an app on his own iPhone.

"I'm not giving you that! There's a lot of personal business on all those phones," Byron declared.

"I really would only need the data from Amanda's number, but I doubt if it's a separate login, is it?" James asked his newest client, a man whom he could tell was quite uncomfortable, but a scenario he was quite used to.

"No, probably not." Byron wrote the username and password on a small sticky note and slid it across his desk, watching as James punched them in.

"Okay, Mr. Cook, you should receive a security notice any second. I'll need that code."

Byron complied, making a mental note to eventually change his password.

"Could you give me some names of some of her best friends, boyfriends, and anyone else she would converse with on an ongoing basis?"

"Well, her only boyfriend other than Moretti has been Kyle Williams, Bud Williams' son. You know, the biggest car dealer in South Carolina. Her best friend is Trisha Shyree, who lives right down the road from us. Other than that, mostly calls to her family."

"And calls to Moretti," James added as he made some notes. "I assume Amanda has a credit or debit card. I'll need that account login information."

"That's over the top now, James. You're getting into areas a bit too sensitive," Byron stated, suddenly having second thoughts about dealing with this *private eye*.

"Mr. Cook. Are you serious about nailing this man who violated your little girl or not? I can hand you your check back and just walk out of here."

Byron sat silent, momentarily looking away, out the window toward the Panther's stadium. "All right, James," he replied begrudgingly while he accessed the family personal accounts information on his terminal and gave out Amanda's account information James needed, making a personal note to periodically keep an eye on the two daughters' accounts himself, something he had been ever lax in doing.

"How would you describe the relationship between Moretti and your daughter now?" James questioned.

Byron stiffened in his executive chair, thinking it to be a foolish question. "He had sex with Amanda and she got pregnant. Then a few weeks later, he almost killed her in a serious car accident and she aborted the baby. What do you think, Cotton?"

"I don't know. That's why I'm asking, Mr. Cook."

Cotton James had confirmed by checking Moretti's Facebook account, which had just recently seen some more robust activity, that he would be racing at a dirt track in southern Minnesota for the entire upcoming weekend. He had staked out the lakeview condominium for several hours before dusk to confirm that no one was in residence.

At just past 1:00 AM, he broke into the front door using his handy door lock tool. Confirming there were no active security devices, he slowly and thoroughly checked out the place using a small flashlight. *No question this is the right place,* he thought, noticing all of the motor racing paraphernalia all over the place, including several framed photographs of the Morettis.

The place could definitely use a woman's touch, he observed, as the kitchen sink included dirty dishes and the bedroom had an unmade bed and multiple worn and wrinkled clothing items scattered about. In addition to the large master bedroom, there was a guest bedroom that also had bachelor written all over it as it included a large piece of workout equipment and a small desk in one corner with a large computer monitor placed on top of it. Unfortunately for the private investigator, it appeared the occupant had a laptop computer that he undoubtedly unhooked and took with him when traveling. *That would sure have made my job easier,* Cotton pondered, as his abilities to log in through the standard Windows password security were quite practiced.

His prospects brightened however when opening the desk drawers that were consumed with paper envelopes full of bills and receipts, containing a treasure trove of information from three credit card and bank accounts, as well as several months' worth of mobile phone bills. He assumed correctly that Moretti had his banking with Unibank and could have had Cook supply him with that data, but having done so could plant a seed with his wealthy client that too much of his service was easily accessed without his $200 per hour efforts.

Taking time to get snapshots of each and every page of every record, the unsavory PI's final task was to place two microcams in strategic locations in the condo, one easily placed on top of a framed presentation on the wall in the master bedroom, and the other in the front room on a main lighting fixture.

Careful to leave the place as untouched, James ran down to the covered dock down on the lake, planting a third microcam inside the boat cabin, identification of the boat made easy by seeing the many photos of it on Moretti's Facebook page. All of the microcams recorded data to a secured server and were easily accessed and studied through website access or an app on James' phone.

Many hours of analyzing data, cross-checking, and so forth, produced some very interesting stuff. Several particular items popped up that warranted further study and the P.I. began to search for data online and make a few phone calls.

James dialed a stored number and left a voicemail. "Mr. Cook, this is Cotton. Call me."

Byron heard the buzz of his mobile phone and asked the two department managers to step out of his office for a break. He then returned James' call. "What do you have for me?"

"I'm checking out some data and I need Moretti's social security number and confirm his date of birth. Do you want his Unibank checking account number?"

"Sure, Cotton. Shoot," Byron replied, knowing he could find it, of course, but James having that number would save time. He also knew that disclosing that information from the bank was illegal, but that wouldn't stop Cook now, in his own mind believing this minor breach would serve the cause of justice.

"1-0-0-3-8-9-7-6-5-3-7-8-2," James rattled it off slowly.

Byron took a couple of minutes and had the information. "You ready?"

"Yes, Mr. Cook."

"His date of birth is February 4, 2001. His social is 359-34-0887. When will you have something for me?"

James slowly wrote down the digits and replied, "Soon."

He made a few visits to check or confirm some information including a stop at the CVS Pharmacy store in Lake Wylie. Confronting the store manager, he presented a fabricated Private Investigator license, explaining he was conducting an investigation related to the Amanda Cook rape case, and needed a copy of a receipt for a purchase made on the morning of July 25th, 2020. Providing the receipt number and last four digits of the card used to pay, Cotton explained to the fellow that he could save himself some aggravation, as failure to produce the simple receipt copy would result in a warrant and much more red tape.

Confirming the purchase had not included any information on prescription medications, the gentleman complied, perplexed several weeks later when a deputy sheriff showed up with a warrant requesting the exact same item again anyway.

James waited seven days before again phoning Byron Cook, informing him that he had sufficient information for submission to the Solicitor General's office, suggesting that he hand it over to Edmonds, not mentioning that Ferrell's office wouldn't receive himself favorably, all because of *issues* they had with Cotton James in the past.

He had caught Moretti on the minicams late a few days after James had planted them, but there was nothing incriminating from the data, only a young bachelor coming and going from his residence, and not a single time being inside his boat. The app did have a warning feature of motion, something that may serve a purpose moving forward, assuming Moretti didn't discover the mini cams, which was likely.

It was two weeks later and Byron had taken the day off early, motoring down I-77 when his phone buzzed, seeing it was James Edmonds calling. "Talk to me James," Byron yelled into his Cadillac's speaker system.

"I spent a better part of this morning in Ferrell's office. The case of Alex Moretti's statutory rape has been reopened."

"That's great, James!" Byron asked gleefully. "So, what do you think?"

"The evidence that Cotton found is pretty damning," Edmonds replied.

"But is it enough without Amanda's testimony?"

"Honestly, I think it is. I don't see how Moretti defends it. Ferrell's people will have to subpoena and reacquire all of Cotton's evidence again," Edmonds stated, leaving out the word *legally*. "Don't expect a trial to happen next week, Byron."

"That's okay. At least now something is happening. Great work, James!" Byron exclaimed, suddenly having a bit higher opinion toward Mr. Cotton James.

Trisha and Amanda had the cabin all to themselves the second evening as the Shyrees went out to take in a show. They had taken a ton of photos and videos that day and busied themselves posting their stuff on social media. Ever since the accident, Amanda kept receiving tons of friend requests on her Facebook, many of whom were quite surly and rude people wanting to post things that were everything from grotesque to hateful.

215

Amanda had gotten into a habit of waiting until she and Trisha were together and the two would have fun checking out each of these potential Facebook *friends* before deleting them.

"Check this gal out, Amanda, a stripper from Las Vegas," Trisha stated.

"I think she and this one would go well together," Amanda replied as she denied *friendship* with the ex-Hells Angels guy. The next one caught her eye, a teenage girl around her age.

"Check this out, Trisha. A race girl. Oh my god! Her Facebook has pictures of Alex!"

"Chasity Younger, Region Sprint Car Champion. Says she raced against Alex! Wow!" Trisha returned excitedly.

Amanda studied the various photos on the girl's Facebook page. "Gee, Trisha. She's just a young girl!'

The two went over Chasity Younger's profile in detail and Trisha commented, "Those are all photos from way back when she started racing. Nine years old! How is that possible?"

"No, it says here she won a championship last year, at fifteen!" Amanda recited, sharing a look with Trisha.

"That would make her sixteen now, Amanda... Come on! I know what you're thinking."

"She is cute, Trisha."

"So are you.... And so am I!" Trisha replied jokingly, trying to lighten up Amanda's mood before she entered the mental doldrums again.

The girls were having a better time the following day as Trisha's parents gave her some cash and let the two roam free through the downtown area of Gatlinburg, truly one of the few busy places left on the planet that parents could consider totally safe for two very attractive sixteen-year-old girls like Trisha and Amanda.

They marveled at the view from the Ober Gatlinburg tram lift and traveled up the mountain to the top, where a facility rented skis during winter and also had an ice skating rink. Following a robust forty-five minutes on the ice, the girls checked in their skates and sat down to enjoy an ice cream together.

"Jeremy keeps texting me, Amanda. I'm going to tell him to stop being a bug," Trisha claimed humorously.

Amanda stared momentarily toward the crowd circling the rink. "I wish my boyfriend would bug me."

"You really need to stop calling him that, Amanda. For better or for worse, you were so popular before and now you have every cute guy on the planet checking you out!"

"I just cannot get over his not calling me, Trisha," Amanda told her friend for the *umpteenth* hundredth time.

"Why don't you moon him over the phone," Trisha replied, finally getting some semblance of laughter out of Amanda. "How about I do it?"

Amanda knew her spirited friend may do just that, and laughed some more. "What, here?"

"Might get his attention. I'd be afraid he'd tell me your butt looks better than mine,... and hurt my feelings." The two shared another round of laughter.

"I'll just send him a text," Trisha stated, and began searching for her phone.

"Let me give you his number," Amanda added, playing along.

The mischievous teen punched in the number on her phone and then took a close-up selfie sticking her tongue out, blown up to not reveal her whole mug. SEND

They shared more laughter prior to each having a sudden quiet look as Trisha's phone beeped right away.

She turned her phone toward Amanda who reviewed the text. *"Who is this?"*

Before Amanda could calm down and think about how they should reply, Trisha had already pecked out a long answer. *It's Trisha, you shit! My best friend can't see why you never contact her. I thought more of you than that, Alex! Don't you even think about her anymore?* SEND

Amanda saw Trisha had that *cat ate the canary* look. "What did you say, Trisha? Let me see."

She grabbed the phone off the table and digested the message, not sure whether to kiss her best friend or spank her hind end.

"Sorry, Amanda. I just had to do that."

A short moment later, a beep indicated another incoming reply... *"I'm not a shit! I don't know you, Trisha, and I'm tired of getting all these weird calls and messages from an 803 area code. My name is NOT Alex. It is Gertrude, I am a 76-year-old recently widowed woman and I will have my granddaughter block this number!"*

"What is this, Amanda?"

"I haven't the slightest idea, Trisha."

"Are you sure that's Alex's number you have there?"

"Of course I'm sure," Amanda replied. "I've never changed it since he gave it to me that night in Long Beach over two years ago!"

The two compared notes, verifying that Amanda had indeed given Trisha the correct number from her phone.

"I don't know, Amanda. Maybe he changed it? Can you go back and access your old phone records?"

"I guess," Amanda replied, still confused. *I know I didn't change anything, though.*

Trisha immediately held her phone up again and began entering data.

"Who are you texting now, Trisha?" Amanda asked curiously.

"That Gertrude. I apologized and asked her how long she's had that phone number. Hopefully she'll reply back."

Four minutes later Trisha's phone beeped and upon review of the new message, Trisha's eyes went wide. "Check it out, Amanda."

"Since my daughter got me this fancy iPhone in 2009".

Chapter 10

The Eccentric Lawyer

A lex stopped by the shop to meet with his defense attorney and retrieve some personal items from his car.

His father had found him the personal lawyer for his South Carolina criminal case, and as Andy was helping to foot the bill, he insisted the attorney meet with them here at the team facility. His name was Lawrence Frye and he had successfully defended and won a domestic abuse case brought against a former crew chief on Moretti's recently acquired NASCAR team. It was believed to be a very tough case and Frye was credited with doing a masterful job in combatting an overjealous Solicitor Circuit prosecutor who had seemed to have an open and shut case. The three sat in the company's large conference room where Frye and Alex were introduced.

"Your case may just come down to a simple he said, she said," Frye began. "When you say *"I don't know"* regarding where you and the victim engaged in sex, you're attempting to convince the jury that the actual location may or may not have been on the South Carolina side of the state border. In effect, you are testifying that you did indeed have sex with a fifteen-year-old girl from the State of South Carolina. Do you understand or even dispute that, Mr. Moretti?"

"Could we not refer to Amanda as the victim, Counselor," Andy interceded. "It's not as though my son physically raped Miss Cook."

"I'm afraid the law in South Carolina sees this as much the same. When Ferrell or his Assistant Solicitor addresses the court, Amanda Cook will be referred to as the victim, gentlemen."

"We're not in court yet, sir. So could we just refer to Amanda as Amanda?... Please?"

Frye leaned back in the comfortable leather chair. "Very well, gentlemen. Now, Alex, if Amanda agrees to give a deposition, will her testimony corroborate your own?"

"I don't know, sir. I honestly don't know what she would say. I don't think she's very happy with me. I believe she has my number blocked and hasn't returned a single message or call since the accident."

"So, it could be a maybe?"

Andy and his son shared some uncomfortable eye contact. "I truly don't know what she'll have to say."

"I'm sorry to say this, but this case looks very tough, very tough indeed. You see, outside of Amanda testifying with authority that she knows exactly where you two were on that river, each and every time you chose to drop anchor and conduct privacies in your boat cabin, a guilty verdict is likely. That jury is going to be made up of Rock Hill area citizens who may know the Cook family. Moreover, they all know the Bud Williams family whose two sons are known to have romantic connections with both of the Cook sisters. Many on that jury will convict on the mere fact that you admittedly had sex with Amanda Cook prior to her sixteenth birthday."

"Could we talk to her, first?" Alex asked innocently.

"Absolutely not," Frye instructed immediately. "That may be tampering, and if that is remotely established in that courtroom, you could have Perry Mason as your lawyer, Mr. Moretti, and you would still face conviction.

The meeting with Frye concluded and Alex couldn't leave without saying hello to those who were on his crew, several of whom had been some of his best friends. He also met Jon David Hill, another Brit who had inherited his number "5" ride on the team.

"I trust your bloody court case gets fixed in short order, Alex. In the meantime, I'll try to put on a really good show," Hill stated smiling.

It was of small significance that Louis Newberry happened to be his new agent, and that Hill and Evelyn were rumored to be involved more so than just as teammates and competitors on the racetrack, a development Newberry had not included in his plan.

Alex took the comments from Hill that he supported a quick resolution to his court case with a grain of salt, as the rumors about him and Stevens aside, it was no secret this opening had been a fantastic career opportunity for Hill, indeed the way many young drivers get their start in a major racing series, and for the former IMSA pilot to get this chance with a winning Indycar team was just peachy in that regard.

Alex had made a token effort to avoid Evelyn, who happened to be in the building for a change. The two intersected in the shop break room and sat down briefly over a soft drink.

"How are you holding up?" Evelyn asked in an attempt to break the ice.

"I guess as good as can be expected... Congratulations on Toronto. Great drive," he responded, seriously impressed with her second season win. "Second in the points now, I see."

"I was right there with O'Ward and Ericson at Indy," she replied. "That last pit fiasco was a killer."

"Yes, I saw it. How are the teammates?" Alex asked, subconsciously wanting a comment about her relationship with Hill.

"Too soon to tell actually," she answered.

"Well, having Louie as the agent for both of you might make it better for things," Alex stated.

Evelyn didn't really want Jon David's name to come up in this unexpected encounter. "I still communicate as friends on social media with Allison."

Alex knew she was getting a steady litany of news about his cases, but chose not to inquire about it. "I hope you do well in St. Louis, Evelyn. I'll watch some of it."

The two were stuck making small talk and uncomfortable with it when Evelyn spoke, "Alex, if you ever need me to"...

Jon David suddenly walked in as the conversation stopped... Now all three were uncomfortable.

There was good news for Alex Moretti to help him deal with the black cloud that seemed to overshadow his whole life the past year.

Tim had succeeded in negotiating a very good contract for Alex to compete in the World Rally Series next season with the factory Hyundai team. The package was structured as a retainer plus performance bonuses at or near what his previous year's take would have been had he driven the entire season for Moretti Motorsport. The Hyundai folks must have been quite impressed with his few races a year earlier, choosing to take him on despite his pending legal issues.

As Tony would be competing in his second full Formula One season, driving the new Moretti FM-022 model, he looked forward to their being in close proximity again in Europe occasionally as their schedules allowed.

Tim and Sherri planned to celebrate the deal by spending an extended vacation in Europe, meeting Alex and taking in the rallies in Croatia in late April, and concluding in Portugal three weeks later.

Alex worked on a last sprucing up before the second party was scheduled to arrive. He had listed the boat just ten days ago, disappointed that he had not received more inquiries, although the broker had warned him that his asking price was quite high, especially since the bulk of boating season had passed.

Suddenly he received a call, seeing the incoming was from his attorney's office. "This is Alex Moretti," he answered.

"Hold for Lawrence Frye, please," a female voice replied before placing him on hold.

"Alex, Larry Frye. Do you have a few minutes?"

"Of course, Larry," Alex replied., anxious as he had not discussed his case with the attorney for several days.

"I've gone over the case with the office staff and I regretfully must inform you that I cannot represent you," the attorney stated.

Frye had been excited initially at the opportunity to represent Alex Moretti in what would undoubtedly be a case garnering nationwide, if not worldwide, attention.

Alex was shaken. His first arraignment hearing was less than three weeks away and now he had no lawyer. Given the fact that he had financial resources well in excess of what most criminally charged clients would have, this news didn't fare well. "Tell me why, Larry."

"The case is very complicated and we're just not equipped to properly handle it. I'm sorry."

"Could you recommend another lawyer?" Alex inquired nervously.

"You may try Floyd Ramsey, there in Rock Hill. His office is right across the street from the courthouse. We'll send you an invoice for the time we have in your case. Good luck to you."

Invoice for time spent, huh? Great. Alex disconnected, quickly checking Google for Floyd Ramsey. He called and got a voicemail, which didn't exactly inspire confidence. Alex called a second attorney, Mason Pearson, one whom Alex planned to ask if he was related to the late David Pearson, the NASCAR legendary Hall of Famer. Following a brief discussion, an early morning appointment was set.

Alex drove to Pearson's office and was met with a handshake, now knowing that wouldn't be the case regarding the late racing legend as Mason Pearson was an African-American man. The two had a few minutes of small talk about racing before Alex gave him the short version of his sudden predicament.

"I'm fairly familiar with your case, Mr. Moretti. Frankly, it's the talk of the legal community around here unlike anything I've ever seen or heard in all of my thirty-two years of practicing law. I'm afraid I could not take it, though," Pearson declared sympathetically, not telling Alex that he had represented a school teacher, a man who was married with three children and was co-defendant in a case against the York Public School District. It involved a sexual harassment complaint filed by a high school freshman student. Pearson lost in court and the young teacher's career and ultimately his marriage were ruined. The student's name was Allison Cook. It became accepted knowledge in York County, South Carolina, that one did not take on the Cook family, particularly when it involved one of the daughters.

"I would suggest you attempt to get a change of venue," Pearson informed him, knowing it was mixed advice as many of the more rural circuit court districts would offer a jury pool even more hostile toward a midwestern Chicago transplant of Italian descent than the less conservative York County that was effectively part of metropolitan Charlotte.

"Well, I assume I would have to get a lawyer first," Alex responded in obvious dismay.

"I know the man you truly need to be your attorney in this case, Mr. Moretti. If you could get him to take your case, that is. He's sort of retired, and very much an eccentric character, I'll tell you," Pearson explained. "His name is Earnest Flannery."

Alex got out his iPhone and prepared to type in the name.

"Oh, you would have to go see him. Earnest will not answer the phone on an out-of-state call," Pearson advised.

"Perhaps you wouldn't mind me calling his office from here then, Mason?"

"Earnest is not local to Rock Hill, either," the local attorney stated. "And he doesn't have an office. I can call down there and he would tell me you just need to plan on going there."

"Sounds like you know this Flannery pretty well," Alex observed.

Pearson grinned, showing off his pearly white teeth with one diamond inserted gold. "He taught me everything I know. Allow me to write down his address for you."

Alex took the small scribbled notepad slip. "Meggett, South Carolina? Where is that?"

"Right outside Charleston."

Alex left early the next morning for the three-plus hour drive straight south on I-77. He again swapped vehicles with Dominic, always a man happy to parade around in Alex's two-seater. Unaware of what he was getting into, Alex thought a first meeting with the natives may go a bit better with him showing up in a Chevy truck rather than an Acura NSX.

Following the GPS, he got close but expecting to find a house with a number on it or a roadside mailbox with the same, Alex drove all along the patch of blacktop before driving up the road to a corner gas station to ask and hopefully get some local advice regarding this lawyer named Flannery.

The heavyset middle-aged woman who worked as a clerk smiled. "How are ya?"

"Fine Madam," he answered, "I'm looking for a local attorney. His name is Earnest Flannery. According to my GPS directions, his place has to be right down the road from here, but I didn't see"...

"You're not from around here, are ya? Everybody knows Mr. Flannery. Just head back that way," she explained pointing to the left. "And it's a big black gate on the left, right past where the old river church burned down."

"Hmm," Alex replied. "Must have missed it. I may as well buy something from you. I'll take one of those corn dogs."

"You're that race driver guy, aren't you? I thought you looked familiar," the clerk claimed, pulling a tabloid magazine from under the counter. There was his mug on the front cover along with a picture of Amanda being loaded into the ambulance.

He smiled neutrally, unsure of what this strange woman may have thought.

"Are you going to get Mr. Flannery to lawyer for ya?" she asked while a couple of other local customers tuned in.

"Maybe... Is he good?" Alex asked, not truly believing the woman's opinion had much value but having to ask nevertheless.

"He used to be real good," an old man standing there stated. "But I think he's got that dementia now."

"Really?" Alex replied as he studied the old man, who seemed to have nothing to do but hang out on this corner all day. "How long has he had that problem?"

"Oh, I don't know. Just rumors I hear."

Alex paid for the corn dog, nodded to the small bunch, and walked out. *Dementia, huh? How lucky can I be?*

A few minutes later, Alex located the large black gate and pulled in, following a gravel lane down through an impressive grove of moss-covered trees that led to what appeared to be an old historic antebellum-type mansion.

Alex noticed a couple of young black men riding lawnmowers and wondered if he hadn't stumbled onto one of those touristy old plantations he had visited years earlier outside of New Orleans, both who looked up smiling and waved at him.

Alex parked in front of the home and walked up a wide front stairway to a pair of ornate red double doors. He looked around for a moment, thinking the place had that eerie feeling about it, and finally rang the doorbell and waited.

A few moments later, an upper middle-aged black fellow answered, one very fit and donning a dark pair of sports pants and a tee shirt. Smiling pleasantly, he greeted the unfamiliar guest. "May I help you, sir?"

"Yes," Alex responded, somehow expecting a different figure. "Would you be Mr. Flannery?"

"No, I'm Samuel. Could you kindly state your business, sir?"

"I am Alex Moretti and have driven all the way here from Charlotte. Mr. Mason Pearson recommended Mr. Flannery to me as I am in need of a good attorney."

"Mason, huh? Are you a friend of his?" Samuel asked skeptically.

"Just met the man yesterday, in fact. Is Mr. Flannery here today?"

"Alex Moretti, huh? Name sounds familiar," Samuel stated. "Just wait right here."

Alex stood on the large veranda, realizing how humid it was. Two other young black teens walked by, giving him a quick nod as they chatted away together.

The red doors opened again and Samuel reappeared, motioning for Alex to follow him in as they walked through the historic looking home to the rear portico, where a stately old gentleman sat in an old rocking chair, dressed in an off-white suit, white large brim hat, and sporting a bright red bow tie, giving Alex a first thought of Colonel Sanders.

He looked up through a pair of very thick glasses, motioning for his guest to sit down in an adjacent chair. "Would you like some tea?"

"Yes, that would be good, sir. I can pour it," Alex stated as he moved to the small table between them that featured a teapot, three cups, and an ashtray with a thin spent cigar.

"So, Mason sent you down here, huh young man?" Flannery asked.

"That's right, sir. I have a problem and am in need"...

"I know all about your case, Alex Moretti. Even down here, our papers are full of it. I must confess that I didn't expect to see you this early. How about I show you around while you tell me all about it?"

Samuel helped Flannery up and handed the old man his cane. He pointed it toward the garden and he and Alex walked down a rear set of steps and toward another large building. Housed within the structure was a rather impressive car collection and Flannery began a tour explaining every single vintage automobile in detail.

"I know this one would interest you, Alex. This is the car that Junior Johnson drove in the Southern 500 in 1960."

"Are you familiar with my family, Mr. Flannery?" Alex asked, fascinated by the old man's interest in historic automobiles. "Our racing history, I mean."

"Not so much. My knowledge about racing is mostly about NASCAR, and all in the old days. Ask me about Fireball Roberts or Buck Baker. I remember being at the Firecracker 400 in 1966. Cotton Owens had two young drivers running for him that day who would become legends, David Pearson and Mario Andretti. You being Italian, I thought that might interest you," Flannery stated.

This old fella may be more cognizant upstairs than they give him credit for, Alex was now thinking.

They exited the building, moving to another impressive structure that housed a historic-looking horse buggy, saddles, and harnesses. "I sold off all my horses years ago after I stopped riding. When are you going to ask me about the slave quarters?"

Alex looked embarrassed, not knowing why he was being asked that.

"Yes, this was a plantation and had almost two hundred slaves back in the day. My great, great, great grandfather was a colonel in Wade Hampton's calvary, killed just outside Columbia in 1864. I fell out with the family when I was young. I went to law school and became a prosecutor. Locked up a Grand Dragon of the local Ku Klux Klan. I was a pariah in the family, not welcome here for years. When the old folks passed on, I inherited the place, and I've worked to right the past sins of this property ever since. All those black kids you see around. They're all on parole. They get paid good money, get a good place to live, kids educated, everything. When I'm gone, Samuel and his family will inherit it."

Alex was intrigued by the tale, getting the feeling that every new guest to the property received the same historical tour, and the old man relished in playing host as if it was some sort of redemption.

"The evidence against you is pretty overwhelming. You know that, don't you?" Flannery asked as more of an observation. "How long were you involved with that girl?"

228

"Almost a year, sir."

"Did you love her?" The veteran litigator asked seriously, as he halted their walking and stopped to look his new prospective client in the eye.

Alex was stunned, expecting many questions from the old legal warrior, but not this one. "Yes.... I still do."

"And how did she feel about you?"

"The same, I'm certain."

"And now?" Flannery asked, again seriously.

Alex had to break the old man's stare. "Honestly, sir, I don't know."

"Don't ever preface a statement with the word *honestly*. When you qualify your statements that way, it implies you're not always truthful," the scratchy-voiced Flannery scolded.

"Samuel will have you sign some paperwork giving us *Power of Attorney*. I'll file a motion for a delay and give us a little more time to prepare our case. Samuel will let you know when to come back down here next."

"I hate to ask this, Mr. Flannery.... How much is this going to cost me?"

The old man laughed. "Let's just say that you probably can't afford me. But you're here because there's not another lawyer in the South who will take you on. So, to that end, let's just say you can't afford not to hire me."

The two made their way back toward the house, sharing some small talk about the rest of the grounds, crops, etc. As the two prepared to part ways, Alex asked, "How do you feel about my case, Mr. Flannery?"

"I need to get a look at all the evidence before I can judge. The mere fact that you're even here tells me it's quite serious."

Alex felt his skin tense up with fear. He figured this old guy had probably seen about everything in his day, and if he thought things were that serious, they were no doubt critical.

"I used to be a big fan of car racing you know. Not so much with those Indianapolis cars other than that young man from Texas, A.J. Foyt. He used to come down here and race our southern boys sometimes. Good lord that Foyt was good. If I keep you out of jail, you'll treat me to one of those VIP suites in Charlotte, or maybe Atlanta... Now, good day."

Alex was escorted into a room that served as a resident law office and shown their standard paperwork to hire Earnest Flannery and his associate attorney, Samuel Mayne, as his lawyers.

He prepared to depart, sharing mobile phone numbers with Samuel when Flannery's right-hand man asked, "So, how are you feeling now?"

"I'll be better after this trial business is over," Alex replied.

"I mean physically. I was watchin' last year when you hit that wall real hard."

"Oh? Fine, Samuel. Never been better."

"Don't worry about the lawyer bill. Mr. Flannery don't take on but one case a year at most. He don't need the money."

Alex prepared to depart but turned toward Samuel as an afterthought. "Samuel, if you don't mind me asking, how is Mr. Flannery's health?"

"Well, he takes heart medicine every day. Other than that, he does pretty good for a man eighty-six. Why would you ask?"

"Oh, they were saying some things down at the corner gas station."

"Like he has Alzheimer's?"

"Something like that," Alex replied blushing.

Samuel began to laugh. "Don't you worry none. Mr. Flannery's mind is sharp as a whip. I'm not sure who started them rumors, Mr. Moretti. Truth be known, old Ernest is glad people think that, especially when he's at work in a courtroom."

"Thanks, Samuel. That's good to know. And you can just call me Alex."

"Okay, you have a good trip back home,... Alex."

Amanda met a young man named Ricky Harfour who worked with her at the clubhouse. They had gone out a couple of times and were mostly just friends, at least in her mind. He had come by her home a few times and met Amanda's parents. He was no Kyle Williams in Byron's eyes, but both he and Sarah were pleased to see Amanda seeming to become normal.

The two went to a movie together and left afterward for a drive. Ricky pulled over into a Walmart Parking lot, away from other cars, and shut off the key. The young man had his arm around her and attempted to pull her closer, an effort that wasn't playing out like he had planned or hoped. "Amanda, is there something wrong," Ricky asked.

"No, Ricky. Nothing is wrong. It's just that,... I just want to be friends," Amanda replied knowing that wouldn't be what he wanted to hear.

Amanda's parents heard a car door abruptly open and close prior to her entering surprisingly early as both parents were still up at just past 10:30 PM. This was her second date with Ricky and only the third date overall since recovering from the accident months earlier.

Byron and Sarah shared concerned looks as their daughter ascended the stairway rather quickly as if wanting to avoid any questions. Sarah gave her a few minutes before tapping on Amanda's bedroom door.

"Come in, Mom."

Sarah entered slowly to a teary-eyed daughter, lying on her stomach as not wishing to face her mother, knowing she would be most curious why her date with Ricky Halfour had ended so prematurely.

"Amanda? Would you care to tell me about it?" Sarah asked in a tone that told her girl that no explanation was expected.

Amanda hesitated before rolling over. "Mom, kids my age really don't do dates anymore. Ricky just really wanted to hook-up."

"Hook-up?" Sarah replied.

"Yes, Mom, hook-up. Kids just hang out together, smoke pot and have sex together. And before you lose your mind, Mom, yes you did raise me better than that, and no, I haven't gotten into that, either."

"I can only assume that after what you have been through, you would know the consequences of such behavior," Sarah stated.

"Mom, I miss Alex so much. I know Dad hates him and all that, and I know you think I was too young. But it wasn't all his fault. I cannot live with the idea that Alex could spend the best years of his life in prison because of me."

"According to the law, Amanda, Alex should have known better, or at least waited until you were sixteen," Sarah answered sympathetically.

"This is wrong, Mom! It just sucks!"

"I know, baby," Sarah answered as she embraced her youngest child. "I know."

Weeks passed and Amanda's mood had gone farther south as her whole problem with Alex's phone number added new depression on top of her general sadness. *Had Alex changed his number? That number I have stored in my phone seems correct. But I haven't actually punched it in digit by digit since that first night we met in Long Beach(?)* She recalled his commenting about eventually getting himself a 704 number.

Her phone was part of the Cook's family plan with Southern Wire and she couldn't access any of it as the administrator. *Dad wouldn't give me the login, she thought. If I asked, he would get more weird toward me than he already is. But Mom?* Amanda recalled that Sarah was quite upset herself at Alex as he hadn't called to even check on her back when she was recovering in that hospital.

She opened the account login page. Her mom was fairly basic in setting up passcodes. She tried her birthdate entered in reverse... Didn't work... Amanda attempted a few more with their address... Nothing, and now she was locked out of the system, flagged because of too many login attempts. She would have to wait until Sarah returned home from shopping.

Choosing to jog down to the pool, she caught something on her phone's home news page. Far from being any type of news junkie, the headline nevertheless jumped out at her.

Moretti Hires Veteran Charleston Lawyer

She read the article stating that Alex had retained the services of longtime defense attorney Ernest Flannery to represent him in his upcoming trial in York County, being charged with third-degree statutory rape. The story continued to outline the South Carolina laws on the books regarding

232

adults having sex with minor children, designated by those under sixteen years of age. The writer also quoted Solicitor General Circuit attorney Brad Ferrell as stating the evidence against Moretti is quite substantial and speculated that Flannery may negotiate a plea deal for a lesser sentence, which could involve less than three years imprisonment, a substantial fine, multi-year probation, and a permanent listing in the National Sex Offender Public Website.

Oh my god! Amanda thought, tearing up as the enormity of what faced Alex had just slapped her in the face.

Choosing the right moment, Amanda knew Sarah would check on her before retiring to bed, as she had always done.

"Mom, do you remember when you called Alex last year and got upset that he wasn't even calling to check on me?"

"Of course, I remember, honey. Why do you ask?"

"I want to look back at a record of those calls and texts. I think I may have missed something," Amanda stated timidly.

Sarah looked at her daughter, still emotional about an incident almost a year past. "Are you sure you want to relive that, Amanda? I'm afraid of that just digging up bad memories for you and setting you back."

"Please. Mom," Amanda begged. "I think just the opposite. Maybe if I see those numbers back and forth just stopping on those days, it will give me some closure."

Sarah knew the pending trial, whenever that may come to fruition, would be the true closure if there were any, but chose not to bring that up. "How can I help you, honey? I will do anything to help you get through this. You know that."

"I just need the admin login for our mobile phone records. Let me pull that page up."

The two sat in front of Amanda's desk and she pulled up the desired screen, Amanda hoping her mother would know it without getting her father in on it.

Sarah looked at it, pondering. "I can't recall the last time I logged into this," she stated truthfully. She attempted a couple of entries, which failed.

Oh no, she's going to get locked out! Amanda feared.

Sarah tried a third login and did indeed get locked out. She looked up at Amanda and both shared expressions of disappointment. The screen threw up a *forgot username/password* link, which Sarah entered with little confidence, prompting her to enter an account phone number. Her entry failed, throwing up a message that an administrator number and password was required.

"I'll have to get it from your dad, Amanda."

"No, Mom. Don't worry about it," Amanda responded. "Dad's already on edge enough as it is. We won't go there."

A couple of days later, Amanda returned from school to an empty house other than the housekeeper, when she gathered a thought. *Those old phone records must be here somewhere... The den?*

She entered the home office and began to rummage through the desks drawers and file cabinets, happy that none of them were under lock and key. She did locate a batch of envelopes from Southern Wire, hoping they would go back that far. *This stuff is all online now. Thank God Dad believes in a paper trail on everything.*

She finally located one of the thick envelopes with a postmark of March 22, 2021, a statement which listed all of the calls and texts incoming and outgoing from February 20th through March 19th and had detail of all the family's numbers. She studied her own list of calls and text messages, noting the volume was scant between March 6th and March 10th, the days I was in the hospital and unconscious.

A closer inspection. *Oh oh! The digits of Alex's number changed from 847-269-8596 to 847-269-8956(?).* The old number had a last listing on March 9th of last year, the fifth day of the accident! There were three text messages incoming before the 10th, messages that she had not seen appear(?) The new number began on the 10th, outgoing messages on her part only. *This all happened while I was still recovering.*

Couldn't have been Mom, Amanda thought. *Dad? No, he would just take my phone away from me and lecture me about all my communications.* She further considered and it hit her. *"I should have known. How friggin low, Allison!"*

Amanda started to dial Alex's number but hesitated. *I better think about this,* she pondered while studying some of the other numbers back then she interfaced with. Over eighty percent were between her and Trisha, of course. *What's this?... Yes! Why didn't you think about this before, Amanda!?*

She dialed the number and received a voicemail prompt. "You have reached the voicemail box of Crissy Moretti. You know what to do. Bye."

Twenty minutes later, she received a callback. "Amanda? Wow, long time no speak," Crissy stated.

"Oh, Crissy! I am so glad to talk to you! Do you have a minute?"

"All I have are minutes right now, sweety. I'm expecting again, so I don't do all the Grands Prix with Tony," she answered, suddenly feeling it strange to be talking to Amanda again after so much time. "I'm so sorry about what happened, Amanda."

"Crissy, I have been in such a mess. I lost Alex's phone number. How is he?"

"Well, he's been better, Amanda. You had better not call him. He has been strictly prohibited from communicating with you, at least until all the litigation is over with, and that may take years," Crissy stated seriously. "I'm not even sure I should be"...

"Oh, please, Crissy! Don't hang up on me!"

"I'm not going to hang up, Amanda."

"How is he, Crissy? Has he moved on? I see on social media about this Chasity Younger."

"Chasity Younger? She's more or less his part-time business partner for now, Amanda. It's not like they're romantic or anything. He doesn't even have a girlfriend now, that I know of."

Amanda could hardly hold her tongue. *Oh, that's great!* "I miss him, Crissy."

"Amanda, listen carefully. Alex is in deep trouble now. He has two states trying to convict him of felonies, and if either succeeds, he'll likely go to prison and we'll all be out of business. I'm telling you, he has strict orders not to contact you. You may likely have to testify against him in court, Amanda. You do realize that, right?"

"Will you get in trouble for talking to me, Crissy?" Amanda inquired, now worried.

"I don't think so. After all, you called me. But I had best not say anything to Tony's dad. Andy has enough on his plate now. I'm not directly involved in any of those conversations, but I have heard enough of the words *witness tampering* connected with Alex being prohibited from reaching out to you."

Amanda was now more emotionally shaken up than before, abet in different ways. "Crissy, could you please tell him I called?... And tell him that I still,... that I'm alone."

The two disconnected and Amanda was quite pleased with herself that she and Alex's sister-in-law had spoken. As much as she wished to just dial up his number, she held back. *The last thing I want to do is hurt him,* she considered as she began to place some of the envelopes back in her father's desk when her curiosity got the best of her. She began to browse through a few other drawers when she found a large brown envelope tagged important personal.

There were various documents enclosed related to family trusts, her parents' will, and so forth. She found a packet of her parents' wedding pictures, matching the main one that was framed atop the family room fireplace. In the file, she also found the original marriage license along with copies of both of their birth certificates, which provoked serious thought. *Oh my god,* Amanda thought as she heard Sarah enter through the garage and rushed to put everything back as if untouched.

Seven weeks following their initial meeting, Alex received a call from Samuel instructing him to return to Flannery's home and to plan on being there for at least two days. In an age of electronic communications, zoom calls, and so forth, Alex felt that everything about Flannery was behind the times, but desperate times called for desperate measures.

"Quite a ride you got there," Samuel complimented, smiling as Alex had driven his NSX down this time.

"Thank you, Samuel. It's grown on me."

The two entered the old mansion and Alex was seated in the den, hearing the distinct sound of Flannery's cane on the hardwood floor approaching.

He stood as the old man entered, still wearing the same light-colored suit, hat, and bow tie as before.

"Sit down, young man," the attorney instructed as he shuffled around his large and cluttered desk and sat down himself, pausing to light up one of his signature thin cigars. "How are things up in the big city?"

"As good as can be expected, sir. Frankly, I've been traveling around quite a bit, different races and such."

"Don't preface a sentence with *frankly*. It implies you are perhaps not *frank* all the time," Flannery lightly scolded as if Alex was his small grandson or someone of the sort.

Alex took the ridicule in stride, recalling a similar rebuke from the last trip.

"We've looked over the specifics of your case, Alex. The evidence is quite damning, I must say."

Alex sat there, unsure if he was to comment, and figured the old man would prompt him when needed.

"You and this Amanda seemed to like Lake Wylie, didn't you?"

"Well, she lived on the southern part of that lake, I lived way up on Lake Norman. She couldn't drive, I had a boat, and it just sort of fit," Alex replied.

"Indeed," Flannery responded back. "You do know that if the two of you would have restricted your boating activities to Lake Norman, you and I would not be having this conversation."

Alex simply looked at him, words at the moment unnecessary.

"Samuel printed out some pictures of Amanda from that social media," Flannery stated as he browsed through a file folder on his desk. "Quite pretty, I must say. Lucky for you, there are few photographs of the two of you on there."

"I wasn't aware there were any. I thought we were very careful about that," Alex stated surprisedly.

Flannery sifted through the folder, suddenly sitting back as if short of breath, and grabbed his chest.

"Oh my god!" Alex yelled as he jumped up out of his chair, quickly moving around the desk to offer aid to the obviously distraught senior citizen. "Samuel, help!"

The assistant promptly ran in with a prescription bottle and a glass of water. "I had these in the bathroom by his shaving bottle. He didn't take them this morning."

"What are those?" Alex asked, calming as the apparent emergency seemed to subside.

"Mr. Flannery's heart medicine. He knows he's supposed to take two every morning without fail," Samuel stated as if lecturing the old man.

The veteran attorney seemed to recover after a few moments. "Enough fuss! Now, where were we?... Oh yes, photographs," he added while grabbing three color prints which he slid over and in front of his young client.

"Oh, yes," Alex said smiling. "I forgot about that." Emotions crept back to him as he reviewed the illustrations of him and Amanda taken at the Indy 500 parade a year and a half earlier. *Yes, Mr. Flannery. She is beautiful.*

"If Amanda was sitting in your chair right there, right now, and I asked her, have you ever had sex with Alex Moretti in the State of South Carolina prior to your sixteenth birthday, what would her answer be?"

Alex felt stressed and thought about his answer. "I don't know what she would say."

"Not yes, or definitely, or for sure?"

"I don't know," Alex replied. "I mean she was like me. We weren't keeping track of it. It wasn't that many times, considering how long we were seeing each other. And that lake is the border between North and South Carolina right there."

"I'm well aware of that, Alex. Samuel, roll out those charts while Alex and I break for some tea.."

Alex had spent a good ten hours with Flannery and his assistant Samuel going over detail after detail of his case, much of it very personal and uncomfortable, warned that much of it would have to be repeated on the witness stand in court and under oath.

He walked down the famous street in old Charleston, entering a corner bar and grill for a light dinner before turning in for the night at a historic hotel. Amanda had often told him about the old city, one of the places she had spent with the family along with Myrtle Beach and Hilton Head. He fantasized about having Amanda here with him, letting her be his guide for a change, and walking with her along the beach nearby, something they had not done since that first night in Long Beach.

His thoughts would then wander to a darker place, as he pondered the old lawyer's question. *What would she say? Her testimony could convict me for up to ten years! She wouldn't do that to me,* he tried to convince himself. But Amanda had not replied to any of his messages in the hospital. *Perhaps she is extremely bitter at me? My lord, the terrible accident, the miscarriage. I don't know. Damned communication blackout!*

Chapter 11

Just Seventeen

The new year had rolled in and Amanda declined her parents' desire to have a large birthday party for her with many of her friends and classmates. She preferred just a small celebration with a few of her very best friends, and Byron noted with an ongoing concern that none were boys.

"It's been almost a year, Sarah! Amanda has to get passed this," Byron stated, mindful not to mention Alex Moretti's name as part of the discussion.

"We should try to give our daughter a normal teenage experience, Byron. Nearly all of her friends have cars. She remembers Allison getting a new car for her seventeenth birthday. Let's get her one. Then your party will go over much better with her."

Byron didn't care for the idea but hesitated in arguing with Sarah about it. It had been such a stressful year in the Cook household and his own relationship with his spouse had taken some major hits. "All right, I'll give Bud a call."

"Why don't we find out what Amanda wants, Byron? We allowed Allison to pick out her own car, that Camaro convertible."

Sarah's initial part in the surprise was to get Amanda out of the house for the afternoon in the guise of shopping and purchasing the girl a birthday present of her own choice. They pulled into the driveway at just past 6:00 PM and entered to a huge "surprise" as the house was crowded with friends and family.

Once birthday wishes and all of the individual birthday gifts were opened, the crowd heard a repeated horn blowing from outside and exited the front door to a shiny new red Mustang convertible, complete with a big gold-colored bow attached to the front of the hood. The entire party jumped with excitement and Amanda, herself, was a bit overwhelmed. Her excitement, however, became quickly subdued and her smile disguised as the driver who had delivered her new car was none other than Kyle Williams.

Throughout the remainder of the evening, Amanda remained extremely uncomfortable around young Williams, thankful that Trisha was there and her best friend went out of her way to run interference for her by constantly pulling her away from Kyle's sphere. Thinking for months that her father's efforts of pushing her on Bud Williams' son had subsided, Amanda suddenly felt new discontent toward her father, the enthusiasm for the new car notwithstanding.

Samuel answered on the second ring, knowing the number had likely pertained to their current case. "Samuel Mayne."

"Mr. Mayne, this is Elizabeth Toney from the York County Circuit Court Clerk's office," she stated, noting that Mayne's name was listed as co-counsel for the defendant on the case in question. "Can you hold for Judge Layton?"

"Certainly, Elizabeth."

A few minutes passed before the judge announced. "Samuel Mayne, is it? This is Janet Layton calling about this yet another request for a court order.... Walmart receipts? Really, Mr. Mayne?"

"If you please, Madam Judge. Mr. Flannery saw something in Discovery that piqued his interest."

"Well, I'm glad something has piqued, but you tell Earnest the next request for a court order or continuance had better have a smoking gun attached to it!" Layton stated in a matter of ridicule. "Request denied!"

"Yes, Madam Judge. I'll be sure and tell him."

Samuel hung up the phone, not looking forward to giving Flannery the bad news. He proceeded to the rear veranda where he looked out back and saw the old man walking around the property, cane in hand. He approached him with that grim expression that Flannery had seen on occasion where words would become unnecessary, but the old man looked up at him smiling.

"Mr. Flannery. Me telling the judge something new had piqued your interest seemed to set her off. She denied the request."

"That's all right, Samuel. And don't tell me, Layton brought up something about a smoking gun," Flannery added chuckling. "It's not my own piqued interest that matters. When Ferrell objects, it'll be hers."

Bryon sat in his office with two financial administrators as they prepared to issue the upcoming end-of-quarter report when the light on his desk phone beeped. "Excuse me, Mr. Cook. I have a Debra Smith from the consumer credit department on line three."

Consumer credit department? Byron thought, slightly annoyed. "Carole, could you take a message? You know I'm in an important meeting."

"I know that, sir, and Miss Smith apologized. But she says it concerns your daughter, Amanda."

Amanda? Consumer credit? He thought seriously. "All right, put it through."

He picked up quickly and asked, "Yes, Miss Smith. What is it?"

"I am so sorry to bother you, sir. I have a deputy sheriff here who handed me a court order requesting copies of some Visa card records. They are all for the accounts assigned to Amanda Cook from June 15th through October 31, 2020. I am in the process of complying but I felt you would wish to know about this," Debbie Smith stated, actually believing she would face his ire if her department had not informed him of it.

"Very well, Miss Smith. Kindly send me copies of whatever you're turning over," he ordered before disconnecting.

"If you folks would pardon me for a short break, I have a couple of calls to make," Byron directed his staff, prior to dialing Edmunds' personal number.

"Yes, Byron."

"James, we just got a court order requesting some bank records for Amanda. Find out what this is all about and get back to me ASAP."

Edmunds had become used to Cook's short demands, which didn't equate to his taking them kindly. "I will holler at my son-in-law over at Ferrell's office and call you back," Edmunds replied, noting that Cook had disconnected on him before his full response was even made.

Just following the lunch hour, the family attorney called the rigid-tempered CEO back. "It's a court order for Amanda's credit or debit card accounts, just for June through October, 2020. Does Amanda even have a credit card?"

"No. She only has a debit account. What's this all about, James?" Byron asked sternly.

"They wouldn't disclose what it was they were after. Probably nothing, Byron. It's all part of the Discovery process. I'm afraid I also have some more bad news."

Byron's temperature began to rise. "Now what?"

"John informed me there has been another six-week continuance for the trial date to begin."

"Are you kidding, James!?" Byron unloaded, beside himself over this ongoing saga. "This will never get resolved!" He then disconnected.

Edmunds heard the call disconnect on his mobile phone, reminding himself that Byron Cook was one of only a select few clients of his having his direct mobile number. *You would think the man could have a little more respect,* he thought shaking his head.

The next morning Byron opened the internal email and examined the attachment which comprised multiple PDF pages. *There's nothing in here that a court should be interested in,* he doubted. *These kids do waste a lot of money,* his last thought before turning the page to more important affairs.

They had moved in on the fourth floor, two women appearing to be in their mid-twenties. One was an Oriental gal while her roommate appeared to be Hispanic, somewhat lighter skinned and perhaps Brazilian. He had only seen the women individually a few times passing each other in the parking garage or in the elevator.

He had a passing curiosity about them as they both appeared to work professionally and drove nice late-model cars. The two were both rather fit and attractive women, and failing to notice any males accompanying either of them, he began to suspect their personal relationship was closer than simply two girls sharing the rent.

Alex busied himself looking through his mail when he heard a knock on the door and had an initial thought, perhaps more of a flashing desire, that it was Amanda. He opened the door and there she stood smiling, the new Oriental neighbor. She wore a short and light silk robe while she appeared barefoot in dark stockings, rather suggestive attire considering the frigid February weather.

"Hello," he greeted smiling, curious about the nature of this late evening visit.

"Hi," she said smiling. "I'm Cher. My roommate and I moved in last month."

"Yes, I believe we've bumped into each other in the parking garage."

"Would you by chance have some extra salt and pepper?" she asked.

"Salt and pepper?" he asked. *It's nearly ten o'clock.* "I probably do. Oh, come on in and get out of the cold."

Cher gracefully strolled in, stopping to look around. "You're that race driver, aren't you?"

"Yes, I'm Alex Moretti... Would you like to sit down while I see if I can find",... he hesitated, losing his train of thought as he couldn't help admiring her very attractive figure,... "some salt and pepper."

The surprise guest sat on his leather couch, looking around and noticing the various plaques and awards on the walls, as well as numerous magazines, all motor racing related, assorted on the coffee table. As their complex housed mostly retirees along with a few mostly middle-aged married couples, her thoughts were of how he stuck out,... as did she.

Alex began to break some silence and casually carried on a conversation with the woman from his kitchen while he searched his cabinetry for the spare inexpensive salt and pepper pack, which he was certain he had somewhere. "So Cher, do you work here locally, or just wanted to live on the lake?"

"A bit of both, really. And you?" Cher asked.

"Oh, our race team relocated down here and"...

He stopped short as he re-entered the front room carrying the salt and pepper pack. She now lounged on the length of his couch, the thinly clad garment she wore now open to expose her small but firm breasts, and a skimpy thong atop stockings covering a pair of very thin and shapely legs.

"Do you have anything to drink,... Mr. Race Driver?"

Alex froze while gathering his thoughts and his next act. He had experienced many young women come on to him in his brief adult life but rarely one so brazen. "Cher, I would offer you a beer, but I must tell you that I am already involved with someone."

"Involved? Is she the race girl, Evelyn Stevens?" Cher inquired, making no effort to alter her erotic physical presentation.

"No, it's not Evelyn. Someone else."

"I see... Well, Alex. She isn't here... Is she?" Cher asked as she stood and approached him, motioning forward for her lips to meet his.

He grabbed her by the shoulders, holding her back. "I'm sorry."

She backed away slowly, smiling as she pulled her silk garment back around herself while backing away toward his door, strangely not appearing disappointed and still wearing a seductive smile. "Perhaps another time, then?" she asked, more of a promise as she walked out his door with Alex watching her depart, noting she had forgotten the salt and pepper, which he had dropped to the floor.

"Did that really just happen?" he asked himself... *Amanda, what have you done to me?* Alex was thinking shaking his head.

Thoughts of the erotic Oriental quickly dispersed when he got to the bottom of the mail pile, stunned by the contents of an envelope from the United States Department of State. The only real tonic he had to treat the immense loneliness and missing Amanda was getting behind the wheel in a race car. Now this remedy had a crushing wrench thrown in it... Due to a court order, his passport had been suspended.

She knew her mother would get an email from school by mid-afternoon reporting her absence. Amanda would tell Sarah she just didn't feel like going to school today and went shopping, as she planned to stop and pick up some new shoes on the way home. Thus, she technically wouldn't be lying to her mom.

Her Google Maps indicated a two-hour and forty-seven-minute drive and she motored down I-77 at seventy-five, thinking she would be there before 11:00 AM. She had called a few days before but received a voicemail box, choosing not to leave a message. The early spring weather was a very pleasant seventy-three degrees and she pulled over at a Columbia exit to open the top and run the last hundred miles with her hair blowing in the wind, smiling and waving slightly as she received her share of complimentary toots of the horn.

Amanda knew her parents would immediately suspect that she would drive up to Lake Norman, and as such she chose a Friday when Alex would be in Mexico for his second World Rally event. Her dad would give her a hard time for even knowing that but she would at least have covering proof that she hadn't been visiting him. It had been weeks since she had spoken to Alex's sister-in-law and was disappointed that she had still not heard from him, but yet understood. *Crissy may not have even told him I called,* she had been thinking and upon reflection, she knew the Morettis were all afraid,... afraid for Alex, and indeed afraid for themselves.

She parked in front, walked up to the large veranda, and knocked on the door. Waiting patiently, a young Hispanic man finally opened. "Good morning," he said pleasantly.

"Good morning. I'm here to see Mr. Flannery," Amanda replied nervously.

The young man looked her up and down. "Please come in, Miss?"

"Cook... Amanda Cook."

"Miss Cook, is Mr. Flannery expecting you this morning?"

"No, I just drove all the way down from York County in hopes of meeting and talking with him," she replied with a pair of big blue sad eyes.

"Please wait here in the parlor and I'll see if Mr. Flannery is available," the young man instructed.

Amanda sat looking around the room which was adorned with high ceilings and ornate wallpaper. The place was nothing like any law office she imagined, giving her the feeling she had stepped back in time,...as in two centuries' time.

Ernest Flannery sat on the rear veranda when his latest intern approached. "Mr. Flannery, there is an Amanda Cook here to see you."

Flannery moved his spectacles a bit lower on his nose, as he looked upward. "Amanda Cook?"

"Yes, sir," his bubbly intern replied. "I swear I think she must be Miss South Carolina or somethin'."

The old lawyer directed Felix to bring her back and Amanda approached two minutes later.

"Hello, Mr. Flannery. I am Amanda Cook. I hope I am not visiting at a bad time." She looked at the old man, who appeared of age to be her great-grandfather.

I'll not stand if you don't mind, but please sit down and join me in some tea. Allow me a moment to clean my glasses," he stated, himself appreciating the beauty of this young Cook woman. "Just so I am clear, you are the Amanda Cook being referenced in this article?"

Amanda's eyes widened as he held up a newspaper in front of her with both she and Alex's picture featured under a headline that read:

TRIAL SET FOR YORK COUNTY STATUTORY RAPE CASE

"Yes, sir. That's me."

"And to what purpose do I owe this pleasure, Miss Cook?"

"I read that you are Alex's new lawyer. I wanted to talk to you about it," she responded.

Flannery paused, looking at her seriously prior to speaking. "Miss Cook, I must inform you that I am the legal counsel for Alex Moretti, and anything we discuss here today may be open to disclosure in a court of law."

"Okay," Amanda answered.

"Now, what can I do for you, young lady?"

"Please, just call me Amanda, Mr. Flannery," she began. "Alex didn't do anything wrong. I never wanted this, sir. Can I just have the charges dropped?"

Flannery listened to her, seeing full well why his famous client was so attracted to her. The sincerity and lovely innocence were striking, the old gentleman thought. "I'm afraid it isn't that simple, you see. The state has strong evidence they possess and believe that proves a felony has been committed."

"Alex never pushed me, Mr. Flannery. If anything, I pushed him."

"I'm afraid the law won't ask for your opinion on that. If the state can prove that my client had sexual relations with you in this state prior to your sixteenth birthday, that is by definition third-degree statutory rape."

Amanda began to get emotional to the point of tears. "If that is the law, then Alex is not the only one breaking it."

Flannery handed her a clean handkerchief and waited for her to compose herself. "Alex has informed me that he doesn't know if you two shared intimacy on the South Carolina side of that river. What would be your testimony on that, Amanda?"

Amanda proceeded to answer as Flannery sat and took notes. "The SG's office subpoenaed your bank credit card records which we were able to examine and received copies of during Discovery. There's a very curious purchase you made on the same date and time you and Alex had dinner at this restaurant, Papa Doc's. Perhaps you could shed some light on it?" Flannery asked as he pointed to the line item in question.

Amanda answered along with other questions during the interview, and finally asked, "Would it cause problems if I contacted Alex, Mr. Flannery?"

"I can tell you care deeply for him, Amanda. I have given him the same advice I will give you now. Do not attempt to have any contact with Alex until this trial is over. The SG's office has gone to great lengths to gather the evidence they have now. Ferrell would not have touched anything this explosive if he wasn't very confident in getting a conviction. You must assume that the both of you will be watched, in effect travel, phone, everything. I would have to assume your visit here today may even be disclosed. Do you understand?"

"No one knows I came down here today, Mr. Flannery. I wish I could just talk to him."

"I would be obliged to instruct any client facing such a serious felony charge to stay totally clear of the alleged victim. But if it makes you feel any better, I believe Alex cares very deeply about you, Amanda."

A half-hour later she departed the old plantation property, heading back north with mixed emotions. She didn't know if her visit was fruitful for Alex's behalf nor had it helped her with some piece of mind, but she had spilled her guts to the old gentleman and would have to live with it come hell or high water.

I had to do something, she kept thinking, though now hearing from Alex's own lawyer how serious things were would make for many more restless nights.

Amanda arrived back home just before her father was getting in himself. Sarah had received the email notice that she had been absent from school, as Amanda told her mother she just didn't feel like going to school and offered no further explanation.

Sarah indeed thought her daughter may likely have driven north to see Alex Moretti, but she chose not to press her on it, nor mention her absence from school to her father.

The Cook dinner table was tense and Sarah's efforts at small talk did little to alleviate that tension as Amanda avoided eye contact with her father, a man who obviously had something on his mind.

This was much the case at their family dinner table ever since the accident over a year prior. Byron constantly suspected that Amanda was still somehow in contact with Alex Moretti, a young man he desperately wanted behind bars.

Sarah wished the whole affair would just go away, including the pending trial, and that her youngest girl could just move on from it all. Both of Amanda's parents appeared to have aged years from the constant stress and bickering, as Sarah tired of her husband reminding her how stable their oldest daughter's life seemed to be in comparison.

"Bud Williams bought out the Honda dealership down in Richburg. He sent me a message that he passed you, Amanda, in your new Mustang on I-77 this afternoon, heading back north toward Rock Hill. I didn't know you knew anyone that far down south," he stated as more of a question.

Amanda hesitated, angry that she still felt as though her dad considered her to be a child. "I just decided to let the top down and take a drive."

"Down the interstate?" Byron asked sternly.

"May I be excused?" Amanda asked as she began to push back from the table.

"I just would like to know what you were doing down there, Amanda. I am your father!"

The table froze while Sarah and Amanda shared looks as if both knew this was a breaking moment that had been brewing.

"I know you think I was with Alex!" Amanda shouted back. "Do you want to know where he is right now? Let me show you." She then pulled her phone from her pocket and opened the racer.com website, featuring an article about the World Rally event in Guanajuato, Mexico. "He's there, three thousand miles from here, Dad."

"Reilly? How did he manage that when his passport has been suspended?"

Amanda hesitated, obviously not knowing that fact. "I knew you would accuse me of seeing him, so I pulled the information up online. I did not drive to Davidson, North Carolina!"

"You're not going talk to me like that, Amanda!" Byron yelled as he stood up abruptly, nearly knocking over his chair.

"What are you going to do, Dad, ground me for life!?" she screamed back.

"Amanda! That's enough," Sarah interjected. "I think you should go to your room."

The two adults watched as their daughter scrambled out of the dining room and up to the second floor. This was the first time in all of her seventeen years that Amanda had lost it like that with either of her parents.

"I think we had best keep that convertible in the garage for a while," Byron said, still nearly shaking. "I hope to God this trial doesn't get any more delays. Maybe then our lives will get back to normal, Sarah."

She began to clear the table on her own, not waiting for the housemaid nor looking at him while he stood there. "You think so, Byron?"

"Whose side are you on, Sarah?"

"I'm on the side of my family, Byron," she replied quickly. "I know what side you're on. You had better start thinking about whose side your daughter is on."

Herrera smiled after he'd hit par on the ninth hole. He and Wally Remington piled into their golf cart as they motored toward the next tee-off box. Since the accident in Vegas, the man responsible for the Unibank-Moretti sponsorship deal had kept his head down regarding direct communication with CEO Cook, and he now reported directly to Remington, a man recently promoted to Chief Financial Officer, and now responsible for all corporate expenditures. As the VP of Marketing, Herrera had an ongoing mission to justify the cost of Unibank involvement in motor racing, a job more tenuous since the accident, at least in the mind of their CEO.

It was noteworthy that Byron Cook was facing uncomfortable pressure by other members of the board while the lawsuit between Unibank and Moretti Motorsports dragged on and on, and the overbearing sympathetic press coverage toward the Cooks had subsided. The Unibank logos were still circling the world's race tracks on Andy Moretti's cars since he had long since removed his son, Alex, from the team, and Amanda Cook had fully recovered from the accident appearing none the worse for wear, at least physically.

Moreover and quite ironically, the extra publicity that was generated worldwide had actually been a boost to Unibank's business. Whether due to sympathy for the Cooks, newfound support for team Moretti, or coincidentally the maturity of Evelyn Stevens' popularity, Unibank had gained consumer customers steadily since the accident occurred.

Led by Marilyn Forsythe, some on the board were calling for the lawsuit between Unibank and Moretti Motorsport to be dropped altogether considering the ongoing legal expenses, claiming Unibank was throwing good money after bad, and even dropping subtle hints that Cook should step down as CEO due to his ongoing emotional state being detrimental to overall corporate interests.

"You're going to have fifteen minutes in front of the board Monday, Adam. You know Byron would like nothing more than to kill the entire motor racing program," Remington stated. "Be on point, but not argumentative."

"I'll have a detailed presentation ready, sourcing data from three solid market analysis groups. I'm still waiting on the SCX Report, but the program looks really good Wally," Herrera replied, knowing his reputation and indeed entire career hedged on the success, be it perceived, of Unibank's motorsports initiative.

Remington was quite nervous, in fact. He had been the one who had pushed to promote Adam Herrera as the head of the marketing department, thus his young protégé's actions would always reflect on him, up or down. He also knew a fine line needed to be walked as he did not want his old friend and associate, Byron Cook, to be exposed which would open the door for a longtime rival, Marilyn Forsythe, to possibly replace him.

The quarterly board meeting was called to order at 10;00. Wally Remington gave an overall presentation on the past quarter's performance, covering each segment of their business from commercial finance to personal checking and savings revenues, followed by regions geographically. Always strong in the American South, the board was pleased that growth in other markets where they had been weak, or in some cases non-existent, was growing at a steady pace. He then proceeded to give the other Division VPs the floor for a few minutes to present their own reports which included some heady Q&A.

At 2;30 Adam Herrera appeared and presented his report, fine-tuned on PowerPoint like all the others. Being a sales and marketing guy by trade, his presentation had added sizzle and included samples of the various Unibank video commercials being run. With the increased revenues the bank had enjoyed over the past few years, his budget had increased in concert and he summarized the costs for each segment.

The great irony was that most advertising segments had substantial cost increases with the exception of their advertising in motor racing, which remained substantial but had increased nominally in the past two years in spite of the excellent return. Every board member could not keep from beaming at the various Evelyn Stevens commercials which were aided in no small measure by the North American growth in Formula One, even though Stevens was not the driver of the Unibank-BP F1 car. Adam emphasized that Unibank was getting a huge bonus on commercials Stevens performed for other totally separate products such as insurance, physical health products, and makeup, as the flashy Unibank race cars were always there in the background, giving Unibank massive exposure while costing them nothing. Cook wanted to crunch his teeth every time Marilyn

Forsythe would wax enthusiasm and compliment Herrera on what was quite brilliant on his part.

The announcement was made during a press conference at the US Grand Prix in Austin. It shook the world of motorsports in a fashion unlike anything since the deaths of Ayrton Senna and Dale Earnhardt decades earlier.

The Monaco Grand Prix, long considered the crown jewel of Formula One, would not be held the following year due to financial issues unresolved between the Monaco monarchy and the US-based corporate ownership of Formula One. Critics had claimed for years the circuit to be obsolete for modern Formula One cars, and its lack of passing zones had made the race appear too much as a parade.

Given the municipality was such a staple for Formula One, indeed many drivers past and present resided there, the decision had shaken much of the establishment to the core. For years, the monarchy had paid no sanction fees while some nations were now having to fork out tens of millions of dollars to get F1 to show up. Other nations were waiting in the wings with cash in hand but the packed schedule had limited consideration for open expansion.

While many pundits had claimed that a high-stakes game of chicken was being played out by both sides over the course of many months, it was a foregone conclusion in most circles that a deal would get done. However, negotiations failed to reach an agreement and the late announcement forbade any possibility of replacing the Grand Prix on the traditional late May weekend. Requests for additional comments from the monarchy or the new Formula One ownership executive representatives had yet to be released, other than to state that a deal couldn't be reached and the race would not be held during the upcoming season.

Within no time, articles began appearing throughout the motor racing media speculating on whether certain Formula One drivers would be competing in the Indy 500, as both the qualifying and race weekends for the American Memorial Day classic would now be open on the F1 schedule.

The sports media began a frenzy of promoting, denying, and speculating about all of the different teams and drivers' plans for a rare one-off influx of F1 drivers at Indy, most of whose contracts forbade, but made for good social media fodder nonetheless.

Andy and his NASCAR team manager, Myles Delcanton, had breakfast with Roger Penske and Tim Cindric, Team Penske President, at the Wynn Resort Hotel, all in town for the NASCAR Cup Series race weekend at the Las Vegas Motor Speedway.

As the IndyCar season had concluded in September, Moretti Motorsport and similarly, Team Penske, were now focusing more on the home stretch of the NASCAR season. Penske driver, Austin Cindric, who was Tim's son, was in a strong battle for the NASCAR Cup Championship, which would cap off a breakout year that started with victory in the Daytona 500.

To the consternation of all involved, most of the media attention in Las Vegas, even among the rest of the NASCAR teams, was dwelling on the Alex Moretti court case, and less on the preferred focus of the NASCAR driver's championship. *The Captain* was a man always concerned about image, indeed his white-collar approach to Gasoline Alley in Indianapolis had literally changed the sport, had mixed feelings about the entire affair. While some were of the opinion that Alex Moretti had cast a dark cloud over his series, it couldn't be ignored that the worldwide press had brought added attention to the sport of motor racing in general.

While many racing venues still struggled to fill seats, and indeed some tracks had gradually removed some whole stands, network and cable TV ratings were up as were online streaming customers. The post-Covin uptick had been largely credited to Evelyn Stevens' popularity, but recent marketing analysis revealed much of the increase was directly attributed to the Moretti-Unibank saga and the media's newfound obsession with it.

Another phenomenon was the accompanying coverage and interest in alternate series, such as sprint cars, often referred to as *outlaws,* and the World Rally Series, There was a common denominator that was arguably connected to these recent successes – *Alex Moretti.*

To that extent, the news regarding the Formula One race in Monte Carlo was welcome news to Roger Penske, Indianapolis Speedway President Doug Boles, and company, recalling the added international interest in the Indianapolis 500 when Fernando Alonzo had shown up a few years before, a man who quickly announced his intention to pursue a ride following the recent F1 news.

"I know you'll have a ride for Tony," *The Captain* stated. "What about Leland?"

"I haven't seriously discussed it with him, yet," Andy replied. "I'm not certain Honda and Dallara can step up on such short notice. What are you getting from the Chevy people?"

"I spoke to them briefly and I think I have them thinking. I know both Chevy and Honda see this as a huge PR opportunity, as do I. Pity this couldn't happen the following year with Ford coming back in," Roger added, knowing the upcoming year would be a rare opportunity for the 500 as Formula One would either resolve the issues with Monte Carlo or have an alternative race on the calendar for the following year. He had visions of the 500 back in the 1960s, when Team Penske was still developing and first entered a car with Mark Donohue. Many of the Grand Prix stars in Formula One came *across the pond* and raced against the best Indycar drivers, along with NASCAR legends like Cale Yarborough and the Allisons. Unfortunately, supplies of chassis and engines were limited in the modern era and may not accommodate too many guest drivers, although the thought of the packed stands for Pole Day and Bump Day at the speedway were still pleasant to contemplate.

The underlying issue hanging over the Las Vegas racing community in general was the pending involuntary manslaughter case against Alex Moretti, on a perpetual hold because of the state's election for Attorney

General, which was just three weeks away. Moretti had pleaded no contest and paid a $305 fine for his part in the accident, which would likely settle things in Nevada should Juanita Martinez win the election, due to her personal views and political pressure from the pro-choice lobby. Should her opponent win, all bets were off and Alex would face yet another legal challenge, as though his plate was not full enough already.

Aaron Williams was a big NASCAR fan and flew out to Vegas for the weekend, taking advantage of the opportunity to spend a weekend with his fiancée, Allison Cook, who flew in from LA and had reached out to Adam Herrera who arranged VIP Garage Passes for the two. The couple showed up at the track on Saturday to more than a few stunned whispers in the garage area,

"Let's go, we get a free brunch at the Moretti hospitality tent," Allison stated arrogantly.

"You are joking, right?" Aaron replied. "I thought you and your family despised that outfit."

"Come on, Aaron. Don't be a wimp," Allison chided. "We'll have that whole place squirming."

They entered the hospitality area and were indeed met with a stunned silence for a moment. The only representative of Unibank there was Adam Herrera, sitting there with Evelyn Stevens and her agent, Louis Newberry. Ignoring the many uncomfortable stares, Allison led Aaron past several tables to where Herrera and Stevens were sitting.

"Why Evelyn, I'm surprised to see you here," Allison observed. "You're not driving, are you?"

"No, I'm just here as a guest, supporting the team. I didn't expect to see you here, either," Stevens added, of the belief that Allison knew her presence would pinch some nerves, but obviously seemed to relish in it.

"We're here on business," Newberry interjected. "We were in Austin for the Grand Prix, and I arranged for Evelyn to show up here for some local engagements this weekend. This town is buzzing about the prospects of the new F1 race here."

The five sat and chatted over brunch. Herrera was the one individual who was quite uncomfortable as he had become very close friends with both Andy Moretti and NASCAR team manager Mike Delcanto, knowing how they would take this surprise incursion. Allison picked up on the fact that a new contract was in order for Evelyn, as Newberry bragged about his part in structuring the original deal with Unibank, including exclusions and options related solely to his client.

As Evelyn had a breakout year, indeed nearly winning the Indycar Championship, Newberry had planted seeds with two other teams that she may be available and could bring some Unibank dollars with her. Herrera was well aware of this and quite nervous, knowing there were other sponsors chomping at the bit to grab Stevens. Should she bail to another team and sponsor, his entire support from the Unibank board would collapse along with his upward career there.

"We would prefer to keep Evelyn in the Moretti camp," Adam stated, not adding that having Stevens appear in their advertisements for Formula One was viewed as priceless by nearly the entire Unibank board. "We're meeting in Huntersville in three weeks to iron this out."

Allison picked up on that quickly. "We'll be in town then for Aaron's five-year high school reunion. Perhaps we could get together for a night out. Why don't you text me, Louie, and let me know where you and Evelyn are staying?" Allison directed before giving Newberry her phone number and collecting his.

Adam and Aaron shared an uncomfortable look, knowing Allison had already shared calls and texts with Evelyn for quite some time. The inappropriate gesture of openly giving out her number to another guy was of no consequence to the very forward woman, a trait Aaron despised but said nothing.

Following the scene at the Moretti NASCAR trailer, Aaron and Allison took a shuttle back into town and back to the Rio where they were staying. With a few hours remaining prior to dinner, one in which they had invited

Evelyn and Newberry to join them, Aaron was hot to trot to jump his long-time girlfriend's bones again, an itch she was all too willing to scratch.

Two hours later, Allison showered while Aaron sat in the suite hot tub following a very long session in bed. He was proud of himself for having satisfied his fiancée's physical needs following weeks of being apart. Allison played along as always, laughing to herself in the shower, while always believing she was much too precious to ever be the sole lover of one man.

She would soon marry Aaron Williams which would make her father happy, placing herself in a good position to inherit his estate, particularly since her younger sister was on such a downward progression to fall out of favor with him totally. Aaron would inherit no less than eighteen car dealerships, and should he ever tire of her personal proclivities, she would simply divorce him and walk away with millions.

Chapter 12

Trial of the Century

York County Circuit Court, Rock Hill, South Carolina

The local news reporter prompted her cameraman to approach a bit closer, as she had headlined her biggest story ever, competing with space on the courthouse lawn with well-known journalists worldwide. The expected ESPN and Fox Sports contingent were there, but also crews from the Associated Press, the New York Times, Reuters, and the BBC to name a few.

"Hello, this is Melissa Townsend reporting to you live from the York County Circuit Courthouse in Rock Hill, South Carolina, where the much-anticipated and delayed trial of Alex Moretti enters what's expected to be its next phase following an exhaustive jury selection. At issue facing Mr. Moretti, the exiled race driver and son of racing legend, Andy Moretti, are the charges of third-degree statutory rape of then fifteen-year-old Amanda Cook. Miss Cook is ironically the youngest daughter of Byron Cook, the well-known and respected CEO of Unibank Corporation, headquartered in nearby downtown Charlotte, and the major sponsor funding Moretti Motorsport.

The final verdict could have far-reaching implications beyond this criminal case and one that could land Alex Moretti in prison for up to ten years. Even though a maximum sentence is not expected, a guilty verdict would impact other large civil lawsuits pending and affect the highly volatile relationship between Unibank and Moretti Motorsport, the very prominent race team based just north of Rock Hill in Huntersville, North Carolina. We will be keeping you up-to-date on this very important and emotional trial as it develops. Back to you, Brian."

The courtroom was packed and many would-be observers were turned away. The entire Cook family was in attendance with an abundance of associates and friends, while the Morettis were also well represented with nearly half of the Moretti team staff along with other prominent members of the motor racing community, including Dale Earnhardt, Jr. and Chip Ganassi to name a few. Seated behind the Cooks were the Williams family, Bud and his wife Lisa, as well as their two sons, Aaron and Kyle, with Allison Cook seated beside the oldest son, both of whom had taken off from school a few days to be home for a high school reunion, and attend what was expected to be a very explosive trial. The whole town was tense with many knowing the Cooks quite well, as well as the prominent Williams family who had such a close connection with the Cooks.

Judge Janet Layton pounded the gavel to call the court to order. "In the case of the State of South Carolina versus Alessandro Moretti, the defendant is charged in violation of the state criminal code 16-3-654, Third Degree Statutory Rape of a Minor. The defendant has entered a plea of Not Guilty as Charged. Is the Solicitor General prepared to proceed?"

"We are, Your Honor."

"Mr. Moretti, you are represented by Mr. Ernest Flannery. Mr. Flannery, have you prepared a defense?"

"We have, Your Honor."

"Very well, then," Judge Layton stated. "The prosecution will make its opening statement."

The Sixteenth Circuit Solicitor General, Brad Ferrell, had chosen to handle the high-profile case personally and stood before the court, outlining the evidence against the defendant and the state's plan to call witnesses to corroborate that evidence, all in order to prove beyond any reasonable doubt the guilt of the defendant.

Ernest Flannery followed with his opening, driving home the fact of the jury deciding the guilt or innocence of the specific state statute, an attempt to draw a line in the sand against the SG's effort to try the defendant for any and all outside incidents.

Having concluded the opening statements, Judge Layton instructed Ferrell to call his first witness.

"The state calls to the stand Miss Serena O'Gara."

The courtroom was silent as a tall, shapely, and well-dressed young woman walked down the center aisle and up toward the bench where she was sworn in and seated.

Ferrell smiled as he approached. "Miss O'Gara, could you please state your full name and address for the record."

"Serena O'Gara, 651 East 8th Street, Charlotte, North Carolina."

"According to the record, you were employed as a waitress at Papa Doc's Shore Club in Lake Wylie, South Carolina, on July 25th, 2020. Is that correct?" Ferrell asked.

"Yes, I was."

"Miss O'Gara, do you recall back on that date speaking to the defendant, Alex Moretti?"

"Yes, I waited on him and Amanda."

"That would be Amanda Cook?"

"Yes, it was."

Ferrell retreated to his desk and returned toward the witness box with a piece of paper, handing it to the witness. "Miss O'Gara, does this receipt look familiar to you?"

"It looks like one of our tickets we used at Papa Doc's."

"Your Honor, I would like to submit into evidence Prosecution Exhibit 9B, a receipt for a meal and drinks dated July 25th, 2020, retrieved by the Solicitor General's office via subpoena," Ferrell stated confidently.

Upon review, Judge Layton declared, "Without objection, the evidence will be entered into the record."

"Now, Miss O'Gara, do you recall what time it was that day when you last saw Mr. Moretti and Miss Cook?" Ferrell added while glancing toward the jury.

"It was just before midnight when we were closing. They were on his boat which was tied up in one of our slips."

"Did you see the boat back out of that slip, as if leaving?"

"No, he had asked me if he could stay there for the night. I told him I doubted anyone would hassle them about it," she replied.

"And did you actually see them physically that late?"

"Yes. His boat is one of those cabin cruiser types. I saw them inside through the small windows."

"It must have been quite dark there, Miss O'Gara. How is it that you recall that so vividly?" Ferrell asked in an attempt to preempt the anticipated questioning from Moretti's attorney.

"Yes, it was dark, but the cabin lights inside were on, which made it quite easy to see inside," she responded.

"And was there anything distinctive that piqued your interest?"

"Yes. They were naked and"....

"She's lying!" Amanda screamed from her seat behind the SG's desk. She then broke into tears and buried her head into her mother's chest.... "She's lying, Mom," Amanda repeated in a whisper.

The courtroom crowd erupted as Judge Layton pounded the gavel. "Order in the court!... Miss Cook, you will compose yourself or I will have you removed from this proceeding. Is that clear, young lady!?"

Amanda struggled to compose herself and looked up toward the judge, giving a slight nod.

"Miss Cook, is that clear?" The judge repeated, not satisfied with a simple gesture.

"Yes," Amanda replied while throwing Alex a brief glance.

"Proceed, Mr. Ferrell," the judge continued.

"Now, Miss O'Gara, I'm sure the jury, and no doubt Mr. Moretti and his lawyer, are quite curious how it is that you could make that declaration of two individuals naked in a boat after dark when the area where you work is many feet away from where Mr. Moretti's boat was docked. Would you please explain?"

"Well, he is quite famous since he was Evelyn Stevens' boyfriend and all. I'll admit that as we were closing I couldn't help but stroll down the dock for a closer look," O'Gara replied lowly, looking straight toward the jury as careful not to catch a stare from Alex Moretti or Amanda Cook.

"Miss O'Gara. speak up and clearly into the microphone and repeat, please," Judge Layton ordered.

"I was curious since he was so famous. I couldn't help myself and walked down the dock and up to his boat, as we were closing."

"No more questions, Your Honor," Ferrell stated and strolled back to his seat.

"Mr. Flannery, do you wish to cross-examine this witness?" Judge Layton inquired.

"Yes, Your Honor," Flannery replied. He and Alex shared some whispering talk. Then Flannery turned and consulted quietly with Samuel before standing and approaching the witness.

"Miss O'Gara, what time was it when you first waited on my client and Miss Cook?"

"I think it was probably around 8:00 PM or so," she replied.

"Now, the receipt Mr. Ferrell produced a while ago had a date and time stamped at 8:43 PM," Flannery inquired. "Would that be the time when you checked out Mr. Moretti?"

"If that's what the receipt has on it," O'Gara answered.

"You testified earlier that you saw Mr. Moretti and Miss Cook at just around midnight, correct?"

The witness looked toward Ferrell, hesitating before answering.

"Miss O'Gara, would you like for me to repeat the question?" Flannery asked politely.

"We close at 11:00 and take an hour to clean up. So, it would have been right about then," she replied.

"If you checked Mr. Moretti out at 8:43, but did not close until 11:00 PM, did he and Miss Cook hang around all that time after he paid his tab?"

"No, they left and went out to his boat after that," she stated.

"Miss O'Gara, you have made a couple of references to *his* boat. How did you know that it was *his* boat?" Flannery asked.

"I guess I just assumed it. Usually, it is the guys who own them."

"Is it fair to say, Miss O'Gara, that there was a period of at least two hours when you would have lost sight of them?"

"My section was the tables out overlooking the dock. So I could see all of the guests' boats there."

Flannery shuffled around a bit, scratching his head. "I wasn't inquiring about the boat, Miss O'Gara. Can you confidently state right here, in front of God and this court, that you never lost sight of either Mr. Moretti or Miss Cook the entire time between 8:43 PM and midnight?"

"Well, I didn't actually follow them around the whole time," she answered while appearing flustered.

"How many dock slips are there at Papa Docs?"

"O'Gara quickly stared upward as if thinking. "About twenty, I believe."

Flannery looked toward Samuel and nodded who approached the floor with an easel and a large poster-sized image on it.

"Miss O'Gara, this is a recent aerial photograph of the Papa Doc's establishment. Would you agree with that?"

"Yes, that's Papa's," she replied.

Positioning the easel between the witness stand and jury box so the entire courtroom could review it, Flannery instructed, "Miss O'Gara, using my cane here, could you please point out for the jury which slip was occupied that night by Mr. Moretti's boat?"

Serena grabbed the cane and tapped on the end outer slip, which Flannery repeated, repossessing his cane and tapping on the poster-sized photo in the same spot. "So, that one right there?"

"Yes," she answered.

Flannery stood back and nodded at Samuel, who replaced the poster-sized image on the easel with another. "Now, Miss O'Gara. Does this photograph appear familiar to you?"

"It looks like another picture taken from Papa Doc's," she responded.

"This was taken by my assistant, Samuel Mayne, in August of last year, from one of the outside tables at Papa Doc's. Would you say this is a fair representation of what a customer of Papa Doc's would see when looking out toward the boat slips?"

"Yes, it would."

Flannery nodded at Samuel, who promptly approached the easel with a replacement poster-sized photograph.

"And the second photo was taken the same day but two hours later. Would you say this, Miss O'Gara, is a fair representation of what a customer of Papa Doc's would see when looking out toward the boat slips near dusk?" Flannery asked while pointing toward the easel with his cane.

"Yes, it would," she answered solemnly.

"Do you recall about how many boats were moored there at around 8:43 PM that night?"

She thought a moment. "I would say, fifteen or so."

"Fifteen or so?"

"Yes, about that."

"Could it have been twelve boats?" he asked with a look of genuine curiosity.

"Maybe, she replied. I didn't count"....

"Objection Your Honor!" Ferrell yelled as he rose. "Does this court really expect this witness to recall how many boats were in attendance where she worked at 8:43 PM, on a night over two years ago?"

"Sustained," the Judge ruled. "Get to your point, Mr. Flannery."

"So, Miss O'Gara, it's fair to say that most of the boat slips at Papa Doc's were taken at the time you checked out Mr. Moretti and Miss Cook?

"Yes, we were busy."

Flannery walked back to the defense table and made a scene out of seriously studying some notes pushed forward to the edge of the table by Samuel, before strolling back toward the witness stand.

"During your earlier deposition, Miss O'Gara, you testified that you had waited on Alex Moretti and Amanda Cook. Do you recall the content of your conversation with her?"

"Objection, Your Honor!" Ferrell declared loudly. "The state has established the defendant and Miss Cook were present at the witness's place of employment on the date specified. Is chit-chat between Miss Cook and her waitress really pertinent to this case?"

"I'm simply trying to qualify the full credibility of the witness, Your Honor. I would ask for some leeway here," Flannery defended.

"I'll overrule the objection. Make sure the point of this questioning is made valid, Mr. Flannery."

"Thank you, Your Honor.... Miss O'Gara?"

"Could you repeat the question?"

"Miss O'Gara, you testified that you had first waited on Alex and Amanda around 8:00 and that you checked them out at 8:43. In that timeframe, did you have any conversation with Amanda Cook while she was sitting there?"

"Not so much. She had on a wide-brim hat and big sunglasses, and she sort of kept looking away from me. He did most of the talking," she stated.

"And when you say she, you are speaking about Amanda Cook, am I correct?"

"Yes, sir."

Flannery made a movement toward the jury box as to clear the view between O'Gara and the courtroom attendees. "Is Amanda Cook in attendance here today?"

The jury members all looked at Flannery, thinking it a strange question, as did Ferrell and Judge Layton as well as the entire courtroom at large, particularly in the aftermath of Amanda's outburst just moments earlier.

"Well, certainly. She is right there sitting behind those two lawyers," O'Gara stated as she pointed toward Ferrell and his associate.

Flannery removed a handkerchief from his suit pocket and made a gesture to clean his glasses. "I'm sorry. Just for my clarification, I believe Amanda Cook and her sister, Allison, are seated one in front of the other in the first two rows. Would you please state which of the rows you are referring to, Miss O'Gara?"

Ferrell whispered to his Associate SG, both seated at the prosecution table. "What's that old bird up to?" A question replied to with a shrug of the shoulders.

"It would be the first row."

"Thank you," Flannery replied chuckling. "My eyesight is not what it used to be. No more questions for the witness at this time, Your Honor."

"You may step down, Miss O'Gara," Layton stated. "Mr. Ferrell, your next witness."

"The state calls Mr. Alessandro Moretti to the witness stand your honor."

The courtroom was filled with hushed chatter as Alex, dressed in his finest blue suit and tie, approached the bench and was sworn in.

The state's attorney went through the standard motions of getting the witness's full name and address for the record prior to his questioning. "Mr. Moretti, how long have you known the victim?"

"Objection, your honor!" Flannery stood abruptly and stated, raising his cane straight up toward the ceiling, a motion that would become his signature throughout the trial. "The court has not established the existence of a victim in this case."

"Objection sustained. You will rephrase your question, Mr. Ferrell."

"Of course, Your Honor," Ferrell acknowledged, not questioning the objection but wanting to establish that term with the jury, nevertheless.

"Mr. Moretti, how long have you known Amanda Cook?"

It had been considered a possibility that Alex would simply take the *Fifth*, but surprised many when he willingly began his testimony. "It would be two years this past March," Alex replied.

"And during the initial introduction, were you aware that Miss Cook was barely fifteen years of age?"

"'Yes. She did inform me of that."

"But despite of that fact, you engaged in a romantic relationship with her anyway. Is that correct?" Ferrell continued.

"It wasn't despite"...

"Please, Mr. Moretti just answer the question yes or no. You chose to engage in a romantic relationship with her anyway, correct?" Ferrell continued.

"Objection, your honor! Flannery jumped up again. "There is no evidence that my client engaged in a relationship with Miss Cook despite her age, to quote Mr. Ferrell."

"Overruled, Mr. Flannery," the Judge stated. "I'm sure that may or may not be established through the witness's testimony.... Mr. Flannery, are you all right?"

The old attorney seemed to appear lost for a few seconds before falling backward into his seat and collapsing while holding his chest. Both Samuel and Alex rushed to gather around the stricken senior while the remainder of the courtroom sat in shocked horror as Moretti's attorney was having what appeared to be a heart attack. The judge quickly ordered the bailiff to call for an ambulance before pounding the gavel and calling for a trial recess until ten o'clock the following morning.

At 10:00 AM the following morning, the court gathered for the trial to reconvene, only to learn that Earnest Flannery had indeed had a severe cardiac arrest and remained in an intensive care unit at a local hospital. Judge Layton announced the court would recess until such time as the defendant's attorney had sufficiently recovered or that alternative counsel could be assigned and properly prepared.

Louis Newberry arrived on Friday with his typical show of being a big shooter. He had been not so subtle in reaching out to more than one competitive racing team regarding their interest in Evelyn Stevens, all of whom were intrigued if not fully enthusiastic as most every Indycar outfit had secured their driver line-ups for the following season.

He had arranged dinner on Friday evening at Bricktop's, one of Charlotte's finest dining establishments, with Adam Herrera and his two clients, Evelyn Stevens and Jon David Hill, along with last-minute guests, Allison Cook and her fiancé, Aaron Williams.

The courtroom drama regarding Alex Moretti's attorney was the initial buzz of the engagement, along with the final contract signings for Stevens and Hill, scheduled for the following Wednesday morning. With the effects of a bit too many cocktails, Newberry was quite open to some of his negotiating ploys, somewhat to Hill and Steven's embarrassment. Like everyone else in sports, she wanted the best deal she could get from her employer, but she had developed a strong sense of loyalty to Moretti Motorsport despite her failed romance with Alex, and fully expected to continue there and compete for next season's series championship.

Newberry had lobbied privately that his prized client separate her professional relationship with Hill, as the condition that any prospective team owner provide a second ride for him as part of any deal involving Stevens had become quite a barrier for doing business. The other overriding issue was Stevens' Formula One connection, namely her continuance in producing ads featuring the Unibank badged F1 cars, gold in the eyes of the sponsor. He had reached out to Zac Brown to explore interest in her, as McLaren was the only other Indycar team in the paddock involved with Formula One, but their stable of drivers was fully set and Brown answered with a thanks, but no thanks, as he already had plans for one or two guest drivers from F1, available now due to the Monaco situation.

Evelyn's former team, IndyWest, certainly lacked the wherewithal to accommodate all of Unibank's requirements, but with some added sponsorship revenue could provide a competitive Indycar package. Santos had bought out Lynch lock, stock, and barrel since Stevens had departed three years prior and had upgraded the team in every aspect from facility to equipment to personnel. When Newberry had reached out toward the end of the season, what began as talks that were little more than fantasy had turned quite serious. Other than the lack of the F1 connection, Santos was offering triple the retainer money for Stevens than Moretti had been paying.

All throughout dinner, Allison observed with a scheming curiosity, noticing that Adam Herrera had little input, which was a surprise since he represented the money behind Unibank. If anything, he seemed a bit too timid in exploring options, and Allison saw this as an opportunity,... and a huge one at that.

The topic of the trial and the overall legal feud between the Morettis and Allison's father was discussed only briefly at the family dinner table on Sunday as Sarah kept shooting her husband and oldest daughter unpleasant stares, knowing Amanda was quite on edge about it.

After dinner, Allison entered her father's den where he sat alone nursing a glass of Jim Beam. She had always displayed her *Rebecca of Sunnybrook Farm* face in front of her dad, a complete ruse that a normally astute Byron Cook had always been blind to.

"How is the legal suit going between the bank and Moretti, Dad?" she asked feigning concern and empathy.

"As slow as molasses, I'm afraid. Once that young son-of-a-bitch, Alex, is behind bars, it should move forward quickly," Byron stated, happy that he had at least one member of the family who seemed to be on his side and needing some good news, following the bad news out of Nevada that Juanita Martinez had won the election for State Attorney General and her own assistant would be taking over as District Attorney in Clark County. Any action on prosecuting Moretti in Vegas on a vehicular manslaughter charge was simply not going to happen.

"Is it true that Evelyn Stevens is open to signing on with another team next year?" Allison asked.

"Where did you hear that?" her father asked.

"I overheard Adam Herrera and her agent, Louis Newberry, talking about it over dinner last night," she replied, knowing that would pique his interest.

"Herrera, huh?" Byron asked for confirmation.

"Yes, Dad. Adam believes Newberry is just playing him and Andy Moretti, though."

"Did he tell you that?"

"Not in so many words, but everyone knew it," Allison added, thinking of a new angle. "With you being the boss, maybe you should throw some weight at it, Dad. Newberry was claiming that Evelyn has a full option to drive for another team next year. That would surely torpedo Moretti Motorsport, would it not?" Allison asked, as though just curious.

"Yes,... yes, it just might," Byron observed smiling at his daughter, who was working on a postgraduate degree in marketing. "Maybe Adam Herrera should be working for you," he added, only half-joking. "Perhaps I should have another assistant whom I have confidence in reviewing these options." *And I have the perfect candidate in mind,* he pondered smiling.

Late that evening, Newberry received a text, one that rapidly opened his eyes. *"Meet me in your hotel lounge in thirty minutes. I have something important to discuss with you. Be alone."* It was from Allison Cook.

True to form, she later walked in and spied Newberry sitting alone at the end of the bar. Being a Sunday night, there were few patrons in the lounge catching the NFL game, their attention refocused momentarily as she approached him smiling. She straddled the bar stool adjacent to the wide-eyed Louie, discarding her lengthy coat on the empty stool next to her, revealing a short leather skirt and crossing her legs facing him, an act that had always worked to pique a male's interest.

"I must say, Allison, this is a pleasant surprise," Newberry stated. "How was the reunion last night?"

"It was a hoot... Order me a Martini," Allison replied, conscious of the time and not wanting to be seen with this bellowing slubber any longer than necessary.

"And Aaron?" Newberry asked, having a genuine curiosity that the beautiful Allison Cook would be here in a hotel bar with him, a good forty-minute drive into downtown Charlotte from Tega Cay on a Sunday night.

"He left this afternoon to head back to California. He has to report first thing tomorrow morning," she replied as her fiancé was now a US

Marine lieutenant assigned to San Diego. "How final is your deal with Andy Moretti?"

Newberry leaned back a bit, taken off guard by the unsubtle question. "Most of the specifics have been agreed to and we're to meet in his office Wednesday morning to wrap this thing up."

"I thought you were still talking with that Santos gentleman," she replied quickly.

"I have been. But Santos was mostly just a bargaining chip used to get a much better deal out of Moretti," Newberry boasted.

"What if Santos could beat Moretti's offer? There would be some interested parties who would really like to see Evelyn Stevens drive for her old team again."

"There are always interested parties, Allison. But you know the old saying, money talks and bullshit walks."

"Oh, that's funny," she replied giggling. *What a pompous ass.*

"Without mentioning names, Louie, there are some really influential people who do not want Evelyn driving for Moretti Motorsport. There may be something special in it for you if you could engineer a deal with Indywest," Allison stated with that mischievous smile of hers as she placed her right hand on his left thigh. "Shall we adjourn to somewhere more private while I share some details with you?"

Newberry was smitten as he called for the bartender to bring forth his tab as he and his evening guest got up to leave. Allison walked out with him in escort fashion while neither of them paid much attention to the small dark-haired woman sitting quietly in the corner, one sporting a large hat and dark glasses to dissuade unwanted recognition. She also paid her tab and promptly departed a few paces behind them.

Just past midnight, Allison was in Newberry's suite bathroom in front of the vanity to freshen herself up a bit prior to departing. He came up behind her, placing his hands on her shoulders, and began to kiss around her neck.

She hoped he wouldn't notice her eyes being shut a bit too tight as her skin crawled.

"You are quite certain that Adam Herrera will play ball, Allison?"

"If I said he will, he will," she replied, angry that he would still question her and anxious to get dressed and out the door.

"I'm so happy that you and I will be working so closely together," Louie stated softly as he moved his palm down to get one more feel of her shapely rear end. "And when will this bonus be wired into my account?"

Again, she was incensed at his implied mistrust. *Getting me in bed for nearly an hour should be bonus enough for a pig like you, Louie!* "I'll arrange payment as soon as I hear the official press announcement."

"Fine, and when could you and I have another,... meeting?"

She turned to look at him, disgusted as he stood there stark naked as though he was a candidate for the defunct Playgirl magazine. "Just get that deal done, Louie. Then we'll talk."

She opened his suite door and walked out, not noticing the small minicam device attached high up on the corridor ceiling with Velcro.

It was early on Tuesday morning and Adam made his way to the top floor, informed only that Cook wanted to discuss the status of the Moretti contract with him immediately. He had called Wally Remington to inquire if he knew anything and had been told his immediate boss had not. Very busy himself with staff in his office, the CFO told Herrera to just have all his facts and figures in a row before meeting with the big man, and then quickly discarded any concerns.

Herrera entered the CEO's office where Cook was joined by a sharp-dressed, very attractive woman from the legal department, Carolyn Tyler. Casual greetings were exchanged and Cook motioned for Herrera to be seated.

"Adam, Carolyn here tells me this contract we have with Moretti has some intriguing loopholes, mostly regarding Evelyn Stevens," Byron said. "Carolyn, please repeat again what you told me earlier.".

"Well, gentlemen, this contract is most unusual in its makeup, particularly as it relates to Evelyn Stevens. She has a year-to-year option after the second year and she may take a portion of the Unibank sponsorship with her to another team, with our consent of course. The other quirky part of the contract has to do with our monetary commitment based on overall team performance, and it's based on a combined team quotient. In the first two years, Moretti Motorsport exceeded the minimum performance standards without issue," the contract attorney explained.

"This past season, Tony Moretti moved to Formula One and that team achieved mediocre results, the NASCAR team just did okay, the standards of Indycar were only met largely because Evelyn herself had a breakout year. The IMSA sports car champion, Vito Caruso, didn't bring the team's overall score up very much as there were not as many IMSA races.

The team's performance quotient effectively sets funding for the following year. The language in the contract is somewhat vague regarding the potential departure of one driver, namely Evelyn Stevens. Should Stevens leave the team, the contract could be interpreted as the team's overall performance quotient for the previous year being calculated without her numbers, which would technically be grounds for Unibank to lower its overall funding to Moretti Motorsport by over sixty percent."

Herrera sat there listening, seeing the wheels turning in Byron Cook's mind while recalling how uncomfortable Andy Moretti was in signing the terms of their contract three years earlier. *It was Newberry who fabricated such extraordinary details back then,* Adam recalled, knowing had it been any driver other than Evelyn Stevens, Andy would not have agreed to it. *But who could have predicted the bizarre circumstances of these past two years?*

"Well, Adam? My first thought is why we didn't explore this more in detail a year ago. What do you have to say about that?" Byron asked expectantly. All three in the office knew Cook was chomping at the bit for a chance, any chance, to damage Moretti Motorsport in any way possible.

Herrera gathered his thoughts, knowing he had glossed over the topic regarding Stevens' renewal option the previous year, and it was now biting him in the butt. He was also thinking it all too coincidental this meeting taking place the very morning before he, Stevens, Hill, and Newberry were expected at Andy's office for an extension signing the very next morning, one that all had agreed to in principle weeks earlier and the signing to be a last formality, as had been the case previously.

Cook never called for meetings on important issues like this at the last minute, Herrera pondered. *It couldn't have been Newberry. Byron Cook would never so much as take a phone call from him. Evelyn, herself? No, she always allowed Newberry to handle everything contract-related, as foolhardy as that was on her part. Who else could have tabled this with the CEO near the midnight hour?*

"As Stevens kept improving in her second year, she was quite happy where she was, and her agent, Newberry, was content and even giddy to get the generous raise they received for this past year," Herrera explained defensively. "And it is quite a stretch to claim that Moretti Motorsport's first year in Formula One was mediocre. On the contrary, their finishing sixth in the constructor's points standing was seen in most circles as extraordinary."

He could tell Cook wasn't happy with his explanation, but the CEO chose to let it go for the present. "What is it you would like me to do, sir?"

"I would like to meet with Evelyn Stevens as soon as possible. If she is unhappy with what Moretti is paying her, I suspect she'll entertain offers to move to another team.... And if I understand this correctly, we would have the option of taking Unibank sponsorship with her," the CEO responded. "Am I right, Carolyn?"

"Yes, sir. That is the way I would interpret it," she replied.

"Are you sure you want to do that, sir?" Herrera asked, knowing the answer already. He thought about suggesting they bring this to the board, knowing they would not convene again until after the first of the year. "I've already agreed in principle to terms with the parties for next season. If Newberry lets the market know that Stevens is still available, other sponsors may pounce. We'll be forced to dramatically increase our budget for her services, well over what she will cost us if she sticks with what's in the current agreement."

"You mean the current agreement with Andy Moretti," Cook stated as he shot a questioning glance toward Tyler. "Set up a meeting. I want to have a conversation with Evelyn and this hot shot agent, Newberry," Cook demanded, his previous disdain for Louis Newberry suddenly diminished. "If she is that much of an asset to us, we'll increase that budget. You'll work with Carolyn here to make certain the terms of any new contract get us the best return on any added investment in Miss Evelyn Stevens."

Tyler could hardly contain her smile at the opportunity to involve herself in something so important, following years of toiling in a cubicle on the fourth floor, never having a direct conversation with Byron Cook until recently, when a chance after-hours encounter had flourished into a full-blown affair with a man who'd always seemed as straight as an arrow, and one with a beautiful late thirties spouse at home to boot.

Adam Herrera's smile was forced, knowing this ambitious and forward woman would now effectively be in charge of all things related to their motor racing sponsorship contracts, despite his title of VP of Marketing. He left Cook's office, thinking their meeting had concluded, curious that Tyler seemed in no rush to gather up her items.

She sat silently until Herrera had closed the office door behind him, then stood as finally preparing to leave. "Are you going to stop by later, Byron?"

"How about we take off early today? I don't want to get home too late," he replied.

"I'll be waiting."

Adam Herrera was now a very troubled man. He had developed a strong friendship with Andy Moretti over the past few years despite the tragedy in Las Vegas. He was of the solid belief that any and all of his endeavors regarding the Moretti sponsorship were done in the best interest of his employer, but he knew all too well the serious accident in Vegas could not be reversed and that Byron Cook still had an extreme vendetta toward his friend. It was his hope that the passage of time would heal some of the bitterness Cook had for the Morettis, but the meeting he just attended revealed that hatred in the man was burning stronger than ever.

He called Newberry and requested that he and Evelyn meet with him and Byron Cook at the Unibank building as soon as possible, which turned out to be later that very afternoon.

So far as Andy Moretti was concerned, Herrera felt he owed it to the team principal to hear of this development in person, thus he wrapped up the items in front of him, left the building, and headed up I-77 to break this to Andy, news that he knew would devastate the man, as if he hadn't been thoroughly deflated enough these past couple of years as it was.

He entered the Moretti Motorsport facility and was greeted by the receptionist, who quickly announced his arrival to the boss. Andy quickly came out of his office and approached to greet the bank executive. "Adam? Do I have my schedule crossed up? I thought we were all on tap for tomorrow morning?"

"We were, Andy. Could we speak privately?"

"Of course, Adam, right this way," Andy directed, knowing by his guest's expression that something was amiss,... something not good. "Alicia, could you please get us some coffee?"

The two sat down in Moretti's office and even though Herrera had been there many times before, he always appreciated the legendary majesty of the place, years of history and glory on the world's race tracks in plain view among all the trophies, framed pictures, and awards.

"What is it, Adam?" Andy asked. "May as well get to the point. I know you have news that isn't good."

Thirty minutes later, the two shook hands as two close friends who expected their future partnership was very much in doubt. Andy was indeed devastated although not shocked. He had known by catching tidbits of Louis Newberry's tone the past several weeks that something negative was developing. Like all driver contract renewals, particularly one in which a driver had just come off a very strong season, the owner would be expected to increase the driver's compensation. Andy was prepared to do just that, but the rub with Newberry would not only involve a pay increase for Evelyn but the upcoming season's compensation for Jon David Hill as well, a driver whom he would normally replace. This revelation that Stevens may jump ship from a team that had nearly carried her to a championship without so much as an opportunity to at least match any competitive offer, was news that was quite stunning and upsetting, to say the least.

Herrera started thinking about shoring up his networking around the various paddocks. He had grown to where he loved the sport over the last few years, relished being involved at such a high level, and began to think of other possibilities that would allow that privilege to continue should his position with Unibank become untenable.

Even as Adam sat in front of him, Andy received a call from Newberry and he feigned surprise as not to break confidence with Adam Herrera.

"Andy, Louis Newberry here."

"Good afternoon, Louis," he responded on the speaker. "What can I do for you?"

"I'm afraid I will need to postpone our meeting tomorrow. I have some issues with my clients to clear up prior to our signing?"

"Issues?" Andy replied questioning as he looked at Herrera shaking his head. "I thought we had all agreed on everything but finalizing the paperwork."

"You know that nothing is final until we actually sign," Newberry replied in an arrogant tone that was to denote a position of strength.

Andy wanted to tell Newberry that he considered his word to be worthless, but held his tongue. "When should I expect to finalize this, Louis?"

"I'll let you know, Andy. Gotta run now." *Click*

I'll let you know(?) Andy thought. "There is one silver lining in all this, Adam. I won't have to deal with that horse's ass anymore.

Andy took the news very hard. Evelyn Stevens, his leading Indycar driver, was moving back to Roberto Santos' team, taking a large portion of Unibank's sponsorship dollars with her. With Stevens gone, the chance of getting Unibank back onboard in any capacity for future years was now pretty well hopeless. This added to Moretti's ongoing worries regarding the huge lawsuit, which had now dragged on for two years. British Petroleum was still on board, but the huge oil company had never shown the appetite for funding a full Formula One effort on its own, and would likely back out totally if Andy failed to sign another major sponsor to partner with them.

He had almost a year to find new funding, hoping and believing sponsorship for his two-car F1 team shouldn't be an issue, as advertising space on an F1 car seemed priceless, even for a mid-pack team. Getting a solid multi-year sponsor for his overall operation in the States was quite tentative, though, particularly since Alex's criminal trial was again headline news. Right now, his immediate challenge involved stabilizing the Indycar squad, which added additional stress when he and Ward were busy enough readying the team to support extra drivers for the 500 in May.

He announced the signing of veteran Ryan Hunter-Reay, a former series and Indy 500 champion, to replace Marcus Newsome. Ryan, who carried the nickname *Captain America,* had likely passed his prime years but was a solid competitor and Andy had always viewed him as a team manager someday, given his professional persona and popularity among sponsors. The hiring had also brought hope of his helping to support the two other teammates, one of whom could likely be a rookie.

It had always been assumed that Jon David Hill would accompany Stevens but that had not been the case as Santos' deal only involved the popular female. This was another bone of contention for Andy, as Newberry had always insisted that any deal for Evelyn Stevens would have to include Hill in the package. Little did he know that Evelyn had quietly lobbied her agent to get her a new deal without Hill, as her still fledgling paddock romance with the fellow Brit was not all the wine and roses that everyone believed.

As the effects of the changes were playing out, Andy found himself in the unenviable position of having to keep Hill in a car, a driver whose past year's low championship result in the final standings had contributed to the impetus for Unibank's move on the guise of the team's subpar overall performance. It also meant his still dealing with Newberry for another season. There would be one consolation, however, that being a pay reduction for Hill, a stick in the eye that Louis Newberry, who still represented Jon David, had not considered.

Byron had long since lost his guilty conscience over his ongoing sexual relationship with Carolyn Tyler, as he and Sarah had shared little or no intimacy since the accident. He just could not comprehend his wife's tendency to want forgiveness toward the Morettis, the very people who in his mind had destroyed their lives.

The Christmas season was the least festive ever in the Cook household and Sarah was quite upset by it. The uproar from the interrupted court case had sown bitterness within her family that had in some ways been brewing for years. For the first time since their moving to Tega Cay, they had chosen not to throw a large Christmas party for friends and family. Inquiring friends were all told the trial had simply zapped everyone's holiday spirit, despite the somewhat upbeat attitudes of both Byron and for unknown reasons, Allison, over the news about Unibank and Evelyn Stevens.

Byron Cook and Bud Williams nor their wives had spoken little since the trial suspension, a result of their perceived disappointment in Amanda's standoffish behavior toward their younger son, Kyle, in spite of the fact that an Aaron Williams–Allison Cook wedding was planned for late the following spring.

Amanda was especially distraught, to the point that she and her father seldom spoke, a fissure so intense that formal family dinners had basically degraded into a scenario where everyone just began fending for themselves. She would be eighteen soon, graduating from high school in May and yet not committing to any college or university, causing her father to hint that his financial support should not be taken for granted, which embroiled the family into yet another dispute.

"I just cannot countenance the fact that Amanda is that screwed up, Sarah. Why couldn't she have just spent her teenage years normally, like,... like"...

"You mean like Allison, right?"

"Did we not give Amanda everything? Most teenage girls would walk through fire for the life she has," Byron stated. "All of our lives have been turned upside down over this, Sarah."

"You just cannot stand it that she fell in love with a young man who's not of your choosing, Byron!"

"She was fifteen years old, Sarah! She became infatuated with a celebrity. How could a girl that age know what love is?"

Sarah stared back with a strong mixture of anger and sadness. "I fell in love at that age, Byron, and I married him... I now wonder what happened to that guy," she exclaimed sadly. "What are you going to do when you run out of people to hate, Byron?"

She felt this was potentially a pot of gold beyond her wildest dreams and resisted the urge for the quick hit. This was just too good for what she originally had in mind. She dialed a number and was promptly greeted with his voicemail prompt.

"It's Remi. I have a project I need help with. Call me ASAP."

The Waffle House on Pineville-Mathews Road was fairly busy with their normal morning crowd. She looked at her watch as she waited impatiently in a booth for him to show. He was fifteen minutes late. She held up her arm and mockingly pointed at her watch when he finally arrived.

"Nice of you to show, you shit."

"That's what I always liked about you, Remi. You're such a classy broad," James replied sarcastically.

"Screw you, Cotton. I can tell by your old boots and that worn-out hat that your business must not be that booming, so you better be nice to me."

The two paused while ordering coffee and the waitress to move out of earshot.

"Well, now that we've had our pleasantries and you've suggested getting physical with me, what's up?" James asked, smiling mischievously.

"Allison Cook? Do you know her?"

"Everyone down here knows who she is,... and her sister,... and that whole Cook outfit," James responded, choosing not to disclose that he had recently done a job for Allison Cook's father. "What about her?"

"Listen to this, Cotton," she instructed, and laid her iPhone down on the table between them after accessing and opening a lengthy audio file, playing it through the speaker.

He listened with interest, her pausing the audio briefly a couple of times when their waitress and other patrons passed close by.

"Looks like you're muscling in on my trade," he noted. "Quite explosive."

"Amazing the cooperation you get from the housemaids there for fifty dollars cash," Remi boasted.

"I'm impressed. So, what's my angle?" Cotton James asked of his former flame, who had already appeared to have stolen his thunder.

"I need to know everything you can get about this contract they're talking about. Louie Newberry has treated me like dirt since he started making the big bucks and I'm going to stick it to him."

"Their names aren't on there, Remi," Cotton stated. "And what you're doing could get you in hot water. How do you know it's her?"

"I have more than just this recording, and so far as the hot water, I'll worry about that," she responded.

"I just don't want you to get in over your head, Remi."

"Oh, sure, Cotton. Like you dream about me every night. Give me a break... How much?"

"My usual.... Shouldn't take that long. I normally need a thousand cash to get started. But for you, I'll take three hundred."

"I can only spare two right now."

He got up, removing his wallet to pocket the cash, less a twenty for the tab.

"Are you buying, Cotton? Don't hit a girl with too much shock this morning," Remi asked.

"I've got it," he replied, preparing to walk out. "And by the way, I do still dream about you at night... Sometimes."

Studying the file, she could barely get over it. *Oh, Cotton! I owe you one... I knew Newberry was a sleaze and a snake, but this was unbelievable. Petty cash would never have gotten him a female this hot. I knew it had to have been something more.*

Her first inclination was to go to Evelyn Stevens. That would have been the moral and ethical thing to do, but as a former prostitute turned paparazzi, Remi didn't feel that charitable. No, she had two and possibly three targets, thinking she could possibly even fleece this Carolyn Tyler, whose fingerprints were all over that contract.

She started sending him text messages and voicemails for the first time since he cut her off almost three years earlier. She had been on a mission to get even with him ever since and that time was at hand.

Newberry was annoyed at her bugging him and had indeed stopped responding to Remi about the same time Evelyn had stopped romancing Alex Moretti. But now, just when he was about to block her number on his iPhone, a thought hit him that motivated him to return her call.

"Well, Louie. Long Time."

"Yes, Remi. I've been rather busy. But I think I may have some work for you."

"I'm all ears."

She listened intently and was nearly aroused at what he was telling her. *This is too good!*

"So tell me, Louie, since her dad is already your piggy bank, what are you after?" Remi asked, as if she already knew nothing.

"That's my business."

All the more reason to stick it in your rear end, Louie. "This Allison Cook, she's sexy but not a star like Evelyn Stevens. It wouldn't be worth much except to maybe blackmail her with her husband-to-be. They're in California. I'll need expense money."

"What do you mean, expense money? If you want an entry to these people, you pay me, as always," the arrogant Newberry nearly yelled into his phone.

"No deal, Louie!" Remi barked, assuming that he should be desperate by now. She then hung up.

"Although most of the team had two weeks off for the holidays, Andy was putting in fourteen to fifteen hours per day. He and Ward were working diligently on plans to field two more cars with all the accompanying equipment, personnel, and expenses required to run at Indy in May. Andy had sold British Petroleum on stepping up to sponsor his son, Tony, the result of the positive impression he had made on the BP contingent during his first full season in Formula One.

Tony was excited to the gills, having run the Indy 500 seven times and nearly winning twice prior to missing the classic. The Team would also feature a car for Vito Caruso, their ace sports car driver and past year's IMSA driving champion.

Daniel Riccardo would be joining the McLaren stable along with Fernando Alonzo, returning after not qualifying last time out at the speedway and on a quest to follow Graham Hill as the only driver to ever win at Monte Carlo, Lemans, and Indianapolis.

Adding to the excitement for the upcoming month of May were interests from former world champions Jensen Button and Nico Rosberg, as well as former NASCAR champions Tony Stewart in a joint venture with Michael Andretti, and Kyle Larson, who would pilot a car also provided by Zak Brown in a partnership with legendary NASCAR team owner Rick Hendrick.

It was Christmas morning and the Cooks awoke to the holiday somewhat grasping for that traditional warm feeling. The girls weren't kids anymore and had yet to have their own, thus the early morning magic of experiencing a child awakening to their special holiday gifts wouldn't occur but Sarah put on her best face to create an atmosphere of joy and happiness despite the year's challenges.

Amanda's phone beeped with indications of a number of holiday wishes as she sat on the family front room sofa, taking her time to read and respond to each message. Her expression brightened when she caught a Merry Christmas text from Crissy Moretti. *"Amanda, I want to wish you a very Merry Christmas and hopefully a joyous and Happy New Year. ALL our love, Crissy (and I do mean ALL)."*

Sarah had given their house servant the weekend off and worked herself to prepare a hearty breakfast, calling for Byron and both girls to come hither and enjoy it. She couldn't help but notice a sudden spark in Amanda's eyes as she approached the dining room table.

Amanda embraced her mother heartily while Sarah glanced up toward Byron, a tear running down her cheek. "Merry Christmas, Mom."

"Merry Christmas, honey," Sarah replied, not knowing what had gotten into her little girl but thrilled for whatever it was.

Amanda even turned toward Allison and shared holiday greetings, her older sibling feigning a smile in return, but with her always cynical mindset suspected something unforetold was up.

Amanda couldn't quite bring herself to hug her father as the rift between the two of them, nearly two years in the making, would take more time to heal, if ever. In his own twisted way, Amanda knew her dad loved her,... but there *was* that twisted way, one they may never be able to reconcile.

Chapter 13

Sworn Under Oath

I t had been nearly four months since Flannery's heart attack and the old lawyer entered the courtroom aided by his assistant, Samuel. The crowded courtroom sat and waited anxiously for Judge Layton to appear.

Upon her entry, the bailiff stood and instructed, "All rise."

"You may all be seated," she instructed. "Mr. Flannery, I trust you are in good health today. Shall we continue this trial?"

"Yes, Your Honor. I thank you for the court's indulgence."

"Mr. Ferrell, is the Solicitor General prepared to proceed?"

"We've been ready, Your Honor. If it may please the court, I would like to repeat a question with the last witness that was recorded prior to the trial's extended recess, due to the unfortunate and lengthy delay."

"Without objection, Mr. Moretti, you will again take the stand and I remind you that you are still under oath," Judge Layton stated.

"Thank you, Your Honor," Ferrell stated.

The courtroom quieted as Alex Moretti walked solemnly back up to the witness stand, a young man who had been torn mentally for two years, the despair only interrupted by his scattered moments behind the steering wheel in a race car. Thus far, Ferrell had not hit him with any questions Ernest Flannery had not prepared him for, keyword – yet.

"Mr. Moretti, you were fully aware of the fact that Miss Amanda Cook was under sixteen years of age while you engaged in sex with her, correct?"

"Yes, I was aware," Alex answered.

"And when was it that you and Miss Cook first had a sexual encounter?"

Sarah held Amanda's hand as the room remained silent. Alex couldn't help but gaze at Amanda, the first time they had shared eye contact of any length for the four-month trial delay. "I believe it was the last Saturday in June, almost three years ago."

"The last Saturday in June, 2020," Ferrell stated as he turned and spoke toward the jury. "So, again, you knew at that time that Miss Cook was still fifteen years of age?"

"Objection, Your Honor!" Flannery declared, standing robustly with his pointed cane, if nothing else a signal to the court that he was still on his game, despite his health challenges.

Sustained. You're being repetitive, Mr. Ferrell."

"I'm sorry, Your Honor. I will withdraw the question... Do you believe your sexual activities with a fifteen-year-old were morally acceptable?"

"Objection, Your Honor! Are we engaged in a legal proceeding or a religious confession?" Flannery declared.

"Sustained," The judge ruled. "Mr. Ferrell, this court will be in judgment of violations of state law, not moral or immoral behavior. Lord only knows we would have time for nothing else should we open that door."

The courtroom crowd began to buzz with a peal of mixed laughter, causing the judge to pound the gavel and call for order.

"Did Miss Cook's age give you pause at least, Mr. Moretti?"

"Give me pause? Would it have been better if Amanda had been closer to my own age? Of course. But there was nothing we could do about that," Alex testified.

"Did you consider the fact that you may have been committing a felony, Mr. Moretti?" Ferrell asked sternly.

"No, I was not aware of that. I'm not a lawyer, sir."

The courtroom erupted into another loud buzz as the judge pounded the gavel and again demanded order.

Ferrell moved toward the jury box before asking, "Where did this first act occur, Mr. Moretti?"

"It was at my condominium in Davidson, North Carolina," Alex replied lowly.

A nineteen-year-old man had sex with a fifteen-year-old girl from South Carolina. And Miss Cook spent the weekend at your place, did she not?"

"She stayed over on Saturday night," he replied, not able to avoid glancing toward Amanda again despite her father's piercing stares.

"And you and Miss Cook spent three nights together on Lake Wylie on your cabin cruiser boat. Is that correct?" Ferrell continued, by now confident he had the jury in his pocket.

Alex hesitated as if unsure of himself. "I think that is correct."

"Ohhh! Maybe you and Miss Cook spent the night so many times you cannot recall how many."

"It was three," Alex corrected.

"If it will please the court," Ferrell stated, "I would like to turn everyone's attention to the large monitor. This is a GPS map of Lake Wylie, overlayed with phone records taken from both Mr. Moretti's and Miss Cook's smartphones, indicating the two had spent several times together on the large lake starting in June of 2020, with the last data points tagged in October the same year. Were you and Miss Cook together on Lake Wylie all those times in the year 2020, Mr. Moretti?"

"That's about right," Alex answered.

"You don't sound certain, Mr. Moretti. Maybe it was eight, maybe ten or twelve times."

"You have the record right up there. I take that as correct.."

Ferrell smiled as if he was preparing to open the grand prize, strolling again over in front of the jury box before his next question. "Mr. Moretti, on the 25th of July, it appears, according to both your and Miss Cook's phones, you two were both together overnight on the South Carolina shore of the lake. Did you and Miss Cook spend the night together on your boat that night?"

"Yes. That was at a dock slip at a waterfront restaurant near the ramp where I parked my vehicle," Alex replied. He noticed Flannery squinting his eyes at him as if reminding his client to never help the prosecution with unnecessary detail.

Ferrell moved quickly back to his desk and was handed a document by his assistant prior to re-approaching the witness stand. He handed the sheet of paper to Alex which contained a photocopy.

"Mr. Moretti, this is a receipt dated July 25th, 2020, at 11:46 AM. It is for a purchase at the CVS Pharmacy in Lake Wylie, South Carolina, charged to your Unibank Visa account. Would you read for the jury the items purchased on that receipt?"

Alex stiffened, warned by Flannery this would come out in the trial but extremely nervous and embarrassed nonetheless. "It was for a card, a bottle of perfume, and a prophylactic."

"Would you repeat that last item, and closer to the microphone, if you please?" Flannery asked, which was more of a demand.

Alex reluctantly pulled the microphone forward. "A prophylactic."

"A prophylactic, a condom,... or rubber as many would refer"...

"Objection, Your Honor!" Flannery declared. "Mr. Ferrell is appending the defendant's testimony for effect!?"

"Sustained," the judge declared. "Not a question, Mr. Ferrell."

"Sorry, Your Honor. Let me rephrase... Mr. Moretti, a prophylactic is the same thing as a condom or rubber, is it not?"

Alex glanced at Flannery, who was whispering to Samuel, admitting his error in the objection, which had given Ferrell another opportunity to have those damaging words repeated in front of the jury.

"It is."

"What is a prophylactic used for, Mr. Moretti?"...

"Objection, Your Honor!" Flannery hollered as he appeared to stand and shake as he pointed his cane upward.

Judge Layton appeared to indeed shake her own head for a second. "I'll have to regretfully overrule your objection, Ernest," she stated in a rare moment of addressing an attorney by his first name during a legal proceeding. "The witness will answer the question."

"It's a protection device worn on a male's penis to protect from disease and to prevent unwanted pregnancy," Alex answered reluctantly.

The courtroom again began to buzz loudly and the judge again pounded the gavel.

"Could you speak a little louder"...

"Mr. Ferrell, I believe the jury heard his reply," Judge Layton interrupted, believing the SG was overstepping his bounds a bit.

"Very well, Your Honor... And again on August 25th, and on September 23rd, as the data points would indicate, you two are documented as being on Lake Wylie together after 9:00 PM and then also at just prior to 8:00 AM the next morning. Do you recall those instances, Mr. Moretti?"

"I recall the other two nights," Alex stated.

"Your Honor, I would like to submit into evidence documented data from the year 2020 showing that the defendant's phone and the victim's phone were mapped together on multiple occasions at locations on Lake Wylie. Two dates reflect data points at both 9:04 and 9:08 PM and at 7:35 and 7:34 AM the very next mornings respectively at locations on Lake Wylie that fall within the border of South Carolina, in addition to the data previously on July 25th," Ferrell stated.

"Without objection, the evidence will be admitted into the record," Layton ruled.

"Thank you, Your Honor," Ferrell replied and continued. "Mr. Moretti, how many times since you have known Miss Cook have you two engaged in sexual relations?"

Alex hesitated as he and Amanda held momentary eye contact together.

"Well, Mr. Moretti?" Flannery asked as more of a directive while he glanced toward the jury.

"I don't know."

The courtroom again exploded in chatter prompting the judge to pound the gavel repeatedly. "To all of the attendees seated here, I will not allow these outbursts in my courtroom. One more such outburst and I will have you all removed!"

The room got very quiet which tended to increase the tension. "You may continue, Mr. Ferrell."

"Thank you, Your Honor... Well, Mr. Moretti, since you seem to have such a lack of memory for a young man your age, perhaps you could give us your best guess then."

Alex studied briefly, raising yet another eyebrow toward Amanda who sat staring at him misty-eyed. "In total, maybe twenty times."

The hushed chatter began but the crowd kept themselves relatively calm, heeding the judge's order.

"Mr. Moretti, were you aware during all this time that you and Miss Cook were engaged in these sexual encounters, that the laws in North Carolina and South Carolina regarding having sex with a minor under sixteen years of age were slightly different?" Ferrell asked, attempting to nail the case down.

"No, I was not aware of that," Alex conceded.

"So based on your testimony, is it fair to say that you would have made no precautionary effort to ensure that your vessel was navigated and moored in such a way as to not land within the border of South Carolina while these sexual relations were occurring?"

The entire courtroom became glued to the edge of their seats with every following question, and while many in the assembly tended to disagree with the law as written, very few by this point in the proceeding had doubt as to his guilt or innocence of that law.

"Yes, that is fair to say," Alex replied.

"I have one last question, Mr. Moretti. Have you ever had sexual relations with Miss Cook in South Carolina prior to January 19th, 2021?" Ferrell inquired.

The entire courtroom remained frozen waiting for the answer. Alex again could not avoid his gaze upon Amanda, who sat beside her mother in tears. He finally repeated his previous answer. "I don't know."

"You don't know?" Ferrell asked showing an air of skepticism. "You seem like a very smart young man. I assume you must have a sharp mind and quite a sense of geographic awareness to drive a racing car at 230 miles per hour. Reilly?"

"I'll repeat. I don't know."

"I have no more questions," Ferrell stated and leisurely returned to his station.

"Mr. Flannery, you may cross-examine the witness," Judge Layton instructed. *Well, Ernest? You had better have quite a scheme on this one,* she thought curiously, herself having a long and storied legal history with Flannery and now suspecting the old warrior to be long past his prime.

The entire courtroom paused in anxiety, wondering what Flannery had for his client.

"If it will please the court, I shall have lunch with my client and recharge my strength before recalling Mr. Moretti as my first defense witness."

Ferrell looked over at the old man, indeed appearing to have one foot in the grave. *What's ole Earnest up to now?* he thought.

"Mr. Ferrell, you may call your next witness," Judge Layton instructed.

"The State of South Carolina rests, Your Honor."

The court adjourned for a long lunch break and everyone began to file out. Andy and his mother, Matilde, entered the stairway leading to the ground floor at the same time as the Cook family. While Andy and Byron shared quick but stern glares, Matilde and Sarah both acknowledged each other with a courtly nod. Allison and Amanda departed together with opposite expressions toward the Morettis, and for his part, Alex continued to resent the fact that he couldn't even speak to Amanda.

They all fought their way through the crowd outside the courthouse as reporters kept after them to get their televised comments in. As the Morettis walked down the street, all while catching some unpleasant shouts from the many protesters, Alex would join his father, mother, and their attorneys for lunch in a small café with much of the lunch crowd giving Alex and his family more unwelcoming looks.

Alex could tell by his father's expression that he didn't feel good about the way things were going, particularly since the old lawyer chose to wait in cross-examining his son.

"Twenty times, Alex? Really?" Andy asked while shaking his head.

"We were seeing each other for almost a year, Dad. Do the math," Alex snapped back.

Matilde chose to intercede. "Let's not bicker among ourselves.... You haven't appeared too worried, Mr. Flannery," she said as more of a question as the four settled into their café booth.

The cagey old lawyer never appeared worried, an image he knew could sway a jury. "We have a good case."

Andy was not appeased. "I don't know?... That was a terrible answer! Anything would have been a better answer than that."

"No, Mr. Moretti," Flannery replied calmly as he reviewed the menu. "That's precisely what he needed to say."

Meanwhile, the Cooks were lunching at a nearby grill owned by longtime family friends. The mood was extremely somber as everyone could tell Amanda was quite upset by it all. Ferrell had informed her that he would avoid having her testify if possible, but circumstances may require it.

"Twenty times! Can you believe that, Sarah?" Byron expressed quietly as the two walked together toward the establishment. "The bastard is making our daughter appear as some sort of wild teenage harlot!"

"You wanted this trial, Byron. Be careful what you wish for," Sarah stated in retort. All throughout their marriage, she had stood side-by-side with her husband on every issue that had arisen over the years, just as the pretty wife of a wealthy southern businessman was supposed to do. Now she found herself building an ever-increasing resentment toward him, seeing him enraged with hatred toward the young man's entire family, as if all the kind hospitality the Morettis had shown since meeting them had never existed.

"Amanda's testimony will ice this thing. And then maybe the healing process can begin," Byron exclaimed.

Sarah hesitated while very much in doubt. "You think so?"

Amanda had no appetite, sitting at the long corner table just across and down from Kyle Williams, who kept attempting to catch her glance and was bothered that she seemed to go out of her way to avoid looking over at him, much less speak.

I would forgive you, Amanda, the young football star told her through his own internal thoughts. *Let's just put this behind us and get back together.* Kyle had his own mental demons as he sat next to his older brother, who would soon get married to Allison Cook, his longtime girlfriend sitting at his side. The younger of the two Williams boys had his own history with her, extremely bothered that Allison could just casually talk and glance toward him as if nothing had ever transpired between them.

The judge again pounded the gavel. "This court will now come to order. Mr. Flannery, you may call the defense's first witness."

"I now recall to the stand, Mr. Alessandro Moretti."

Flannery stood while studying some notes, as the judge reminded the defendant that he was still under oath. The veteran litigator then approached the witness stand.

"Alex, you have seen the data displayed by Mr. Ferrell showing all of the three dates where your phone was logged late at night at three so-called data points, all located on the South Carolina side of Lake Wylie. Do you have any basis to dispute that data?"

"Regarding the phone location and times, no I don't," he replied.

"And you saw all three cases showing your phone, and Amanda Cook's phone, placed right near there, in fact just a few GPS points away, before 8:00 AM. Do you have any reason to dispute that data?" Flannery asked, glancing toward the jury whose members watched in fascinating curiosity what this line of questioning was leading up to.

"No, sir. No dispute."

The courtroom could not contain itself as the many attendees were all questioning why the defendant had just apparently pleaded guilty. The judge pounded the gavel. "Order in the court!"

"Now Alex. The prosecution's detailed data report appears to be blank for several hours on two of the dates, showing no data whatsoever for nearly ten nine hours. I'm sure the jury would want an explanation of that. Could you shed some light on that for us?"

"Yes, if my recollection is correct, and I don't keep a diary, that location is right at or near the marina where I launched my boat and parked my vehicle and trailer overnight. I anchored my boat overnight across and down the lake on the east side, returning the next morning."

"And the reason for no data?"

"Amanda and I agreed to turn off our phones for the extended period.

Ferrell could not contain himself. "You've got to be kidding!"....

"You're out of order, Mr. Ferrell!" The judge scolded. "You will have an opportunity to re-examine and question the testimony. Continue, Mr. Flannery."

"Thank you, Your Honor.... Okay, Alex. There are the data points documenting the first time your phone, and we all assume your boat with Miss Cook on board, was emitting a signal all night," Flannery stated. "This would indicate, as the prosecution has so blatantly displayed, that you and Miss Cook spent the night in the state of South Carolina on July 25th. What is your response to that?"

"Amanda kept complaining about stomach cramps that night, so I chose to stay put and not expose her to the ride across and up the lake."

"Did you and Miss Cook engage in sexual relations that night, Mr. Moretti?" Flannery questioned.

"No."

Ferrell made a show of rolling his eyes as if to mock the whole testimony, an act of theatrics Flannery was fully expecting.

"Your Honor, I have no more questions at this time for this witness," Flannery informed the judge. "I would reserve the right to recall him later for rebuttal."

"Very well. Mr. Ferrell, do you wish to cross-examine?" The judge asked.

"Yes I would, Your Honor," Ferrell responded quickly while jumping up from his chair and pacing quickly toward the witness stand.

"Mr. Moretti, just a few hours earlier, when I asked you if you ever had sex with Amanda Cook on South Carolina soil, you testified that, and I quote, I don't know."

Alex sat and stared neutrally at the prosecutor, not changing any expression.

"So, Mr. Moretti, do you really expect the members of the jury to believe that you were documented in South Carolina after 9:00 PM, not once but twice, traveled after dark across the lake to moor your boat in North Carolina, and returned to South Carolina before 8:00 AM the very next morning, indeed on both occasions?"

"That is correct," Alex answered.

"And, indeed, you would have them also believe the one time your two phones happened to emit GPS signals for the full night on the South Carolina side of the lake, you didn't have sex because Miss Cook had a stomach ache?"

"Yes, that's right."

"Well, Mr. Moretti, since you seem to be so positive about these particular details on these specific dates, how is it that when I asked you if you had ever engaged in sexual relations with Miss Cook in South Carolina, you testified, I don't know?"

Alex thought about his reply, considering the question. "I do recall rather vividly that Amanda spent three nights with me on the boat that summer. On the first night, we docked at Papa Doc's all night. The next time, and the time thereafter, I was allowed to use the covered dock owned by an acquaintance from our team, whose parents have a weekend place there. Amanda was nervous about the crowd at Papa Doc's, and we also didn't have an electrical hookup there. So after that night, I made alternate arrangements for the next trips."

"But again, Mr. Moretti. You just testified earlier that you didn't know if you had sex with Miss Cook in South Carolina. Do you really expect the jury to believe that?"

"Objection!" Flannery yelled, jumping up from his seat and pointing his cane toward the ceiling again.

Alex paused, glancing at Flannery briefly and waiting for the judge to respond.

"Sustained."

Ferrell feigned a look of confused resignation. "No more questions, Your Honor."

The judge called for a thirty-minute recess, and the courtroom emptied out temporarily. Alex entered the men's room and stood up to a urinal beside Aaron Williams.

"I heard about you, Moretti. I hope they lock you up and throw away the key," the young uniformed officer declared.

"I don't believe I know you," Alex replied.

"Aaron Williams," he replied. "I'll be Amanda's brother-in-law someday, and you had better hope you never get to know me better."

"Sounds like a threat," Alex responded, as he stood over the sink and washed his hands.

Williams made a move to shove him against the towel cabinet when the bailiff officer entered. "Gentlemen? Is everything all right here?'

The three dispersed without additional incident with Alex thinking, *You don't know half of what you think you know, sir.*

Amanda clung to her mother, not wanting to talk to anyone. She was now convinced she would be called to testify before this was all over and was extremely nervous about it.

Ignoring the emotional wall created in the courthouse foyer between the Cooks and their friends and the Morettis and theirs, Matilde Moretti walked up to Amanda, further ignoring the shocked stares of others. Sarah looked at her, smiling lightly as if to voice some sort of tacit approval.

"Amanda, at least some of my prayers have been answered. You're looking well," Matilde expressed sincerely. She then nodded at Sarah who replied in kind. Byron saw the exchange and grabbed his wife by her arm, escorting her with Amanda in tow back into the courtroom, a girl who could not avoid looking back over her own shoulder and smiling warmly at Alex's grandmother.

"Mr. Flannery, do you have further rebuttal questions for this witness?" Judge Layton inquired following her calling for the court to come to order.

"Yes, thank you, Your Honor."

"Mr. Moretti, I remind you that you are still under oath," the judge stated.

Flannery reapproached the stand. "Alex, When the jury hears you testify regarding those three nights last summer in detailed specificity, but then in another testimony you don't know if you ever engaged in sexual relations with Miss Cook in South Carolina, they may be confused. Could you explain to the jury with some clarity what you meant by those conflicting testimonies?"

"Yes, I'll try. I recall the details of all three times that Amanda and I were together overnight because each of those had to be well planned out. We both knew we weren't supposed to be together, and it was often several days on end before we were. As such, I do recall those weekend details quite well. There were many other times, often during the middle of the week, that we would spend just an afternoon, sometimes just a couple hours together on the lake, and I don't have any kind of detailed record of the when and where on those." Alex explained.

"And on some of those occasions, you two did engage in sexual activity?" Flannery led.

Alex had been coached not to appear upbeat when answering such questions. "On some, yes."

The judge returned to pounding the gavel again to quiet the resumed hushed chatter in the courtroom.

"Alex, let's return to Long Beach, California in April, 2020. Was this the first time you met Amanda?" Flannery asked.

"I think we may have been introduced at our team facility ribbon-cutting ceremony a month prior. But I didn't recall that too well. I would say we met formally at a hotel reception party in Long Beach."

"She was with her sister, Allison, at that event, correct?"

"Objection Your Honor! Is this relevant?" Ferrell jumped up and asked.

Judge Layton hesitated before looking to Flannery and Moretti. "I'll allow it. Mr. Flannery, you must soon display the relevance, however."

"Yes, Your Honor... Upon meeting Allison and Amanda Cook at that reception, explain to the jury what occurred that night, Alex."

"Allison invited me to a party she was hosting later that night. I chose to go to the party, but knowing I had to wake up early the next morning, I left after spending a short time. It was then I found Amanda taking a late walk out on the beach and ended up escorting her back to the hotel."

Flannery shuffled back to his table to study some notes. "You mentioned you left that party early. Amanda's older sister, Allison, was not happy about that, was she?"

"I object, your honor. Parties three thousand miles west of here that happened three years ago? What is the relevance to this case?" Ferrell asked sternly.

"Objection sustained!"

"Sorry, Your Honor. Scratch that... Alex, when you met Amanda on the beach and escorted her back to her hotel, you two had quite a conversation, didn't you."

"Yes, sir. We did," Alex replied, anxious to expand on it.

"What was that conversation about?"

"Objection, Your Honor!" Ferrell hollered. "Mr. Flannery is filibustering in hopes the jury will forget about his client's earlier testimony!"

"Overruled. You'll have the opportunity to point that out during your summation, Mr. Ferrell," Judge Layton ruled.

"Thank you, Your Honor," Flannery responded. "Alex?"

"I was surprised by the conversation. It wasn't as though I was chatting with a fifteen-year-old. The shy little sister I had met earlier was quite open about some things. We talked about our ages, our families, things like that,"

"And how had that changed your opinion regarding the two sisters over the course of that evening?" Flannery continued.

"I started to feel close to Amanda after that," Alex stated, speaking slowly as he went while looking straight at Amanda, a vision quite apparent to the entire courtroom.

"And what did she tell you about her sister that night, Alex?" Flannery plowed on.

Alex's muscles tightened as he prepared an answer. "She told me that her sister wanted to sleep with me."

"You son-of-a-bitch!" Aaron Williams hollered as the crowded and stunned courtroom erupted. He jumped up and ran headlong toward the stand, tackled by the bailiff while Judge Layton pounded the gavel. The judge ordered the two attending sheriff's deputies to escort Williams out the rear door, now facing charges of contempt of court and assault. Meanwhile, a now very angry Allison Cook moved to the first row, sitting just on the left of her father.

"I will not tolerate another outburst in this court!" Layton exclaimed. "Anyone who violates this order will be immediately arrested and charged with criminal contempt of court. You will now continue, Counselor."

"Thank you, Your Honor," Flannery expressed, appearing to be in deep thought.

The muffled courtroom audience was no less tense. Allison was now so blitzed at her sister following the previous testimony that she could hardly speak. Neither of her parents looked forward to confronting either daughter during the coming adjournment, both wishing to avoid internal family problems and in the back of her mind at least, Sarah feared the testimony was true. Adding to the anxiety, Byron was in dread of the personal aftermath from his friend and major longtime client, Bud Williams. While he knew Sarah was quickly growing weary of the road this legal action was taking, Byron's rancor toward Alex and the Morettis, in general, was growing ever more intense by the minute.

Flannery nodded and moved forward. "Okay, Alex, when you heard that comment from Amanda, that her sister wanted to sleep with you, what went through your mind?"

"I thought Amanda was pretty bold to state such a thing... I tried to just make light of it," he answered, again sharing emotional stares with her.

"And did Amanda have further comment on that?"

"She wanted to make it clear that she was not like that."

"Based on your limited experience that evening, did you agree or disagree with Amanda's assessment of her sister?" Flannery asked him.

Alex became quite uncomfortable, suddenly avoiding everyone's stares. "I thought it was likely so."

Byron reached to his left, clutching Allison's hand, as if assuming she would be quite hurt after hearing this. In reality, she now became more determined than ever to exact vengeance on Alex Moretti,... not to mention her own sister.

Flannery strolled back quickly to study his notes. "Alex, how would you compare the two Cook sisters physically?"

"I think them both to be beautiful young women," he replied.

"I object!" Ferrell stomped up yelling. "This is becoming a circus, Your Honor!"

"Overruled," Judge Layton quickly reacted. "I want to see where this is headed."

Ferrell sat down before looking back over his shoulder at Byron and shaking his head.

"In fact, isn't it true that upon first meeting the two Cook sisters, you thought they were almost twins?" Flannery inquired while standing near the stand but looking toward the jury.

"Actually, I did think that, yes."

"And Allison Cook is just a few months younger than yourself, correct?"

"Yes."

Byron stirred uncomfortably, leaning over and whispering in Sarah's ear. "Where's Flannery going with all this BS?"

"Like I said, Byron, be careful what you wish for."

"You already told me that," Byron replied in a loud whisper, disappointed that his wife was not more supportive.

"So, Alex," his attorney continued. "You felt both of the Cook sisters were extremely attractive, indeed appeared nearly identical, and yet you apparently shunned any physical overtures by the older sister, and instead engaged in a courtship with the younger Amanda. You would have to have known this would cause immense consternation, would you not?"

"I did," Alex replied in resignation.

"How many times were you and Amanda together prior to having your first sexual encounter?" Flannery asked seriously.

"I'd have to think," Alex quickly replied before providing a more definitive answer. "I would say six or seven times."

"I have no more questions for this witness, Your Honor," Flannery said, addressing the judge.

"Very well, Counselor. Mr. Ferrell, do you wish to redirect?"

Ferrell acknowledged in the affirmative and approached Alex. "Mr. Moretti, you testified that you agreed with Amanda's assessment that her sister, Allison, wanted to sleep with you, correct?"

"I said I thought it likely. Allison never came right out and said that," Alex replied nervously.

"You were romantically involved with your teammate, Evelyn Stevens, for quite some time prior to having sex with Amanda Cook, isn't that right, Mr. Moretti?"

Alex shifted in his seat, knowing Andy definitely did not want Evelyn's name brought up in the trial, particularly any intimate details about her and his son, knowing the press would have a field day with it. "We lived together for a while."

"Isn't it true that Miss Stevens was indeed still residing in your condominium while you were spending time courting Amanda Cook?" Ferrell pushed.

"She didn't actually move her things for a while but",...

"Just answer the question, yes or no, Mr. Moretti. Did Evelyn Stevens officially reside with you while you were involved romantically with Amanda Cook?"

"Yes," Alex replied, unsure himself that was correct but feeling boxed in.

"Mr. Moretti, how many women have you had sexual relations with since turning fifteen?" Ferrell asked.

"Objection, Your Honor!" Flannery yelled. "Is the personal life of my client prior to his relocating to the Carolinas relevant to this case?"

"I'll withdraw the question, Your Honor," Ferrell offered, just wanting to get a seed planted with the jury. "Mr. Moretti, you were recently involved in a serious auto accident in Las Vegas, Nevada, one which resulted in both yourself and Amanda Cook being hospitalized"...

"Objection, Your Honor!" Flannery yelled. "The defendant is on trial for an event or events that occurred in 2020, allegedly in our state!"

"Sustained. You will restrict your questioning to the case in front of this court, Mr. Ferrell."

"Of course, Your Honor," Ferrell replied, knowing he would be shut down in referencing the incident in Las Vegas, but wanting to remind the jury of it, nonetheless.

"No more questions, Your Honor," Ferrell announced as he again withdrew to his station.

Andy sat nervously, very concerned about how the trial was going. On the opposite side of the aisle, Byron Cook sat seething as the memory of Las Vegas was reconstituted and angered that the judge had not allowed that dialog.

"This proceeding will adjourn until 10:00 AM Monday morning," Judge Layton declared before pounding the gavel.

The Cook home was stressfully quiet Friday evening following the weeklong trial proceeding. Allison sat at the dinner table, unable to even look at Amanda, while Byron and Sarah made feckless attempts at small talk to distract from the tension. The older daughter excused herself to call Aaron Williams, still suspended from the courtroom following his earlier outburst, and quite upset with the statements regarding her that came out in court earlier and shocked that his own girlfriend was now brought into this courtroom saga.

Byron made things worse by making an ill-advised comment that both girls would have been so much better off had they never accompanied him and Sarah to Long Beach three years earlier, really pouring gas on the fire by suggesting how much better off Amanda and the whole family would be had she just kept dating Kyle Williams.

Amanda began to break down in tears at that remark and abruptly got up from the table and scurried upstairs without any semblance of asking to be excused, as was the long family custom.

It would be a long weekend in the Cook household as all the family members could think about was the trial and their individual ill feelings toward each other. Sarah approached Allison, who sat out by their pool, ignoring everyone while being glued to her smartphone screen.

"Allison, you avoiding your sister like this is not what this family needs right now," Sarah stated.

"You heard what that little bitch,... Amanda said about me," Allison decried.

"She's been through a lot. You know that."

"Mom! Everyone in town thinks I'm a slut now, including my own boyfriend! If he even keeps speaking to me, that is," Allison responded, not truly worried about what Aaron was thinking. He would just be led around the nose and believe whatever she told him, as always.

Later in the evening, Sarah checked on Amanda, a girl who just seemed to want to lay in her bed now and try to sleep. "Honey, do you want me to fix you anything? You have to eat."

"No, Mom. I'm not hungry."

"I know this whole trial business has been really hard on you. You could stay home, Amanda. Everyone would understand," Sarah expressed in support.

"No, I want to be there," she replied, always having in the back of her mind this was her only chance to be close to Alex. "I may get called to testify, Mom. That's what Mr. Ferrell told me from the get-go," Amanda added.

Sarah and her daughter both knew that Ferrell wanted Amanda sitting there beside her family, upfront in the courtroom audience both sad and heartbroken, all for the jury to see, knowing she wouldn't be called to testify the first few days, if at all.

"I saw you and Alex staring at each other while he was on that stand, Amanda. You want to tell me about it?" Sarah asked sincerely.

"I don't know what to say, Mom," Amanda said as she laid her head on Sarah's shoulder. "That whole time in that courthouse, I sat there feeling that he wanted to see me, to talk with me.... But we could not.... No, as hard as this has been, I want to be there."

The Morettis dropped Crissy off at the airport, scheduled to fly south for the Miami Grand Prix and join Tony. Alex drove north with his father, grandmother, and aunt, blowing off an idea to dine out on Friday night as they didn't figure they could go to any restaurant and have a sit-down relaxing meal in private.

Thus they all gathered at Andy's home, recently custom-built on the shore of Lake Norman and just a short drive away from both of his boys, Tony and Alex. His sister, Marie, and mother lived on the property, both of whom prepared a hasty but tasty Italian dinner.

The personal atmosphere between Andy and his youngest son remained tense, and Andy had tried to lower the temperature a bit by agreeing to pay much of Flannery's bill to represent Alex in a trial that had captured the media's fascination unlike any since O.J.

The trial and its potential repercussions had kept a constant emotional cloud over the entire Moretti family, and Andy had often been accused by his mother of putting the interests of his team over that of his family. In his own mind, it was all related of course, as he loved both his sons but also wished the family as a whole would appreciate what his success had given them, pretty much everything from a roof over their heads to a lifestyle that most could only dream about.

With that as a backdrop, Andy was frustrated with Ernest Flannery, believing the prosecutor had gotten the better of him for the most part thus far, and hoped he had something in his bag they hadn't seen yet. One comfort Andy did take from the trial, as small victories were taken, was the realization that Alex had never deceived him regarding any involvement with Allison Cook at all, and he now understood that his youngest boy had been truthful regarding Allison as he was involved with the other Cook girl all along,

He also looked back at the events two years earlier in Lemans, now realizing Amanda could never have been there then, appreciating the faithfulness his boy had toward Byron Cook's youngest daughter in the face of such temptation that her own sister had planned to throw at him there.

Alex sat outside on the second-floor veranda with the elder family contingent as they watched the outside monitor of the first day of practice in Miami. Tony was running ninth currently out of twenty-two, not a place that a Moretti was accustomed to nor happy with, but not bad considering a second-year team. The bright silver white and green Moretti car, decked out in the Unibank and BP livery was beautiful and the broadcasters gave the team ample screen time though much was due to the added dialog regarding Tony's brother's trial several hundred miles up north.

Andy was preoccupied momentarily with an incoming call, prompting Maria to ask her nephew how he felt sitting in that courtroom with Amanda, having not spoken openly with her since the day of the accident two years earlier.

"It was emotional, I'll tell you that, Aunt Maria.," Alex replied.

"So sad, that Amanda is such a beautiful girl. I hate seeing such vibrant young people in such a state," Maria added.

"He still loves that girl," Matilde added. The question is what does he do about it since Andy's lawyers are prohibiting him from even talking to her? That's if he's found not guilty, that is."

"Well, we haven't been communicating, and the good lord only knows when we'll be able to," Alex said in resignation. "I just wonder if she'll come to see me when I'm in prison?"

"I wouldn't get too down," Matilde stated with mature confidence. "I suspect that Ernest Flannery has something up his sleeve. He didn't become that wealthy and successful by being an old fool. He has that Ferrell intimidated. I can see it."

The following Monday morning, the courthouse crowd was back in a frenzy. The reporters and their crews were in force, and the Observer reporter got a quick comment from the State Solicitor General District Attorney, Ferrell.

"Mr. Ferrell, will you call Amanda Cook to the witness stand today?"

"I can't comment on future witnesses who may or may not be called."

"How do you feel the state's case against Alex Moretti will conclude?"

"I believe that Alex Moretti took advantage of a young underage South Carolinian girl and had sex with her too many times to recall, not even knowing where he was at the time. I believe justice will be done and hopefully today. Thank you."

"You heard it, ladies and gentlemen. The world motor racing community and certainly the public in general watch anxiously as the new trial of the century is nearing conclusion. This is Melissa Townsend coming to you from the York County Courthouse. Back to you, Brian."

Bud Williams was not happy in having to post bail to get his oldest son released from custody, shocked as he and the Cook family were close friends with Judge Layton and her family.

The bailiff prompted everyone to "all rise" and the judge took her place on the bench and repeated the case numbers and details.

"Mr. Flannery, are you ready to proceed?" Judge Layton asked.

"Yes, I am, Your Honor."

"Then without objection, proceed."

"I call to the stand Miss Valerie Hampton."

A young woman, one of medium height and slightly overweight, strolled down the aisle and was sworn in by the bailiff. She then proceeded to take her seat.

"Would you please state your name and address for the record, please?"

"Valerie Hampton, 24 Hudson St, York, South Carolina." the witness responded.

"And where were you on the night of July 25th, 2020?" Flannery asked.

"I was working the evening shift a Papa Doc's Shore Club."

"Miss Hampton, do you recognize anyone in this courtroom from that date at your place of employment?" Flannery asked.

The courtroom began to stir, wondering who this new witness was and what part her testimony could have in the case.

"Honestly, not really," she said. "They weren't in my section. I recognize Alex Moretti over there and Amanda Cook now, like mostly from their pictures all over the social media and tabloids at the grocery store regarding this court thing."

"So you didn't recall them from that night?" Flannery continued, consciously not approving of her prefacing her statement with the word, *honestly*.

"No, both had dark sunglasses on. He had a Firestone baseball cap on and she had like a big white hat that sort of hid her face."

"Miss Hampton, I'm confused," Flannery stated. "How is it that you could recall such details about their attire, even to the point of the logo on his hat, from nearly three years ago when they weren't even your customers?"

"They were in Serena O'Gara's section. She asked me to take a photo of them for her on my phone. I still have it right here," she replied and reached into her purse to produce her iPhone.

"If it pleases the court, Your Honor, I would ask the witness to pull that image up for the jury's review," Flannery stated.

"By all means," Judge Layton instructed. "Miss Hampton, please hand the bailiff your phone so the court may review these photos you possess."

"Objection, Your Honor!" Ferrell exclaimed loudly. "It has already been established the defendant and Miss Cook were in attendance at the Papa Doc's establishment at the time and date in question. This photograph was not presented during pre-trial discovery?"

"Approach the bench, gentlemen," Layton directed.

Ferrell and Flannery both stood before the judge as all spoke in lower tones, somewhat overshadowed by the now excessive mixed chatter in the courtroom.

"Your Honor, Mr. Flannery is wasting the court's time with this! This photo was not presented to the Solicitor General's office in advance," Ferrell complained vigorously.

She looked toward the defense attorney for his expected response. "Mr. Flannery, tell me there is a point to this."

"Your Honor, Miss Hampton is a rebuttal witness and made no mention of any photographs to my staff. A witness for the prosecution previously testified right here that she saw, with her own eyes, my client and Miss Cook naked together in his boat at around midnight," Flannery retorted, while Ferrell displayed an obvious expression of disgust. "Could the jury be so bothered by seeing a photograph of them sitting fully clothed in a restaurant together?"

"I'll allow it, Mr. Flannery, but I want to see the point you're making, and soon."

"Thank you, Your Honor."

Judge Layton pounded the gavel once as a prompt for the attendees to cease their chatter, as Flannery reapproached the witness while Ferrell returned to the plaintiff's table and sat down. On the surface, he saw no point nor advantage to the picture but knew the cagey old Flannery had some agenda related to it.

As each member of the jury had an opportunity to quickly look at the photos, the judge ordered the bailiff to meet with the witness following her dismissal to accommodate the transfer. Some of the jury members were indeed bewildered as to their pertinence to the trial.

"And why would Serena O'Gara ask you to take these photographs?" Flannery asked, as if extremely curious.

"My phone was newer than hers, and she didn't want them to know a picture was being taken," Hampton answered.

"I understand the part about the phone, I guess. But did she explain to you any reason for such clandestine behavior with the phone camera?" Flannery inquired, again expressing much curiosity.

Hampton stirred uncomfortably, looking down momentarily as if thinking seriously about her reply. "She told me it was Allison Cook cheating on her boyfriend."

"Excuse me," Flannery stated. "You mean Amanda Cook, correct?"

"No. We were both up at the bar waiting for our beverage orders and she nodded toward them and told me it was Allison Cook."

The courtroom couldn't contain itself, as Judge Layton pounded the gavel repeatedly and called for order.

"So, Miss Hampton. To be clear, Serena O'Gara told you that the young woman in question, the one she asked you to photograph, was Allison Cook?"

"Yes."

"And what did she tell you about the male you were photographing?"

"Nothing, just that Allison Cook was cheating with some other guy. She knew who her boyfriend was."

The courtroom started to buzz again, with their focus now very much on Allison Cook, who now sat there frozen and happy that her boyfriend Aaron was excluded from attending. Her future in-laws were there, however, and obviously affected. Byron Cook could not even glance at his longtime friend and business customer, Bud Williams, or his wife. Sarah sat between him and Amanda, now steaming in her own way. *Byron, you wanted this. Now you've got it!*

"Miss Hampton," Flannery continued. "The defendant, Alex Moretti, is quite a well-known sports figure, all the more so at that time because of his lengthy relationship with Evelyn Stevens, herself a worldwide celebrity. Despite his hat and sunglasses, did neither you nor Miss O'Gara recognize him?"

"I don't keep up with that racing much. My boyfriend is into it, but I don't think Mr. Moretti does NASCAR. So no, I had no idea who he was."

"And the girl? Did you know who she was?" Flannery asked.

"No, or at least not until Serena told me. Most everyone around Lake Wylie knew or had heard about the Cook sisters," Hampton answered. "But I didn't go to Fort Mill High, so I didn't know them personally."

"And Miss O'Gara?" Flannery kept going. "Did she indicate a familiarity toward Alex Moretti?"

"No. She just kept talking about Allison Cook and another guy. We both commented that he was quite good-looking. But it was mostly about getting a picture of her with another guy."

"Did you know why she asked you to snap the photographs?" Flannery asked.

"Serena wanted to post it on TikTok and Instagram. She had something against Allison Cook and was always into posting stuff on social media. I didn't send the images to her, though," she stated.

"Didn't send them to Serena? And why was that?" Flannery asked while looking toward the jury.

"I like my job at Papa Doc's. I still work there and got to thinking it could come back and bite us."

Flannery strolled back to the defendant's table. "Your witness," he stated to Ferrell.

The Solicitor General's District Attorney sat momentarily, feigning a whisper with his associate before standing to approach the witness.

"Miss Hampton, how long did you work with Serena O'Gara?"

"She worked at Papa's for about four months I think. We worked the same shift sometimes," she replied.

"Were you two friends?"

"No, I wouldn't say that," Hampton replied.

"Isn't it true that you despise Serena O'Gara?"

Hampton stirred again, obviously uncomfortable. "It got to that, yes."

"And the reason for this rift between co-workers?" Ferrell asked, looking to the jury and trying to regain some momentum.

She looked over at the jury, struggling to compose herself. "One of the bartenders was my boyfriend at the time. He was cheating on me,... with her."

"So it's fair to assume then that you wouldn't be inclined to speak positively on any subject involving Serena O'Gara, would it?"

"I have testified truthfully here today," she replied quickly before Ferrell even had a chance to demand she answer with a yes or no.

"No more questions, Your Honor."

The judge called for a thirty-minute recess. As those in the courtroom stood and most hit the exit to hit the restroom, check emails, messages, and other necessities, Alex and Amanda stood and shared an emotional stare, in some way both realizing the long saga may be coming to an end, although both still feared the outcome.

The court officials, participants, and observers were all now confused if not intrigued by this latest witness. The SG prosecutor obviously had made a last-minute ploy to discredit her, but every member of the jury now wanted more information about this seeming misidentification on the part of a previous key witness and where that would play out in the overall picture of the trial.

Sarah and Lisa Williams gathered together in the women's restroom line. The two lifelong friends missed the friendly meetings, joint charity work, and routine chit-chat together, all that seemed to be gone with the wind now.

"Bud's getting really pissed off about this, Sarah. It's not the kind of publicity he wants," Lisa declared.

"You know I never wanted this, Lisa," Sarah responded, attempting to show empathy. "May the good lord help it be over soon."

The two strolled together back to the courtroom, both hoping that when the trial was over things would get back to normal.

Judge Layton pounded the gavel and called for the trial to resume. "Mr. Flannery, your next witness?"

"I would like to recall Miss Serena O'Gara back to the stand, Your Honor."

The courtroom audience buzz resurfaced and Judge Layton repeated her previous threat to remove anyone whom she deemed as out of order.

O'Gara nervously reapproached the stand and was again sworn in.

Flannery made a scene out of staring at her while shifting his gaze down toward the many notes in front of him.

"Mr. Flannery, do you have questions for this witness?" Judge Layton inquired as everyone was getting testy.

"Sorry, Your Honor. My old brain doesn't process as well as it once did." He finally stood and approached the witness.

"Miss O'Gara, you are quite an active person on this social media, are you not?"

"Most of us in this generation are, sir," she replied with a somewhat snide expression.

"My associate here, Mr. Mayne, saw a post you placed on Facebook, a photograph of you and Luke Kuechly, a star football player for the Panthers, isn't he?"

"Yes, he's retired now," she answered.

"And there's also a picture taken on there of you with Chase Elliott. He's Bill Elliott's son, is he not?"

"Yes, that was right after he won his Cup Championship," she added.

"A chip off the old block, isn't he?" Flannery continued.

"He's NASCAR's most popular driver and has been since Dale Junior retired."

"Oh yes, speaking of Dale Earnhardt Junior, you have a close-up photo on your Facebook page of Dale along with you and several others in his Whisky River bar. That's near the Charlotte airport, isn't it?"

"Yes, sir."

"How did you get all those celebrity sports figures to sit still for a picture?" Flannery asked.

"Objection, Your Honor! Ferrell yelled. "Are we really going to have Mr. Flannery go through a litany of this witness's lifelong Facebook postings?"

"Overruled, but let's get to a valid point, Mr. Flannery."

"Yes, thank you, Your Honor... Miss O'Gara, would you like me to repeat the question for you?"

"No, I got it. Most of our local sports celebrities are quite willing to get pictures with them, so long as you're prepared and don't take much time."

"I see. And if Dale Earnhardt Junior showed up at Papa Doc's while you were working there, and he and his wife were dining at one of your tables, you would undoubtedly have asked for a photo to be taken with them, wouldn't you?"

The witness began to squirm a bit, believing she now knew where this hostile attorney was taking her. "I probably would, if they had time and it wasn't too busy."

"Well, Miss O'Gara, during your previous testimony, you claimed that you well recognized the defendant, Alex Moretti. In fact, I'll quote from your previous statement made right here under oath, "Well, he is quite famous since he was Evelyn Stevens' boyfriend and all."

The jury began to glance sideways at each other for impressions as the trial spectators began yet another buzz, prompting the judge to pound the gavel twice.

"Miss O'Gara, since you are apparently quite adept at getting your photo taken with many sports figures, why did you not ask Mr. Moretti for a close-up photograph?"

Serena's face was quite blushed now as she struggled. "Well, he didn't know me from Adam, so"...

"Are you trying to tell the court that Luke Kuechly, Chase Elliott, and Dale Earnhardt, Junior all knew you personally and that's the reason you managed to get their photographs?"

O'Gara was really intimidated now, her nerves frayed as she struggled to come up with an explanation. "I didn't know Amanda and thought she would not like it."

"Miss O'Gara, did you tell your co-worker, Valerie Hampton, that it was actually Allison Cook at that table with the defendant and not Amanda?"

"It was a long time ago! I could have been mistaken! But I did see them having sex in his boat!"

The judge again pounded the gavel. "Order in the court!"

"Miss O'Gara, you testified earlier that you had looked through the small windows on Mr. Moretti's boat, and that both he and Miss Cook were naked. Now you're claiming you saw them having sex. Is there a reason you didn't mention that act specifically before?"

"I thought that I had stated that," O'Gara replied, now frustrated and avoiding eye contact with the members of the jury.

"I have no more questions for this witness, Your Honor."

"Mr. Ferrell, do you wish to re-examine?"

"Yes, Your Honor." The prosecuting attorney gathered his thoughts momentarily before re-approaching.

"Miss O'Gara, that was a long time ago, three years now. How well did you know the Cook sisters?"

"Not all that well. They were fairly well-known around the area then, I think."

"And you would agree that being four years apart, they do look strikingly similar, almost as twins?" Ferrell lead.

"Yes. I may have assumed it was Allison there because of Alex being around her age," O'Gara responded, so happy to now be questioned by a friendly lawyer.

"And it is your sworn testimony here today that you did see the defendant and one of the Cook sisters in his boat cabin around midnight naked together, correct?"

"Yes."

"I have no further questions, Your Honor," Ferrell stated, trusting that he had regained the trial initiative.

"Mr. Flannery, call your next witness," the judge ordered.

"Yes, Your Honor. I call to the stand Miss Amanda Cook."

The whole courtroom exploded with chatter now, as everyone expected the possibility that Brad Ferrell may call the *victim* to testify, but not the defendant's attorney.

Alex, as shocked as anyone in the courtroom, placed a hand on Flannery's shoulder while Amanda was being sworn in, a signal to hesitate before rising to approach her on the witness stand. "Are you sure this is a good idea?" he whispered in the veteran attorney's ear.

Flannery replied with no indication of concern and in a low tone. "No problem, so long as she just tells the truth."

The entire courtroom was as silent as a mouse as the defense attorney shuffled up toward the witness stand.

"Miss Cook," Flannery began. "I'm sure you really didn't want to testify in this trial did you?"

Amanda couldn't help but throw a glance at Alex. "No."

"In fact, you have never wanted this trial to even occur, isn't that correct?"

"It is."

"Do you recall the events of the evening of July 25th, 2020, Miss Cook?" Flannery asked.

"Yes, very well."

"Very well, you say? That was nearly three years ago, Miss Cook. God knows you have been through a lot during that time. How is it that you recall that date so well?"

"Because it was the first time Alex and I were spending the night together on his boat," she answered, mentally forcing herself to black out all the stares toward her from the court spectators, with one exception - the defendant.

"Miss Cook, you and Alex had dinner at a place on Lake Wylie, Papa Doc's Shore Club," Flannery stated. "Were you content or happy about stopping off at that place?"

"No, not really. Papa Doc's is a very popular place, probably more so than any place on our lake. I was worried I would be seen by someone who knew me and my family."

"Do you recall the waitress who serviced you that evening?"

"I do now from her testifying here. Not so much from that night, though," Amanda replied. "She and Alex talked too much but I didn't say anything to her."

"Amanda, were you jealous that your boyfriend was sitting there in front of you having a friendly chat, perhaps flirting with an attractive waitress?"

"Objection, Your Honor!"

"Overruled," Layton declared. "I want to see where this takes us."

"Well, Amanda?" Flannery asked again.

"No, that wasn't it. Alex never did that, at least not in front of me. He was talking to her mostly about parking the boat overnight in one of their slips. I just didn't want to be recognized. I wanted to leave there."

"I see," Flannery added while putting a hand up and pressing his forehead, as if in deep study about something. "Miss Cook, You began dating Alex around the time shortly after the 2020 Indianapolis 500, correct?"

"I don't know if dating is the right word. We never could go out on a regular date together, but started seeing each other after Indy, yes."

"Yes, well, I suppose the younger generation doesn't use that term as much as we did back in the day," Flannery chuckled. "But tell me, did you and Alex ever go "Dutch" as they say, each paying their own way when together?"

"No, never."

"Never? But there was a purchase you made yourself at a Walmart at 10:38 PM that very night, July 25th, 2020, as documented in the case record. It was their store in Lake Wylie, just a short drive from Papa Doc's Shore Club. Were you both not together?"

"Yes. We left Papa Doc's and he drove me there. I wasn't going to have Alex pay for my tampons," Amanda stated softly as she looked downward toward her lap.

"Tampons?"

"Yes, my period began that night, which was another reason I was uncomfortable in the restaurant."

Ferrell was jolted as the entire courtroom around him was buzzing again. *I'll be damned,* he thought, struggling not to display his sudden consternation. Judge Layton even took a few minutes to pound the gavel.

"So that is why the defendant claimed that you had a stomach ache that night?" Flannery led, as his entire case began to become clear.

"Yes, it was."

"Amanda, knowing your menstruation period was coming on, why didn't you and Alex just postpone this river rendezvous until another day?"

"I didn't know if my period would start that soon. Back then, we couldn't just go out whenever we wanted and our times together had to be planned in advance. As bad as I felt, I was happy to be with him." Amanda answered.

"Amanda, your waitress has testified here earlier that she had seen the two of you without clothing in Alex's boat. Your response?"

"Never happened. We were never like that on that night and I would never allow prying eyes in by having his curtain slides in the cabin open, even if we were. I'm a very private person," she added emotionally while giving him a glance in the process.

"So, Amanda," Flannery continued. "Could Miss O'Gara have been mistaken?"

"She made that up!" Amanda answered showing obvious conviction. "And I know Alex was the same way about his privacy on that boat."

"Amanda, Alex has admitted that you two engaged in sexual relations multiple times during that year, 2020, and early 2021. Some of those times occurred on Lake Wylie, or the Catawba River as we always knew it. Prior to your sixteenth birthday, how many times did you and Alex engage in sexual relations on the South Carolina side of that river?"

Amanda studied momentarily and slowly shook her head. "I don't know."

"But your family lives on Lake Wylie. You must know that geography pretty well. You can't recall a single time having sex with the defendant in your state?"

"I was never paying attention to that. It wasn't that many times. I just didn't know exactly where we were, sir."

"No more questions, Your Honor."

"The court will recess for twenty minutes, at which time Mr. Ferrell may cross-examine," the judge declared and pounded the gavel one time.

The scene in the courthouse foyer was tense. Sarah had run forward and embraced her daughter before escorting her out of the courtroom. Byron was beside himself, angry at her as knowing that her testimony could have iced the case for the prosecution, literally set the entire stage for victory in the Unibank civil suit against Andy Moretti, and bankrupt those contemptible *wops*.

Ferrell was beside himself. For Amanda to take the stand and state "I don't know" was just too much. She and Moretti had to have pre-planned their testimony, they had to have. He had to get her to admit to it under oath, lest his career path would go up in smoke.

Andy approached the old litigator outside on the courthouse steps as he enjoyed a cigar. "I underestimated you, Mr. Flannery. You had all this in your bag from day one."

"Let's not break out the champagne bottles yet, Mr. Moretti. She still has to hold up under cross-examination."

"Right, well I just want you to know how much your diligent work means to my family," Andy replied, patting the old man on the back.

"Well, thank you. That is very kind. You had best thank Samuel before you leave, too. He's the one who does all the leg work, you know."

The trial came to order and Amanda again took to the stand, reminded by the judge that she was still under oath.

Ferrell approached with a different attitude than originally anticipated, believing from day one that Amanda Cook would be his final ace in the hole if he needed it. He would now have to break her down on the stand and confess to what everyone had always known.

"Miss Cook, how many years have you and your family resided on Lake Wylie?"

"I was in kindergarten when we moved to Tega Cay," she answered.

322

"Over a dozen years, then. And your family has quite a nice big boat docked at your home, isn't that correct?" Ferrell asked.

"Yes."

"How many times over the years have you been on the family boat cruising up and down Lake Wylie, Miss Cook?"

"I couldn't say. Quite a few," she stated.

"Quite a few. Is it fair to say that you are familiar with every home, dock, launching ramp, and business establishment on Lake Wylie, Miss Cook?" Ferrell asked, his tone getting gradually more aggressive.

"I wouldn't go that far," Amanda responded. "As a kid growing up, my friend Trisha and I were busy together when we were on our parents' boats. We paid little attention to landmarks."

"Miss Cook, let me remind you that you are under oath. We all know that you were involved in that tragic accident in Las Vegas two years ago"...

"Objection, Your Honor!" Flannery declared, his cane pointing upward.

'Sustained. Mr. Ferrell, we've been over this before," the judge scolded.

"I'm sorry, Your Honor. I will rephrase.... Miss Cook, how many times since March, 2021, have you and Mr. Moretti been in contact?"

"The day of the accident is the last time we've spoken," Amanda answered, emotion showing as she looked toward Alex as if to communicate that she couldn't believe it had actually been that long.

Ferrell was beginning to grasp at straws now. "Miss Cook, you would prefer this jury to issue a not guilty verdict, wouldn't"...

"Objection, Your Honor!"

"Sustained. You are totally out of order, Mr. Ferrell. The jury will disregard that question and it will be struck from the record," Judge Layton ordered, getting angry for the first time since the trial was reconstituted.

"I am sorry, Your Honor... Miss Cook, let's back up a bit. So, you do admit that you and the defendant, Alex Moretti, did engage in sex prior to your sixteenth"...

"Objection, Your Honor! Repetitive," Flannery yelled.

"Overruled, Mr. Flannery. This witness has not been asked this question."

"Thank you, Your Honor. Miss Cook?"

"Yes, I have had sex with Alex."

"Prior to your turning sixteen?"

"Yes."

"How many times have you and the defendant engaged in this intimacy in our state?" Ferrell plowed on.

Amanda hesitated.

"How many times, Miss Cook?"

"I do not know?"

"Miss Cook, have you and Mr. Moretti ever had sex in any form at any place in your state?"

Amanda closed her eyes momentarily prior to looking toward the jury. "I don't know."

The judge again pounded the gavel as the courtroom repeated a noisy buzz. "Order in the court!"

Ferrell put on his best smirk as he asked, "Do you truly want this jury to believe that you never engaged in sex down here prior to turning sixteen?"

"No," Amanda stated flatly.

The whole courtroom became silent as even the Solicitor General District Attorney Ferrell was momentarily speechless.

"No?" he repeated back to her.

"I answered your question, sir."

"So, you and the defendant did engage in sexual relations down here prior to"...

"That's not what I said!" Amanda recoiled loudly.

Ferrell almost flinched as the rest of the courtroom froze on the edge of their seats. "Well, please be clear then, Miss Cook."

"You ask me if I had ever had sex here in South Carolina prior to my sixteenth birthday. That question did not include the words with the defendant, sir," Amanda came back sternly.

"You are talking in circles, Miss Cook!" Ferrell directed, a man obviously frustrated.

"No, you're asking questions in circles," an emotional Amanda replied.

"Miss Cook, let me remind you the strict penalty for perjury"...

"May I say something, Your Honor?" Amanda interrupted.

Ferrell pounced. "Your Honor, would you order this witness to answer?"...

"Mr. Ferrell," Judge Layton cut him off. "You have purported this witness to be the victim in this case. I believe her desire to make a statement is quite appropriate. Miss Cook, you may make your statement and then you will answer the remainder of the state attorney's questions."

"I did have sex before I turned sixteen. It occurred one time before I turned fifteen and it was not consensual. The wrong person is on trial here! Alex didn't do anything to me! I was drugged and raped," Amanda stated as she began to break down. "I was drugged and raped by Kyle Williams!"

The entire courtroom sat in complete shock as most attendees who knew the prominent Williams family were staring over at their youngest son. Kyle was wide-eyed as he kept looking around for support that was not forthcoming. After a brief period of stunned inaction, Bud Williams rose from his seat with his wife, Lisa, who grabbed Kyle by the arm.

"We're not going to stand for this," the senior Williams stated. "Let's get out of here."

Judge Layton then ordered the bailiff and deputy sheriffs on duty to arrest Kyle Williams for questioning, and he was escorted out of the courtroom while the rest of the Williams family vacated, totally devastated and in a near state of shock. as the state's largest car dealer prepared to deal with their own potential scandal, one of epidemic proportions.

The judge pounded the gavel. "Order! Order in the court!... Miss Cook, would you like a recess until tomorrow morning to continue?"

"No, Your Honor. Can we please finish this?" Amanda stated, still in tears but showing unforeseen strength in the face of such dramatic conditions.

"Mr. Ferrell, do you wish to continue with cross-examination?"

"Sure, Your Honor," Ferrell stated, his tone lacking the same level of arrogance from twenty minutes earlier.

He re-approached the stand as he attempted a mental rewind of how to deal with this girl, one who all this time had seemed so shy and fragile but one who had turned out to be the biggest challenge as a witness he had ever encountered.

"Amanda, I'm sure I speak for the Solicitor's office when I say how sorry we are for what you have gone through. But I must still ask you, have you ever had sexual relations with the defendant in this case, anytime or anywhere in this state prior to January 19, 2021?"

She looked around the courtroom again, so spent yet so relieved now that her whole family knew what had happened between her and Kyle Williams. She saw an expression on Alex, who appeared mentally spent but emotionally supportive. She saw the old lawyer, Ernest Flannery, who appeared as calm as a cucumber, and then her family sitting there, a wide mixture of love, disdain, and shock.

"I don't know."

"No more questions, your honor."

Amanda stepped down and moved to return to the front row, somewhat blank of expression as she was devoid of all emotion. The attending courtroom audience remained fairly quiet as though they were all emotionally exhausted.

The judge saw Ferrell retreat to his desk, hiding a feeling of dejection. "Mr. Flannery, call your next witness."

"The defense rests, Your Honor," Flannery stood and stated.

"The court will recess until nine o'clock Monday morning when we will hear closing arguments," Judge Layton stated while pounding the gavel.

The atmosphere in the Cook residence was frigid as the whole family was on pins and needles. Amanda's testimony regarding an allegation that Kyle Williams had raped her three years earlier had shocked the entire Rock Hill community, overshadowing the previous explosive testimony impugning Allison Cook's fidelity. Byron was shocked at the disclosure and of the belief that nothing he could say at the moment would be the right thing.

Sarah was totally upset as a parent and angry that her husband was not as outraged as she was. "What do you think about this trial now, Byron?"

"Why didn't Amanda say anything about this business with Kyle before?" he replied, much to his wife's chagrin.

"What's that supposed to mean, Byron?" Sarah came back. "Are you insinuating that it never happened?"

"I think it's time for this family to have an open and honest conversation about some things," he replied.

"Yes, Daddy. It is time we had an open and honest conversation," Amanda stated, surprising her parents as she strolled down the stairway and into the front room.

The three of them all sat down in a formal setting and both Byron and Sarah knew they were no longer addressing a child.

"Amanda, I don't know what happened between you and Kyle Williams three years ago," Byron spoke. "But you do realize that such accusations may potentially ruin the young man's life as well as destroy a lifelong family relationship."

"Byron! Let's allow Amanda to just tell us what happened!" Sarah yelled back. "This is serious!"

"I have no desire to explain in detail what happened that night with Kyle Williams. I only want to say that I spoke the truth but I do not seek to persecution of Kyle... But this trial... It's just wrong!"

"Amanda, you almost lost your life over your getting involved with Moretti. He had no business getting involved with a young"...

Amanda cut her father off. "I thought you wanted to have an honest family conversation, Dad."

Byron and Sarah both shared a confused and concerned look.

"What is your point, Amanda?" Sarah asked sincerely.

"This trying to make Alex a convict is wrong. I wanted to stop it."

"You were not even old enough to drive, Amanda," Byron stated.

"Do you believe Alex should go to prison, Father?"

Byron and Sarah shared another look as Amanda had rarely if ever addressed him as "Father", which had a more serious connotation than the simpler words "Dad" or "Daddy".

"He broke the law, Amanda."

"Have you ever broken the law, Dad?" his daughter replied, catching him off guard and injecting a bit of anger on his part.

"I'm not on trial for a felony, Amanda."

"Maybe you should be," Amanda stated sternly.

"Amanda! That's your father you're talking to," Sarah decried while raising her voice.

Amanda sat firm while collecting her thoughts, some that she had rehearsed for days on end. "Just before Alex's trial resumed, we celebrated your birthday, Mom. Thirty-nine years old, remember?"

Sarah shot a look at Byron. "What's your point, Amanda?" he asked, impatient with their conversation.

"My point is that Mom is not thirty-nine, she is thirty-eight. She was born on January 10, 1985, just two days and sixteen years before your wedding day,... and six months before Allison was born."

Sarah began to tear up while Byron sat frozen, his face blushed red.

"And you were five years older than Mom, Dad. If Alex is found guilty, this is going to be publicly exposed," Amanda stated with conviction.

"Amanda! You had better consider what you're saying," Byron stated. "It would damage our reputation, yes. And that would cost us all, including you."

"I don't care, Dad. This has to stop!" Amanda stated, then got up and retreated to her upstairs room.

Byron and Sarah sat staring at each other, unable to speak for several minutes.

"I can't believe this, Sarah," Byron stated, his anger still ever-present.

"You can't believe what, Byron, that our daughter knows we've lied to her all these years?"

"She's hell-bent on equating her own parents with her escapade with a race driver. You know it's not the same thing, Sarah."

"No, it's not the same thing. We were lucky enough not to get in a serious car accident," Sarah responded.

"Do you realize what she has done, Sarah?" Byron asked. "If what happened with Kyle Williams was that serious, why did she wait until now, until this trial to say something? It doesn't look good, Sarah. Amanda coming out with such an accusation now, right at the end of her testimony on the witness stand. Just doesn't look credible, that's all."

Sarah was stunned that her husband, Amanda's father, seemed to have little interest in what did actually happen between her and Kyle Williams. "Well, let me tell you what is credible, Byron. Our family birth certificates, that's what. You had best figure out something now. I know my daughter, and if Alex Moretti is found guilty in that courtroom on Monday morning, she'll be talking and there will be no shortage of reporters there. What are we going to do then?"

Byron watched his spouse run upstairs while he retired to his den. He downed a straight glass of Beam in three quick gulps, slamming down his fist on the hard oak desk. He sat there thinking about what to do, a man who had always been decisive, always having the challenges in front of him under control. He had never felt so helpless, so much in a box.

He then retrieved his iPhone, looked up a number, and dialed, hating it when getting a voicemail prompt. "James, we need to have a conversation with Brad Ferrell. Call me back immediately."

Chapter 14

Trial Aftermath

"This is Melissa Townsend reporting from the York County Circuit Courthouse in Rock Hill, South Hill, South Carolina. In an abrupt and shocking development, State Solicitor General Circuit Attorney Brad Ferrell began the court session today in the trial of Alex Moretti by submitting a motion to drop the charges against the well-known race driver, followed by Judge Layton's ruling of dismissal."

Half of the courtroom seemed to jump for joy while Alex exhaled in an obvious state of relief and received immediate encouragement and accolades from his family, while Amanda strongly embraced her mother while her many tears began to soak Sarah's wool sweater.

Alex then stood and faced Amanda, who then scurried toward him as the two embraced as if there was no tomorrow while the remainder of the courtroom attendees stood in stunned silence, including some of those who struggled to hold back the urge to applaud the two as they all prepared to clear the courtroom.

Ferrell walked out of the courtroom while refusing to answer any questions from reporters, an unnatural act for him in the least. The various other media representatives busied themselves sticking their microphones in front of any member of the Moretti family who would stand still.

"Andy, will this decision today open the door to reinstating your son, Alex, to drive for your team again?" Andrew Maddox, a reporter for Motor Racing magazine, asked boldly.

The Moretti Motorsport principal, fully thrilled with the court outcome, replied. "Well, I don't have a car or a crew for him right now. We still have some obstacles to overcome, but this is certainly a great day for Alex, our family, and the team in general. Thank you."

Melissa Townsend of the Observer approached the defense attorney. "Mr. Flannery, it appears this was a great day for you and your client, Alex Moretti. Your comments?"

"Yes, young lady, it was a great day for justice. The state simply could not prove my client was guilty of anything."

"Mr. Flannery, do you believe a similar charge will be brought against Kyle Williams?"

"I'm afraid you'll have to ask the Solicitor General's office about that. Thank you very much."

"There you have it, ladies and gentlemen. This is Melissa Townsend reporting to you live from the York County Courthouse in Rock Hill, South Carolina, where the case against well-known racing driver, Alex Moretti, charges of third-degree statutory rape in the case involving his relationship with Amanda Cook, the daughter of Unibank President and CEO, Byron Cook, were suddenly and shockingly dismissed this morning. Back to you, Brian."

As all the key players gathered outside the courthouse, an awkward and emotional scene developed. Alex stood by Amanda, her hand in his arm, while her father and mother waited to depart.

Byron was quietly steaming under the collar, still reeling from the dismissal while standing there in front of his youngest daughter, referred to as the victim for the past two years and now appearing inseparable from the very young man who in Byron's view should be behind bars.

Sarah stood near with extremely mixed emotions, happy for Amanda in her own way but knowing another firestorm would now be brewing over the trial disclosure regarding Kyle Williams, not to mention the problems they would face should the issue of she herself being pregnant as a minor become public.

Despite Andy's feeling of joy, he still felt the personal conflict between himself and Byron Cook as the two shared some awkward eye contact.

Crissy Moretti sensed the pending standoff and seeing Sarah Cook in tearful emotion, chose to approach Alex and Amanda, starting with a heartfelt embrace of the girl before initiating a silent discussion with the two. "I know it's difficult, but you should go home now, Amanda. Alex will be here for you," she spoke, prompting her brother-in-law to agree with a repeated nod.

Amanda looked at Alex for a few moments with tears of joy. "I wish you could take me home, and help bury this hatchet once and for all."

Alex and Sarah shared a look as he pondered the best response. "I don't think the time is right yet. Let's allow these wounds to heal a bit first. You had best go now, Amanda. I'll call you later."

"Promise?"

"Yes, I promise," Alex responded, and he and Amanda embraced again prior to her walking away to join her mother and father.

The drive home to Tega Cay was silent and cold as the emotional aftermath for each family member was quite dissimilar, to put things mildly.

Byron Cook could bite a ten-penny nail in two as all he could think about was how the outcome had harmed his civil case with Unibank, hurt his older daughter Allison's reputation, and damaged his long-time relationship, personal and professional, with Bud Williams and his family.

Sarah avoided speaking to him nor turning to chat with Amanda in the rear seat but was personally thrilled by the outcome and overjoyed for Amanda, notwithstanding the impending bitterness it would cause Allison to harbor toward her younger sibling.

Amanda smiled as she stared blindly out the rear window, thinking of little else but reconstituting her longtime but interrupted relationship with Alex.

Matilde planned a celebratory dinner at Andy's home as the Morettis hadn't such good news in a long while. She had invited Ernest Flannery and his assistant, who both happily accepted and the old man had Samuel re-book their lodging to a hotel in closer proximity to Lake Norman.

Alex had ridden with Tony and Crissy and they had barely passed downtown Charlotte when his phone beeped, a text from Amanda, which was the first in over two years, at least that he was aware of. *You can call me anytime. I'm home.*

He smiled to himself and dialed, getting a pickup on the first ring. "Hi."

"Hi, stranger. It's been a long time," he joked.

"You don't know how much I've missed you. The shores of the lake won't matter anymore."

"Especially now, Amanda. I sold the boat quite a while ago," he said. "Needed the money.... My lord, I'm so glad that's over. How about you?" he asked.

"Yes. I was so scared when I was on that stand," Amanda stated, still in a state of excitement. "But Mr. Flannery had told me to just tell the truth, so I just let go."

"You definitely dropped some bombs, all right.... Wait, what do you mean, Mr. Flannery told you?"

"He didn't tell you? I drove down to Charleston to see him," she replied.

"No!" *Well, that old scudder!* "When was this?"

"A long time, like right after I got my car over a year ago. Are you mad?"

"I sure wish I had known, that's all," Alex replied. *Water under the bridge now.*

"Oh! Mom's knocking on my door. Talk later?"

"Sure."

"Love you, bye."

Allison had arrived at the family residence early as she abruptly left the courthouse and raced home. "I'll get even with that little bitch, and her asshole boyfriend, too," she rambled on to herself while continuing to empty out her closet, an act mostly symbolic as she had moved out months earlier when she relocated to San Diego.

The rest of the family entered twenty minutes later and could hear the shuffling going on upstairs. Sarah strolled into Allison's room confronting an angry daughter. "Allison, what's going on here?"

"I'm packing up the rest of my stuff."

"Your pillows, your bedspread?" Sarah asked, feeling the horrid emotion from earlier in the day now coming back to her.

"Mother, so long as she's in this house, I'll not set foot in here again!"

"Allison, we had better talk about this. You'll be back for the wedding and"...

"Wedding!? Wedding? Get real, Mom. Aaron's parents won't even look at me now. They will disown Aaron if he doesn't break off our engagement. My life is just ruined!" Allison nearly screamed as she thundered out and down the stairway toward the door.

"What's going on?" Byron asked sternly as Allison practically ran by him, pausing just for a few seconds to give him a quick peck on the cheek before walking out and forcefully slamming the front door behind her.

Sarah followed down the steps while in tears again, giving her husband a look that told him without words, *I don't want to talk to you right now.*

Byron ran quickly outside and up to his oldest daughter, just as she was closing the trunk of her car. "Allison, you don't have to leave this way."

"Yes, I do, Daddy. I'll never step foot here again so long as Amanda is here."

"I'm so sorry this happened, baby," Byron stated as he placed his hand on her shoulder.

"Do you realize what Aaron's brother must think? What his parents must feel now? Now Kyle has been arrested over all her lies, Daddy! I can't even face them now. I hate this town, and I'm gone, Daddy. Don't forget that I love you," Allison cried as she and her father hugged.

He then stood in his four-car driveway and watched his oldest daughter back out and drive away. The family patriarch was slumping as he appeared back in the house and retired to his den,... to drink.

Sarah entered her youngest's room and could see the mixed emotions. "How are you holding up, honey?"

"I'm fine, Mom. Better than I've been in a long time."

"Amanda, you do know that Kyle Williams was arrested."

"No, I'm not thinking about Kyle Williams."

"Amanda. You testified that he raped you. Are you sure you wouldn't like to tell me about it?" Sarah asked sincerely.

"Mom, this wasn't about Kyle. It was about Alex. They were trying to put him in prison for rape. He never raped me, Mom. Alex didn't even pressure me to have sex with him until I was ready. I really don't want Kyle Williams or anyone else to get hurt, and the last thing I ever want is to testify in any court trial again. It happened over three years ago. I just want to move on with my life now. Do we have to talk about it anymore?"

"No honey, we don't," Sarah replied, *at least for now.* "You know I'm always here for you."

Matilde Moretti and her daughter, Marie, worked to put on a huge feast of fettuccini and spaghetti with meatballs, along with some fine Italian red wine. Flannery and his right-hand man were treated as guests of honor and Andy stood to offer a toast.

"Here is to Ernest Flannery and Samuel Mayne, if not before, they are now legends of the courtroom!"

All stood to drink to the two and applauded.

"Mr. Flannery, you didn't tell me that Amanda had paid you a visit last year way before the trial began," Alex stated, in a tone that implied an explanation should follow.

"No, I didn't disclose that as we couldn't have you contacting her. Could you sit here in front of me, your family, and our god above, and swear you wouldn't have?" Flannery asked, his mannerism no different than that of being in court.

"You told me not to," Alex replied defensively.

"Yes, and I advised her accordingly," the old man added as he helped himself to some of Matilde's Italian cuisine. "I was pleasantly surprised that she took that advice. I knew that Ferrell would test her with two important questions; had she been in contact with you, and had you two gotten *cozy* in South Carolina. Had she answered *yes* to the first question, or even hesitated before answering *no*, the jury may not have believed her answer to the second one. In the end, she told the truth and that made our case."

"Just curious, Mr. Flannery. What was the whole purpose of that questioning about Long Beach and that whole Allison Cook opinion business?" Andy asked, something he had been very curious about, knowing that would sow even more bitterness in Byron Cook, as if there was not enough as it was.

"I needed to establish in the minds of the jury that Alex was not some ruthless playboy, just waiting to jump in bed with every lovely young female he could find. I think it served its purpose."

"What are your thoughts regarding the civil suit we're still facing, Mr. Flannery?" Andy asked seriously with all of the rest of the family members tuning in also.

"Well, civil litigation isn't my specialty. Samuel actually handles those cases, when we choose to take them on."

The table's attention shifted suddenly to Mayne who considered a response. "I'm sure the enormity of the suit against the team and counter-suit you've filed are way above anything I've ever dealt with,"

Samuel commented thoughtfully. "I will say that our getting this case dismissed today, which is way above what we expected going in, should strengthen your civil case considerably."

"Then I should be unrestricted so far as seeing Amanda," Alex added promptly.

"No, I wouldn't go there just yet, young man," Flannery responded. "I would strongly advise you to keep a very low profile, at least publicly, until that litigation is concluded. You don't want to just rub it in Byron Cook's face."

Matilde chose to change the subject slightly, seeing her grandson was not taking his lawyer's advice real well. "Alex, one thing puzzles me that came out in the trial. I've known you for twenty-two years now, and other than on race morning, you've never been much for waking up early on a Sunday. What's with you waking up and running that boat of yours across that lake so early?"

"Amanda worked at her club pool on Sundays. Plus she wanted to get home early enough to accompany her mother to church," he replied.

His grandmother sat and looked up briefly at him along with the rest of the dinner table... "Oh."

Little had any of them known that night that in spite of Ernest Flannery's brilliant lawyering in the courtroom, Ferrell's decision to petition for dismissal, without so much as a closing argument, was totally due to a certain discovered birth certificate and marriage license.

It was getting late and Alex headed home to the condo, just twenty minutes drive down the road. He had sent Amanda a text earlier that the family was celebrating and that he would call her afterward. He wasn't happy about breaking the news to her that Flannery had suggested they still keep a low profile for a while.

He couldn't wait to get reacquainted with her again. He had thought she was quite attractive before, but now at eighteen, he thought, *Wow! And to think that she waited for me all this time.*

The two chatted for over an hour about anything and everything since they had last been together nearly two years earlier. Alex saw a call come in from Tim but chose to just let it go to voicemail. Amanda told him the atmosphere at the Cook home was toxic and made all the worse by Allison exiting the way she did. Her father knew she would be in her bedroom talking to him, which made it worse but she didn't seem to care.

How about I drive up tomorrow night?" Amanda asked. "I'll cook you dinner, and you haven't even seen my car yet."

"Sounds good, Amanda. We have a lot to catch up on."

"Yes, we do," she replied. "I love you... Good night."

"I love you, too, baby."

He had forgotten about Tim and apologized when he called back a second time at just after 11:00 PM.

"Alex, are you sitting down? I already have you a gig to qualify for the Daytona 500!" Tim declared excitedly.

"What!? When? With whom?"

"Gordon Rostell was following the trial and called me about three hours ago," Tim responded.

"Gordon Rostell? Who is he?" Alex replied, not recalling the name.

Tim began an air of disappointment, figuring his rather volatile client would be jumping for joy since it had been quite a long time it seemed since he had booked anything with a major series or event. "Gordon used to be a crew chief years ago working with Harry Gant. He's been mostly involved in vintage sports car events for the past twenty or so years. He's retired or semi-retired now and living down here in Venice. He's got a golfing buddy here with money to burn, they made a deal with Len Wood for a car, and they want to go and run Daytona."

"Harry Gant?" Alex inquired. "Isn't that the guy who they always called *Handsome Harry*?"

"Indeed they did," Tim replied.

"And who is Len Wood?"

"Who is Len Wood? You must have had your head buried in depositions too long, my man. Len Wood, the Wood Brothers, the team that invented the fast pit stop, and the team of David Pearson... Hello!"

"Oh, that Len Wood," Alex responded, the deal sounding better now.

"No retainer, buddy. It's a straight 50-50 prize money split. If you don't qualify, we get zippo," Tim detailed. "Sherri's out of town visiting her daughter who's expecting a new grandbaby. I'm heading up and we can room together if you want. You'll have to be in Daytona tomorrow."

"Tomorrow!?"

"Yes, qualifying starts Saturday. You'll need some practice time in the car."

"Tim, I really need a few days to unwind from the trial," Alex exclaimed, knowing this would upset his reunion with Amanda.

"Alex, I already had to cancel that commitment with Taylor for the Daytona 24. You're going to be standing out on the corner of a racetrack holding up a cardboard sign before long."

"All right, Tim. Text me where we're staying," Alex closed. *So much for spending a weekend with Amanda. She won't be happy.*

Newberry knew Evelyn would not take kindly to the upcoming week's schedule. He had set her up to be a guest on Danica Patrick's Daytona 500 pre-race broadcast and informed her that she would have some other *lesser* appearances. Following the 24-hour IMSA race in Daytona, she had been so focused on keeping up with the daily and hourly events of the trial, she had just informed Louie that she would just discuss the details with him when she arrived.

Mickey Raines was Evelyn Stevens' crew chief at Moretti Motorsport and she credited him as a big reason for her stellar result the previous season. She had pushed Newberry to try and get Indywest to hire him, but Andy Moretti had already given him a promotion to team manager for his entire Indycar operation, along with a generous raise in pay.

She began to have an immediate personality conflict with her new chief, Matt Van Brough, largely because he couldn't handle all of her celebrity distractions which amounted to more than all of the rest of the series' drivers combined. Even Pato O'Ward, who spent an inordinate amount of time with self-promotion to his many fans, had not allowed this activity to distract from his time with the team. Van Brough wanted her to be in the team shop for most of the weeks preceding the series opener at St. Petersburg, a wish that was not forthcoming.

A large part of the problem the prickly crew chief had yet to learn was the new contract his driver's agent had put together, which looked great with a tripling of pay but the beautiful Stevens went nearly bizzerk when she and Louie sat down together in the front room of her Daytona Beach hotel suite and went over the fine print.

"Did you read all this bloody rubbish, Louie?" Evelyn asked in a dress-down tone he was not accustomed to.

"I got you a sweetheart deal, Evelyn. You're the highest-paid driver in Indycar now! You know sponsors tend to expect a lot when they spend that much money," Newberry replied defensively, not wishing to discuss the fact that this new deal was put together at the midnight hour and that he hadn't bothered himself with reading every word.

"Expect a lot? Really?" she stated in retort as she switched back to the page in question. "Monday, February 13th: Unibank branch office in Ormond Beach, Florida, Show up in my bloody Unibank racing suit, greet walk-in customers, sign autographs, and get pictures taken from 9:00 AM to 6:00 PM!... Tuesday, February 14th, Unibank branch office in Daytona Beach South: Same bloody thing!... Wednesday, February 15th, Unibank branch office in Port Orange: Again, 9:00 to 6:00! There's seven pages of this bloody garbage!" Stevens shook her head as she threw the multi-page stapled document to the floor.

"You stayed busy with sponsorship commitments last year, Evelyn," Newberry came back in his defense.

"Yes, Louie. Busy last season meant flying to Barcelona for two days to shoot a few thirty-second Unibank commercials with Tony and his Formula One car! That commercial played thousands of times all season long."

Newberry struggled to find the right words, knowing this schedule was unrealistic and in denial that it was his responsibility to screen all such documents thoroughly before agreeing and having his client sign. "Calm down, Evelyn. I'm sure this can be worked out. Herrera knows you wouldn't be able to do all that."

"Well, you had better get on the horn and bloody fix this, Louie. I'm not showing up at some bank facility to greet customers all day as if it were Walmart!... Now, I have things to do," Stevens stated angrily and abruptly stood up, an unspoken signal that her long-time agent should just beat it.

"Call me when you get a chance," was the text message on Amanda's phone as she pulled into the school parking lot. Running late for her first class, she just sent him a quick reply that read, *"Will call after my math class."*

Alex had packed up early and left for Daytona before sunrise, cruising on I-95 at seventy-five miles per hour when his speaker phone began ringing, the word *"Amanda"* showing up on the Acura dash monitor.

"Good morning. How's my favorite girl?" he asked.

"I decided to go ahead and go back to school. I've missed so many days that I thought it best. It's so weird here, you know. It's all over the local news about the trial and my testimony. I'm getting looks from everyone," Amanda added. "I need to throw the Long Beach teddy bear at someone to let off some steam. What do you want for dinner tonight?"

Alex took a breath before distributing the bad news. "I'm sorry, Amanda. We'll have to take a raincheck on that. I'm ten miles north of Savannah heading for Daytona."

"What?... You didn't tell me about that!"

"Just got the call late last night. I'm qualifying for the Daytona 500," he replied, knowing she would be pissed.

"Oh, Alex, we haven't been together for two years and you take off the very day after the trial? This sucks!"

"I still have to pay the bills, babe. I called NASCAR and Fox Sports to request a delay on our behalf but they hung up on me," he joked.

Amanda wasn't amused. "Are you going to call later?" she asked, her mood now completely soured.

"I'll call this evening. Love you."

Amanda didn't reply as she opened her student locker.

"Amanda?"

"Yes, I love you, too," she replied finally. "I'm not happy about this, Alex."

"I know. Neither was I. I'll Call you tonight."

Amanda was not a happy girl. She had stood by Alex Moretti for two years, possibly the most beautiful girl in her high school class, and now when this excruciating trial was finally over, Alex leaves for Daytona the next day to drive again.

"Trisha, he called me last night and told me he was headed for Daytona to race," Amanda disclosed. "I'm crushed."

"You don't have to live like this, sweet bug," Trisha responded. She had seen that spark in her best friend's eyes return after a solid two years of dismay, and now a few hours later Amanda struggled to maintain it. "You could go to Clemson and have a boyfriend in no time."

Amanda heard her best friend's advice, knowing that Trisha had already committed to attending Clemson herself. "That would sure make my dad happy," Amanda responded, unclear if she considered that a positive or negative at this point in her life. "And Kyle Williams will be there."

"Oh, it's a big school, Amanda. Plus he might be in jail by then."

"Not funny, Trisha. Plus, I just have one problem."

"What's that, girl?"

Amanda looked at the young woman who had been closer to her than her own sister since they were kindergarteners, tears now forming in her eyes. "I still love him."

Tim introduced Alex to his new single race boss and all of his upstart crew members over dinner at the well-known Sloppy Joe's, located right on the beach. Most of the bunch had not worked together as a pit crew in years, feeding into a skepticism on Alex's part that he tried hard to disguise.

Their lead engineer, a term Alex thought was much too generous, looked like a man who had just walked out of a terrorist biker film. He introduced himself as Jake and mumbled under his breath that this gig was causing him to miss out on his favorite weekend hobby, that of a Confederate corporal in an Alabama infantry regiment performing Civil War reenactments. His sidekick, an overweight and bearded lad who didn't have a tooth in his head, appeared twenty years older than his age and kept ribbing the make-believe soldier that even if their driver qualified and finished in last place, the two would make more money than they had in the past year.

Leaving the joint, Alex followed Tim as they headed up the A1A beach highway toward their hotel, with Alex already disgruntled that Rostell had not paid the whole tab, insisting that Tim or Alex pick up half of it, with all of their part ending up on Alex's bank credit card.

"Those boys do drink a lot of beer, Tim," Alex observed as he and Tim were connected on each of their car speakerphones.

"They just got to Daytona themselves, Alex. Can't blame them for being a bit excited," Tim replied, *especially since they're not paying for it.*

"I suppose not," Alex replied, struggling to focus on the mission at hand while still thinking about Amanda.

"You only have to beat out three drivers, Alex. You can do that," Tim stated, knowing that his running in the top four out of seven cars and drivers for the last two rows would mean walking out of the famous racing town with at least a little money.

Alex worked to build up his mental confidence, knowing he had been fast in every kind of racecar he had ever driven in his life, but he and Tim had to be realistic. Coming down here and taking on the great teams and drivers that had been running here for more than a generation, teams like Hendrick, Penske, Gibbs, and Roush, not to mention his dad's own Moretti team, would be a very tough mountain to climb.

His concentration was broken as he noticed the crowded rows of hotels, condominiums, and businesses had given way to a bare and open beach on his right and a scant spattering of houses now on his left. "Where is this place, Tim?"

"Just a bit farther," Tim replied. "Daytona is packed now, in case you haven't noticed, Alex. This is the only hotel I could get at an affordable price, and it's still over two hundred bucks a night, plus tax."

"Great," Alex came back, still looking forward to a good night's sleep following the seven-hour drive to get here, and then having to suffer through that rollicking and costly dinner.

The two pulled into the hotel parking lot as Alex was now regretting his driving the NSX down, with one too many signs that read:

NOT RESPONSIBLE FOR VEHICLE THEFTS, BREAK-INS, OR DAMAGES

Charming, Alex thought. *If Amanda would only see this seedy joint.*

Tim checked in and the two had their bags in tow as they entered the second-story exterior door to their room when Alex was confronted with a single queen-sized bed.

"Uh, Tim... I like you, but I don't like you that much," he told him, regretting this trip more by the minute.

His agent chuckled. "That couch makes into a pullout bed. I'd flip you for it, but with my bad back and all, age before beauty. You know how it is."

Alex frowned as he began unpacking. *Great, Tim. Just great.*

Following their each showering, Alex stepped outside and sat in his car while dialing up Amanda. He received her voicemail and sat there for what seemed like an eternity waiting for her to call back.

Oh, oh. She's never done this before. Always a quick text at least. Alex worried that his last-minute dash south, happening the very morning after their two-year separation over his criminal charges, may have been too much for her.

He sat in his car, checking his phone for other messages, his social media, and news which was still dominated by the news from his trial. Nearly every story featured a photo image of him and Amanda together on the courthouse steps with the various pundit's twists on the trial itself.

After nearly an hour, she called. "I was having dinner with Mom and Dad. I chose not to interrupt it and excuse myself, mostly for Mom's sake. It's still pretty tense here, you know."

"I miss you, already," he stated. "I'm starting to get a nauseating feeling about coming down here."

"That's good to hear... The missing me part, I mean," she replied. "We had a long conversation about me going to college."

Alex paused, not knowing how that would affect things. After the long saga following the crash, he had not thought about the fact that Amanda would be graduating high school and would or should think about her education. "I see."

"You don't approve?"

"Amanda, I'm not sure that's any of my business," Alex replied, unsure of what else he should say.

"I want it to be your business."

Oh, that's good. I suppose my sudden venture to head to Daytona didn't kill her after all. "What do you want to do, Amanda?"

"I just want to be close to you."

"You know how my life is, Amanda. I'm gone nearly every weekend at least nine months out of the year," he added. He wanted to state that he would just like her to be with him all the time, but couldn't bring himself to say it, not after all that she had been through.

"I know. Maybe I'll just take off for a year," she suggested, the thought just coming off the top of her head.

"We had better spend some time talking about this, Amanda."

"When are you coming home, Alex?"

"If I don't qualify, I'll be home in less than a week. If I do, two weeks. Maybe I could sneak back a day or two early next week, even if I do make it," he stated, knowing that would be a stretch but thinking she may like to hear it, and wanting to believe it himself.

"You don't sound like yourself, Alex. When we first met, you were one of the best drivers there. You're just hitting your prime now."

"Thanks for the vote of confidence. I don't have the greatest team behind me now. A bunch of drunken has-beens actually. We'll see," he told her. "Listen, I better get in and get some sleep. You too, baby. Love you."

"Keep me in your dreams, Alex Moretti. Good night."

He had been drinking heavily the past couple of days. He had never bothered to keep such a close eye on his girls in the past, choosing to allow Sarah to tend to that function. Lately, he checked the details on Amanda's debit card account a couple of times per week for any evidence of chicanery related to Alex Moretti. Thus far he had found nothing that would offend him, other than his usual opinion of teen girls and women in general, wasting so much money.

Being somewhat intoxicated, on this particular night he chose to tap silently up the steps and approach Amanda's bedroom door to put an ear against the wood, all in an effort to listen in on her chit-chat over the phone, which seemed to be his daughter's main hobby as of late.

He thought a moment about simply barging in and yelling at her on the spot but something caught him, even in his near drunken state, and he chose to save it for a morning conversation with Sarah.

His wife knew something was up the next day when Byron had called his secretary early to inform her that he would be delayed in getting in. Once Amanda drove off for school, he composed himself and prepared for a difficult conversation.

"What do you think Amanda is going to do about her college education, Sarah?"

"I don't know, Byron. She has been rather preoccupied as of late," she answered.

"Did you know she's thinking about just taking a year off,... to chase that Moretti boy around the globe from race track to race track?" Byron asked his wife of twenty-three years.

She looked up at him, unsure of whether his question, which was more of a challenge, was to test her or if he knew something she didn't. "Where did you ever get that idea?"

"I heard her talking to Alex Moretti on the phone about it."

"What do you mean you heard her?" Sarah responded.

"I heard her, Sarah! This has to stop and I mean now. We need to go ahead and get her enrolled at Clemson," Byron demanded.

"No, we won't. We allowed Allison to choose her own college path, and we'll do the same for Amanda," Sarah stated firmly.

"Amanda's in no proper state of mind to make those types of decisions. As responsible parents, we have to make them for her. She'll thank us later, Sarah."

"Bullshit, Byron! You know that Kyle Williams attends Clemson. Does that not even bother you? You've said virtually nothing about that!"

Byron was stunned. Sarah had never used that type of foul language in her home before. "Sarah, we cannot stand by while our daughter throws her life away and takes up with some,... some race driver."

"He seems much more honest than most car dealers I know."

"What's that supposed to mean, Sarah?"

"Throughout that whole trial, he didn't hold anything back. He was"...

Sarah was interrupted by a knock on the door. Both she and her husband were surprised as in their exclusive private development, they didn't get random visitors much. Byron walked over and opened the front door, confronting a middle-aged very fit male in a suit and tie, accompanied by a thirty-something-year-old woman, also professionally attired. "Yes?"

"Are you Mr. Byron Cook, sir? she asked.

"Yes, I am Byron Cook."

"Mr. Cook, I am Detective Maria Saint John and this is Lieutenant John Reed. We are from the Tega Cay Police Department. May we come in?"

"What's this about, detectives?" Byron asked defensively.

"Byron, let them come on in," Sarah ordered and they both stood aside as the two officers entered. "Won't you sit down? Would either of you like some coffee?"

"Thank you, Madam," Reed replied. Black for me.

"I'll be fine," Detective Saint John added.

Sarah went to the kitchen somewhat shaken. She knew why the police were there.

"Why would the Tega Cay Police Department pay us a surprise visit?" Byron asked as though he was somewhat offended.

"We just have a few questions regarding your daughter and her relationship with Kyle Williams," Reed stated slowly, wanting to await Mrs. Cook's return. "Would your daughter, Amanda, be home by chance?"

"No, she's at school," Byron replied as Sarah re-entered the front room with a tray full of coffee cups.

"We have a referral from the York County Solicitor General's office. It's regarding a statement your daughter made during her testimony at a trial a few days ago," Reed stated after thanking Sarah for the coffee.

"Has Kyle been arrested and charged with anything?" Byron asked.

"He was arrested and held for questioning following testimony at a trial. He was released shortly thereafter."

"Amanda has been under a lot of stress," Byron offered. "I think we should talk to her and get back to you."

"We would really need to speak directly with Amanda, Mr. Cook," Detective Saint John stated. "Perhaps we could return sometime after she returns from school?"

Byron and Sarah shared a look, one of obvious worry.

"Could I call you?" Byron asked expectantly.

The two detectives themselves glanced at each other and Reed gave his partner a nod.

"Very well, Mr. Cook. If we don't hear back from you in a few days, we'll contact you. We wish to avoid questioning Amanda while she is at school. You do understand."

The two police detectives departed and Sarah could barely hold her anger.

"This is an absolute disaster," Byron stated shaking his head. "A lifetime of friendships will be destroyed over this."

"Amanda says she was raped by him, Byron! I don't give a damn about friendships right now. I care about our daughter."

"We still need to sit down and talk to her, Sarah... Before the police do."

"Why?... Why, Byron? So she can be sure and lie? We all know she didn't do a good enough job lying to suit you at the trial, don't we?"

He received the text message late that read, *"When will you be arriving in Daytona?"*

"Be there by tomorrow night, Louie. What's up?"

"Need to meet. Have some potential conflicts with Stevens' schedule," Newberry's return message stated.

He smiled as he could just see the arrogant Newberry right now and how Evelyn Stevens would be reacting to playing banker for a few days. *You could have re-signed with Moretti, Louie,* Herrera thought to himself.

Alex struggled the first couple of days to get up to speed with the car. The Woods' supplied Mustang had come with a basic generic setup and had told Rostell that much tweaking between their driver and crew would have to be done to get that final mile per hour or two that would be necessary to make the race in a very fast and competitive field. The latest NASCAR models from the participating manufacturers GM, Ford, and Toyota were down overall on performance from previous years as NASCAR endeavored to keep competitive speeds under control.

The fastest drivers, Austin Cindric, Kyle Larson, and Chase Elliott were lapping the 2.5-mile high-banked speedway at just under 182 miles per hour. Alex was lapping at 178, which would make the field as things stood on Thursday, but was dicey as drivers up and down the paddock were constantly making adjustments and improving by the hour.

Something Alex should have expected but was somewhat blindsided by was his being completely deluged by the media with questions regarding the trial, and more specifically his relationship with Amanda Cook. Even Evelyn Stevens, who unexpectedly appeared in the paddock, had constantly been thrown into the mix as an additional distraction.

Alex called Amanda late afternoon on Saturday, full of glee after qualifying on the fifteenth row for the race, to be run the following weekend.

"I saw you on TV! It was so exciting!" Amanda stated, holding back on informing Alex of the events around Rock Hill the past few days. "So, I guess that means I won't see you for a while."

"Surely another day won't kill you. I'll be back home by midnight."

"What? Don't kid around Alex Moretti. This is Amanda you're talking to now." she added.

"I'm passing St Augustine now. You have no idea how much I miss my own bed."

"Oh my god. You're serious. I was planning on going to church with Mom late in the morning," she said, somewhat to herself, wishing someday he would be welcome to go with her.

"Don't put that off, Amanda. The man upstairs has been awfully good to me this week," he stated, not jokingly. "I may sleep real late anyway. Call me when you get out of church and we'll figure out something."

Newberry entered the Daytona Grande Oceanfront Hotel, meeting Adam Herrera in the lobby lounge. He assumed the Unibank executive would be catching hell by now over Evelyn Stevens having left each bank branch at 11:00 AM this week, spending just two hours at each and not the expected nine as her contract called for. She would be joining them in one hour, which the nervous and sweating agent arranged, hoping to condition Herrera for the adjustments she wanted by the time she arrived.

Adam approached, surprisingly giddy while slapping Newberry on the back as he sat down and ordered a cocktail. "How go the wars, Louie?"

He hasn't heard from the locals at his banks yet. "Great, Adam. Business is great."

"Very good. Now, what can I do for you, my friend?" Adam asked, looking like a man who may have just won the lottery.

"It's about Evelyn's schedule. You see, the hours and consecutive dates are,... well quite unreasonable, if I must say."

"Hmm, really? Why may I ask, Louie, did you so willingly accept the requirements?"

"It all happened way too fast. You folks were so anxious to get it done," Louie claimed as he grasped for air in a vain attempt to deflect blame.

"No, Louie. I was anxious to get the contract with Moretti Motorsport done. It would have cost the bank about the same amount if you included her part in the royalties she would continue to earn as a bonus on the Formula One commercials,... which have now ceased of course."

"Adam, she will be here in less than an hour, expecting us to come up with a revised and more reasonable schedule."

"Well Louie, you're talking to the wrong guy. I submitted my resignation notice to Unibank this morning. I'll be on the payroll for another month, but I won't be overseeing any more projects."

"No? Well, who should I be dealing with then?" Louie asked nervously.

"Her name is Carolyn Tyler," Adam informed. "She hasn't officially been promoted yet, but that appears to be Byron Cook's plan."

"How is this Tyler in working on such details?" Newberry asked.

"Oh, from what I've seen, Carolyn Tyler is very astute on details."

"I suppose she cannot be reached until Monday then, huh?"

"That would be likely correct, Louie."

"What are you going to do, Adam?"

"Become an agent,... for race teams. I'll specialize in getting sponsors for teams."

Newberry was stunned. Herrera had been such a close business associate from day one, the guy who helped put his original deal together connecting Unibank with Evelyn. He was quite certain that he would fully understand that Unibank's demands on his client were unreasonable. Herrera was the guy who would help him fix this but now he would be dealing with an unknown.

"Well Adam, I do wish you well," Newberry stated with his usual insincerity, a trait that Herrera had seen through from day one. "Would you mind setting up a meeting with this Carolyn Tyler? I'm sure the three of us could get this resolved."

"I'll just give you her direct number... It's 704-329-3006. Good luck with it, Louie," Herrera replied smiling as he stood and waved over the waitress for his tab.

They walked out of the church sanctuary together and it seemed everyone wished to give their regards to Amanda, with many embracing her as though she had just returned from some sort of hostage crisis, while Byron and Sarah looked on.

Byron had wanted the three of them to have a heart-to-heart conversation about Kyle Williams ever since the police visit on Friday morning, but he chose to have Sarah initiate it, which she had thus far declined to do.

They had taken two vehicles as Amanda had told them she had things to do after church, while Sarah elected not to question her about it, and Byron at that point thought better of it, himself.

She drove through Mecklenburg County thinking of nothing but spending time with him. *Two long years,* she kept thinking. *They all thought I needed a shrink. Have the two of us changed? Would our relationship still be the same? Would the lack of excitement, the rush of a forbidden romance change us? That clandestine part of our connection would soon disappear. Is that the reason I was so drawn to him, because I shouldn't be? No! Your name is Amanda, not Allison.*

She knocked on his door at just past 1:00 PM, choosing not to text him first as she wanted to surprise him. She knocked again with no answer. She then called him.

"I'm down at the dock, Amanda. Come on down."

She retreated to her car and motored around the condominium building and down to the private boat dock, where he ran up and greeted her.

Following an emotional embrace and deep kiss, the two decompressed finally and he stated, "Come check it out. A friend at the shop is trying to sell it to me."

"What, another boat?" Amanda asked. "I was so excited to show you my car."

"Oh yes, I forgot about that. Come on, the boat first."

He held her hand and led the way as they checked out the thirty-four foot Formula cruiser. "What do you think?"

She looked the craft over, believing it looked similar to her father's boat, a feeling that gave her pause. "How can you afford that? I figured you would be broke by now," she observed.

"Hopefully, I'll be making some money soon. Nothing too good for my southern belle."

She stood still for a moment, looking out over the lake.

"Amanda, is something wrong?"

She turned and put her arms around his neck. "Alex Moretti, I don't need expensive boats or expensive cars, or anything like that. I just need you."

They embraced while their lips were pressed together, the two frozen in time for several moments, oblivious to their surroundings. A sarcastic old retiree snickered finally, knowing they hadn't seen him. He had been Alex's neighbor for over two years but they had rarely even spoken. "You two really ought to get a room. If my wife still looked like that, I know where I would be."

Amanda gave the old man a snide look before looking back at Alex for his reaction.

"That's one hell of an idea," he replied while laughing and reached down, wrapping his arms around Amanda's buttocks, and lifting her up over his shoulders like a sack of feed before retreating up toward the small parking area.

"Put me down! Alex Moretti, put me down or I'll scream!" Amanda hollered while her arms and legs were flailing in the wind as she caught a backward glimpse of the old man, now laughing at them.

"This must be it, huh?" he asked, still laughing as he released her to the ground before the bright red Mustang convertible.

"Have you any more juvenile acts in store for me, Mr. Moretti?"

"Not for the next twenty minutes," he replied grinning.

"So, what do you think?" Amanda asked as she playfully punched him a couple of times in the arm and reached up to fluff back her hair.

"Looks like fun. When did you get this thing?"

"It was a present for my seventeenth birthday last year."

"I didn't know?" he said, as his expression became blank as if in deep thought.

"How would you have?" she replied, her thoughts and his seemingly synchronized. "It's been a long time, Alex."

"Yes, it has. Come on, let's go."

He sat out on his third-story balcony, lounging in his new matching checkered flag bathrobe that Amanda had bought the two of them as a coming-together gift. Sipping on a light drink, he looked out over the lake, enjoying the evening that was cool and breezy as he watched the sunset, still early in the Lake Norman winter. He and Amanda had showered together and shared a repeated intimacy after spending most of the afternoon in bed together. She remained in his bathroom a bit longer, as women will do, and finally appeared through the sliding doors, sporting the same racing tee shirt she had worn that morning after the very first night she had spent there.

"You remembered," he said, admiring the woman he had so missed, noting that father time had been very good to her. "I'm surprised you didn't wear your bathrobe. You would match me."

"I know you like me in this," she replied. "And you kept all my stuff."

"Oh, so you've been pillaging through my drawers, have you?" Alex exclaimed playfully.

"Are you offended?"

He looked back out to the water and smiled, knowing she would be pleased and assume that no other female had been there, at least on an ongoing basis. "Everything is still pretty well as they were since you... Since the accident."

She retreated back indoors and returned shortly thereafter with a wool blanket, grabbing a seat next to him in the cool breeze.

"I dated a couple of guys. It was summer before last," Amanda stated solemnly as she stared out toward the lake herself in earnest thought, as she didn't want any secrets between them.

"Okay."

"My family pushed me to,... and I"...

"Needed to try and move on," Alex cut her off, finishing her statement as he knew it word for word.

"I didn't sleep with either of them," Amanda continued, believing he would want to know.

Alex was silent, sifting through his emotions.

"And you? Has there been anyone?" she asked.

Alex paused, not certain how Amanda would react but himself wanting honesty in their relationship. "There was a girl from Sweden. It was also summer before last. We spent a few weekends together back and forth with the races. She wanted to come back home with me but I declined. And there it ended."

Amanda sat and began to become misty-eyed.

"I thought I needed to move on. I felt so bad in that hospital,... and kept sending you text messages. I got no response from you, Amanda. My grandmother told me about the baby and I just thought you were through, I guess."

Amanda had thought many times about this conversation, knowing their disclosures could be emotionally devastating. *If Allison had not scrambled my phone. What if Alex and I would have kept in touch?*

"I didn't know I was pregnant. I suspected and was going to get a test and then... What if I would have told you?"

"I would be a proud father now, wouldn't I?"

"I guess you would be," she replied as she got up from her chair and approached to sit on his lap, an emotional test between them she felt had now been bridged, always unsure of how she would react had he suggested an alternative. "You'll be heading back down tomorrow morning?"

"Leave at the crack of dawn."

"Such a long drive to spend one day," she observed.

"I'm not complaining,"

Suddenly they heard a knock on the door. He chose to ignore it and the knock persisted.

"Alex, open up!"

He looked up surprised. "That sounds like Crissy."

"I guess I better run into the bedroom," Amanda stated hurriedly.

Alex moved swiftly through the condo and opened his front door, surprised to see his sister-in-law standing before him.

"Well, well. Don't you look spiffy," she stated as she looked at him in his fluffy checkered flag bathrobe.

"Come on in," he replied. "Where is Tony?"

"He's on his way back from London with his dad. I'll see him for just a few days and then they're both going to Daytona... Where is she?" Crissy asked smiling as she looked past him as if expecting to see company.

"Where's who, Crissy?"

"Who do you think? You sent us a text that you were driving all the way up here for just a day, and you have your phone turned off, Alex. There could only be one possible explanation I could think of for that. And I wanted to see her, just to say hi."

He smiled and shouted, "You can come out, Amanda. It's just Crissy, my sister-in-law."

Amanda came out into the front room and the two girls warmly embraced each other, seeming to have a genuine affection as though they'd known and were close to each other for years.

"Wow, don't you two look cozy together," Crissy observed as she admired both wearing the matching robes.

"I bought these online," Amanda replied as she snuggled up next to Alex.

"Well, why didn't I ever think of something like that?" Crissy asked herself. "Send me the info... So, tell me how you've been, Amanda."

The three shared small talk for nearly an hour and Alex could tell the two had a certain connection.

"Amanda, I just wanted to tell you that I am so sorry for not telling him about our phone conversation last year. I just knew"...

"It's okay, Crissy. Trust me, I understand. It's probably for the best that you didn't tell him... He would have called me, and that could have hurt him in the trial, right Race Man?" she added as she elbowed Alex softly in the ribs.

"Probably... I was pretty busy," he joked.

"We all knew he would have," Crissy added as the three shared some laughter.

It had been a long week. Alex had kept working with the crew chief, Mark Nettles, to improve the handling of the car. The rest of the crew seemed enthused in spirit but how good would they perform under pressure in the race? *It was anybody's guess,* Alex thought, often shaking his head.

Limiting his nightlife, he tried to keep a low profile and looked forward to his conversations each evening with Amanda. He knew she was quite anxious when he emphasized their still having to limit their time together until the civil suits between Unibank and he and his father's race team were settled. He chose to appear optimistic in order to keep Amanda's spirits up, but knew that expecting lawyers to move with haste would be futile.

Tim began to encourage him to press for clearance on his passport and was becoming disgruntled with his client's lack of initiative in that regard. Alex would have secured a ride with Hyundai running in the World Rally Series again, but he pushed back, not really wanting an international gig just yet.

On a better front, Alex's father and his brother were flying in, giving him a chance to stay in their suite at the team's hotel, as well as accompany them to an annual Saturday night cocktail party with Ford Motor Company. This would hopefully give him a good chance to discuss the status of the Unibank lawsuits in detail.

Late Friday afternoon, Amanda called, telling him that she and Trisha may drive down there if he could help them arrange lodging.

"I have a party invite with the Ford people Saturday night, Amanda. I can't take you to that," Alex recoiled.

Amanda was devastated, thinking he would be so excited about her driving all the way down there. "Why not, Alex?"

"We talked about this, Amanda. Look, Dad and Tony are coming down. I haven't been able to spend any time with him since the trial and I'm going to discuss this lawyer business with him in detail. Until then, we're just going to do the best we can. I'll be home late after the race on Sunday and should be open for a couple weeks after that. Okay?"

"Well, me and Trisha can find something to do then," she answered.

"No, Amanda. We couldn't be seen together and I would have to get you a room outside of town. Our time would be so limited."

"Like we're not used to that?"

"I plan to stick with Dad like glue the whole weekend so I can hound him mercilessly about the lawsuit," Alex stated, the whole idea of her and Trisha running around Daytona with that partying crowd not sounding appealing. "Just be patient. It'll only be a few more days."

He waited for a response as the line was silent. "Are you still there?"

"Yes."

"I love you," he added.

"Me too. bye," Amanda closed, so disappointed as thinking he would be thrilled with her driving down there.

The reception was held at the Hard Rock Hotel on the beach, crowded with personalities from all sectors of stock car racing, past and present. It had been quite a while since Alex had spoken to or even seen many of them, including Roger Penske, in town hoping for another Daytona trophy, along with team president Tim Cindric, cheerleading for his son, Austin, of course.

Andy would spend ample time with the Ford execs, excited about their next season's re-entry to Indycar following a near thirty-year hiatus.

Alex and Tony would make the rounds together, confronting a familiar face.

"Congratulations, Alex," she said pleasantly as she moved to give both Alex and his brother Tony a brief welcoming embrace. "Unchartered waters here, is it not? How do you feel, starting 30th, aren't you?"

"29th actually. We do what we have to do, Evelyn. There's no money left to pay any of the rest of us, not with you cashing in," Alex joked. "It does appear Louie struck gold for you. I never would have thought."

"Yes, you don't know bloody half of it," she responded with a smile he recognized as disingenuous, a look she would wear when deeply disturbed about something, also as evidenced by her downing Martinis one after another.

"Evelyn, are you okay?"

She repeatedly feigned a smile, waiting for the lingering passersby to clear. "Alex, could I talk to you about something?"

"What's on your mind?" Alex responded, by now conscious of being seen with Stevens a bit too long.

"I need some air. Would you mind?" she asked, nodding toward the glass doors that led from the ballroom outside to the pool area.

"Over here, love," she paused addressing and halting a passing waiter, grabbing yet another drink off of his silver-coated tray, while knocking two other of his cocktails to the floor in the process.

The two exited the ballroom, with Alex having to grab Evelyn by the arm and assist her as each sat down on adjacent pool lounge chairs, catching the attention of more than a dozen touristy fans still buzzing on the beach with the weekend race crowd.

"I'm in big trouble, Alex," she began.

He looked over at her, feeling extremely uncomfortable by now. "Trouble, huh? A word all too familiar."

"That new contract I signed. It sucks."

"I heard you got a huge increase," he replied, having a hard time with empathy considering his situation over the past several months.

"It's all the bloody bullshit they have me doing. I'm about to drop."

"I don't get it, Evelyn. You were always so gung ho about all those PR functions Newberry set up for you, all the photo shoots, the commercials. That's what cooked our relationship."

"They expect me to work nine hours per day, three bloody days per week at local bank locations preceding every major race weekend on the *friggin* calendar, Alex."

"I would get with Adam," he advised, having never recalled his former girlfriend looking so distraught, angry, and loose with such salty language, while also of the belief that she must be grossly exaggerating in her present state. "He'll be fair with you. Have him rearrange things that you can live with. Where is Newberry? He should be Johnny on the spot here. Ain't that what you pay him for?"

"Adam has left Unibank and says he's going to be a sponsor agent, whatever that is. He gave Louie his replacement's number, a woman named Carolyn *Tiller*, or *Tailor*, I don't bloody know." Stevens was slurring badly while showing more and more effects of way too many cocktails. "She is a real piece of work. The corporate bitch won't budge a bloody minute or a *friggin* penny. Seriously, I feel like quitting, just blow off the season and head home. Let the bloody scoundrels just sue me."

Alex looked around, wanting to get back inside but knowing he couldn't leave Stevens, not in her condition.

"I had better go," Evelyn stated and nearly fell down stumbling over one of the pool lounge chairs.

"You had best call a cab," Alex claimed looking around, suddenly wondering where Newberry was, a man who would never in the past allowed his prized client to devolve into such a state, particularly in public.

"Why don't you drive me, love?" she said while hanging all over him. "It's just down this bloody beach."

"All right. You just sit here and be a good girl while I head back in and inform Tony and Dad," he directed. "Take me about five minutes tops. Okay?"

"You're my bloody man,... or I mean *the* bloody man, love. Hurry."

Alex went inside shaking a few hands and found Andy and Tony, informing the two of them what he was about to do.

"How about you?" Andy asked, looking him up and down. "The last thing we need right now is for you to get in trouble with a DWI or something."

"Dad, I've had maybe two cocktails all evening. Stop worrying."

Alex retreated back out to the pool area, lifting the lovely but well-intoxicated Stevens up out of her lounge chair and holding her up as he made his way through the lobby to the elevator and down to the parking garage.

The two were well recognized by some of the many hotel guests onlookers, some shooting photos from their phones at them despite his best efforts to hold his hands up in a vain effort to block his and her faces from view. He practically carried her out to his car, struggling to pour her into the low-profile two-seater, which was never designed for easy access.

He raced down the street for three miles, pulled into the Four Seasons lobby, and escorted the overly liquored-up Evelyn Stevens to the first-floor elevator, gladly accepting help from a well-meaning hotel porter. They rode up to the fifth floor and the two helped her get inside her luxurious oceanview suite as she immediately crashed on the bed in her formal gown while Alex removed her high heels before throwing the bedspread over her. The bubbly porter by then knew who he was helping and thanked Alex as he handed the young man a twenty-dollar bill as the two departed the suite and headed out and down the hall.

Chapter 15

Daytona Fireworks

The Daytona 500, dubbed America's race, was NASCAR's main event, and in some circles rivaled Indy as the Super Bowl of racing. Scheduled on the weekend right after the Super Bowl and prior to most other series openers, NASCAR took advantage of a motorsport-hungry public who clamored for racing after the lull of winter.

Indeed, winning at Daytona was a huge box to check off in a stock car racer's career. Many of the great legends of NASCAR had won there, icons like Petty, Allison, and Yarborough, with more recently Gordon, Earnhart, and Johnson. Even two of Indycar's greatest, Foyt and Andretti, had challenged Daytona as interlopers and had come away with victory.

Should Alex endeavor to win here, it would certainly be huge. His confidence was much higher than when he arrived nearly two weeks earlier, but he was not naïve. This was not Indy, a place where he and his brother were always among the drivers to beat. Here, he was a rookie, a literal David going up against Goliath. Though many in the paddock wouldn't speak out publicly, a number of teams and their drivers resented all the media attention Moretti was getting, as every reporter on the scene seemed to pass them by for a chance at a question and comment or two from Alex Moretti. On the seemingly rare occasions when another driver would get some press exposure, they were always asked something about what they thought of Moretti. Whether it was fair or somewhat justified, to many in the Daytona starting field, Alex was a marked man.

Amanda and Trisha watched with intense focus from the Bustle family room, a retired couple who lived close by and would hire the girls to house-set for them while they enjoyed their frequent travel. It was a convenient alternative as Amanda didn't need the constant implied pressure of her father's disdain for her watching Alex race.

The network broadcast began with the annual extensive pre-race show anchored by Danica Patrick.

"Happy Sunday everyone and welcome to the Fox Sports Daytona 500 Pre-Race show. I'm Danica Patrick coming to you live from Daytona International Speedway and joining me on the set as my co-host is Dale Earnhardt, Jr. We wish to welcome as our special guest, British racing phenomenon Evelyn Stevens."

Amanda felt a thought creep into her conscience. *As Evelyn didn't drive in NASCAR, I didn't expect that she would be down there.*

Danica continued, "Evelyn, I know you have raced here at Daytona a few times in the 24-hour IMSA race, but I believe this is your first time here for the 500. What would you like to say to all of your fans in the UK about the atmosphere at America's premier NASCAR event?"

"Well, thank you for having me," Stevens replied. "I must say the overall energy here is electric. It's as close to that of our own British Grand Prix as anything I've witnessed, at least over here in the States, excepting the 500 in Indy itself."

"Evelyn, I know the last couple of years when you drove for Moretti Motorsport, there was often talk here, on David Land's podcast, and on social media that you may possibly race in NASCAR someday," Dale Jr, stated. "I know your new team doesn't have a presence here. Is that still something you ever think about?"

"Never say never, Dale. Before I came to America, I had an opportunity to run in the Australian Supercar series, back when my friend Scott McLaughlin was the hot shoe down there, and those cars are pretty similar. I'm still more in my comfort zone on the road and street courses, although we do run on ovals in Indycar. I've watched these guys here and the way they race is bloody terrifying. Folks in London will display the middle finger at you for closing to within ten meters of them at forty kilometers per hour. Your chaps race lap after lap at nearly 200 miles per hour while kissing each other's back bumpers and constantly trading paint colors on your fenders and doors. Shocking!"

"Evelyn, the entire racing world has been enthralled over the past several months with the trial of Alex Moretti," Danica stated. "You've been quoted many times since the trial began that you would not attend the court sessions as you did not want to be a distraction. Others have strongly speculated the prosecution wanted to have you in attendance and appear as some sort of secondary victim. Would you care to comment on that and tell our listening audience how you feel about the outcome?"

Stevens had been prompted during the pre-show prep that a question about the trial would need to be asked. She was not thrilled about it, especially considering her mood following such a tough week as a designated bank branch host.

"I don't know about the prosecutor's motives and so far as the outcome, I spent much of the evening with Alex last night and expressed my sincere happiness for him and the whole Moretti family. I have missed him dearly and look forward to seeing him in our paddock again."

"So Evelyn, what is your prediction for today's race?" Dale Jr. asked.

"Oh, far from me to predict these things. It seems these races always end up in a shootout. I like Chase Elliott, who looks like he has taken over the mantle of *golden boy* here since you retired, Dale. My close buddy, Tony Kanaan, keeps claiming that Kyle Larson is one of the best drivers in the world. I don't have a bloody dog in the hunt, as you fine people here in the States like to say. I would like to see Alex Moretti prevail. He's such a love, even if he is a long shot."

"That witch!" Trisha yelled in a mocking fashion. "She looks like she's aged twenty years since I last saw her."

I spent time with Alex? I miss him dearly? He's such a love? Amanda kept mentally hearing her quotes over and over. *He never mentioned her being down there.* "Oh, come on, Trisha," Amanda responded. "Evelyn is a babe and everyone knows it." *And she's down there and I'm not,* Amanda thought to herself. *And it will be that way almost every weekend!*

"You come on, sweetheart. Have you looked in the mirror lately? You're the hottest woman south of the Mason-Dixon Line, and Alex knows it! So cheer up."

Alex started conservatively and by lap ten he was running thirtieth. He felt this racing was like a tightrope with all of the cars running as though they were stuck together with glue. When he would attempt to pull out and run high or low in order to make some passes, he would find himself losing two of three places and have to work to get himself back in line. But despite his still being toward the back of the field, he crossed the finish line less than four seconds behind the leader.

Mike Joy led the race announcing crew, joined by Clint Bowyer and Terry Labonte.

"We've reached the halfway point of the race, Terry, and it seems there are still a good dozen drivers who look strong enough to win this thing."

"It could be more than that, Mike. It's amazing the race has been run totally under green flag conditions thus far and only seven cars have dropped out over various mechanical problems."

"Clint, Alex Moretti is now running a solid twelfth. Considering the team, which could only be described as makeshift, he's having quite a run."

"Quite a story there," Bowyer commented. "He's been fast his whole life in every car he's run in, so I can't say I'm surprised."

"The yellow just came out! there's been a major pile-up in turn one. I believe Ryan Mackey may have hit Sam Yancey which started it," Joy exclaimed. "I count nine, maybe ten cars damaged and likely out of the race. Look for the entire field to come into the pits."

Alex followed the leaders in front of him down pit road for his third stop. He had worked his way up to eleventh place as fully seventeen cars had dropped out by either some sort of breakdown or crashes on the track. The few seconds in the pits were the only time during the race he could relax a bit mentally. He was quickly learning that the constant concentration here was perhaps more intense than anything he had competed in before and lap by lap he gathered some new respect for the NASCAR regulars, although he doubted their reciprocal regard every time his car collected a bit of foreign paint colors.

He returned to the mix as the field slowed behind the pace car, dropping a couple of positions in the pits. As his car picked up speed, Alex was quick to get on the radio com to Nettles. "Mark, this damn thing has a bad vibration now, coming from the right rear. I think."

"Come back on in. Hopefully, we can get you back out without losing a lap," his crew chief replied.

Alex pulled back in and came to a stop, while his chief held up a hand, dropping his arm and waving him back out after just a few seconds. "What was it?" Alex hollered on the com.

"Right rear tire lugs weren't tight," Nettles replied. "It's all right, you still have eighty more laps. Just run hard but keep it steady."

Keep it steady, he says, Alex thought to himself. *Bumper-to-bumper at over 180 miles per hour, and my crew chief wants me to keep it steady.*

The few laps under yellow flag conditions did serve to allow the drivers to relax a bit. Alex was now at the back of the field and looking at over twenty similar race cars ahead of him. He thought about Amanda, assuming she was watching. *Not exactly making her proud, Alex,* he thought to himself.

He thought about the conversation with his father the night before, the senior Moretti being adamant that he should not be seeing Amanda until he had a better grasp from the attorneys regarding the state of the ongoing corporate lawsuits still unsettled. *She's not going to like this,* Alex knew, as he headed toward a green flag start.

With just ten laps remaining, Alex had miraculously avoided another huge on-track incident that took out another nine competitors and the Rostell team crew was ecstatic as he was suddenly running eighth with just two rows of cars separating him from the leaders.

"Just stick to Elliott like glue, Alex," Nettles kept coaching. "All the teammates are going to run together. Make sure you're not caught out of line or you'll fall back like a discarded beer can!"

Alex considered Nettles, like the rest of his crew, to be extremely rough around the edges but had helped get him this far. *I'm right here amongst these multi-million dollar teams, Gibbs, Hendrick, Penske, and Moretti with this bunch... I love it!*

Amanda was glued to the Bustle's seventy-five-inch TV, crossing her fingers on one hand that Alex didn't get in a huge crash as seen twice earlier, and throwing her fist up in the air with every pass of the finish line.

With just two laps to go, Alex crossed the line in the lead with his dad's own leading driver, Alan Allison, right on his rear end and a line led by Chase Elliott followed by Kyle Larson close on his right side.

"Keep your foot in it, boy! Don't let up!" Nettles now yelled as the rest of his rag-tag crew were nearly hysterical.

"If I had my foot down any harder, I'd be pushing on the radiator! This thing won't run any faster!"

"Just keep up the scare! Once that white flag drops, the whole friends and family deal is gone, buddy!"

Keep up the scare? What the hell is he talking about? Alex thought, too intense to laugh. He quickly returned to the mission, his crew chief reminding him that his father's best NASCAR pilot, who had filled Alex's rear view mirror for several laps, would not ride back there and be content with a second or third-place finish.

This is crazy, he kept thinking. *Here Dad has his guy on my ass and this could just come right down to me and him. Unreal.*

Mike Joy displayed the anticipated excitement of a green flag shootout at Daytona, one of the most thrilling moments in racing.

"Alex Moretti leads the pack as the white flag is waved! What an incredible achievement that young man would experience with a win after all the turmoil over the past two years."

"But how many times have we seen the car leading on lap 199 lose over the years, Mike?" Bowyer added. "All these front runners are going to make their move here."

"The field is now heading down the backstretch and there's Allison pulling down to the inside, making his move to get around Moretti. And there goes Elliott and Larson with Joey Logano right behind on the high side! And now Truex is behind Moretti!" Joy spoke loudly into the microphone. "We may be in for a three-wide finish, Terry!"

Amanda and Trisha were jumping up and down on the leather sectional, both screaming themselves. "Come on, Alex! Go baby! Go!"

"Here they are coming out of the final turn, Elliott, Moretti, and Allison all three at the line and... Oh! it's Alan Allison taking the win in a near photo finish, beating Chase Elliott by just inches, and Alex Moretti maybe another two feet back coming in third. This may be the most exciting finish to the Daytona 500 we've seen in years, Clint."

"You're so right, Mike. Alan Allison wins the Daytona 500 for Andy Moretti, with Chase Elliott finishing second by an eyelash! This will undoubtedly make the highlight reels for years to come."

"And the biggest story of all, Mike," Labonte added, "could be Andy's son, Alex, just two weeks out of a potential felony conviction, and nearly wins this thing, all with the most inexperienced crew the speedway has seen in decades."

Amanda was now deflated. She just knew Alex was going to win when she saw the white flag and he came oh so close. The two girls watched as Alan Allison performed the now traditional donut before jumping out and standing atop his car as his crew and excited boss, Andy Moretti, came running out onto the track from the pitlane to join in the celebration.

A bubbly Rusty Wallace, the broadcast pit reporter, was given the honors of interviewing the winner. "Alan, you just won maybe the most exciting Daytona 500 finish in history, surely in my lifetime. What is going through your mind right now?"

"I just can't believe it. It's like a dream come true. I'm so thrilled for all of my teammates and crew. I wish to thank my sponsor, Unibank, and here's one for Andy," Allison added.

"Let's move over and get a comment from the winning owner, Andy Moretti. Andy, you've had such a storied career, both as a driver and more recently the founder and principal of your own team. How does this victory rank along with all of your other achievements?" Wallace asked as he held his microphone up in front of the excited winning car owner.

"This is the Daytona 500, the biggest prize in NASCAR. I'm so proud of the whole team for the effort put in down here, I just can't put it all into words."

"Andy, what were you thinking as the laps counted down, seeing your driver running right behind the race leader, who happened to be your youngest son, Alex?"

"I was on pins and needles for sure. I always told Alex that Morettis raced to win, so I knew he would give it his best shot. My hat's off to him and that team, one that was just put together days before qualifying. You know we weren't about to give him anything. With Roger and Rick and all the other great teams here, nobody can let off the gas, not for a second, lest the rest will just roll over you."

Chase Elliott was very gracious if disappointed as the runner-up in his interview. NASCAR's most popular driver, and son of legend Bill Elliott, expressed surprise that he and Kyle Larson failed to pass Allison and Moretti. "We had the perfect setup going into the last lap. I figured Alan would pull out on the inside and let Kyle and I run to the front, but

Trux and Joey filled the void and helped them keep the speed. It was a great and clean race, at least up front. No complaints."

"Now we have Jamie Little with Alex Moretti," Joy announced.

"Alex, you came home a very close third in your first Daytona 500. What are you feeling right now?"

"I'm quite exhausted, Jamie. This is the most mentally intense race I have ever run. I've driven at Indy, at Lemans, Rally cars, even the Chili Bowl, and this race just requires so much focus all the time. My hat's off to all of those who have done it multiple times. Congratulations to Alan for winning and also to my dad. I know this is huge for him after a tough season last year."

"Alex, you came down here to drive for a quickly arranged team less than two weeks ago and almost won. Should we be surprised if a more permanent ride in NASCAR is in store?" Jamie asked.

"Who knows, Jamie. If I may, I would like to shout out some love to all of those close to me who were not here physically to share in this. You know that I love you!"

"There you have it, Mike. Alex Moretti, a bittersweet but impressive third-place finish in the Daytona 500."

Amanda was anxious to console Alex on not winning and discuss the coming week. She chose to skip the texting and just call him, slightly disappointed at getting his voicemail.

Despite not winning the crew were beside themselves in celebration, knowing their driver had bested most of the very best NASCAR had brought to bear. Alex finally made his way through the post-race accolades and interviews to settle at the team bus for a beer or two, when he spied her missed call. He stepped out in the garage area between the team tractors and dialed.

"Alex, I'm so proud of you," Amanda stated. "Are you disappointed?"

"Well, yes. I know I shouldn't be, coming down here a day after the trial and qualifying, then almost winning. I'm mentally tired, though."

"I'm exhausted myself from jumping up and down and yelling at the TV. Are you still coming home tonight?" she asked anxiously.

"No, not until tomorrow. Dad wants me and Tim to join them for a team victory celebration party tonight."

"Ohhh! I was so anxious to see you!"

"Amanda, you have school tomorrow anyway. I should be home by late afternoon or so. Then I should have nothing on the schedule for a week or two," he added in consolation.

"All right. You better be ready for me, buster," Amanda replied jokingly. "Your woman has a week's worth of energy ready to unleash on you."

"Sounds good, baby," he added, covering his phone as best he could to void all the ambient noise.

"Okay, I can tell it's loud there. Have a good time at your dad's party, and be thinking about me."

"Trisha, I'm going up to his place right after school tomorrow. I want to surprise him. What should I wear?"

She saw her best friend just staring at the small screen on her phone. "What Trisha, you look like you just saw a ghost... What's wrong?"

Trisha couldn't bring herself to say anything and just turned her phone around for Amanda to see.

MORETTI-STEVENS LOVEFEST AGAIN?

The headline on Safari's news entertainment page featured a photograph of Alex and Evelyn, dressed in formal attire and appearing together at a party. The article, dated the day before at Daytona Beach, Florida, seemed to suggest that Alex Moretti and Evelyn Stevens' romance was back on and the two were all smiles with cocktails in hand.

It hit Amanda like a ton of bricks. *His spending so many days down there, his not wanting me to drive down, and Stevens stating in front of the entire planet that she had been with him the evening before the race.* Her eyes began to well up.

"Now, Amanda. Don't jump to conclusions. You don't know for certain this is as bad as it looks," Trisha said, trying to console her but not sounding overly convinced herself.

"What would you think, Trisha? If this was Jeremy, tell me. What would you think?"

The two kindred-spirited lifelong friends sat dejected, momentarily staring down at the floor.

"I don't know, Amanda. Jeremy is not Alex. You know I love him to death, but he's not an international sports celebrity and as knock-down good-looking, either."

Amanda looked up at her, tears now running down her face. "It's going to be like this every weekend. I'll be at college somewhere,... and he'll be at another racetrack, with her there."

"That's if he lives that long. You know what he does is dangerous, right Amanda?"

Amanda returned home for the night, very down and not knowing what to do. She did her best to disguise her melancholy in front of the folks and spent the bulk of the evening in her room, online searching for information. She pulled up Google and plugged in the words *Alex Moretti and Evelyn Stevens.*

The web was awash with articles about the two dating back almost four years. She found the stuff punishing and couldn't help admiring Evelyn's beauty and class in front of a camera. The low point came when she came across the YouTube video of the two of them on what appeared to be a high-rise balcony, with Stevens straddling him nude, making her think immediately of herself on Alex's balcony and who could be spying on them with a camera.

Tired of it all, none of the online information appeared to be anything new or recent. Suddenly a chat message popped up in the lower corner of her monitor from Trisha. "Amanda, this is a Facebook page I found. It's some sort of luny racing fans with their new pictures and videos from Daytona."

She clicked on the link, a page filled with many photos taken at what appeared to be the beach. One caught her eye with a caption that read, "Moretti and babe Stevens lounging outside at the Hard Rock Hotel pool. The image was date and time stamped, Saturday, February 18 2023 10:39 PM.

Amanda now buried her head in her pillow, not wanting her mom and dad to hear her weeping. The devastation of the accident two years earlier, the news about a baby, the long saga of waiting and enduring the trial, and now this. She turned and curled up under her bedroom blanket, feeling completely nauseated. The betrayal was nearly unbearable. Through it all, she had stayed loyal to him.

I feel like such a fool, she thought as she struggled to fall asleep, the pain she felt seemed as the worst feeling ever.

The Moretti Motorsport celebration party was loud with an abundance of food, drinks, and laughter, as it was among the greatest overall victories in the team's history.

Alex attempted to corner Andy for a few minutes in order to discuss the status of the Unibank lawsuits, and namely when he and Amanda could come fully out of the closet. To his dismay, his father seemed to want little of it.

"It's critical that you behave yourself for as long as it takes to end this business with Unibank. I'm telling you, son, you have to stay clear of that girl for a while."

"How can you say that, Dad?" Alex replied in near exasperation. "You were there in that courtroom. She could have fried my ass on that stand and it would have made her dad all the more happy to see me go away to prison. But she didn't."

"Alex, we do need to clear this thing up with Unibank and Byron Cook as soon as possible, if nothing else, so I can reinstate you to the team. After all that has gone down, do you really think our two families could ever look each other in the eye again?"

Alex gave his father a stern stare. "I love Amanda. I'm not going to stop seeing her, not now after all we've suffered through for two years. I would like to have your support, Dad, but this is something I'm going to do."

Both remained speechless before Andy just shook his head at his son and walked away.

Newberry popped another pill as he was moping around and about to blow a gasket. He had just gotten off the phone with Carolyn Tyler, a woman who acted as though she controlled the entire Unibank operation, and blistered him over Evelyn not keeping to the schedule at their Daytona area bank branches the previous week.

When he suggested they meet soon and revise a plan that was more reasonable, she slammed the door on him. "A contract is a contract," he was told. Adding insult to injury, Roberto Santos just forwarded an email received from Tyler, informing him that funds would be withheld from the team in accordance with their contract, and that further insolence by his driver may jeopardize the entire sponsorship as well as subject him to a lawsuit.

Adding to his list of woes was the fact that Allison Cook had yet to transfer a single penny of the so-called bonus she promised him for putting this whole ill-conceived deal together.

Evelyn was calling for the third time in thirty minutes, a call he dreaded answering.

"Hello, Evelyn."

"Okay, Louie. Talk to me."

"I don't have any update for you, just yet," Newberry replied, trying to sound calm.

"Bullshit, Louie. Roberto just called me madder than bloody hell over my bank appearances."

"He shouldn't be badgering you over those types of details," Newbery replied defensively. "I'll have to give him a call on that."

"Tell me what that Carolyn Tyler had to say," Evelyn snapped.

"I'm trying to set up a face-to-face with her."

"Don't lie to me, Louie. I'm not showing up at another bank, not for one second until this gets resolved. I don't need this. I can go back to the UK and drive in the WEC for a year. I should have never left Moretti Motorsport. Tony told me his dad was prepared to give me a generous raise, and I wouldn't be dealing with all this bloody garbage you got me into!"

"Evelyn, please calm down," Louie pleaded, choosing a different tact. "You know, Fox Sports or NBC would sign you up in a heartbeat. You were pretty good as Danica Patrick's guest on Sunday."

"Yes, they told me that. Despite a miserable hangover and a pissed-off attitude, they told me I was pretty good... And I wouldn't need you to help me with the details of their contract, either," she barked before hanging up on him.

Alex pulled out of the hotel parking garage at just past 9:00 AM. He worried about how he was going to deal with Amanda, telling her they still needed to sneak around for the time being as if nothing had changed, even though his criminal trial was over and she was no longer a minor, but a beautiful and bright young woman who had just been relieved from a state of despair after two long years.

Tim called to suggest that he be prepared to entertain some new offers, as his performance on Sunday had raised more than a few eyebrows. His agent was quite upbeat in telling Alex the check for finishing third at Daytona would be in access of a million dollars, and thus Alex himself would be netting well over 400 thousand, a hefty sum that would put a huge dent in his debt load, pay his share of Flannery's tab, and leave him a few thousand left over after taxes.

He fantasized as he approached the first of the Rock Hill exits about he and Amanda's father actually being able to face each other civilly someday, a scenario that seemed all too far over the horizon.

He sent Amanda a text that he was an hour from home, feeling odd that she hadn't responded, even though it should have been well past her school hours. About the time he passed the sign that he was entering North Carolina, he sent her a second message, and still no reply. *Something is not right*, he thought nervously.

He pulled into the complex parking garage at just past five, dialing her phone as he got out of his car and worked to gather his things, this time getting her voicemail.... "Amanda, I'm back. Call me."

He took the elevator up to his floor, concerned about her now. He couldn't recall her ever not responding to him quickly in some fashion, even dating back to the first day they had met, three years earlier in Long Beach.

He walked into his place and through the kitchen, checking the frig for a beer or soda, grabbing a Bud before strolling into the bedroom where he was greeted with a large envelope propped up on his bedspread against his pillows. Immediately, a bad feeling started to gather in his abdomen. Inside was a handwritten letter that had him speechless.

Dear Alex,

After all considerations, I believe I should move on with my life and you yours. I was so hopeful that once the trial was over, you and I could enjoy a normal relationship and perhaps even a future together. I can see we don't always travel in the same circles and I cannot be with you at all the races.

I gathered up most of my things but left you the two bathrobes. I think mine should fit Evelyn just fine. I hope that you and her find happiness together.

All my best,

379

Signed Amanda

PS: I recall your leaving a spare key in the light fixture. I will l put it back when I leave.

Alex was simply crushed. *What happened? Was she that upset that I didn't want her down at Daytona? Or was it something else?*

He called numerous times and kept getting a voicemail. By the following morning, he felt like driving down there but knew he wouldn't be welcome at her parent's home and it might make things with the lawsuits worse, at least according to his dad's lawyers.

He kept sending text messages but to no avail. He was just shocked and disheartened that Amanda would not respond.

Newberry was angry and desperate, He had attempted on numerous occasions to contact Allison and she wasn't returning his calls or messages. The standoff between Evelyn and this Carolyn Tyler showed no sign of getting resolved and he was stuck in the middle as both women placed the blame squarely on him. He needed someone to intercede and with Adam Herrera now out of the picture, there was only one person he could think of - Allison Cook.

Sure, he was angry at her for reneging on the bonus, but right at this moment his biggest problem was getting the terms of Evelyn's contract renegotiated into something realistic or the golden girl, who accounted for over ninety percent of his income, would just walk and go back to the UK for a while.

He had to put pressure on Allison to help, not to mention drop a hint about his bonus, not to mention getting her back in the sack periodically. He sent a message requesting a call back right away and his phone quickly buzzed.

"You want to apologize?"

"Get real, Remi. When could you start on the project we spoke about a few weeks back?"

"It was several weeks. Depends on what you're paying."

Newberry was pissed, not accustomed to getting a dress-down from a former prostitute, but desperate times called for desperate measures. "What do you need?"

"A thousand to start and"...

"A thousand!?" Louie grasped. He started to lash out and remind her that she only charged him two hundred for the first time she,... but thought better of it. "Agreed."

"I need to know the background on this," Remi stated.

"I told you, that's not any of your business," Newberry scolded.

"No deal, Louie. If I'm going to travel all the way out to California and get dirt on an engaged woman, I want to know why."

"Since when did you get religion!? She's a gorgeous babe who sleeps around on her fiancé. It'll be a piece of cake."

"I'll send you a PayPal request every few days. You'll pay me right away. Money is tight," Remi stated, smiling to herself as they concluded their conversation and disconnected.

I already know she's a hot woman who's unfaithful to her future hubby. But that's not all she is,... Right, Louie?

Tim Malloy was not a happy camper. While he had yet to succeed in acquiring a ride for Alex in the NASCAR series, surprising due to his performance in Daytona, Tim did have not one but two offers on the table from factory-backed World Rally Series teams.

To Tim's chagrin, Alex had kept procrastinating in contacting the State Department to reinstate his passport, which took time under the best of circumstances. In his case, the federal officials must receive a rescinding order from the State of South Carolina whose bureaucrats must first acquire the proper documentation from the York County Circuit Court

Clerk's office. Only then would the federal agency begin processing, a six to eight-week endeavor.

It would often take two days for Alex to return Malloy's calls, and even then he would sound incoherent on the phone, as though he had been drinking,... or worse.

It had been nearly four weeks now and it had all but appeared that Amanda would not respond to any of his communiques. Alex was just miserable and in a nauseated state of flux over it.

He thought a few times more about just showing up at her home but talked himself out of it. Feeling he had to do something, he drove down to Rock Hill one day in the early afternoon, driving around the Fort Hill High School student parking lot, and spied her bright red Mustang. He stopped in front of it, left his Acura running, and jumped out to place an envelope under her windshield wiper blades.

At just past three, the building bells rang out and Amanda and Trisha approached the car and paused. Trisha could tell Amanda knew where the envelope came from and suggested she just throw it away without opening it. Amanda was curious and emotional, grabbing the envelope and once the two of them got in her car, choosing to open it.

Dear Amanda,

Please call me and let me know what is wrong. If I did something to offend you, kindly tell me what it was. And I wish to give you your bathrobe back. I love you.

Nothing has changed, Alex

PS: Whatever gave you the notion that Evelyn and I were back together?

Amanda broke down in tears as she got to the end before handing the handwritten note to Trisha, who solemnly read its contents herself.

"Amanda, we've talked about this and I know what you're thinking. You have to be strong. You can't go back, Amanda. You'll set yourself up for another heartbreak all over again."

She didn't respond right away, starting the engine and pulling away. *Where did I get the idea that something was brewing between you and Evelyn? That's insulting, Alex.* "I'm not going to call him, Trisha."

"Are you going out with Mathew? He keeps asking me about it, Amanda?"

"I'm not quite ready, Trisha," she replied. *I'm just not ready.*

Tyler entered Remington's office with an ample number of printouts including the contracts and all the related emails related to the conflict between Unibank and Roberto Santos, his driver, Evelyn Stevens, and her agent, Louie Newberry. She could tell the corporate CFO was not a happy camper.

"Carolyn, tell me this mess is on a path to getting cleaned up."

"Well, sir. I'm overseeing this and saving us hundreds of thousands of dollars in withheld funding. Mr. Cook insisted the contract with Evelyn Stevens' new team have a maximum return," Tyler stated, assuming the bank's senior bean counter would like the sound of that.

"Maximum value, huh?" Wally Remington mumbled as he browsed through the documents. "In my position as Chief Financial Officer for this corporation, when you talk about saving the bank hundreds of thousands of dollars, it should be music to my ears. But this has been one public relations disaster," he stated angrily as he slammed the paperwork down on his desk. "We're well on the way toward bankrupting not one, but two race teams now, ones that feature Unibank all over them. We made Evelyn Stevens a star and now it's all over the press and social media that she is threatening to leave the sport altogether because of what Unibank is doing to her!"

"Mr. Remington, I just drew up the contract with her agent. If they had a problem with it, they should have objected at the time. Then we could have negotiated an agreement."

"I cannot believe Adam would have let something like this pass by him," the CFO stated in disgust. "I knew he was just riding out his thirty days, but this fiasco thoroughly disappoints me."

Tyler sat silently, not reiterating that Byron Cook had purely tasked her with the details and relegated him to a non-administrative PR role, the key reason he had resigned. Her designs on being promoted to Herra's old position as Vice President of Marketing was now looking tenuous at best.

"That's not all, Carolyn. I want you to respond to this email from Marilyn Forsythe regarding the impact of the Unibank Formula One ads being discontinued. I see you were copied on that," he stated as he looked up at her expectantly.

It was common knowledge that Forsythe had been lobbying the other board members to make some changes at the top, specifically making her the President and CEO. It was also no secret that she and Wally Remington did not see eye-to-eye, a big reason he continued to support Byron Cook, a position the CFO was finding ever more untenable.

"We could entertain doing some updated spots, sir. Of course, the Grand Prix race crowds and the Moretti F1 cars wouldn't be featured in those."

"It was that along with Stevens that made those advertisements so appealing. You had better find somebody, anybody, to come up with some new ads."

"There is a problem with that, sir. Our funding for that was tied to Moretti Motorsport and his Formula One team. That was cut off along with Stevens' move to Indywest."

"That's just great, Tyler! You've been handed the keys to this project. The next board meeting is in three weeks. You had better come up with an answer, like tomorrow."

"I'll get on that, sir."

Tyler left Remington's office knowing she was caught in a box. The cutback of funding to Moretti Motorsport was the main task handed to her directly by Byron, himself, a decision that was made in her own bedroom. Not a fan nor having any sufficient background knowledge of Formula One, in effect not knowing one open-wheel race car or track from another, she had acted in ignorance and naivety. *I should have taken advice from Herrera,... before he walked.*

Remi sat enjoying herself as she watched the swimmers and surfers from the Mission Beach outside tiki bar, sitting straight across from Allison Cook, who was joined by a male, perhaps thirty, tanned, fit, and one she knew was not Lieutenant Aaron Williams, her fiancé. *At least this one is better-looking than that sleazeball Louie.*

She had possessed the goods on the woman and that snake, Louie, prior to departing for California and she was shadowing Cook mostly for sport now on Newberry's dime. She had never truly gotten ahead in her life, working in the *sexual entertainment* business before having to move on to a more *stable* occupation. After all, performing as a stripper and prostitute were not occupations that generally got better with time.

She didn't know how he had done it, but her old flame, Cotton James, had gotten the full detail of the contract they so adamantly discussed, initiated during and after Cook and Newberry engaged in their carnal activity. Every time she went back and listened to the recording, she had to chuckle at the noises Cook was making, pretending that slob Louie was actually satisfying her. *I know the drill, honey britches. You need more practice.*

Cotton assisted in helping her set up a site on the dark web from which to operate, one that he assured her could not be traced back to either of them. The question now became how Remi would use the extremely toxic information she now possessed and against whom. All of the players were somewhat well-off, as she assumed Louie was by then, as was Evelyn

Stevens, who was surely knocking down some big bucks, and Allison Cook, whose family and future in-laws were both quite wealthy.

If I play this right, I may never have to work another day in my life, Remi thought to herself.

Crissy had shown up to drop the baby off prior to her and Tony preparing for the long flight overseas. Their three-year-old, Adrian, had been with Grandma Matilde for a few days and she was all too happy to babysit him and her new grandbaby while Tony and Crissy would spend a long weekend in Melbourne for the Australian Grand Prix.

The conversation between the Moretti women had always migrated toward Alex as both Matilde and Crissy had assumed some proper family stations in watching out for him, or at least attempting to.

"He's become a hermit, Matilde. Since Amanda has left, he seems to just spiral down into a constant drunken depression," Crissy advised.

"Yes, so very sad," Matilde replied. "I could tell in that courtroom, they seemed destined to have a great relationship."

"Something has happened. Amanda and I started texting each other back and forth again, just after the trial. I was beginning to feel so close to her, too. So much is different now. I hardly ever see or communicate with Evelyn, either."

"I know, Crissy. I was thinking how good it would be if Amanda's mother and I could become friends. She's such a thoughtful and sweet woman... You should reach out to Evelyn. I know Andy sure misses her."

"Out of the question, Carolyn!" Byron responded, practically yelling. "There's no way we're paying Alex Moretti to help us produce commercials. Why would you even come up with such a cockimany idea?"

"It's what Adam suggested," Tyler answered, knowing beforehand that her clandestine lover wouldn't like it.

"Herrera? When did he throw his two cents in on this? As an ex-employee, his opinion means nothing to me, Carolyn."

"Well, Byron. He *is* their agent now," Tyler stated.

What are you talking about? Agent for who?"

"He's the agent for Moretti Motorsport, in charge of acquiring and working with sponsors. According to his new website, he has almost half the teams in Indycar and now three in NASCAR as clients... I'm really uncomfortable, Byron. Mr. Remington wants all these open issues regarding funding cleaned up before the board meeting.

We have to do something about Evelyn Stevens. She's boycotting our banks and threatening to just take a sabbatical from racing altogether. You wanted Unibank out of motor racing, Byron, and you're about to succeed.

Our CFO says Marilyn Forsythe is preparing to start a firestorm in front of the board over this," Tyler concluded.

"Forsythe needs to get on her broom and fly on out of here," Byron stated. as he shook his head and just stared at her momentarily. "You didn't hear me say that... Let's release Stevens from branch appearances for now. Contact Santos and tell him you'll release all pending funding so we may get her back in the car. Why can't we do some new spots using the car she driving now? Ninety-plus percent of our customers couldn't tell the difference between an Indycar and a Formula One car anyway."

"So, are we updating the Indywest contract?" Tyler asked while making some notes.

"No, not yet. Just let them know that we're not going to penalize them over the bank branch appearances, at least yet."

It appeared Evelyn was placated for the time being. Tyler informed her the bank branch appearances were all on hold and was working with a contractor in LA to produce a new series of commercials to be run on various television sources and online.

Her spirits slightly improved, Stevens had run strong in Long Beach, finishing second to Graham Rahal and talk had resumed about her challenging for the championship again. The folks at Penske Entertainment and the Indianapolis Motor Speedway, in particular, were especially pleased as they didn't want the dust-up with Evelyn Stevens to be the main story leading up to this year's 500, which promised to be the most anticipated in decades considering the additional *guest* drivers competing from Formula One and NASCAR.

Newberry's blood pressure had gone down a bit as Santos had received a substantial funding transfer from Unibank, glad to confirm with Evelyn that her bank branch duties were being suspended for now, although she kept pressing him on when her contract would be amended.

"Evelyn, just drive the car and leave all the contract details to me," Louie said to himself after she had hung up her phone. He would still need some leverage to use with Allison and felt the time was at hand for him to pressure Remi on when he would get it, particularly since he had already sent her over four grand.

He dialed her up and was aggravated when he kept getting her voicemail. Four glasses of Jim Beam and half a pack of cigarettes later, he finally received a callback.

"When I call your ass, Remi, you answer. Is that clear?"

"Are you sitting down, Louie? I can give you something that is very clear," Remi responded.

"I don't need to sit down. What do you have for me?" Newberry questioned.

"Just listen."

An AI-simulated male voice narrated.

Ivey's Hotel, Suite 903, Charlotte, North Carolina, November 13, 2022 10:51 PM

"I don't care what it takes, Louie. I want Evelyn to sign with Roberto Santos." -*Allison*

"Perhaps we can both shower together." -*Louie*

The sound of a champagne bottle's cork popping off.

"Be a good boy and I'll think about it. Now be serious and pour me a glass." -*Allison*

"It's a huge deal. It'll take some time, sweet lips." -*Louie*

There was a sound of ice cubes rattling into a glass.

"You stand to make out like a bandit. Don't get too greedy." -*Allison*

"I would make just as much if I signed a new contract with Moretti." *-Louie*

"That would not make me happy" *-Allison*

"And what about making me happy?" *-Louie*

"Lay back, while I give you a sample." *-Allison*

A few sighs and groans were heard. "I am getting a bit happier." *-Louie*

A pause

"Hey! Why are you stopping?" *-Louie*

"When will this deal be done?" *-Allison*

"This week." *-Louie*

"If this is publicly announced by Friday at noon, I will give you a $25,000 bonus." -*Allison*

"We won't bore ourselves with the other fifty-plus minutes. Would you like to see the photographs?" Remi stated, clicking off the audio.

Newberry was shaking. *After all of the gigs I have put her onto. You bitch!* He thought. "What do you want?"

"I'll take that twenty-five grand bonus, plus another twenty," Remi declared arrogantly.

"I've never received that bonus!" Louie yelled, exasperated and already thinking of ways to get at her.

"Maybe accounts receivable isn't your strong suit, Louie... That's not my problem. You've got forty-eight hours," she replied in a calm voice which irritated him further.

"I'll need more time than that!"

"I don't have the time. If this sounds like a raw deal, Louie, I have another party or two who may be interested. I know a guy like you appreciates the concept... I'll start with Evelyn Stevens."

The quarterly bank board meeting in late March was explosive with the topics of the new commercials and advertisements featuring Evelyn Stevens dominating the agenda.

Byron had Carolyn Tyler present the motor racing sponsorship segment to most of the board members, led by Marilyn Forsythe, blasting her with criticism and tough questions. She had contracted with a Hollywood production company to produce commercials with Stevens in her new Indycar. Some of the spots were fine but efforts to film on current Formula One circuits conflicted with the FIA over licensing. Andy Moretti held a license as a Formula One Team owner that he could renew annually, which he had done as BP was running numerous advertisements in Europe, the Middle East, and Asia.

This had been brought up by Herrera when CEO Cook was forcing the change, thinking at the time it would be a minor issue. To deal with the problem, Tyler had arranged and paid eight thousand British pounds to rent the old Brands Hatch circuit in England for one day during the week and filming was completed with Stevens in her Indycar, including a mockup of a pit stop.

Worldwide criticism from the huge Formula One fanbase appeared immediately on social media and became rampant, as fans from all international markets were accustomed to Stevens strolling in front of Tony Moretti's Unibank/BP badged F1 car with actual Grand Prix event footage as a backdrop. The new ads were universally lambasted as amateurish and unrepresentative of a modern-day Formula One circuit, making the story more about Unibank's poor production while ignoring the targeted goals of the spots themselves. The viral social media spilled over into the mainstream motor racing community, which included key media outlets in places like Indianapolis and Charlotte, and in turn, reopened the whole can of worms about Evelyn Stevens' contract fiasco.

Forsythe continued to criticize the decision to sue Moretti Motorsport, emphasizing the fact that Unibank had basically transferred their star athlete, Stevens, back to a small and relatively unaccomplished team, while creating discord with her and the team by requiring an overbearing and unworkable appearance schedule. She managed to get a majority of the other members to agree that some arrangement needed to be entertained with Andy Moretti regarding the use of his FIA license for their advertisements.

Tyler kept glancing at Byron to lend some support but to her disappointment, he was mostly silent. She would have a stern talk with him the next time he visited her apartment over it.

Byron Cook was embattled and angry that he had gradually found himself consumed by the problems with Unibank's racing sponsorship when he should have been spending time on investments, acquisitions, and mergers, all the things that had grown Unibank into such a worldwide financial giant during his tenure.

The decision to hand Carolyn the keys to manage this major contract had blown up in his face, and his retention as bank president and chief operating officer was now being openly challenged. While confident their clandestine affair remained secret, Byron felt his ability to manage Tyler had gotten strenuous at best.

"I have an interesting proposal that Adam laid out, Byron," Tyler stated expectantly.

"What is it?" Byron asked skeptically, disgusted he was still having to deal with Andy Moretti and to add insult to injury, Adam Herrera, who was now serving as his agent, the man who had sold the board on all this motor racing business in the first place.

Adding insult to injury, his plan to replace Herrera with Tyler had been a fiasco, as now it seemed that Herrera was managing her, despite his no longer being on Unibank's payroll.

"He believes Andy would be receptive to an arrangement with us to utilize his FIA license and team for Stevens' commercials if Unibank would agree to drop all pending litigation against him."

"I'm sure he would. That's just not going to happen unless he agrees to pay a substantial settlement to us, Carolyn. Once this Memorial Day race is over with, this will all blow over."

"I'm not so sure, Byron. Do you know who David Land is?"

"I haven't a clue."

"Neither had I until I took it on my own to educate myself about this racing. He does a very popular podcast that appears on YouTube weekly and has hundreds of thousands of followers. I want to show you this," Tyler offered as she pulled up the targeted screen on her laptop.

"Welcome to the greatest race course in the world, the Indianapolis Motor Speedway. This is David Land, reporting that

the month of May is shaping up to be the most exciting in years, and perhaps in my lifetime. The sport of motor racing is still reeling from the cancellation of the Grand Prix of Monaco, which has opened an opportunity for Formula One drivers to compete here at Indy if they are contractually released to do so.

Two very notable drivers who are on tap to run are Danial Riccardo and Fernando Alonzo, the two-time world champion who had run here previously, running very strong in 2017 but vowing never to return, siting the dangers of racing near walls at 225 miles per hour. But the man is a racer and may not pass on a golden opportunity to join the great Graham Hill as the only two drivers ever to have won at Monaco, Lemans, and Indianapolis.

One driver here lacking confidence right now is Evelyn Stevens, Indycar's star celebrity who had a breakout season last year before a surprise return to the Indywest team as their sole driver following three seasons at Moretti Motorsport. As we've covered extensively on previous podcasts, Stevens has been extremely disgruntled and has even threatened to leave the sport over claims of unreasonable new demands by her longtime sponsor, Unibank.

The legal feud between Unibank and Moretti Motorsport continues to place a black cloud over Andy Moretti's team, which saw a huge chunk of their funding depart with the loss of Stevens. Sources within the team tell me the ongoing civil litigation is still blocking Alex Moretti's return to the team, Andy's youngest son who has not raced here for the past two years.

Please leave you comments below, and don't forget to hit the like"...

Tyler closed the file, looking at the boss' reaction.

"Well, this isn't exactly the New York Times," Byron stated, trying to find some solace.

"Byron, I could spend all day here reviewing all the other online media that can't seem to get enough of Evelyn Stevens, especially since her relationship with Alex Mor"...

"I don't want to hear about that!... Reach out to Herrera and see what you can get worked out with this FIA license business, Carolyn. I'm sick and tired of fooling with this," the besieged CEO replied.

Sarah could tell he wasn't happy when he walked in and threw his suit coat on the front room couch before heading directly to the den to pour himself a stiff drink. These past few months had practically torn the family apart. She had hoped that once the trial was over, some severe wounds would begin the healing process. But the explosive revelation that Amanda had made about Kyle Williams, her revelation regarding their own private past, and now all this blow-up with Evelyn Stevens, had the man who had always been such a steady tower of strength and compassion becoming an alcoholic before her very eyes.

"Do you want to talk about it?" Sarah asked as she appeared at the den door.

"That bitch Forsythe is gunning for my job, Sarah, all over this Evelyn Stevens bullshit!"

She had given up on lecturing him about his language, as his rage had become all too commonplace now and Sarah thought it best to just allow him to vent. "So, what are you doing about it?"

He looked at her as if unprepared for such a question. "There's not much I can do. This is the last year for our involvement in motor racing, Sarah. I just hope I can survive that long. I'm even having conflicts with Wally Remington now over this. If I lose his vote on the board, Forsythe is as good as in as President and CEO. She is actually organizing the rest of the board to travel to Indianapolis and populate our VIP suite for the race. As bad as I hate it, I'm going to have to be there, also, just to show face."

It had now been three years since they had last attended the 500, and Sarah actually had such fond memories of it all.

"But, Byron? What about Amanda's graduation? That's on the Saturday evening of that weekend," she asked seriously.

"I can't be in both places at once, Sarah!" Byron declared. "If I'm not up there, Forsythe will all but orchestrate a mock election to oust me."

The very idea of his not being there for his own daughter's graduation did not set well with his wife, but on the other hand, having him removed as head of Unibank would destroy him. They were already extremely wealthy and the loss of income was of little consequence. *No,* Sarah thought. *Having him home every day moping around and drinking would serve to destroy what semblance of a family we still possess.*

"You go, Byron. I'll handle the graduation."

Sarah woke Amanda at 9:00 knowing she had been out late at the high school's prom, held at the Tega Cay Golf Club Community Center just down the road. "Are you going to church with us, honey?"

"Sure, Mom."

They sat down for a hearty breakfast as the family was still stressed over the events of the past few months.

"How was your date last night?" Byron asked, trying to act neutral toward her as their relationship had improved, if ever so slightly.

"It was fine."

That didn't sound very inspiring, Byron thought. "That Mathew seems like a nice young man, isn't he?"

"Yes, he's nice," Amanda replied.

Byron and Sarah looked at each other as acknowledgment they needed to broach another subject.

"Amanda, your father will not be able to attend your graduation ceremony," Sarah declared.

Amanda simply looked up from her meal at the two of them.

"I have to be in Indianapolis, Amanda. It's the last year of our involvement there and we're sponsoring three or four cars... I don't want to go but"...

"It's okay, Dad... I understand... It's okay."

THE RACE GIRL

Chapter 16

May to Remember

The month of May opened at the Indianapolis Motor Speedway with an air of excitement as the entry roster for qualifying was the largest in nearly three decades, the number limited solely by the total available chassis and engine combinations. Speedway President, Doug Boles, was especially enthused at the number of tickets already purchased for qualifying weekend, shaping up to be the largest crowd in as many years.

Following a rocky start to the season, Evelyn Stevens followed her strong Long Beach run with a solid sixth-place finish in Birmingham. The issues with her Unibank relationship improved, at least temporarily, as she did agree to spend some ample time with all of the Unibank guests who figured to have four cars starting with their livery, both Indywest team cars with Evelyn and Santos' second *guest* driver, Horace Ramos, along with Andy Moretti, with Jon David Hill and Ryan Hunter-Reay driving.

Andy would be fielding a third team car piloted by Tony Moretti, whose performance in the first few events in Formula One had helped encourage BP to step up with support, sponsoring his number "5" Honda-powered Dallara fully with their Amoco branding.

All in all, it bothered Andy that he couldn't muster up a ride for Alex, still worried about the pending lawsuits which he knew were still purely personal between him and Byron Cook. His youngest boy had paid exponentially in emotional capital for his lapse of judgment, a painful thought for his father as he now realized that Alex and Amanda were so attached all this time. Andy now blamed himself for their apparent parting of ways, which had now continued to cast a black cloud over the family and team despite the favorable trial outcome several weeks earlier. His son would have to miss out on yet another chance at Indy 500 glory, a race he himself knew could be so difficult to win.

The weary team principal was tired of his attorneys telling him that pushing a settlement with Cook would undoubtedly mean an admission of liability on the team's part, and result in a hefty settlement in favor of Unibank. His best option was to ride it out and allow their own officers to tire of it, a process that could still drag on for years on end.

The first week was busy for the Morettis as the team traveled to Indianapolis with high hopes in what promised to be the most anticipated race in many years. Tony and Crissy had just returned from the San Marino Grand Prix where he finished in seventh, four places above his teammate, for a week off prior to heading to Indy for practice in preparation for the pole. While Tony spent his first day at the shop, Matilda and Crissy dropped in on Alex unannounced, who hadn't returned any calls in two days and was still in bed at 11:30 AM that Tuesday morning. The place looked like a pig sti with unwashed dishes, dirty clothing scattered everywhere, empty beer cans on all the tables, and a couple of empty hard liquor bottles on the front room floor.

The two spent time cleaning the kitchen, gathering all the clothing, and packing it into the washing machine. The two then picked up and took out the trash, while little Adrian got into his uncle's diecast race cars, not realizing some were rare collectibles and worth hundreds of dollars each.

He heard the vacuum cleaner going and finally woke up and walked out of his bedroom, sporting his new checkered flag robe, which also needed washing.

"Alex, you look like hell," Matilde scolded. "How long since you last took a bath or shaved?"

"I don't know. You don't really have to clean"...

"Hush your mouth, Alex," Matilde snapped. "You need to pull yourself together. There are other women in this world who would walk through fire for a young man like you. Get over it."

He could barely absorb his grandmother's lecture as his life was such a disaster. Starting out the year with a dismissal in his trial, a great if brief reunion with Amanda, and a stellar Daytona 500 showing should have launched the year off right. Then it all just collapsed on him. Amanda, for reasons still unknown, wouldn't even speak to him, he had gotten sideways again with Tim and Sherri over the passport snafu, and his father still had not rehired him out of a residual fear of that god-forsaken civil lawsuit with Unibank.

"I know I'm in a rut. This passport dilemma has screwed up my rally gig and Malloy can't seem to get a serious offer in NASCAR for me. I just need some time to get past this," he stated.

"And you think this will help you, young man?" Matilde asked while shaking her head and holding up the empty Seagrams 7 bottle.

They pulled back into Andy's circle driveway just before 6:00 PM. Maria had volunteered to leave the office early to watch the baby and work to prepare dinner for the family, including Alex, who declined the invite to join them.

Matilde was worried about her youngest grandson and upset with Andy, who had flown back to Charlotte for a couple of days but seemed to be consumed with his race team as they had not performed well on the Indy road course.

"Why don't you have a car for him?" Matilde had pressured Andy more than once. "That's what he needs right now."

"It just can't be done right now, Mom. Not until this Unibank suit is resolved."

"And we all thought Unibank would be the greatest thing ever," she bellowed. "I'll be so glad when their presence is all gone and over with."

"At least we won't have to worry about entertaining all of them again. Santos can have all of that," Andy replied. "We'll have the BP/Amoco people and a few more, but nothing like the army that Unibank used to throw at us."

Crissy chose not to involve herself in that debate, knowing that Tony's advancing career in Formula One would not have occurred without Unibank and BP.

"He just keeps harking on the fact of Amanda just cutting off all communication. Who could know what's going on in that girl's mind after what she's been through?" Matilde added. "That boy has to get over her, Crissy... He has to."

"I've always had a good relationship with Amanda," Crissy said, thinking out loud. "Maybe she'll talk to me. She at least has to tell Alex her reasons."

"Your time is almost up, Louie!"

He played that voicemail a second time before deleting it. He had painstakingly sent Remi fifteen grand late the day before, hoping and assuming the woman would be placated and back off of that threatened deadline. He was wrong and could not withstand the backlash from Evelyn should she become exposed to the contents of that recording and photographs. He dialed.

"I need some more time! It would help if you could send me whatever you have on Allison while you were in California."

"No mas, amigo," Remi replied, obviously mocking him.

"Remi, I've sent you almost twenty grand this week, so back off," Newberry stated. "Send me what you have on her so I may pressure the bitch into paying the rest."

"You send me another ten grand and I'll consider it," Remi replied, not disclosing the fact that she had nothing to share with him regarding her trip to San Diego. *I already had the goods, Louie... And I don't need an agent to help me collect the rest of your tab.*

Twenty minutes later, Newberry had a text come in, sent from an obscure website and not Remi's phone. They were images of him and Allison in the bar at Ivey's, a profile of his facing her from his barstool and her having her hand on his left thigh.

You bitch!

Allison had thus far blown him off. After all, he had pushed through the deal and would stand to cash in big time. She had no intention of paying the imbecile another single dime.

What's he going to? Tell Evelyn on me? I have him by the balls and he knows it, she thought grinning. Such scenarios were all part of her business model. Mother Nature had given her a seductive body that could be used,... and was.

She felt no pressing need to call Newberry but did take the time to review the images he had sent her in a text.

"You bastard!"

"Allison, Dad will be so disappointed. You cannot pull something like this," Aaron stated.

"This is too important to me, honey," Allison replied, displaying her well-practiced big sad blue eyes act. "I have to be there to support Evelyn. I'm the one who put this deal together, Aaron. I can't have Dad there having something blow up on it. He's under a lot of pressure and it's partly my fault. Plus, it's my big chance... How about you go ahead and fly to Hilton Head, do the family thing, and I'll fly down there to be with you on Memorial Day, itself?"

"Okay, Allison. You owe me," Aaron responded with feigned authority, as though his fiancée would take heed.

"Of course, baby," she replied. *Sure I do.*

Allison would fly to Indianapolis on Saturday morning of race weekend on the guise of supporting Evelyn Stevens and her new team, while also being beside her father, who had seemed to place way too much faith in Carolyn Tyler to replace Adam Herrera, a woman whom Allison viewed as little more than a dingy lipstick-wearing bimbo.

In reality, she had arranged to spend Saturday evening with Louis Newberry, the two both declining to disclose their private meeting plans with others,... and with each having separate agendas for that meeting.

She had apologized profusely to Newberry for her lack of not returning his calls and claimed to have some money coming in before the end of the month and would pay him his bonus when they met in cash. For his part, the besieged agent held his level of suspicion, but was still intrigued about the sexy Allison's suggestion of a clandestine meeting with him alone and would willfully play along.

Her whole excuse for missing Amanda's graduation was met with a sad rebuke from her mother, but Sarah lacked surprise as the ugly rift between the girls over the trial testimony still lingered, and the idea of their remaining hundreds of miles apart did have its own appeal, at least for the present.

She thought about calling or texting her but decided a personal face-to-face, woman-to-woman meeting was more appropriate. She knew the high school and had pulled up her Facebook page, which featured numerous images of her in the new red Mustang convertible.

Crissy sat patiently in the parking lot for over an hour. She kept checking the time, anxious that she would see Amanda among the host of students and approach her before she drove off. She had no way of knowing if Amanda had any extended hours, activities, or anything of the sort as she waited just a few parking spots away.

The loud ringing sound emitted and in short order, the rear doors opened, the throng of teenagers sprung out into the parking lot, and Crissy soon recognized Amanda chattering away with another girl as both headed for the Mustang. Crissy quickly got out of her Honda CRV and approached the two just as Amanda was opening her door.

"Crissy?" Amanda asked while taken by surprise.

"Hi, Amanda," she responded. "How have you been?"

"Okay, I guess... Oh, this is my best friend, Trisha."

"Pleased to meet you," Crissy stated and took the girl's hand in greeting. "Crissy Moretti," she added.

Amanda and Crissy shared a brief standoff and suddenly, as if both were on the same page, moved forward to embrace each other. After another few seconds, Crissy asked. "Amanda, is there somewhere we can talk?"

The two schoolmates shared a brief look before her reply. "Trisha is riding with me. Perhaps we could all three have an ice cream or something? There's a little place close by called *The Scoop.*"

"Sure," Crissy answered, preferring a private meeting, but she recalled Alex mentioning Trisha once in the past. "How about I just follow you?"

"I'll keep you in my mirrors."

"You promised yourself, Amanda. Are you sure you want to do this?" Trisha asked as they breezed through the Rock Hill traffic with the Mustang's top down.

"What do you expect, Trisha? I like her a lot," Amanda asked her.

"What do you think she wants to talk to you about?"

Amanda looked over toward her briefly. "How many guesses do I get?"

Crissy followed closely behind, smiling as the two teen girls in the open shiny red convertible received their share of honks and hollering from members of the opposite sex along the way.

She recalled back to when she and Amanda had first met at Indy three years earlier, the way she looked at her brother-in-law,... and the way he looked at her. Even though Amanda wasn't even old enough to drive, Crissy had this feeling about her, and about them. *Amanda surely doesn't look like a kid now,* Crissy observed. She recounted telling her the story of how she and Tony met, how genuinely interested and sincere she was, so much different than her older sister, one who seemed to always be looking past her as one who felt herself above everyone. *So different than Amanda.*

They arrived at the ice cream shop and each ordered a small cone before finding seats at one of the small round metal tables.

"I think you two have known each other for a long time. Isn't that right?" Crissy asked, wanting to get a measure of Trisha's station in the pending conversation.

"Best friends since we were five years old," Amanda replied.

"So, I suppose you'll both graduate soon. Have you decided on colleges, yet?"

"Clemson," Trisha answered for the two of them.

Amanda looked at her friend smiling but shaking her head slowly. "I'm not a hundred percent on that, yet."

"So how is your mom, Amanda? She was so nice," Crissy asked, attempting to gather as much neutral information before broaching the serious topic.

"She's fine. Mom is such a strong person," Amanda replied. "That whole accident and saga with the trial, it's been hard on all of us."

"Indeed it has, Amanda. I understand you haven't seen or hardly spoken to Alex since Daytona. If you don't mind sharing, what happened between the two of you?"

Amanda and Trisha again shared a glance. "I think I just needed to move on."

"There had to be more to it than that, Amanda. That Monday before the race when he drove up here just to see you, I saw two people in love with each other. I think I know what that looks like."

Trisha could tell her lifelong friend was starting to get emotional. "I'm sorry, Crissy. But he cheated on her."

"No way," Crissy bit back. "Cheated with who?"

"This image is from the night before the race," Trisha offered while showing a photograph of Alex and Evelyn embracing each other at some formal party. "And there's more," she added, displaying for Crissy's consumption another two photos of Alex and Evelyn lounging together at a pool after dark, and two more of Evelyn apparently hanging all over him in a hotel elevator while he held up his hand in a failed attempt to block a camera. All were date and time-stamped the night before the race in Daytona.

Crissy just looked at the images shaking her head.

"I thought he loved me, Crissy," Amanda exclaimed. "I called two days after you saw me and told him that Trisha and I were driving down to Daytona. He didn't want me to come. I know why now."

"You believe that Alex is still seeing Evelyn?"

"Looks like more than just seeing to me," Trisha added in support of Amanda.

"This makes no sense," Crissy responded, although now understanding better. "I know that if it were up to Evelyn, they would be back together in a heartbeat. But they're not. Alex isn't planning to even spend one day at Indy this month. Not a day, Amanda! And Evelyn, like all the other drivers, will be there all month."

"That's the problem, Crissy. She'll be there at every race and I can't be. How can I ever trust him after that?"

"I can't tell you about this business with Evelyn in Daytona. Tony was with him most of the time and I'll find out... I will tell you, Amanda, he hasn't been with her since returning from Daytona. He hasn't been anywhere. He's started to drink and just lays around the condo all day. He's a mess... You think about it. Call him, Amanda... He needs some sort of closure at least."

"He broke my heart!" Amanda responded.

"I can see that," Crissy acknowledged as she rose up and prepared to walk out.

Trisha embraced Amanda as she was now in tears.

"I did love him, Crissy," Amanda almost yelled.

Alex's close sister-in-law turned for one last thought as she looked back at them before exiting at the door. "You still do, Amanda."

The speedway president, Doug Bowles, was beside himself with excitement as Pole Day was shaping up to draw their largest crowd of the millennium by a long shot. The stars of Indycar were being challenged by three current drivers from Formula One and one of NASCAR's biggest stars, Kyle Larson.

The McLaren stable had added entries for Fernando Alonzo, the very popular two-time F1 champion, and Larson, a top driver from Rick Hendrick's NASCAR team.

Not to be outdone, Chip Ganassi had coaxed former world champion, Nico Rosberg, out of retirement, as well as Tony Stewart, an Indy favorite who had not run at Indy in over twenty years, to team with his solid crew including the legend, Scott Dixon, and two-time series champion, Alex Palou.

Andy Moretti would add a car for Tony, who had won the pole twice before his exodus to Formula One, and signed a last-minute deal with Jensen Button, as suddenly loads of cash to sponsor cars for this one-off event was pleasantly in abundance.

The worldwide press couldn't get enough of Indy with their darling Stevens still garnering much of the attention, but Nico Rosberg had his share of fanfare, along with all the other *guests*.

By Thursday all front runners were lapping in the 232 miles per hour range with Scott McLaughlin setting the pace and Tony Moretti an eyelash behind.

Evelyn Stevens was frustrated as the Indywest car couldn't seem to crack 228 in practice, which put her in serious danger of not making the show. The Indywest team found themselves at a distinct disadvantage in not having two experienced drivers sharing data, as her one-race teammate, Ramos, was a rookie and even slower in practice than she was. By Saturday morning she was on the phone with Newberry, ragging about her contract and the team he had her stuck with.

Pole Day was electrifying as a crowd of over 140,000 filled the stands, all waiting to cheer their heroes on. The hotels and flights to the city were overbooked and a crowd of perhaps 400,000 was expected for race day.

Kyle Larson set a blistering four-lap speed of 233.987 to grab the provisional pole, a speed which held through the late afternoon. Most of the favorites had qualified with the exceptions of Tony Moretti, Will Power, and Helio Castroneves, back for his *Drive For Five*.

Power ran very fast but fell off on the fourth lap and settled for third fastest at 233.853, followed by Helio's 232.934, good for the third row.

The late afternoon run by Tony began as the shadows now covered much of the track and possibly giving him an advantage if his car was set up just right.

Several hours to the southeast, a depressed Alex Moretti sat and watched as his brother began his run, sitting up on the edge of his couch, and beginning to tune into his large TV screen at the end of Tony's first lap... 233.903..."Come on brother. You can do it."

Another forty minutes south, Byron and Sarah heard Amanda and Trisha become animated in the family room, as both scurried down the stairs to see what all the uproar was about.

"Go Tony! Yes!" Amanda yelled... 2nd lap, 233.789.

"I thought she was over this stuff," Byron told Sarah as they watched from the bottom of the stairway.

"Oh, get a life, Byron," Sarah snapped as she ran up behind the girls on the sectional.... Third lap, 233.734!

The broadcast displayed a shot of Tony's wife sitting next to Andy on his pit box, tense with both of her fingers crossed.

"Look!" Amanda screamed. "It's Crissy!"

Back up north, Alex was more subdued but stiffened up as the broadcast showed Tony at just a click off Larson's speed as he sped into the first turn. "You've got it, Tony... Steady... Fourth lap, a blistering 234.786, giving Tony the pole-winning speed of 234.053,

While Byron retired to his den, Sarah and the two girls were screaming, jumping up and down, high fives, and all. They calmed down just a bit as NBC's Kevin Lee worked his way through the crowd.

"Tony, this is your third Indy 500 Pole. With such an outstanding international field, how would you rate this one?

"Well, Kevin, they're all special and I'm so glad to be back here after missing this race last year. I didn't know if we had anything for Larson, but the car was strong and I believe the late afternoon run played in our favor. Now, I just need to win one of these."

"Tony now gets the congratulatory hug and kiss from his wife, Crissy, I'll take it back up to you, Leigh."

Amanda reached for her phone to send a quick text, *"Congratulations, Crissy! Great job, Tony!"*

On his end, Alex smiled while he got up for another beer. *Great job, brother. I guess I'll do the leftover lasagna.*

One driver who was not happy was Evelyn Stevens, who had posted the 32nd fastest speed and waved it off as she would undoubtedly get bumped out of the field the following day, with a good seven cars still trying to make the field. While Van Brough kept trying to reassure her, she had serious

doubts that he and his crew had any more ability to get more speed out of the car. Roberto Santos was upset and began to rant and rave while Van Brough threatened to walk off the job if he didn't get out of the garage, thus his wife grabbed him and took him away, claiming she was going to give him a strong sedative to knock him out for the night.

It also struck Evelyn as odd that her agent was nowhere to be found for the weekend, not that she missed him but thought odd of it as he had always gone out of his way to display himself at Indy in years past. Just as she prepared to leave Gasoline Alley, she was stopped by none other than Adam Herrera.

"You got a few minutes?" he asked.

"That's all I have right now, Adam," she replied, obviously quite dejected and he needing no explanation as to why.

"Where's Louie?"

"I haven't a clue. Makes the place seem quieter, does it not?"

"I have an idea, Evelyn. I think you'll like it."

"I'm all ears, Adam."

"You either need another car or your existing car needs a makeover. Otherwise, you won't make this race," he stated matter-of-factly.

"I know that better than anyone, Adam. And?" Evelyn asked dubiously.

"I have a possible solution for you. Let's go somewhere where we can sit down."

"Get real, Carolyn!" Byron spat, extremely annoyed that he was bothered by this right then, while also disturbed that his mistress was calling him late on a Saturday.

"Hear me out, Byron!... How will it look if Evelyn doesn't even qualify for the race? You know the board will be all over you over it."

She's so right, he reflected. *Forsythe will eat this up.* "I don't like the sound of this, Carolyn. Let me sleep on it and we'll revisit this Monday morning."

"Byron, there's no time. They'll be working on her car all night. She has to qualify tomorrow or the gig is up."

Byron hated these kinds of on-the-spot high-pressure moments. He had always been taught to never make important decisions when you're emotional. Unfortunately, it appeared he had little choice at the moment.

"Are you serious?"

"I just got off the phone with her, Andy."

"Adam, there is no time to complete all this."

"I can get everyone together for an announcement first thing Monday."

"That won't do her much good now, Adam," Andy replied.

"How about we do a four-way call with me, you, Santos, and Cook, like now."

"Good luck with that, Adam," Andy replied as he prepared to disconnect. *I believe in aiming high, Adam. But you're dreaming.*

"Just stand by your phone."

Thirty minutes later, Herrera called back. "I can't seem to get hold of Santos, Andy."

"Roberto won't be a problem. Just get Cook on," Andy stated, still not believing this would all go down like this, anyway.

Five minutes later, Andy's phone rang twice and he took a breath before picking up. "Andy Moretti here."

"Andy, it's Adam Herrera and I have Byron Cook on the line."

After an awkward few seconds, Andy replied. "Good evening, Byron."

"Andy."

The frigid pleasantries out of the way, Herrera began. "Gentlemen, I have discussed the basic details of my proposal with each of you. I believe Andy wants to say something."

Byron gritted his teeth, this being the first time the two had spoken directly in over two years.

"Byron, Adam proposes that I send some of my crew to help Santos' people get Evelyn's car lined out so she may qualify tomorrow. Is that your understanding?"

"I believe so," Byron answered dryly.

"And you and I will agree to totally drop all pending lawsuits against each other if I agree to that, correct?" Andy stated.

"If you can assure me that she'll qualify, yes."

"Huh? No, no. That's not the way things work, Byron. You want to explain this to him, Adam?"

"He doesn't have to explain it," Byron bellowed. "I know you're both on the same team."

"Byron, this decision has to be made now, or Evelyn's toast," Herrera stated.

Everything went quiet for a moment.

"Byron?"

"All right,... all right. Get it done."

"We don't have time for paperwork, Byron," Andy stated. "I'll have a few of my best people down there right away if I have your solemn word of honor that we will complete this agreement unconditionally on Monday morning and issue a public statement that we're both dropping all pending lawsuits, personal and professional."

Adam listened intently for a reply.

"You have my word on it."

"All right, gentleman. We've all agreed and will proceed accordingly. Any other questions?"

"No, Just don't screw me on this, Andy!" Cook's last statement as he disconnected.

"Well, Andy? You still there?"

"Yes, Adam... Do you think I can trust him?"

"I think so. But just to be sure, make sure she qualifies," Adam stated.

"All right, Adam, as you are my witness."

"Should I track down Santos?"

"Up to you, but how could he object? Roberto will just owe me one. So long as Van Brough is wired in, we're good."

"Right."

Andy disconnected, smiling while shaking his head. His best chassis technician, Mike Jensen, who was Evelyn's chief engineer the previous two years, was chomping at the bit to help her. Having all four of their cars safely in the show, the team would have an early evening off to enjoy themselves.

Andy had given Jensen his tacit approval to head over to the Team Indywest garage and offer his expert assistance after the rest of Team Moretti had all left the track, a nod that had occurred a full hour prior to his and Cook's conversation.

Byron poured himself another glass of bourbon. He hated the deal he had just made, feeling Moretti had just gotten completely off the hook while giving up little in return. He would have to get the board members onboard Monday, but that should be no problem. None of them supported that lawsuit anyway.

The ladies will be shocked that I will be anxiously watching race cars on TV myself tomorrow. He swallowed the last five ounces whole.

"He agreed to what?" Matilde asked, not in the mood for jokes.

"I'm serious, Mom. Jensen and Green were there all night working with them. No guarantees, of course, but they changed some things on her car."

"Does that mean you can have a car for Alex, then?" Matilde asked.

"Unfortunately not, Mom. There's no time and all the chassis are taken up anyway. I'll be glad to get him back onboard for Detroit, maybe. How are my grandsons?"

"A handful, God love 'em. Have you given Alex this news?"

"No, but that can be my next call, Mom."

"Give Tony and Crissy my love," Matilde replied as they disconnected. *I hope Alex answers his phone.*

Bump Day at Indianapolis was as intense for some as the run for the Pole the previous day. Not making the race at all was a reality for seven cars and drivers who still planned runs to fill the last few spots on the grid.

At track opening, Evelyn Stevens hit the track for some practice laps, showing slight but measurable improvement right off by averaging just over 229.5 MPH in six laps before returning to the pits, somewhat smiling as was her boss Santos, who had been made aware earlier over breakfast of the late-night support his beleaguered team had received.

Sarah and Amanda were somewhat taken aback when Byron declined to accompany the two of them to church as he was glued to the family room TV screen, himself. *What are they waiting for? Get your butt out there and get this over with!* he sulked.

Starting at just before noon, the sky was partially cloudy in Indianapolis and the remaining few hopeful qualifiers began to make their runs. Evelyn had run a 229 plus for three laps but waved them off as it appeared that wouldn't be fast enough, and returned for some more adjustments. With six hours remaining, she was still cautiously optimistic,... until the dark clouds appeared.

Tremendous tension was building in the Indywest pit as Andy and his man Jensen played coach for Van Brough's crew as Santos burned a hole in the blacktop behind them, dying for a cigarette in the restricted area.

"Tell Roberto to stop worrying, Jensen expressed to Van Brough. The car's setup is right for a cool track. It'll come to her, trust me."

"If it's dry," Van Brough replied in retort, getting exceedingly anxious they had not just completed the earlier run and stuck with it.

By 4:00, three remained and the weather had changed with rain possible at any moment. Evelyn sat nervously in pit lane behind Juanita Legos, a rookie who had not shown sufficient speed all month to qualify but held the place in line ahead of her. If she happened to take to the track when the rain started, Stevens would be holding the bag unless the weather cleared up in time for the track to dry and return to green flag conditions before 6:00 PM, which now appeared unlikely. Her earlier run, as it turned out, had placed her in the 30th spot had she maintained and completed the run, although it seemed ominous at the time with six cars still set to run.

Byron sat on pins and needles aside Sarah and Amanda, strangely asking many questions about the Bump Day rules and surprised that Amanda seemed to know all about them.

"If it starts raining, Stevens is SOL," Amanda stated, unable to pull against her, despite past personal considerations.

"Why don't they go!?" Byron kept yelling at the screen as Leigh Diffey announced that rain looked imminent.

The three sat on edge as Legos left pit lane and began her initial warm-up run. Taking the green flag on her third pass, the young female rookie entered the first turn clocked at just over 231 MPH, Diffey announced, as Byron sank back on the sectional.

"Don't worry, Dad. That's slow," Amanda stated. "Her speed will scuff off in turns two and four. You watch."

Byron looked quickly over at her as Sarah smiled at the rare light and close moment between them,

Legos hit the bricks clocked at 226 MPH and then slowed on the second lap before pulling back into pit lane.

"What happened?" Byron yelled. "Why did she quit!?"

The three all sat there, thinking there must have been a red flag because of rain, but were surprised by Leigh Diffey's commentary.

"What a shocking development! It was obvious Legos did not have the speed and in a great show of sportsmanship, it appears that Ken Tolar, the car owner for Juanita Legos, has waved her run off to give Evelyn Stevens a last shot at qualifying. She is pulling out of pit lane now hoping to get her four-lap run in before the showers open up, which appears will happen any second now."

Stevens quickly got up to speed in her warm-up laps as Roberto Santos stood next to his crew chief, Van Brough, his fingernails all but chewed away.

"Cross your fingers, boss," the crew chief assured him.

She took the green flag as the crowd all stood and cheered, none having departed in spite of the obvious pending foul weather. She was quick on her first two laps and crossed the line on her third lap carrying an average of 232.4. Suddenly raindrops appeared on the first-turn pavement as she passed through at speed. Diffey could hardly contain himself behind the NBC Sports microphone, yelling that rain was coming. Could Stevens complete her run before hitting wet pavement, potentially losing grip and risk hitting the third or fourth turn wall at over 230 MPH?

The track's most celebrated driver entered the last turn just as the clouds broke as she raced down the home stretch, almost as if the showers were chasing her down. Taking the checkered flag just when the rain overtook the entire facility, the clock registered her at 20th fastest with a four-lap speed of 231.566 MPH.

"Oh, wow," Byron stated, showing little emotion although underneath a stoic exterior was most relieved.

The family females were more ecstatic, jumping up and down and hugging each other. Amanda was in tears as Sarah could see her mixed emotions, knowing what her daughter must be thinking. Byron never told them that Evelyn Stevens, with some unforeseen help from Andy Moretti, had probably just saved his job.

Andy shook Adam's hand following the confirmation text from his corporate lawyer, Ed Rothman, confirming that he had spoken to Reggie Morgan and that both Unibank and Moretti Motorsport had agreed to drop all the pending lawsuits against the other, a topic of headline news for later that day to add to all of the other buzz at the speedway.

The celebrations and accolades of Tony winning the Pole, Evelyn making the show with speed to spare, and all of the notable guest drivers qualifying were short-lived as practice for the real thing began in earnest the following day. It would be a week full of practice and adjustments for each team to improve and ready themselves for the upcoming Sunday while the speedway, not to mention the whole city of Indianapolis, was bustling with excitement as the usual buzz of the annual 500 was now the most anticipated of any in most observer's lifetimes.

While Evelyn Stevens carried her usual post-500 media circus, foreign celebrity drivers Nico Rosberg and Fernando Alonso received plenty of press attention, not to discount similar activity around Kyle Larson, Tony Stewart, and Jensen Button.

Meanwhile, the series' stars O'Ward, Power, and Castroneves were running the fastest practice times in addition to Pole sitter Tony Moretti, who was still considered an Indycar regular despite his one-year hiatus to race Formula One.

On Tuesday afternoon, Tony was following George Halbert at speed when the rookie lost control in turn three, hitting the wall and glancing back down the banking right into an oncoming Moretti, who tee-boned Havert at over 220 MPH, causing his Dallara to flip end over end over the top of Havert's car in a horrific crash before sliding to an upside down stop in the middle of the short chute.

The bells rang out signaling the conclusion of her last class. The week was filled with last semester tests and preparation for her graduation on the upcoming Saturday. She walked out into the hallway where Trisha waited by Amanda's locker. She could tell by her friend's somber expression something was dire as they both shared the smartphone news flash.

DRIVER KILLED IN INDY CRASH, POLE SITTER CRITICALLY WOUNDED

Amanda came to tears as she digested the details of the news. "Oh my god, Trisha! Tony,... and Crissy!"

She first thought about calling her, but hesitated. *She'll be busy at the hospital. The family will be all around. I'll send a text and ask her to call me when she feels the time is right.*

Her phone rang within minutes. It was Crissy calling back.

"Oh, Crissy. I am so sorry," Amanda stated. "Has anything changed?"

"No. Thanks for asking, Amanda. He is unconscious now. We don't know anything."

"Is there anything I can do, Crissy?"

"Pray for him. Just pray, Amanda. Perhaps you're living proof of that power."

"I should call Alex," she added.

"He's on a plane already, Amanda. I'll tell him you'll call later?"

"Yes. That would be good. We'll talk soon," an emotional Amanda closed. *Such tragedy. We're all made of it, it seems.*

He sat down with his CFO in the bank cafe early on Wednesday morning, as was routine for them in midweek. Once the small talk and quick update of the numbers were out of the way, the subject of Indianapolis came up.

"That family has been through a lot," Remington stated, sighting the headline of the Charlotte Observer sports section.

"They live by the sword and they often die by the sword, Wally," Byron replied.

"We should send something, a card maybe."

"I'll have Carolyn Tyler handle it."

Remington sighed, long suspecting that Cook had an affair with Tyler and somewhat disappointed the CEO had chosen not to take his longtime friend and associate into his confidence. *I guess I understand it,* Wally pondered. "I'm taking Liz and all the kids to Indy."

"You are?" Byron asked, surprised and disappointed he was not informed of that earlier.

"Byron, Forsythe has already made a big deal out of her representing Unibank in the VIP Suite there. Not a good thing. It would be good for your whole family to be there."

"I know but Amanda's graduation is Saturday night. Sarah is already not happy about my being gone for that," Byron replied.

"Well, Carolyn Tyler will be there to support you," Wally said, a bit too openly. "If any BS comes up regarding Stevens and her contract, she'll be close by to help cover it,.. I guess."

Alex had walked into the restricted hospital waiting area with his grandmother and two nephews in tow at 10:05 PM to a waiting and red-eyed Crissy, who anxiously grabbed and embraced little David and her older son, Adrian.

Tony lay in the Intensive Care Unit in critical condition, still unconscious although his breathing had somewhat stabilized.

Alex himself appeared haggard, not having shaved or had a haircut since Daytona it seemed. His phone buzzed notifying him of another text. *Amanda.*

"*Alex. I am so sorry about Tony. Let me know if there is anything I can do. I'll be praying for him. Amanda.*"

It had been over three months since they had even talked. He wondered if he should call her. He checked the time and dialed.

"Hi," she answered.

"Hi, Amanda."

"How is he doing?"

"About the same," Alex replied, feeling strangely distant with her.

"I am so sorry... How is Crissy holding up?"

"Okay, I guess. As well as can be expected," he answered, wanting to say more but the words just wouldn't come.

"I'm graduating Saturday, so I won't be coming up there with my dad."

"Yes, I knew that. Congratulations, Amanda."

"Thank you," she replied. Like him, she was having difficulty making conversation. "Well, I'm here for all of you if you need anything... Bye now."

He stared downward at his disconnected phone. *Bye, Amanda.*

Stevens had gone to the hospital where nothing had changed and Crissy informed her that Alex had gone to the Union Jack bar for a drink. The local speedway pub was busy as was always the case during race week and the place seemed to stand still as she walked in, strolling around the U-shaped crowded bar and up to him, sitting alone at the far end.

"You look terrible," Evelyn declared, noticing even in the dim light that his eyes were bloodshot red. "What's with all the hair?"

"I don't know. I haven't been up to getting it cut. How are you?" he asked.

"Like everyone else, Alex. I just left the hospital. No news, yet."

He looked straight ahead as he spoke. "I never thought it would be Tony, you know? I was always the reckless one. It should have been me, Evelyn."

"What we all do is dangerous. You know that. I heard your dad has decided to just withdraw the "5" car."

"Oh? I hadn't heard that," Alex responded with a look of surprise.

"I wouldn't be in this race if it wasn't for your dad," Evelyn exclaimed. "He may have just saved my career."

"I'm glad that worked out. So, did you get your contract straightened out with Unibank?"

"Not totally, but thanks for asking," Evelyn answered, pausing as the bartender hinted he wanted an autograph.

"David Land keeps mentioning it on his Podcast," he stated.

"I understand you and Amanda have quit seeing each other," Evelyn said, expecting a reaction.

"That's right," Alex responded.

I can tell. You wouldn't see anyone in your condition. "Do you want to tell me about it?"

"We just kind of fell out after Daytona."

"I see. After what I heard about the trial, I'm surprised," she added. "I need to get going. Are you going to be okay? Need a ride or anything?"

"I'm fine. Thanks, Evelyn."

"Okay. You should really get a shave and a haircut," she stated in parting while patting him gently on the back.

"Andy, you need to put Alex in the car," Crissy stated as more of a demand.

"No, withdrawing it is the honorable thing, Crissy," he said to his daughter-in-law.

"Honorable? Honorable for whom, Andy? Honor Tony! If he was talking right now, it's what he would want."

"And how do you know that?"

"If he doesn't survive, he wouldn't want to be buried in that car. He would want his brother to drive for him."

"I'm not sure Alex could handle it, Crissy. You've seen him. He isn't in very good shape and I'm not even sure that Frye or Boles would approve it."

"Of course they would. That Moretti name still means something around here. Let's put Alex in the car."

Amanda awoke on Thursday morning to a striking headline:

Alex Moretti to Drive for Stricken Brother at Indy

Oh my god! She thought. *I should send him a text.*
"Hey Race Man! I heard the news. Make us proud! Amanda"
Alex looked at it, thinking it strange that she was feeling the need to note her name at the end, as if he would no longer have her stored in his phone. *"Thanks, Amanda. I'll be starting last, but I'll give it my best shot."*
He then proceeded to get into the cockpit, a place he had not been in an Indycar for a while.

Her phone buzzed and she anxiously picked up on the first ring. "Hello."
"How are things, Crissy?"
"Still the same. Thanks for asking, Evelyn."
"I probably won't come up tonight, but I thought I'd check in," Stevens stated. "Is there anything I can do for you?"
"Well, maybe. Have you got a few minutes?"
"Sure, Crissy. Just name it."
The two discussed what Crissy had in mind, a favor that Evelyn had not seen coming. "That will not be easy for me, Crissy. You know that."
"I'm not just asking for Alex. I'm asking for all of us, Evelyn."

She made a habit of just letting unknown area code calls dump into voicemail, letting the call disconnect, and then listening, which eliminated the hassle of talking with too many telemarketers. The message from the caller was quite awakening, and after a brief thought, chose to call back as this voicemail was from someone quite unexpected.

423

"Hello, Amanda. Thanks for calling back so soon," Evelyn began, attempting to get comfortable in the conversation.

"Evelyn, how are you?"

"Bloody tired, I must say."

"I believe it. That was quite a show you put on Sunday. We were thrilled."

"Thank you. This call is in regard to our mutual friend."

Amanda was silent.

"Are you still there, Amanda?"

"Yes, I'm here."

"I understand you believe there may still be something between Alex and I."

Amanda paused. "Evelyn, I'm not sure that I"...

"Hear me out, Amanda. I had my time with Alex Moretti, but he loves you now. Crissy sent me those pictures of me and him in Daytona. That was nothing, Amanda. I was angry over my contract and I wanted to cry on his shoulder. He drove me to my hotel and carried my bloody intoxicated arse up to my room and left. He didn't even want to be at that party. He wanted to be with you, Amanda... It's your business, but he has an important job to do Sunday and he could use a pick-me-up. Can the Morettis count on you?"

""I'm not sure what I can do. I'm not going to be there, Evelyn."

"You have the next best thing, Amanda... A phone."

Sarah busied herself in getting ready for the ceremony, pausing every once in a while as Byron was actually texting pictures back from Saturday's events at the speedway, a time she recalled so favorably from their time there three years earlier. There he was with Evelyn Stevens and her new boss, along with legends Mario Andretti and Johnny Rutherford.

Byron had taken the Lear jet up Friday night, a move to partly undercut Marilyn Forsythe, whose reservation for the corporate plane was usurped at the last minute by Byron, Carolyn Tyler, and Wally Remington with his family.

Amanda couldn't stop thinking about the call from Evelyn Stevens and decided to have an initial conversation with Crissy, who validated everything she had claimed.

"Of course, I called her on it, Amanda. I know my brother-in-law pretty well by now. He's like a real brother to me, and he has been down ever since Daytona. These past three months are probably the first time he has gone this long without being behind the wheel of a race car since he was five years old."

"I feel so bad now, Crissy."

"Well, don't be. Just let him know you're behind him. It'll give him a lift on Sunday, I just know it," *and hopefully my husband, too.*

"I will, Crissy."

"Well, well! Look at you!" Matilde spoke as she arose to hug her grandson, well-groomed and fresh-shaven. "Now I recognize that handsome boy I raised."

Alex embraced her and Crissy heartily, then asked, "How is he?"

"The doc says he's breathing better," Matilde answered, glad for small victories.

"Where are my nephews?" Alex asked.

"Marie has them tonight," Crissy replied. "You seem a bit sprite, for a change."

"I guess it was time I cleaned up a bit," he admitted.

"And talked to someone, I assume?"

He smiled back. "A little bit."

"And?" Crissy added expectantly.

"We'll see... After Detroit, we'll see how it goes."

Chapter 17

500 Miles

S arah was sad that her entire family wouldn't be on hand for Amanda's graduation as she and her youngest girl went out for a late lunch to celebrate on their own. As much as she wanted the occasion to be remembered and happy in spirit, she could tell something was bothering Amanda.

"What is it, honey? You're not yourself today. Are you upset about your dad?"

"No, that's not it. I just keep thinking about Tony Moretti,... and his family."

"And does that include Alex Moretti?"

"I wish I could just be there for them, Mom."

"Well, honey. We'll throw a little party at home tomorrow and watch it together. You can invite Trisha, and Brittany, and"...

"It's not the same," Amanda replied as she stared out the restaurant window. "Maybe I'll go,... late tonight after the graduation."

"Amanda! You can't fly out that late. There probably wouldn't be any flights available, even if you wanted to."

"Let's just see." She began to pull up some apps on her phone and punch in data... *No luck. Mom's right, it seems.*

"This is silly, Amanda."

"I'll just drive. If I leave after the ceremony, I can be there by tomorrow morning,... before the race starts."

"Amanda, you're not going to drive all the way to Indianapolis,... in the middle of the night!"

"Why not?" she responded. "I have a good car."

Sarah could tell the girl was serious. *My little girl has grown up and is hellbent on doing this.* "Well then. I'm going with you."

They chose to take the by-pass around the west side of Cincinnati, passing by the international airport around dawn, and knew they should arrive in Indianapolis with hours to spare before the green flag dropped. As such, Sarah and Amanda chose to pay a visit to the IU Methodist Hospital first, and Amanda sent Crissy a text that they were there.

Earlier that morning, Tony was transferred out of the IC Unit to a private room. While he remained unconscious and was still considered critical, his heartbeat had stabilized a bit and even if the move was largely symbolic, it gave the family a small semblance of optimism.

As the medical staff restricted visitors to family only, Crissy and Matilde met their visitors in the hospital lobby for a surprise greeting.

"Sarah, it is so good to see you," the Moretti matriarch stated as the two embraced as though a long past relationship needed to be revisited. "And look at this beautiful young lady you brought along."

"Actually, she brought me, Matilde," Sarah replied smiling.

Amanda exchanged warm greetings with Crissy and her elder-in-law.

"I had no idea you were coming. You should have given us some notice," Crissy stated.

"It was a last-minute decision to come, to put it mildly," Sarah replied, giving Amanda a quick glance.

"Matilde, would you mind entertaining Amanda's mother for a few? I want her to see Tony."

The two made their way through the corridors toward Tony's room as Amanda questioned whether they would allow her in.

"Don't worry about it. I'll tell them you're my sister," Crissy stated, trying to inject a small bit of humor where she could. "I heard you have experience with sneaking into these types of places, anyway."

Amanda was sad at the sight of him, all bandaged up with tubes and probes hooked up to him everywhere.

"The doctors are saying he doesn't appear to have serious head injuries."

"Neither did I, Crissy."

"I know. Maybe I just wanted you to see,... and say that, Amanda," Crissy replied misty-eyed, and forced a small but emotional smile. "You go. Go to the track and push Alex to do well for him, Amanda. I'll take it as a sign."

The crowd gathered early as fans wished to get a glimpse of their favorite four-wheeled gladiators. It would be noted as perhaps the most celebrated if not talent-laden field in over half a century. Tickets were being scalped out on Georgetown Road for five times their face value. Press pundits from all over the world were on hand as interviews with drivers and dignitaries from the sport were rampant with commentary and debate, often regarding the competitive skills of drivers from different racing disciplines.

NBC Sports' Leigh Diffey had his two cohorts, Townsend Bell and former Indy Pole Sitter James Hinchcliffe, who were on hand to add commentary.

"Well, fellas, this is it, perhaps the most anticipated Indianapolis 500 in my lifetime. Your thoughts, Townsend?"

"It may be the most exciting ever, Leigh, considering all the worldwide media attention. Some of the best drivers in the world are all here. It's going to be thrilling to say the least."

"James, it has been quite a volatile week with the drama of Bump Day to the tragic accident during practice on Tuesday. I know that you have been close to the Moretti family," Diffey continued.

"I certainly have and my thoughts are with the Havert and Moretti families, Leigh. I spoke with Andy earlier who informed me that Tony has been transferred out of the Intensive Care Unit at University Med. His condition has not changed dramatically but we can all hope and pray for his full recovery. I know Andy considered withdrawing Tony's Pole winning entry but the family chose to have his younger brother Alex, who last raced in an Indycar at Monterey two and a half years ago, drive the number "5" on his brother's behalf. The last time Alex ran here, he started on the outside of the last row as he will today, and was himself involved in an opening lap crash that took out a third of the field. He has a very good car under him, so I expect a bit of caution on his part when the green flag drops."

"Evelyn Stevens certainly has had a turbulent start to the season," Diffey added, "and our own Marc Mandell spoke to her earlier. Marc?"

"Good morning, Leigh. Yes, I did speak at length with Evelyn late yesterday and she is quite emotional regarding the Tony Moretti tragedy, as you would expect considering her past connection to the Moretti Motorsport team. She has experienced a frustrating start since her announced return to the Indywest team, as there are some unresolved issues regarding her team sponsor commitments, but she is not thinking about those now. Evelyn knows she has a very good car despite her last row start starting position, and she is cautiously optimistic about her chances in today's event. Back to you, Leigh."

Allison showed up at the Indywest hospitality trailer early and greeted Evelyn Stevens as though they were long-lost friends, joining her for a filling buffet breakfast.

"So Evelyn, I heard you've had some issues with your contract," Allison stated as though uninformed.

"Yes," she replied, looking around to ensure her comments were not overheard. "I'm not happy that Adam Herrera has left and now we have to deal with this bloody Tyler."

"What about Louie? Where is he, anyway?" Allison asked, again appearing genuinely curious.

"I don't know and I don't care. I just want to get this race in," Stevens stated.

"Why don't you use me as a go-between, Evelyn?" Allison asked confidently. "I'll have my marketing degree, and I could just represent you. Don't tell him I said so, but I would be much better than Newberry, at least so far as you're concerned."

Evelyn smiled and said nothing as she looked over and smiled at another admiring passerby.

"Well?"

"I'm not sure that would work out too well, love. I'm going to try and get back to driving for Andy Moretti next year."

"I see," Allison replied, pleased that Stevens seemed to be taking her into her confidence.

"I know you and your little sis are not even talking," Evelyn continued. "That would make things quite uncomfortable for all of us."

"Wouldn't bother me. I have no problem dealing with Andy Moretti."

"Alex will no doubt be back, also."

No surprise there, Allison thought. "So?"

"I expect Amanda to be quite a fixture in the paddock next year, Allison," Stevens added.

Allison picked up an air of acceptance on her part, as though Stevens and Amanda had developed their own personal connection somehow, a scenario she would despise, though not openly.

"Oh? Well, business is business, Evelyn. I could forgive my sister,... over time."

"We'll have all summer to consider it, Allison. But I suppose it's something to think about," the star female driver concluded. I just need to have an agent I can trust and one who would never again saddle me with such a bloody mess. If you do run into Louie this afternoon, don't bring any of this up, Allison. I don't need any more bloody distractions right now."

"Oh, I won't say anything,... if I do happen to see him," Allison stated rather sheepishly.

Amanda drove around the town of Speedway, unaccustomed to the crowded sidewalks and lawns several city blocks away from the speedway, as the last time the Cook family was here they were simply dropped off in front of the main gate after a comfortable ride in a luxury limousine. The cat calls and often obscene signs were flashed at the two while Amanda drove slowly forward, heading east to park as close to the track as possible.

"Oh my god, Amanda! What was that his sign had on it?" Sarah asked blushing, as one of a group of young party animals approached the side of their car with a banner requesting the two females expose their upper body parts.

"I think they're looking at you, Mom!" Amanda declared, trying to keep from laughing. "Forty dollars just to park!"

"Keep going, Amanda. Let's park closer so we don't have to walk by all of these drunken heathens," Sarah directed. "Why don't we just put the top back up?"

Amanda paid fifty bucks to park on the crowded lawn at a residence bordering the packed campground just west of the speedway itself. The accompanying fans were rowdy but friendly and after buttoning up the top and locking the car, Sarah and Amanda took off on foot across a pedestrian creek bridge toward Georgetown Road, and the back of the huge home straight stands that announced the west side of the massive race track.

Unaccustomed to approaching any sporting or entertainment event without a ticket, they burrowed past the throng of ticket scalpers, choosing to just purchase a general admission ticket for sixty bucks each, soon to learn that wouldn't get them access to any fixed seat, much less admission to a VIP suite.

Byron had lost some of his tension following a couple of late-morning cocktails, but struggled while having to smile and carry on a casual conversation with Marilyn Forsythe. He appeared nonchalant in the close company of his mistress, Carolyn Tyler, who seemed to be holding an open competition with Forsythe on who was actually perceived as the party host for the suite.

Suddenly Byron's phone buzzed and he looked surprised at the caller's ID. *Sarah? I thought she would be in church.* He covered one ear to block the ambient noise. "Hello."

"Byron, we're down here below the suite at the elevator," Sarah stated loudly. "I need you to get us a ticket to get in."

"What are you talking about, Sarah? What elevator?"

"Amanda and I are here. Send someone down here. We don't have credentials."

"Sarah, stop fooling with"...

"Byron! Get your butt down here!" Sarah screamed. "We're here! Now hurry up."

Three minutes later, Allison appeared at the elevator door, where a track security guard stood his ground, not taking the word of these two women that they should be allowed entrance to one of the expensive VIP suites, perched atop the Tower Terrace stands facing the home straight and flag stand.

"What are you two doing here?" Allison asked, not liking such surprises and still reeling from what Evelyn Stevens had shared with her about her sister earlier.

"I'll explain later," Sarah replied. "How can we get in?"

The four stood there at a bit of a standoff as Allison seemed to enjoy the problem. Amanda finally talked the guard into getting on his radio and summon a higher level official, one who approached the well-recognized and now famous Cook sisters. After a few more minutes of frustration, the two were awarded the appropriate credentials and made their way up to the Unibank suite.

The command for drivers to get to their machines was given and Alex climbed into his number "5" Amoco-sponsored car, the stress building as his thoughts kept oscillating back and forth between his brother, Tony, and that first turn that had hit him so hard on the start of the last race he had started here. He also thought of Amanda, believing she would be watching at home, but with an all-star international cast and the famous female starting on the inside of the last row to the left of him, he suspected the cameras would play him little regard.

Crissy sat in Tony's room with Matilde, watching the coverage on the wall TV monitor, when she spied a text message pop up on her phone.

"Crissy, Mom and I finally got in the Unibank VIP Suite. They were all in shock to see us. I couldn't see how to get access to anyone connected to Moretti Motorsport, though."

"I know," Chrissy replied. *"You can't just walk in down there. Let me call you back, Amanda."*

Sarah's appearance made Carolyn Tyler extremely uncomfortable as Byron had difficulty acting naturally and distanced himself from his illicit lover as though she had the plague, his sudden attitude hardly unnoticed by the other bank attendees, namely Marilyn Forsythe. His displeasure of being there in general was made all the worse with the addition of Amanda being present, particularly with the ongoing friction between his two daughters.

Allison played the social butterfly for a while but couldn't hold back, grabbing a seat next to her sister on the outside lower row seating as the two overlooked the pre-race pageantry below.

"I thought you and Alex had shot craps after the trial," Allison stated as the two stared forward.

"Yes, so?"

"What are you doing here, Amanda?"

"I could ask you the same thing," Amanda replied.

"I'm here to support Dad,... and Evelyn," Allison stated, noting that her sister sounded quite bold.

Amanda paused and just looked over toward her older sister with a neutral expression. "Well good, Allison. Enjoy the race." She then got up and started to walk back up to the inside of the suite, stealing Allison's thunder as leaving her older sister alone and staring at her backside.

"You can be hateful all you want, Amanda! What happened between Kyle and me was your fault. You should have taken care of him!" Allison declared loudly, drawing some unwanted attention from the several Unibank suite attendees gathered near the two.

Amanda stopped and turned back toward her. "I was fourteen years old, Allison. You did me a huge favor, and I should be grateful for that."

The two shared a deceitful stare and Amanda was tempted to suggest that her sister should be ashamed, but chose not to waste her breath.

"You want me to do what? Crissy, we're kind of busy down here."

"Andy, I think it's a good idea. What can it hurt?"

"No! I need that boy concentrating on the mission at hand," Andy replied. "Not thinking about that girl."

"Do this for Tony. Andy," Crissy replied heartily as her father-in-law clicked off.

The crew chief for the "5" car, Jack Morley, could see the boss was agitated. "What's up?"

"Oh, Tony's wife just informed me that Amanda Cook is here and that I should have her join us here on the pit stand... These women."

"At least it would replace some eye candy," Morley joked, making reference to the team missing Evelyn Stevens.

Andy grunted. "Right... Oh, hand me your headset."

The Moretti Motorsport team owner shook his head, looking back up over his shoulder at the VIP Suites just north of the famous Pagoda, hesitated, and hit the com.

The field headed down the backstretch at pace speed during their first warm-up lap with Alex continuously thinking about that first turn, keeping the car under him, and then making his brother proud. As he passed the massive crowd packing the stands, he had not forgotten about the enormity of the event despite his three-year absence.

Victory here was perhaps the world's foremost single-athlete achievement as winning drivers' names were etched into immortality. No sporting event offered such a thrill to win nor such agony of defeat, a race where finishing a close second felt as crushing in some ways as falling out on the first lap.

He wasn't sure his brother would ever walk again, indeed worse may not survive this place. But the Morettis would return year after year, chasing that Borg-Warner Trophy. There were the great ones who had won multiple times and great drivers never to win, while many, including his father, had tasted the milk just once, heroes all. It was always such an honor to walk up and have a conversation with the likes of Gordon Johncock or Al Unser, Junior.

Perhaps this day another Moretti will join that exclusive club, Alex pondered. *No driver has ever tasted victory here starting dead last. But it is five hundred miles,... and I have a very good car.*

He heard his headset sound off indicating an incoming from the crew. "Alex, your sister-in-law wanted to let you know that Amanda Cook was up in the Unibank suite cheering for you," his father advised.

"What?... When, Dad?"

"I don't know. But she's here,... and hollering for you to win I'm told. Go get 'em, Alex."

Alex felt his nerves lighten as the field cruised down the main straight on the final parade lap, not able to avoid the sudden urge to look up to his left toward the suites above the Tower Terrace stands. *Amanda, here?* he thought quickly, smiling as he worked to refocus on the upcoming green flag start. *Not totally sure where I stand with her,* he thought quickly, his focus returning to the star and that first turn.

Kyle Larson began to pick up the pace, leading the field as the thirty-three cars entered the fourth turn. The field roared past the flag stand at over two hundred miles per hour, picking up speed through the first turn with every one of nearly 400,000 fans standing. Amanda felt her fists tighten and held her breath, so thrilled that all thirty-three drivers had made it through that first turn intact.

By lap ten, two starters had fallen out with various difficulties. The field had begun to spread out with Larson and Scott McLaughlin trading the lead while most of the rest of the field flashed by the start-finish line just seconds behind.

Both Alex and Evelyn had slowly climbed up into mid-pack by lap fifty when the first yellow was flashed as second-year driver Bruno Masten hit the second turn wall, uninjured but out of the race while nearly every driver hit the pits for fuel and tires.

Evelyn entered pit lane just behind Alex and stopped just in front of him, leaving just ahead and gaining three positions while Alex's crew had difficulty with his fuel nozzle. On a more tenuous front, Helio Castroneves and Nico Rosberg collided on the way out of their pitboxes, ending the race for both top ten contenders.

Alex motored on, his car fast and handling well even as the tires began to scuff off, a good sign his setup was right. He seemed to make a habit of thinking about Amanda for just a few seconds while on the backstretch. When the race was over, he would reconcile with her one way or the other, coming fully prepared for all possibilities. Approaching the third turn, his focus would fully return, knowing the slightest mistake at this speed could be catastrophic.

Byron stood by, attempting to hide his scowl while a bubbly Marilyn Forsythe took the lead as the defacto Evelyn Stevens cheerleader in the Unibank suite, with most of their entourage now populating the outside suite seats and roaring every time she would make another pass, her Unibank sponsored car running strong and up to tenth place while giving chase to Penske drivers Josef Newgarden and Will Power.

Amanda seemed to be in her own world as she watched patiently while Alex passed by, averaging just under 223 MPH at race speed. She herself had yet to fully reconcile with him, assuming they would be seeing each other, and just sat there quietly with Sarah, focused on him making it through to the end safely.

Sarah observed the interaction between her two girls during the race, concerned that here was her youngest daughter, who in a strange way seemed so content and having purpose, even though she had just graduated from high school and had yet to enroll in college, while at the same time, inside the suite and somewhat isolated from the crowd stood her oldest girl, having a drink and seeming to have little interest in the action, herself having a solid future established with her degree and pending marriage, yet appearing so melancholy to the point of being miserable.

On lap 112, Alex began to lose time as his right rear tire developed a slow leak. Morley encouraged him to last three more laps if possible to avoid the extra stop as he was close to the pit window as it was, but it wasn't in the cards and the "5" Amoco badged car limped into the pits a lap later. Losing precious track position, he re-entered the track, now trailing the leaders by two-thirds of a lap, tightening his wrist around the steering handles in frustration, figuring his chances for a strong finish had just gone up in smoke.

Evelyn came through the latest round of stops now finding herself in the top six as the Unibank Indywest Dallara was performing flawlessly and she was currently the fastest car on the track, trailing the leader, Kyle Larson, by a mere seven seconds. Even Byron had to animate himself as the Unibank contingent were all in a fanatical rush as Stevens was steadily passing the likes of Fernando Alonso and Colton Herta right in front of them.

During the next round of stops under green flag conditions, Marcus Erickson made a critical error, coming down the pit lane entrance lane hot while his crew chief was hollering for him to watch his speed. Despite slamming on the brakes, his leading Dallara crossed the speed zone line at two miles per hour over the 60 MPH limit and was handed a stop-and-go penalty, costing the Swede half a lap and likely a chance at victory.

Alex kept his foot in it but was still behind the eight-ball as the laps wound down when suddenly a lapped car stalled suddenly entering the fourth turn as leaders Larson and Scott Dixon came up behind. Larson had to swerve to the right to avoid the slower car and hit the wall bouncing off and down toward the inside pit row retaining barrier, catching Dixon and teammate Alex Palou in the process. While all three ended up waving to a cheering crowd, indicating they were all relatively uninjured, all three top competitors were out of the race, forcing a lengthy yellow flag condition as the safety crew worked to clear the massive amount of debris resulting from the wreckage.

Amanda couldn't help herself and started to get excited when another yellow appeared due to a lapped car being black-flagged with a serious oil leak, when all of the drivers cycled through with less than thirty laps remaining and most of the field pitting for their last stop. She quickly typed out a text. *"Are you watching this?"*

From Tony's hospital room a few miles away, Crissy and Matilde watched anxiously as Alex didn't pit and was now miraculously running in third position with thirteen laps remaining, right behind none other than

Evelyn Stevens and the race leader, Josef Newgarden. She caught Amanda's message and quickly replied. "*Yes! Come on, Alex! You can do it!*"

Andy and Morley busied themselves on Alex's pit stand, calculating fuel mileage, tire data, etcetera. Having been out of sequence, Alex could not run the remaining laps without another stop unless another yellow flag condition occurred, and would likely need a lengthy one at that.

"Try to stay as close to Stevens as possible while conserving, Alex," Andy stated over the two-way, disappointedly shaking his head, knowing his son's fuel status was dismal as well as the tires falling off.

"I can't keep up, Dad! I need more speed!.."

"Keep it steady," Andy replied. "She's tight on fuel, herself."

The green flag dropped on lap 193 with most of the field all good to go to the end. It appeared the three leaders would all need a last stop-and-go for fuel, but lumbered on with five laps remaining when the leader, Newgarden, had a rear suspension failure causing his Chevy-powered Team Penske Dallara to spin and slide up into the wall, causing yet another yellow flag condition.

Evelyn Stevens crossed the line now leading her former boyfriend and teammate Alex Moretti with just three laps remaining while the track safety crew hastily worked to clear the track for a last dash to the finish.

"I'm going full setting," Stevens kept exclaiming to Van Brough, as he was crossing his fingers, knowing the Indywest car was practically running on fumes.

"Alex, you have barely a drop left, but go for it," Andy directed anxiously.

All 400,000 were on their feet as the green flag dropped with two laps remaining. The Unibank suite was a throng of excitement at the sheer possibility of their driver, Evelyn Stevens, actually winning from the last row.

"Townsend, we couldn't make this up," Leigh Diffey exclaimed. "Evelyn Stevens and Alex Moretti, both past teammates, both past romantics, Stevens making the race with Andy Moretti's help, and Alex substituting for his injured brother, battling for the win here at Indy in the closing laps! It's a script made in Hollywood."

440

"Yes, Leigh, and both starting from the back row. Just amazing!"

The green flag dropped and the two passed in front of the flag stand side by side with Alex taking the lead in the first turn. Stevens stayed right on his tail and pulled up beside him on the back straight, taking the lead back in turn three as both drivers prepared to take the white flag.

Byron even noticed his wife, Sarah, jumping up and down beside Amanda as both drivers passed in front of them with one lap to go, again side by side. Standing up and behind her father's subordinate cohorts, Allison moved up beside him and placed her hand on his shoulder as both looked on.

Evelyn could do nothing but keep her foot down as she nervously saw her mirrors full of Alex Moretti who pushed to gain position for one last pass out of the fourth turn, his helmet face shield full of his former teammate and intimate's rear wing and gearbox.

Amanda stood, lips pressed firmly together with both of her hands on her head, when the Unibank and Amoco sponsored Dallaras came into view as Stevens' was swerving from left to right to left in a frantic attempt to keep Alex out of her slipstream when her fuel-starved car suddenly sputtered and lost speed, allowing Moretti to fly by her on the inside, crossing the bricks by just a car length and taking the checkered flag while the standing crowd roared.

The Unibank suite became stunned and suddenly subdued other than Sarah and Amanda, two who stood alone taking it all in, hugging each other while both were in tears.

A similar pair stood and struggled to contain themselves in a hospital room, Matilde and Crissy Moretti were both glued to the wall TV screen as their loved one had won the Indy 500, an annual goal of the Moretti family that ranked right up there behind breathing itself.

Alex slowly paced around the track to the tremendous admiration of the crowd, himself thrilled and misty-eyed, nearly in disbelief while the enormity of the moment worked to set in while he and his father traded animated laurels over the radio.

Alex Moretti and his winning car were hoisted up on the recently upgraded victory podium before a worldwide broadcast audience, the Moretti Motorsport crew ecstatic as they all crowded in, each wanting to get their individual congratulatory embrace and handshakes in for their most celebrated and maligned stand-in driver.

The large green victor's wreath was hung over him as Alex took the traditional gulp of milk before dousing himself with a small remainder. The *Captain*, Roger Penske, moved forward to shake his hand just prior to his father, Andy, himself still overcome with emotion as he embraced his youngest son.

Announcer Kevin Lee worked to get a word from the winning car owner while his son still worked to remove his seat belts and helmet.

"Andy, you have tasted victory here as a driver and now as an owner with your son. Congratulations."

"Thank you, Kevin. I still just cannot believe it. We were down at midrace with a cut tire and the race just came to us. I was surprised Alex maintained his speed in the closing laps, holding off those who had much better tires. I want to thank British Petroleum for stepping up for us, Honda and Firestone for giving us the performance we needed. The man upstairs was looking down on us and it just seemed like it was meant to be. I just wish my son, Tony, was here to celebrate with us and perhaps this miracle will make its way toward his full recovery."

"And now Alex, we all know this has been a tough and emotional month for the Moretti family. You have won the Indianapolis 500. What are your thoughts?"

"I just cannot believe it, Kevin. I'm so thrilled. I just hope my brother is somehow savoring this moment with me. I wasn't sure I had anything for Evelyn there at the end, but it was just our time... And, Kevin, if I could have that microphone for a moment?"

Lee looked confused for a second before Alex grabbed the mic right out of his hand.

The masses of fans halted their exit from the stands and stood still at this most unusual request.

"I going to ask for something special here, Mr. Penske, as I know I may never have a platform like this ever again. I have put my family through hell these past three years and I'll be forever grateful to them all for supporting me. There are two individuals who have endured a much worse trauma than I have. One of them, as you all know, is my brother Tony, who was critically injured earlier this week in practice and I would like to dedicate this great win to him"...

Matilde and Crissy were still standing and glued to the TV monitor in Tony's hospital room, each holding one of Andy Moretti's grandsons, speechless and misty-eyed with emotion.

"The second person is a young woman very close to me and one whom I learned just prior to the beginning of this race was in attendance today. I would like Amanda to be here with me to celebrate this moment... Amanda! Come on down here!" Alex yelled into the microphone while looking up over his right shoulder and past the Pagoda toward the Tower Terrace stands.

Lee made a call over his headset, inquiring how much overtime the network would allow him, given this unexpected request. "Whatever it takes," was the response.

Up in the Unibank suite, all of the Unibank attendees, as well as many thousands of the still-standing fans, realized who the race winner was referring to as Amanda stood frozen while everyone stared at her in exciting expectation.

"Amanda, go on down there," Sarah suggested.

"Mom! I can't go down there... Please!"

"Where are you, Amanda!?" Alex inquired, his request now echoed loudly through the speedway's loudspeakers.

Suddenly as if on cue, the thousands of fans still in attendance followed with a chant. "Where are you, Amanda!... Where are you, Amanda!... Where are you, Amanda!"

"Amanda," Sarah added, smiling. "We're not getting out of here until you go down there and join that young man! This is your moment, baby!"

She then took Amanda by the hand and the two headed up past the intrigued smiling Unibank dignitaries and their family members toward a stunned Byron Cook, who stood at the suite exit.

"Reilly, Sarah? You're going to allow"...

"This is Amanda's time, Byron... Not yours," Sarah scolded him as she held the exterior door to the suite open for Amanda to depart.

The massive crowd had even halted the exits and by the thousands returned to the stands in anticipation. Three minutes later, the entire front straight crowd exploded in applause when the gathered crowd at the base of the Pagoda parted as Amanda appeared, loudly cheering as she ascended to the podium and approached the race victor, an extremely emotional moment as the two had not looked each other in the eye in over three months. They embraced to the repeated cheers of the crowd while Andy, himself overcome with emotion, stood beside his winning car and glanced up at *The Captain,* a thrilled Roger Penske, who shot him a quick nod and a wink.

"Amanda Cook, here in front of these great fans and before the whole world, would you marry me?" Alex asked as he produced for her a diamond ring, which was hanging on a fine chain around his neck, while the massive crowd stood suddenly silent in anticipation.

Matilde held Crissy's hand as the two moved up closer to the wall-mounted screen. "Did you know he was going to do something like this?" she asked.

"I swear I had no clue, Matilde."

Amanda was stunned, and with tears running down her face, replied. "Yes."

Kevin Lee couldn't contain himself and wanted his whole worldwide racing audience to get in on it. "Excuse me, Amanda. Could you repeat that, please?"

Amanda grabbed his microphone, her natural shyness becoming suddenly suspended. "Yes! Yes, I'll marry him!"

Alex and his new bride-to-be enjoyed a final passionate kiss to the huge extended applause of an admiring crowd, hundreds of thousands who all knew they had witnessed an event for the ages.

There didn't appear to be a dry eye in the place as the huge crowd couldn't seem to get enough of them as *The Captain* called for a final couple of laps for the two to parade around the track, realizing what an exciting and historic moment it was, one that would dominate the sporting news for weeks.

The two made their way down to an awaiting Camaro convertible preparing to slowly chauffer the two around the circuit as an admiring crowd went into a frenzy.

"Does this bring back any memories, Amanda?" Alex asked her, his right arm around her waste while waving to the crowd with the other.

"Why did you have this ring with you in the race car?" Amanda yelled into his ear over the noise of the cheering crowd.

"I kept it around my neck for a good luck charm."

"How long have you had this thing?" she spoke into his ear with genuine interest.

"I purchased it the day before the 500."

"I thought you were at the hospital all day yesterday?"

"It was the Daytona 500."

Crissy sobbed with emotion, proud of herself for the part she had played in keeping this once forbidden relationship alive, not to mention her late priming the pump of a stalled romance that had suddenly become more famous than Harry and Meghan, when she felt a sudden tap on her shoulder.

"How can I help you?" The assigned station nurse inquired.

"I beg your pardon?"

"Someone hit the help button, Mrs. Moretti."

Crissy and Matilde looked around after being so focused overhead to the action on the wall-mounted screen. He still had all the casts and bandages and couldn't speak or hardly even move. The two broke into tears as Tony had opened his eyes at last while he joined them in taking in the post-race victory celebration on his room's TV monitor... He was smiling.

Epilogue

That evening following all of the congratulatory accolades for Alex's historic victory and his and Amanda's surprising engagement, they all made a late visit to the hospital where the entire Moretti family gathered as the atmosphere had changed dramatically in just one day. Tony had still not spoken but had opened his eyes, was smiling, and moving his hands.

The photo of Alex and Amanda graced the front page of every major newspaper and online news site in the world. In the aftermath of an exciting and extraordinary Indy 500 weekend, the worldwide sports media was in overdrive with interviews, articles, and post-race commentary regarding what many considered the most amazing event in motor racing history.

Suddenly ticket sales for the remaining series' events tripled and potential race promoters were making inquiries at 16th and Georgetown about future races from New York City to Sydney, Australia.

Within days, Herrera was flooded with inquiries from sources worldwide offering sponsorship dollars as graphic advertising space on racing cars took off like acreage at a land office. Other race teams, including Dale Coyne and Juncos Hollinger, couldn't wait to sign on as clients.

In a small article overshadowed by the headlines of the 500 and the Moretti family saga, it was reported that Evelyn Stevens' longtime agent, Louis Newberry, had been found dead of an apparent drug overdose in his downtown Indianapolis hotel late on the morning of the race.

Despite her recent consternation over her contract dealings, Evelyn Stevens was shocked and saddened by the unfortunate death of her longtime agent. The popular British star avoided overtures by none other than Allison Cook, who went into overdrive to promote herself as Newberry's replacement, an effort still hampered by the rumor that Stevens wished to drive for Andy Moretti again the following season.

Allison was confident she had in her possession all of the compromising audio, video, and images that Louis Newberry had on his notebook computer and smartphone. Her part-time lover in San Diego, a talented officer in naval intelligence, would hack into both, as well as Newberry's social media accounts to remove the compromising data. Little did she know that a former prostitute named Remi had the goods in hand and would be in contact with her in short order. A threat to go to the police was now added to the blackmail of exposing the damaging materials themselves.

The plans for an Alex Moretti-Amanda Cook wedding were being discussed despite the lack of zeal from her father, still a sulking and bitter man who refused to accept his youngest daughter's choice of a husband, nor his wife's path to go against his will and support it.

Neither Alex nor Amanda were invited to attend Allison's wedding, a nearly subdued affair as the Williams and Cook families struggled to smile for the wedding photos while they remained at odds over the aftermath of the previous winter's trial and Amanda's well-publicized accusation toward Kyle Williams.

Amanda enrolled at Queens University in Charlotte for the fall semester and planned to accompany Alex throughout the remaining racing calendar. The post-500 media attention finally subsided, if only a bit, and the team packed up and prepared to head north to Detroit, the next race on the calendar the following weekend.

This time, Amanda was driving while a discussion ensued on a plan for the two to head up to the mountains during the next two-week break. She wanted a cabin in Gatlinburg.

THE RACE GIRL

THE RACE GIRL

Afterword

The Race Girl was written as a purely fictional novel with *authentic effect* by referencing actual teams, events, places, and true-life individuals from the international world of motor racing.

Having lived in Speedway, Indiana, myself for a brief period from 1985 to 1987 and having visited the Indianapolis Motor Speedway multiple times, I am quite familiar with the world's largest stadium as apparent in the story. At press time, Italian manufacturer Dallara USA, based in Speedway is the contracted chassis manufacturer for the Indycar Series with Honda and Chevrolet the series' engine suppliers. All references to Ford Motor Company, a corporation rich in motor racing history, becoming a third engine supplier are purely fictional.

While several well-known drivers and teams are noted in the plot for effect, the Moretti racing family and the Moretti Motorsport teams are 100% fictional with any apparent or relative similarity to actual characters and/or teams purely coincidental.

The young female sprint car racer, Chasity Younger, is a true-life character actually depicted in The Race Girl, along with her mother and father, Ray and Michelle Younger. The family resides in St. Joseph, Missouri, racing the *Chasinator* sprint car on various regional dirt track circuits nearly every weekend from Spring to Fall.

David Land features his podcasts on YouTube and is a great source for updated behind-the-scenes information about the sport and Indycar in particular.

Papa Doc's Shore Club is an actual lakeside bar and grill on Lake Wylie in South Carolina, a great place for a gathering, catch a game, or watch a race.

They have great drinks and be sure to check out their Oyster Rockefeller dish. I am not certain if they allow overnight boat mooring, so you had better ask.

While I'm a huge fan of motor racing (like you cannot tell), I wish to give a special shout-out to some who inspired The Race Girl. I've always been a huge Andretti fan and I for one take it as an affront to all American racing fans that Formula One has challenged Michael Andretti's quest to enter F1. Hopefully by the time most readers get to this page, the challenge will be old news and the Cadillac-powered *Andretti* F1 car will be working its way up through the grid (right, Colton?).

I was in the Tower Terrace stands across from the flag stand when Helio Castro-Neves won his third 500 and the memory of Spiderman jumping up on that fence was just priceless. If you're a race fan and not a fan of Helio, you're probably not a fan of anybody.

I don't believe any other man on earth other than *The Captain,* Roger Penske, could have survived the Covid crisis at the speedway and indeed continued to improve and make IMS the world's greatest race track. I cannot wait to see the new museum when it opens.

When I began writing The Race Girl, the spouse of one of my favorite drivers, Will Power, was undergoing a serious illness and to my knowledge is on the road to recovery. To Will and Liz Power, our prayers have always been with you and your passion has been one of the sport's greatest virtues through the years.

Look for the sequel to The Race Girl, the next chapter in the Moretti racing family saga, in Racing to Win, planned for release in late summer, 2024.

Your reviews would be most appreciated as feedback at the origin of purchase and/or check out my website at www.jamesherbertharrison.net where you may check out my blogs and sign up for my newsletter.

About the Author

James Herbert Harrison, a native of Cape Girardeau, Missouri, has lived and worked throughout the continental United States as a businessman and industrial equipment and software sales representative. He currently resides in Olathe, Kansas with his wife, Maryna, and their teenage son. James has an older son who resides in Cape Girardeau, as well as two older stepchildren. The family are active and proud members of Lenexa Baptist Church in Lenexa, Kansas.

James' pedigree as a writer began ten years earlier with the publishing of his first novel. *Quest For Power*, a political thriller to be re-released as *The Programmer*. *Miracle From Ukraine*, a totally different departure in genre, was inspired by the real-life saga of James and Maryna having experienced many of the actual events in the story.

A lifelong motor racing enthusiast and avid collector of motorsport memorabilia, James' novel *The Race Girl*, a tale set around two racing meccas, Indianapolis and Charlotte, is the first in a planned series on the saga of the Moretti racing family and their exploits, challenges, and tragedies competing in the world's great motor racing series.

Made in United States
Orlando, FL
05 January 2024

42161682R00254

"I was always worried about that. Thought it would have a negative effect on your driving, but It hasn't seemed to affect you. Evelyn, though, I'm not too sure. And how do you feel about that now, Son? She is Evelyn Stevens, after all. Reminds me of your mom twenty-plus years ago, except she couldn't drive on a highway, much less a race track."

"Every man's dream, huh?" Alex replied. "I just got tired of Evelyn being Evelyn. I mean, she came to be the whole world's sweetheart, not just mine. I loved to look at her, that's true. She made me proud for certain. But we had no private life. Even when we were at home, Newberry would call 24/7. I think he did that half the time just to piss me off. And I'll tell you, it worked, Dad."

"You want the beautiful and classy woman who's fully content with your stardom, and never caring about her own? Very hard to find that, Alex."

"Is that what happened to you and Mom, Dad? Her not being content with your stardom, or that she wanted her own? Maybe both?" Alex asked, never recalling him and his father as having this conversation before.

"Probably a bit of both," Andy confessed. "We're a hard species to get along with, race drivers. When we're winning we're all happy and everything is positive. When we're not, we bring it home... That's hard on a woman, very hard."

"Do you ever miss Mom?"

"On occasion. Mostly when you boys are doing well. I think it's sad she doesn't share in it," Andy stated, "I couldn't turn it off, the sport I mean. You need to turn it off and be human sometimes. I guess I just want you and Tony to be successful, and to leave your mark. For people to say or write that you were one of the best ever."

"They say that about you now, Dad."

"Yeah, but it would be nice to have a woman to say that in a private moment when you get old and both cheer for your kids and grandkids," Andy reflected. "I would probably trade that for a few accolades. I'm so happy for your brother. Wonderful wife, and now a beautiful son. Tony has the right balance between racing and family. I just hope he keeps it that way, like Dixon. There's a man to look up to, and still great after all these years. I know you boys are different, but I wish that for you, Alex.